WHEN THE WATERS TAKE US

WHEN THE WATERS TAKE US

A Novel

Beth Willstrop

Basking Turtle Publishing
San Antonio, Texas
USA

Although the writing of WHEN THE WATERS TAKE US involved extensive research and reflects in a small part the author's personal transplant experience, the incidents, medical procedures, and characters in the novel are fiction. Any resemblance between the characters of the novel and actual people and events is coincidental and not intended by the author.

ISBN- (Amazon Print) 979-8-9898577-0-8
ISBN- (Other Print) 979-8-9898577-2-2
ISBN- (ebook) 979-8-9898577-1-5

Introductory poem: Carol M. Siskovic
Cover design: Caitlin B Alexander
Cover photography: Willyam Bradberry/Shutterstock
Dedication art: Hannah Willstrop
Author photography: Salina Radillo

Basking Turtle Publishing
San Antonio, Texas

Printed in the United States of America

A special thank you to the individuals and groups—online and in person—who support and provide care for patients, families, living donors, and care givers involved with kidney transplantation.

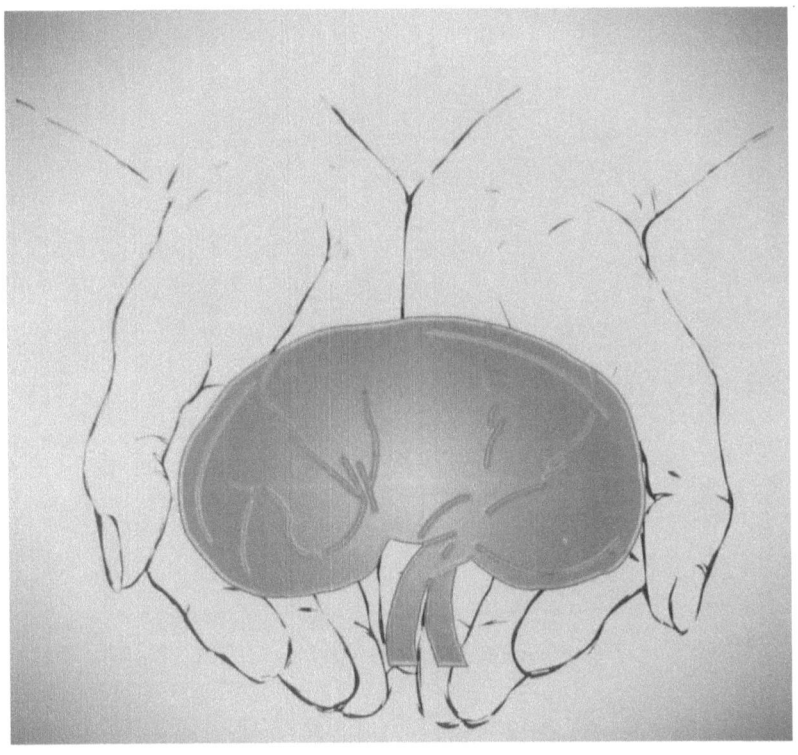

WHEN THE WATERS TAKE US

Not always by choice
we find ourselves midstream,
heading out and away
toward a perceived goal,

sometimes floating,
often lunging and sweeping,
seeking something out there...

a longed-for landing,
a desired destination,
a glorious goal or gift.

In seas calm or stormy,
crowded or solitary, we must
forge forward undaunted,
pursuing our raison d'etra.

Carol M. Siskovic

Chapter 1

July 1, 2015, CiCi's Home, San Antonio, Texas:
Jon kept his eyes straight ahead and gripped the steering wheel as if CiCi's Honda CRV were a three-wheeler ricocheting over treacherous terrain. The wipers squeaked across the barely damp windshield. He had full daylight, little rain, and light traffic. The drive home from the airport should have been a no-brainer, yet CiCi's tales of the Pacific received only grunts that may have meant "That's fine" or "Yes, dear." She studied his face again. Nothing. He couldn't be angry with her—she had just now got home. Besides, they never did silent treatments.

When they rolled her bags into the living room, he stopped beside the recliners, still only responding to her with nothing more than "Mm-hmm." Finally, he spoke. She should have known something was up. Whenever Jon started with "Can I have a minute?" or "Please, sit down," she knew the story would take a while. This time, he used both.

Suitcases blocked her escape to her bedroom. CiCi ran her hands through her travel hair—crunchy from sun damage and cheap shampoo—as she listened and got a grip around her best friend's news. They needed to talk about this. "Kidney failure? What the hell? I go away for six months to come home to 'My kidneys have failed?'" She tried to imitate him with a deep voice, but she squeaked instead—her stress always resulted in a high pitch that embarrassed her and sent her memories back to kindergarten torments.

Jon sighed. "Please don't have a conniption."

"One doesn't decide to have conniptions—they exist because they are." CiCi squeaked faux existentialism as she tried to absorb Jon's news. No more airports—she was finally in her little house, in her soft, snuggly white leather recliner. But her bra—her bra had to go. Fourteen hours in the economy seat had locked her old hips and frozen her back. And her best friend had just told her his kidneys were failing. She would have a bloody conniption if she wanted one.

"In my day," Jon said, "I was a strong, assertive man haggling with tough, wealthy people in business. But when you enter a conniption, my manhood shrivels."

That did it. That broke the tension. Sort of.

She had said she was exhausted when he first asked her to sit down. She had assumed he wanted to present another crazy idea to make millions, and CiCi wished he could have had the decency to save his news until morning. All she could think of was shower and bed. But now, as she looked at his obvious muscle loss and tired eyes, she wondered what kind of friend would not have seen how sick he was.

For three years, she had been roaming the world a month at a time. Thailand came first, hanging out with three new friends and adventuring whenever a zipline or elephant excursion caught her fancy. Then Guatemala, Costa Rica, Caribbean Islands, Fiji, and the list went on. She even learned to scuba dive to visit the undersea worlds. Not a bad life for a retired high school English teacher. She had spent her formative toddler years in Guam, so during her career in Texas, she dreamed of retiring to a little grass shack with hot and cold running water on a deserted tropical island. As a single mom, she had dedicated twenty-plus years to raising her daughter, Kambri. Now the kid was a beautiful thirty-five-year-old woman with an excellent education and a solid career. It was CiCi's turn.

This last trip was to the Big Island of Hawaii, where she spent six months volunteering at the Kalani retreat center in a jungle paradise. No grass shack—it was a tent. For Christmas before she left, Kambri gave her mom a battery-operated lantern and a pink cap with lights in the brim to shine her way past the wild boars to the shared bathroom. Jon made fun of her because she paid for the campsite and cleaned lodges voluntarily for this privilege. But the free food prepared by Britain's Princess Diana's former sous chef—who was also escaping civilization and paying for a campsite while cooking voluntarily—was served on a beautiful lanai overlooking the Pacific. CiCi took yoga and basket weaving and improved her spirit in return for washing sheets and making beds. Jon watched over the home front, letting CiCi enjoy her footloose adventure. The simple life kept her humbled.

CiCi's flight home had its ups and downs, literally. No storm, no turbulence, but the plane dropped so fast it lifted the passengers against their seatbelts. She thought about her author/pilot friend Karlene Pettit's flight safety thriller novels about the lack of pilot training when auto pilot fails. This pilot was on it, but that drop reminded her that one minute everything's all good, and, boom, the bottom can drop out. No choice but to ride it out.

What a gift Jon was—eight years now. No romance, more like siblings, and they bickered like siblings, too. She had found him on *PairForLife.com*. In Jon's picture, he wore overalls that had seen better days and was holding a rooster by the neck while petting a donkey. Unable to resist, she messaged the ass patter to find out if his name was really "John Doe."

Jon was, indeed, Jon Deaux. His father had emigrated from France before he met Jon's mother. Jon didn't speak any French, but he learned to cook in that style—butter on everything—lots of butter. He loved to bake, so CiCi spelled his name Jon D-o-u-g-h. Even though he had heard her say it for years, he laughed every time.

They had decided a few years back to share CiCi's house to save money. It was CiCi's house—that was clear, but CiCi declared herself the winner in this deal. Jon was a trained chef while CiCi

3

burned microwave dinners. CiCi prepared only one meal—a welcome breakfast—before Jon banished her from the stove and took over all the cooking. He even remodeled her tiny space to make room for his master chefery and designed the new coffee pot niche to face into the breakfast nook to keep her out of the kitchen. She was okay with that.

She was not okay with his kidney disease. Jon had given her a cup of coffee to fight off the jet lag while they sat in their respective seats in the recliner sofa. It was Jon's time to speak. As he talked, she struggled to understand how so much had changed while she was off having the time of her life. Boom.

Jon reached across the cup holder that separated the seats, a mutually agreed upon convenience. He took her hand, which he never did because touching was a no-no. "You were excited about your *hippy* tent adventure in Paradise. The kidneys had just started messing up, and the doc thought the problem would resolve with meds. He only noticed it because my filtration score was a sudden drop from my last blood test. We tried to manage it and decided you didn't need to know. If we had told you while you were hula dancing, you would have headed home. For what? There was nothing you could do."

"*We?*"

"Your daughter checked on me. I needed a driver for the biopsy."

"Biopsy?"

"The kidneys are in trouble. Some minor damage because of my past diabetes, but there was lots of inflammation."

"Why?"

"Good question. Doc can't say. I had an adverse reaction to that antibiotic before you left. The huge spreads in my blood pressure and sugar levels because of the prednisone a while back probably didn't help eith…"

"Is there a cure?"

"None."

"Dialysis?"

"Won't do it."

"Transplant?"

Jon paused. "Don't see how."

"You're going to die? That's it?"

Jon lowered his head and went silent.

Chapter 2

7:58 AM December 26, 2004, Patong Beach, Phuket, Thailand:

From her perch in the almond tree that hovered above what was once her favorite Thai massage parlor, Eva watched a young man on a rooftop surf over what used to be a street between what used to be hotels and shops. The roof rider yelled at people to move, to get out of his way. Eva wanted to tell him the dead went where the water sent them.

In truth, she didn't want to tell him anything.

Eva wondered what his life had been like ten minutes earlier, ten minutes before the water. Except for the one thing she never talked about, her life was perfect—American expat, twenty-six years old and living life as a free spirit. She taught English as a second language for affluent families. With no parents deciding her future, she had fallen in love with Thailand and its people. Yes, her life was perfect.

She wrapped her skinny legs around a limb and clung with all her strength to a tree above raging water. Minutes earlier, while preparing her makeshift classroom to tutor a rich hotel owner's son, she had looked out the window of the first-floor storeroom. It was a beautiful place on Patong's beach, just feet from the surf.

This day, however, the shoreline had retreated so far that she couldn't see it. Life paused. The sea breathed, then rolled in, taking Eva and tucking her into a tangle of branches, imprisoning her as she watched her near-perfect life wash away.

The roof rider must have seen the same thing. She wished him luck as the banister he clung to broke into pieces while he *surfed* past the third-story windows of the Kareen Palace Hotel. The sign for *Backpacker Hostel* had remained attached when a second wave pushed the roof and its rider inland. A little place heavily promoted by Internet travel sites, the hostel's charm and price attracted tourists worldwide. She had stayed there upon her own arrival on Phuket Island.

She blinked. The young man disappeared.

Knowing Backpacker's well, she created an imaginary life for the *surfer* boy greeting another day. Breakfast would have been between seven o'clock and ten o'clock every morning with an offering of scrambled eggs, dragon fruit, and Thai noodles that Eva always swore was the soup from the night before. Like other kids who partied too hard, this guy would stagger into the dining room right before the staff took the steam bins back to the kitchen. But not this morning. This morning the roof rider woke up early—a little after seven-thirty—couldn't sleep, so he headed up to the still vacant rooftop.

Eva looked down at the water rushing by—it was much better to think about him right now, not her tree that could topple over at any moment. Roof Rider, yes—she would think about Roof Rider. He would have watched the tide recede and keep receding, the water disappearing into the depths. He would think he suffered a hangover from a mixture of drugs and alcohol. Eva knew the backpackers did that stuff—that's why she never fit in. She imagined him panning the shoreline. Secured boats leaned sideways on their keels, with naked piers towering above them. Other boats floated backward out to sea.

"This isn't right," he would say. Like her, he wouldn't know why, but he suddenly would want company. Out her window that morning, she had seen tourists on the beach bustling around, looking for sea treasures, but the shells had rolled with the water.

The vast, wet sand—now speckled with unfortunate flopping fish—stretched for what seemed like miles. The locals stared and scratched their heads, then called to their friends and family to hurry up the hill, urging stupefied tourists to follow them. When the waves gathered to roll back in, the foreigners still stared out at the sea, exclaiming wonder in all their languages.

Villagers knew. They ran.

But she didn't. She stayed in her little classroom. And now she clung to a tree like a buzzard searching for the dead. The *surfer's* roof broke up—that was that.

Eva climbed a little higher.

****

When the first wave hit, Marco didn't know enough to be afraid. The fear set in soon enough as the second wave hit the roof of his hostel, breaking it loose, taking him along for the ride.

Hours? Seconds? How long had it been? As Marco's vessel crashed against a passing overturned white van, he grabbed the bumper and watched his roof disintegrate to join the mash of lumber, beds, and clothes floating by. He struggled to hold his grip when he saw the clothes had bodies in them.

A hand grabbed him. He stared face to face with another young man. Alive. The two continued floating with the van up the road until they butted into a hotel balcony. While struggling to hold on to the tire, the other man yelled for help to untangle from a pile of debris. His English sounded American, like home.

Marco pulled away rubble and seaweed. "Name's Marco. I, um, I just…" Yes, that felt right—his mother taught him to always introduce himself. This way, if he drowned, this other guy could tell the authorities his name. He yanked a bathtub faucet and a shower rod webbed with curtains off the other man's legs.

"Charles. Thanks for the assist."

While the world moved in slow motion, yet simultaneously at hyper-speed, Marco said, "I saw an old guy in his swim shorts standing on the beach, looking at the wave. He didn't move. He just waited. Then, gone." He gripped the van, frozen. "I don't know why I told you that."

They stared at the wreckage in silence. A hand from the hotel room next to them reached over the balcony railing to pull them from the water. "I'm Hilmi. I hope you are enjoying your stay in Patong."

Marco looked at Charles. He couldn't move, either. Then all three men started laughing that pathetic laughter that comes when pressure backs up inside the lungs and the veins because everything is wrong. Without laughing, every cell will explode. Relief didn't last long—there wasn't time.

"Climb up now. Hurry," Hilmi said. "I think your van will head back to the ocean."

They climbed over the railings and looked back—only debris remained of the busy beach hotels and restaurants. The sea pulled the water, cars, buildings, and so many bodies to the depths. Concrete skeletons poked through muddy tideland like broken bones.

The three men steadied each other and took in their surroundings. A third wave surged inland and rushed back out. That was it—the ocean was done. The van hung onto the balcony by a small part of the bumper.

Marco leaned over the banister and puked.

****

At the peak of the 2004 tourist season and the day after Christmas when the United Kingdom and its colonies would celebrate Boxing Day, a magnitude 9.1 earthquake shook the floor of the Indian Ocean thirty miles below the surface of the earth. One hundred miles from northern Sumatra, the tectonic plates had fought against each other for thousands of years. Most of the time, they would adjust; but this time, the Burma plate subducted below the Indian plate, generating 900 miles of sudden movement. Because the water was so shallow in that part of the ocean, the released energy surpassed 23,000 Hiroshima-type atomic bombs.

There was no tsunami warning system. There had been no time to evacuate. One slip in Earth's framework affected five million people in fourteen countries. The last count of missing or dead—never officially established—totaled over 250,000. In Thailand alone, the walls of water slammed hundreds of miles of coastline. Those who lived had to bury their loved ones and figure out how to rebuild. What should have been a joyous holiday became known as the Boxing Day Disaster.

The Earth's hiccup destroyed lives, devastated land and property, and gathered attention worldwide. But within months, the rest of the world moved on.

****

Marco Herrera never saw himself as a hero, but here he was, a survivor of… well, no one really knew what, yet. Surprised he was still alive, all he could do was respond. He had no thoughts, just fog. People screamed for help, so he helped them.

"Hey, over there." Marco pointed. "A woman is up that tree." Where the water left swamps filled with broken buildings and dead bodies—animal and human—it also left useful items. The men grabbed an unbroken ladder belonging to a building now washed away. Marco found it odd how random items didn't leave with the sea. With the ladder tall enough to get him high into the branches, he still had to climb the next four limbs.

The woman shimmied further up. As he reached for her, she screamed and kicked at him, nearly knocking him off the branch. She looked to be in her twenties, just a little older than he was. Her hair was matted, and chunks were obviously ripped from her scalp, but he saw no other signs of injury. He noticed her torn blouse and looked away immediately, but none of that mattered here at the top of the tree. She kicked him again. He read her eyes. He was trying to take her down the tree. To her, safety was up. Marco finally stopped trying and sat on the branches below. Somewhere in his gut, he found his calmest voice. They talked about clouds, about Buddhist temples, about birds, about anything other than the wave and water. There in the top of a tree with chaos below.

At last, she said, "My friend was here with her husband who had a kidney transplant. He stayed in bed at the hotel this morning to recover a little before flying home. Their daughter was bored but feared the ocean, so no swimming to entertain her. I arranged an elephant ride on the beach for the mom and her daughter this morning. I told her she would be safe. On the beach."

He let her cry, more because he was numb than because it was the right thing to do.

When she quieted, Marco got her name and said to Charles and Hilmi, who were waiting in the mud, "Eva's ready to come down now."

As Hilmi guided her to the rescue truck up the hill, she turned back to Marco. "The medical tourist agency treated my friend's family to a beautiful room overlooking the beach. Right over there." She pointed to what remained of a small hotel. "It was a first-floor suite with sliding doors leading to the sea."

The men watched Hilmi whisper something to Eva, and with renewed energy, she climbed into the truck. Hilmi then walked back to Marco and Charles to continue search and rescue. They avoided talking about the rescues and those for whom they were too late. Instead, they talked of their own lives they had left behind and the visions they had for the future. Charles and Marco only talked of "making it on their own"—there were no plans other than Charles was going to make lots of money. Hilmi's plans were specific.

11

The Malaysian had come to Patong on Phuket Island five years earlier. Hilmi said, "Ajib—my life partner—and I were respected meteorology researchers at *Universiti Malaya*. Professionally, our lives were excellent, but Malaysian laws regarding us—how we lived—are strong, so we had to leave. We came here and built our restaurant with rooms to rent."

Their beautiful real estate faced the bay only yards from the shore. Every morning they took turns waking early to fix breakfast for the tourists. The other one would join for cleanup before they headed to the water for a swim. At night, the sun set right in front of them. "Eva's friends were staying in my hotel," Hilmi explained. "This morning, it was my turn to sleep in. Our home is up the slope five blocks from where I helped you out of the water. Ajib was at the restaurant."

"Why are you here with us?" Marco asked. "Find him."

"We are all looking for everyone. If he is to be found, someone will find him. All must be found."

"Perhaps he's looking for you."

"Perhaps." Hilmi peered out over the devastation. "He was even closer to the water than you were, Marco."

Help for the rescue efforts came from everywhere with no one in command. All understood they needed to deal with the living first. So much danger: ragged metal frames, glass, scared animals lurking in the swamp the ocean left behind. But rescue workers and loved ones did not hesitate.

The three headed to a fishing boat filled with crying tourists. The survivors may as well have been zombies. Falling out of the boat, they crawled through the surf to the beach. Speech left them—only wails remained. The captain explained they had returned from the morning run as the third wave receded. They had no idea the tragedy had occurred. As they came upon debris and saw the dead bodies, they joined the throng of rescuers. One time, full to the sinking point with survivors, they had to motor away while people cried from the water for help. "We could not take them all. We had to leave." The fisherman cried as he spoke to Hilmi, who translated for Marco and Charles.

Marco whispered to his friends, "How do you decide who is left to die?"

The rescuers worked into the night, but it became time to care for the dead. Hilmi suggested the two men needed rest and could stay at his house up the hill. He promised it would be dry. As the day's shock and adrenaline wore off, they talked about their first rescue—Eva—then they vowed to continue after they ate and had a few hours of sleep. Exhaustion overwhelmed them as the rumbles from bulldozers and shouts of rescuers bellowed over the men's snores.

Chapter 3

July 1, 2015, CiCi's Home, San Antonio, Texas:
Jon had sent CiCi to bed to recover from her flight from Hawaii, but she couldn't sleep, not now. She had questions, so many questions, but she needed time to process. Being the queen of phone Googling, CiCi investigated dialysis and transplants, particularly living donor transplants. Research. That's how she faced everything.

She read testimony after testimony of patients with chronic kidney disease who survived years while on dialysis. CiCi's own uncle lived four years while in his nineties and drove himself to dialysis three times a week. When he passed, it was his choice. He was tired. The man was ninety-six—of course, he was tired.

Wide awake, she found herself standing at Jon's study door. She couldn't help it—she started schooling him. With thirty-five years as a high school teacher, her entire life was about teaching others.

Jon did not even look away from his computer. "No, I'm not doing dialysis. If I were younger with children depending on me, I would do it. I would buy the time needed to wait for a transplant. But I'm not young, and my kid is thirty-five. It's a quality-of-life thing."

CiCi marveled at Jon's past. He had had a remarkable existence as a wealthy man, a life that got shot to hell and sent him into bankruptcy during the 2009 recession. His father invented the machine that made double-knit polyester fabric. It was Dad's fault CiCi wore double-knit pant suits in her formative adult years. He was the reason men wore the ridiculous colorful double-knit leisure suits in the 1980s. Jon inherited his father's business and then sold it to invest in other businesses.

A brilliant Jack-of-all-trades, there was nothing he didn't know how to do. He had owned restaurants, which was why he did all the cooking for her. He had licenses in finance and had a lucrative business as a financial adviser in Fort Lauderdale for seven years. Then an agent for the Drug Enforcement Administration thanked him for his open books policy but recommended that Jon close shop and move somewhere else, quickly. Jon's books were evidence in a drug investigation involving some of Jon's clients. That was when he moved to Lake Tahoe to start a contracting business to build multi-million-dollar homes, which was why he knew how to remodel CiCi's kitchen.

CiCi picked at her fingers and bit her thumbnail. "Oh, so it's okay to sign off without a fight and leave your friends?"

"Like I said, if I had young kids."

CiCi tried again to share her wisdom. She wanted to grab this friend by the shoulders and shake him right now. "My hair stylist's sister has been on dialysis for fifteen years. She turned down transplants twice already. Doesn't that tell you it can't be all that bad?" When CiCi had asked her stylist why no transplant, she was told the sister was accustomed to dialysis and didn't want to risk something she didn't trust. As CiCi looked at Jon, she made a mental note to check into why anyone would turn down a transplant.

Jon pulled away from his computer, removed his glasses, and rubbed the palms of his hands across his face. "Look, I've been doing my own research. What do you think I've been doing while you were spinning fire staffs and dancing the hula?"

CiCi should have known she wouldn't win an argument with him—she always lost arguments. He was so smart and stubborn. In her heart, she knew he was right. She had read the material but chose not to absorb all of it, like the part about being tied to the dialysis machine for hours each week and the overwhelming fatigue. And there was the part about a five-year life expectancy on dialysis, but some people such as her hair stylist's sister live a long time.

"CiCi," Jon said, "in this region of Texas, the wait is seven to ten years for a transplant. I'm nearly seventy. I don't have seven to ten years."

His old business as a financial adviser always puzzled CiCi since he was now bankrupt and living in her little, very humble 1300 square foot home. He had told her the first question he asked his clients was about their comfort level for taking risks. He, himself, was a risk-taker and had been bankrupt various times in his life as he would close one business and invest in the next, but he was always working on the next. This current futility crap wasn't part of his story. CiCi would not accept it.

Jon waved his arms around. "Why would I do this?"

CiCi had heard all his stories. He had owned lovely homes in resorts around the U.S., flew his own airplanes whenever he wished, docked his yachts at fancy marinas, and stayed only at five-star anythings. Could all that stuff be so great that his quality of life would now suck? She knew she never would have been a part of his life if he still had all his money. They met while he was reinventing himself with corporate jet interior designs before the recent recession. His pickup line during their second date still made her laugh. They were eating dim-sum at a Chinese restaurant when he said he hoped if they didn't make it as a couple, they would be friends. "I need a friend." Some shtick. "I'm lonely," he had said. That was true—he had moved to San Antonio to work directly with a parts manufacturer. He knew no one other than the manufacturer's team of four men. CiCi thought it was a brush off. They only went on two other dates, but they became best friends.

She left the door and marched into his study to move her glaring eyes closer to him. "Excuse me." And there was that squeaky voice again, destroying any power she had achieved with her Wonder Woman fists-on-her-hips pose. "I didn't realize you disliked my home enough to die rather than live here." Squeaky voice and guilt trip—what would her mother say?

"Hell, CiCi, that's not what I meant." Jon pressed her hand on the desk to keep her from rearranging his pens. "I will forever appreciate this place. You saved me from living in my truck. But I sit here with no strength. I nap all day. I have plans to regain my financial wealth, but I can't get out of bed long enough to interview, much less go to work."

There it was. Whenever they fought, which was rare, it was because CiCi personalized everything.

Jon liked consistency and straight lines—typical of a Capricorn. He joked he didn't have an *h* in his name because it was a wasted letter, inefficient. CiCi was all over everywhere—typical Gemini. She could drive Jon insane, but he swallowed his frustration and laughed at her (or with her). CiCi had xeriscaped in her yard and was proud of her wild-looking bushes that had the most exquisitely scented blooms. The sign at the garden shop had said to let them be free to reach where they wanted, no shaping needed. She liked that. She saw herself in those bushes—scraggly but sweet. Jon could not have foreseen her shock when she came home from work the first spring after he moved in to find her beautiful bushes manicured into nice, tight boxes. Jon meant well, but he had trimmed her. One doesn't trim a Gemini.

"Okay, I'm taking a breath." She knew it wasn't about her house. "I understand you're frustrated. I know you don't do *sick* well. I am just not ready to give up on my friend yet. When your diabetes was killing you, you retired. But you found a way. You're better than freakin' King Sisyphus at defying Death."

"And Hades will have me pushing boulders up mountains for eternity because of it."

CiCi caught him smiling—it was tiny, barely noticeable, but a smile no less. She knew he thrived on his reputation for defiance.

A decade before meeting CiCi, he designed and sold automated window shades for corporate jets. His diabetes was so bad that he maxed out on insulin, and his doctor told him he had two years to live. Retirement sounded right. He sold the shades company and set aside money for his wife's future. They spent what was left to enjoy their remaining time together. Pictures CiCi saw revealed private dinners catered in Swiss chalets, sailing on extravagant chartered yachts, exclusive wine-tastings in Italy.

As Jon's time grew shorter, he learned of studies in Australia where they found gastric bypass surgery cured about eighty percent of diabetics. This was ten years before gastric bypass gained acceptance as diabetes control in America. In fact, even though he was overweight, he still had to gain another twenty-five pounds for a U.S. surgery. He grabbed at the gamble, had the surgery, and no longer needed medication.

Alas, after the surgery, he never felt better in his life, but he had spent his fortune. To restart his airplane interior designs, he needed to use the money from the savings they had set aside for his wife. She had agreed to his restarting his business, but the two amicably divorced, remaining friendly while in separate parts of the country. No wife, no money, but, damn, he felt great.

"In my better days, I would go to Thailand and buy a kidney."

CiCi thought he was exaggerating about Thailand, but maybe not. Jon did amazing things.

His financial recovery had gone as planned. The patent on his latest design, a contract with a parts manufacturer, and a contract with an airplane manufacturer had all come together. Life was grand again. Then the big three automobile industry CEOs flew their private jets to Washington during the Financial Bubble Pop of 2008 to beg for money to avoid bankruptcy. The corporate jet industry became so tainted by the media coverage that large companies, such as multi-state banks, hid their planes in hangars and swore the passengers to secrecy as they boarded. Even though it saved money not to have employees waiting around in airports, the public would not accept the efficiency of such tactics. The plane manufacturer canceled Jon's order at once. He had invested everything into his product. Then it was gone.

Moving in with CiCi allowed him a breather, but it was only supposed to last three months, six at the most—until he found a job, a job in a market with no jobs to be found. University grads waited tables and moved back in with Mom and Dad. Even forty-somethings moved back in with parents. Jon, already in his sixties, had been self-employed his entire life. With three advanced degrees and more years in business than these youngsters had been alive, he had no evidence he could be a team player. He sent three applications a day everywhere. A company in Romania offered him a CEO position. It was a solid "Go" until during salary negotiations his age came up. Nothing.

And now, six years later and still at CiCi's home, he was critically ill.

CiCi went back to her teacher mode. "So, tell me why you refuse dialysis."

"I've had an extraordinary life, and I'm grateful. If I got to do it over and had to choose saving for my old age or daring the Fates to live as I did, I would not change a thing. Now I have to think about my quality of life. I don't want to be relegated to a recliner until I die from dialysis complications."

"But my stylist…"

"She's much younger with a younger heart and younger everything else that fades with age. I love my food. I don't want to watch my potassium levels—it's in everything I enjoy. And fluids, what goes in must come out. But with no kidney function, nothing will come out except during the dialysis three days a week."

CiCi knew he was right—he would be miserable. But she couldn't stop herself. "So, this is all about food?" Of course, it wasn't the food. She had read the research and was undeniably in denial. But then, that was CiCi's way. "You can do home dialysis."

"Why would it be better at home? I'm still stuck. The general advice from everyone is to think of dialysis as a part-time job. And there is that fatigue."

"But you can buy years. You just said so. How long can you live without it?"

"The doc doesn't think I'll make it to my birthday this Christmas."

CiCi gasped.

When they first met, Jon's need for straight lines seemed odd to CiCi since he would only stay at one business for a few years, make his million, and then move on. Then she realized the straight path let him build quickly. But once he completed the steps to the end, he became bored. Then he had to start again, but there was always an again. Dialysis had no end game for him—just wandering forward, killing time for a non-existent transplant, nothing to accomplish since no one relied on him to stick with it. Dialysis would take away his power. But there was a donor possibility—CiCi had two kidneys.

"Be honest—they don't know what caused it?" CiCi asked.

"No, just guesses. Been diabetes-free for years now. The biopsy said it wasn't diabetic damage. My blood pressure's been under control. But what difference does it make? It is what it is. Let's stop for dinner, please."

Kidney talk went on hold while Jon prepared Bananas Dolphin—CiCi's favorite entrée. This was not cute little bananas with grapes in the ends to look like happy dolphins—this was gourmet fish à la Jon. The first time he prepared it for her, long before they lived together, he convinced her he used special spices only found in expensive culinary boutiques. With cooking, he could tell her anything. Once he moved in with her, the gig was over—she watched him use just salt and pepper. But he did it right—the fish tender, sautéed to perfection. CiCi could burn water—fish baffled her.

At first, he let her think the dolphin was Flipper until he saw she wouldn't eat it. This required fast explanation—this was not the bottlenose dolphin that saved small children from drowning. What they called dolphin in the Caribbean were Blue Water Beauties, known as Mahi Mahi in Hawaii, a common fish and not a mammal.

This night, she studied her friend as he feigned enthusiasm while standing at the stove. So tired. Why hadn't she noticed when he picked her up at the airport? He threw bananas in with the fish and caramelized other banana bits to add to the dish. With panache, he drizzled banana liqueur over her entrée and set it on fire. CiCi giggled as he danced with his spatula. It was the flambé that made her clap with joy. When he broke out the vaculator to brew after-dinner coffee, she understood he genuinely wanted to celebrate her return—he had missed her.

They toasted to their friendship with coffee cups. "So, we come back to a transplant," said CiCi.

Jon put down his cup. "I can't wait for a deceased donor. I'll be too old. Other health issues will disqualify me."

"Unless you have a living donor."

Jon pushed back his chair to leave the table.

"Please wait." CiCi told him about her colleague who donated her kidney to a cousin fifteen years earlier, and the colleague never missed the extra kidney. "I loaned Val a bag full of VHS tapes and DVDs to watch while she recovered. She returned them untouched because she recovered much faster than she had expected. She was running marathons in no time, even went to Boston to run." Of course, Val was about twenty-five years younger than CiCi was now, but overall, CiCi was healthy.

His chair slid further back.

CiCi had to stop him before he got to standing, and before she chickened out. "I'll do it. I'll give you my extra kidney."

"You?"

21

"We're a team. When you lost everything, I was there for you. When budget cuts took away my job, bringing about my retirement years before I had planned, you were there for me. When Dad passed away, you were there for me. When I started traveling, I was free because you were here for me and my house." She was winning—she saw it in his eyes. "When I'm hungry, you are in the kitchen for me."

They laughed and toasted coffee cups again.

"The point is," CiCi paused to be sure he was listening, "you are always here for me. We must try."

With a fresh path, CiCi watched Jon head to his computer to investigate living donor procedures in the San Antonio area. Typical CiCi, jump in and then think. It was a crazy idea, desperate, but she needn't worry for herself because what would be the odds he and CiCi would match? And there was her old breast cancer thing from twenty years ago. She forgot about that.

At least he was doing something. It was a step. They agreed to talk with his doctor in the morning.

Chapter 4

December 27, 2004, Hilmi's Home, Phuket Island, Thailand:

The smell of fried bacon fat mixed with kerosene from the gas burner woke the two Americans. Pots and pans clanged like sea buoys while Hilmi cooked everything from the refrigerator—no power meant spoiled food. The groceries in the restaurant had washed into the bay, but there was much stored in the apartment. Hilmi told Marco and Charles that with city-wide rationing imminent, he would give away the food rather than let it rot.

Marco and Charles asked if Hilmi's partner had found his way home, but it was not to be, and the only thing remaining of the restaurant was the golden Thai Buddha mask that had hung on the entrance wall. A friend had found it in the mud and gave it to Hilmi that morning.

The three sat looking out the window at what used to be Patong Beach's posh resort seaside. They tried to eat Hilmi's famous French pastries, but the food stuck to the backs of their throats. The water had returned to where it belonged, as if chaos had never ensued. Down the road from Hilmi's second-story apartment, the pavement looked like heavy rain had come through, yet the balcony was dry. There was a bus on its side, protruding from a shop window two blocks away. Also, Charles's white van still perched on the hotel banister, dangling in the air with debris balancing its rear tires. The shock from the day before had worn off—they couldn't muster the sarcasm they had relied on to keep going when they first met.

There was no relief.

As Hilmi cleared their breakfast plates from the table, he pulled up a chair for himself. He put his elbows on the table and his head in his hands. Just when he appeared to have fallen asleep, he opened his eyes and stared straight into their faces. "You know what *Hilmi* means?"

Marco and Charles sat speechless.

"It means patient, tolerant, gentle, and calm." Then he wept the cries of desperation and anguish that actors never fully master.

This was real.

Charles had never hugged a man before.

Hilmi told the guys he had heard that most rescues had turned into recovery of the dead. Deciding to help at the hospitals higher on the island, Charles and Marco left the beach. From there, they planned to head north and leave the disaster behind.

Hilmi called after them. "He would have worn his shirt with our restaurant logo, the Thai Buddha face with the palm trees behind it."

They had walked only two blocks when Marco sat down in the street. He was a strong young man adventuring the world during his gap year after high school, except Americans rarely promoted the gap year idea—Americans usually graduated and headed at once to a college or the military or had babies and worked at the local fast-food place. Average Americans tended not to travel until they got older and could afford cruises to escape their lives. He had played football in his first year of high school when no pass/no play hit the Texas boy hard. He did not pass, so he did not play—academics were not for him. However, he kept working out and grew handsome shoulders, handy right now.

Marco knew he wasn't college bound, and the military seemed like a dangerous place. Saving all his money from his part-time job while telling his parents he was saving for college, Marco decided he needed enough money for a ticket to anywhere and would work from there. Thailand won the coin toss. The country promoted strong visa requirements in their publications, but so far no one had checked that he had overstayed or that he did odd jobs. The joke was on him. Go figure—an ocean attacked him.

"Dude, you all right?" Charles asked.

Marco looked up. "Yesterday, yesterday was…" Marco felt his eyes sting and face flush—he was about to cry. He couldn't. He wouldn't. He was a man now, and on his own. He must not cry.

"All that water," said Charles, sitting down beside him.

"All those voices."

"And all the silent ones."

Marco stared at Charles—he didn't seem like the poetic type. "And Hilmi."

They sat in the street a few more moments before they pulled each other back up to standing. Charles Snyder was Marco's direct opposite. Marco was only five-foot six and muscular. Charles was six-foot five and a skinny bean pole. They talked about home while trying to make sense of their surroundings. Marco was a ranch boy from Kingsville, Texas—Charles hailed from the suburban elite of Chicago, Illinois. Charles had been an excellent student through ninth grade, but he was too smart and too bored. A self-made person dealing drugs here and there, he never finished high school. The oldest of five siblings, he announced he wanted to go to Thailand to learn more about the world, and his parents were relieved. Charles told Marco his mom and dad paid for his round-trip airfare and gave him a couple of thousand dollars for his journey, hoping he would find himself. That's what they told him, but he knew they just wanted to get him away from the younger children. He said he would never go home.

While plodding down a back road about three miles from the city center, they heard a high-pitched cry. Someone was calling out in Thai, but that plea for help translated anywhere. The men dropped to the ground and started their search. Under a pile of what looked like concrete beach tables and umbrellas, they found a young boy who appeared about ten-years-old. He was so small that he was unharmed in the open space between the table legs, but the pile of poles and umbrella cloth had him trapped.

The kid spoke a little English, shop talk, enough that he told them he had been with his grandmother. "Now I do not know." He sobbed and pointed toward where his family lived—a shack near the beach, now rubble. Then he pointed to a small pickup truck floating in a swimming pool and explained he and his grandmother had been riding to the market in it when the water took them. He had washed out the window and grabbed one of the beach umbrellas floating upside down. "I ride in it, mmm, then table take me."

"I was saved, too. By a roof," Marco told the child, trying to show he understood.

Marco and Charles invited him to go to the hospital with them, but the boy wanted to find his grandmother. He didn't talk about the rest of the family. So young and already he knew too much.

"Come on," Charles coaxed. "Your grandmother might be at the hospital."

Marco decided there was something to the life-changing tragedy thing. Charles had told Marco he had never liked kids because his siblings kept ratting him out to his parents, yet there he was, taking on this kid.

Because the kid could climb into small places, the three rescued more people and got them into hospital trucks. At noon, they started loading dead bodies onto the trucks to go to *wats* (temples) that functioned as temporary morgues for collection and identification. Rescue, even for those who were injured, exhilarated the crews, but recovering the dead sucked the life out of them. They moved the bodies without truly seeing—they had to. Charles was the one who said such a young boy shouldn't see so much death and sent him on a passing truck to a makeshift hospital, hopefully to find his grandmother. He got a description of Grandma's clothing and promised, again, to get word to the kid if they found her.

****

Eva stood outside the *wat*, taking a quick break from receiving the dead to breathe fresh air. The red and gold roofs of the temple rose above the canopies that were placed outside to shelter hundreds of bodies wrapped in white. Eva found it fitting that the trucks brought the bodies to this majestic place.

Passing through life and the questions of the afterlife were the stuff of religions everywhere. But in December 2004, there were too many souls from Phuket and surrounding resorts to fit into the temples, no time for sacraments. Past the front doors, inside the ornate walls, lay hundreds more bodies. People rushed inside to stumble back out, arm-in-arm, crying in all languages.

Inside once again, Eva stood facing away from the entrance and didn't look up from her work even as she spoke to the sound of footsteps. "Speak English? If you're looking to claim a body, sign in over there."

There was no response, so Eva turned. Her rescuer was there, grabbing Charles's shoulders. She had seen it before from others who came in—the need to touch a living person.

"Geez," said Marco. "They can't fit all the bodies inside the building." Then he looked at Eva dressed in her protective gear. "Are all the temples like this?"

She didn't need to answer—Marco and Charles had been working on the beach.

She overheard Marco whisper to Charles, "That's Eva from the tree yesterday. I don't think she recognizes us." Charles whispered back that he couldn't tell because her face had been covered in hair and leaves as he passed her to Hilmi, but her body was about right. Eva had tried to patch up her shredded waist-long hair with the *wat's* scissors, so it was much shorter now than during her climb down the tree.

Eva pretended not to hear—she didn't want to think about the tree, so she put them to work instead of talking.

They watched as she took pictures of a small pile of jewelry and a sun hat. She then entered the details about the items into a spiral notebook and tagged a body with a corresponding number.

"Over there," she pointed, "grab that camera and the spiral. Your assigned numbers are on the first page. We check the body for identifying marks, take pictures of the face, the clothing, and any accessories. Log picture numbers under the first number assigned to you and tag the body. And don't lose track of the memory cards if you switch out. They go in the card box."

"We touch the bodies?" A breeze caught the canopy, blowing it down on Charles. He jerked to run, but there was nowhere to go.

"Bro, we've been touching bodies for two days," Marco said.

"That was search and rescue. This is really, um…"

"Macabre?" Eva asked. "Are you a man or a jerk?" She turned away from them to get back to work. "Help or don't help. Just don't get in the way."

Marco picked up a camera. "I have nowhere else to be, so I'm in."

"All right, I'll join you," said Charles.

"Here, you need to wear one of these plastic cover-ups, cap, mask, and gloves. Since you're human, after all, I'm Eva Davenport. We met in a tree."

"We thought you didn't remember us," said Marco

"I was scared, not blind," she said. "But I am grateful. Thanks."

As they worked, they talked. Marco learned she, also, was from Texas. "I have to admit it's good to connect with home," Marco said. "I'm standing here tagging bodies and don't know why I wanted to see the world. Home sounds pretty good."

"So, call your folks," said Charles. "Me, I'm never going home."

"No, not parents. Not yet," said Marco.

"I get it," Eva said. "I can't go home either."

Marco gave her the why not look.

"Not talking about it." Eva continued her instructions. "Precision. No room for errors in the logs. One doctor told me dead bodies look alike once they start decomposing, and, at this temperature, that happens quickly. We won't even know if they are Thai or European. The only identification might be a wedding ring or a pair of earrings. Mix those up, and we can never reunite loved ones."

A new mantra drifted through the temples: "We will get them home."

Eva finished documenting a young girl's earrings and hair barrettes, then moved to the next body. She put down her spiral and looked out the door where up the hill there was no tragedy. "Yesterday, while the tourists were beginning their Boxing Day vacation on the beaches, I was getting ready to teach a hotel manager's son in a storeroom. When the screaming started outside, I thought it was a large party getting excited way too early in the morning. Then the water poured in through the walls. The room broke. Broke! There is no other way to describe it."

Marco told her he was on a rooftop as it tore loose from the building. So, yeah, he got it.

Eva busied herself with her task but didn't respond like most people would in a conversation. She was relieved when he asked about the manager's son instead of her time in the tree. "He was still up the hill at his home. Safe." She added she had never been religious, but her exposure to the Buddhists and other faiths in Thailand gave her words she needed. "When I was trapped underwater, I started saying all the holy sentences. I was certain I would die, but those holy words must have worked because the wave pulled me under the crest and up the back side. I rolled and rolled, but I'm still alive. I sort of body surfed to that tree and landed in the branches. I couldn't let go to climb down."

Charles took a photo of a bracelet. "Yeah, I said a few things, too, but they weren't so holy. With the first wave, I held on to a door frame, but then the water pulled back. I thought it was over and stayed there. Then the second wave pushed me up, and I grabbed a white van floating by."

Eva gently picked up a little girl's hand to place it across her body to take a picture of her small bracelet. "When that second wave started rolling, I climbed higher into the tree." She looked at Marco. "I watched you ride that roof. I watched you disappear."

"Oh," said Marco.

"I assumed you died. Then you found me in the tree, but I didn't want to talk about it."

"I was scared, too. When the roof fell apart, I was sure I was done for. I brushed against Charles's white van and held on for my life. When the van stopped moving, we needed to get out of the water, but we couldn't let go. I guess when we think we'll die, we grab at anything."

Charles told Eva about the curtains wrapping around him and Marco reaching him just in time. "A man named Hilmi helped us up to an apartment balcony."

Eva's eyes widened. "Hilmi? The one who took me to the truck? He was so calm and told me the sea didn't take me because I have work yet to do in this world. He said his name meant patient..."

Charles cut in, "...tolerant, gentle, and calm."

"He told you, also?"

"Yeah, right before he cried."

They stood quietly in reverence.

Charles broke the spell. "When we first saw him, he hoped we were enjoying our stay in Patong."

They laughed, the first time since they met.

Normally a loner by choice, Eva found the conversation surprisingly easy. "Anyway, he helped me head up to the trucks. I asked the driver how I could help others because Hilmi said I have work to do, so he brought me here."

The guys told Eva about Hilmi's partner. With such a strong connection, the three decided it was their destiny to meet. Their work in Phuket was not yet done.

Chapter 5

July 2, 2015, Central Texas Medical Research Institute, San Antonio, Texas:

The cafeteria was all but empty as Alex and Maura gathered their coffee and sweet rolls to sit at a table where the sun would warm them. Alex's mind was still back in her lab going over the old lab reports again and again.

Maura exaggerated a shiver and wrapped her worn out work sweater around her shoulders. "Why does it always have to be so cold? Put the word *Institution* in a name, and the thermostat drops ten degrees." She hugged her cup. "Yes. Hot coffee."

"Thanks for meeting me here," Alex said, her voice low in case an employee cared to listen. She stirred her coffee like mixing cake batter.

Maura snorted into her mug. Her friend continued stirring her black, sugar-free coffee, never once taking a sip. "So, what's going on?" Maura placed a spoon in her own plain coffee and stirred, making a huge drama out of it. "You sound weird."

"What?" Alex looked around, put down the spoon, and relaxed a little. "Oh, we've just hit some snags. Why does it have to be so hard to save people's lives?"

"Spill it, Sister. What gives?"

Dr. Alexandra Segel had led her kidney research team at the Central Texas Medical Research Institute in writing a grant for six million dollars from the NBIB to develop a remodeled kidney from the patient's own organ, but West Coast Kidney Resolutions won that grant, and now it appeared they were winning the race to market. West Coast had just announced the trials for their artificial kidney would begin in five weeks.

Through Alex's efforts with Senator Gwen Estes, head of the appropriations committee that decided the National Institutes of Health funding, she found a different money source. The senator gave them a year to start the human trials, or she would stop the funds. Her father was to be the first to receive the remodeled kidney. The team had used up nine months. They were close, but West Coast would get there first.

Alex said that even without West Coast's announcement, their research was still in trouble. "We think Senator Estes's timing has to do with the ten-year anniversary of when her father started dialysis."

"But ten years is good." Maura was aware of the limitations of dialysis—her grandmother spent years on the machine.

"Yeah, but his body's giving out."

Because of HIPPA privacy issues, Alex tried to avoid too many specifics. She explained that Mr. Estes had been on a transplant list but was a tough match because he had type O blood—O could give to any blood type but could only receive from donors with O.

When Maura asked about living donors, Alex explained he was adopted and had no way of asking biological siblings to donate. His four children each had their own health problems, so no transplants there. The one friend who was type O had a history of heart trouble, so he wasn't a candidate. It felt good to talk about this stuff, about why her work was so tough. She wasn't really telling anything she shouldn't.

Maura picked up her cup but put it right back down with emphasis, as if she had a brilliant idea. "Estes is rich, so why not just buy a kidney overseas?"

"He considered it, but, if the public found out, it would ruin his daughter's reputation and her standing with Congress and the NIH. He made it clear that purchase was a *no*."

"What? I was joking." Maura laughed. "That stuff is for movies—how can anyone pay a poor person for a body part?"

"You can Google kidney donation and find all kinds of ads from India. Anyway, Mr. Estes's salvation would be a remodel of his own kidney. Someone needed to invent one, which is where my team comes in."

Radical, invasive, and risky. Mr. Estes had decided with only months to live, why the hell not volunteer to be the first to receive a remodeled organ.

"And now you are running out of time? Why don't you invite the Senator to your lab again? Show her how far you've come, thanks to her help with the money."

Alex was kind enough not to smirk at her. Maura simply didn't grasp the urgency. Being first to trials meant strong marketing, which was the future for the Institute. Alex told Maura that Senator Estes was worried about her reputation from supporting this team's floundering research.

"Then she's a fool," Maura said.

Alex knew Maura didn't understand what she, herself, was saying—this stuff was way beyond her diploma level. Yet, she always tried. Maura was a humanitarian surrounded by researchers. Alex half expected Maura to screw her finger into her cheek and say *like* and *no way*.

It wasn't even lunch time, and Alex was frustrated, angry, and exhausted. No career was worth this, but she could never say it aloud, not even to Maura. "We need our kidney to work. Ours is the real deal and will give full kidney function. West Coast's kidney won't. It's artificial. They admit it in their press releases." Then Alex pulled herself over the table within inches of Maura and whispered, "I'm afraid Dr. South is getting desperate."

Alex wished, even as the words fell out of her mouth, that she could take them back. She and Maura never talked about work, a rule of their best friend-ness. *Proprietary* meant secrets. But this was her soul sister. They were Alexandra and Maura—the Rah Rahs.

Maura Menchaca worked at CTMRI with Alex, but in Human Resources in another building. The besties met for coffee whenever possible. They had grown up together and graduated the top two at their high school—Number One headed into medical science, and Number Two into the liberal arts. Human resources appealed to Maura because she helped people find positions that fulfilled their needs—at least, that's what she told Alex whenever it looked like Alex was the one contributing to the world.

"What do you mean by desperate?" Maura asked.

Somehow, Maura had always helped Alex sort through life's challenges: boyfriends, cheating on exams, sneaking out of the house as a teenager, even a period of suicidal thoughts during medical school. Alex counted on her—once Maura promised confidentiality, she would never kiss and tell.

"We can't get past making the right cells stick to the right places." Seeing no comprehension in her friend's eyes, she said, "The kidney is the size of this coffee cup, but only an inch thick, and has about a million tubules. Sometimes we get it right, and sometimes the wrong cells make simple blobs." She paused for a breath. "We're close, so very, very close."

Maura exaggerated an OMG face, imitating her phone's emoticon.

"Look at this cup," Alex said. Maura's flippancy didn't faze Alex as she held up the cup. "Look at the phoenix logo. That's what our team is trying to do, bring eternal life to our patients. Lose your kidneys? We will remake them from your own cells, better ones that will last as long as you do."

"Don't you think you are getting carried away here, Dr. Frankenstein? That phoenix has to burn up to be reborn."

Alex put on her best pouty face. "Well, okay, maybe, but I'm not Frankenstein—I'm not making life out of the dead—I'm making life out of life."

Maura caressed the phoenix on her cup like a pet. "I sit corrected."

"These patients are close to death, though. A transplant brings them back, but transplants require donors, who are rare."

"Then grow a kidney with the stem cells. I thought someone somewhere was working on that."

"They did, they have, we have. Some still try. The problem is all they get is a blob of kidney cells."

Maura cut her off. "The kidneys are miracles." She sang it, poking fun at Alex.

"Well, yes, they are. Go ahead, laugh, but they are." Alex loved kidney talk, but she knew for Maura this was all *finger-in-the-cheek* stuff.

"So, make the tubes."

"We did, sort of." Alex paused. This could be telling too much. "It's amazing."

"Then what's the problem? Why is Dr. South desperate?"

Again, Alex took a moment to answer. But it was Maura she was talking to, and, by the time they finished this break, Maura wouldn't be able to remember anyway. "I'm using our patient's own modified cells that will grow around his own scaffold of tubes to do the actual filtration and secrete hormones like erythropoietin."

This time, Maura really did put her finger on her cheek and yawned.

Alex smiled and drew a house frame on her napkin. "What we're doing is like gutting a house down to the frame and then putting new stuff back on the frame. Our new stuff will decide who comes in and out and adds the laughter and family and mementos."

"Got it. Frame," Maura said. "The problem is your insulation, wiring, and sheet rock nails aren't holding, right?"

"Yes!" Teaching always wore Alex out, which was why she chose research with no professorship obligations. Just now, however, she wanted to reach over and place a gold star on Maura's forehead. "So, we removed one of Mr. Estes's kidneys and stripped it down to the scaffold. We can implant soon. I'm certain. But not soon enough." She had to quit talking before she violated her non-disclosure agreement. But she needed to talk, so she kept going because Maura still looked interested and would smile whenever a word within her vocabulary came through.

The conversation continued one-sided until Alex said her mighty leader had become secretive, and the record sheets sent to the grant audit were not the same ones she had completed.

Maura came to life. "You'll lose your license to practice medicine."

"No, Dr. South would never jeopardize his team," Alex said, but her eyebrows pulled together, and her shoulders slumped. It only lasted a moment, but she knew Maura caught it.

"You said he's desperate, and now he's secretive. If you get caught, your chances of ever working in medicine in a legitimate clinic or hospital would be over."

Alex already knew this, but Maura made it real.

Maura's eyes drilled into Alex's as she said, "I sort through so many applications from people who have fallen into schemes before. I must reject them without even an interview. There are no do-overs."

Alex gave her the frown, the one she had used back in high school when Maura lectured her over stealing a Christmas tree from a sales lot. Maura told her then that she could have ruined her plans for medical school. It had been a fun dare, but Alex still felt guilty after all these years. Maura was good at guilt trips.

Maura said, "Dr. Alexandra Renee Segel, hear me. I'm no scientist, but I know human nature. I make a living with that skill. The lies get bigger as people cover the cover-ups."

Alex hated it when Maura used her full name, especially when she stuck *doctor* on it. She stuck out her chest and tossed her chin around like she always did when she knew Maura was right. "You're so negative. You even complain about the temperature."

"And yet," said Maura, "you brought this up."

Alex said she was sure there was a good reason behind the reporting errors—it had to be a misunderstanding. She had to keep Maura's snooping eyes away from this, so she turned on her sweet charm by promising to speak with Dr. South and begged Maura with a pinkie swear not to say anything about their conversation.

Best friends once again, the ladies clicked phoenix coffee cups to honor the greater good and headed back to work.

Chapter 6

July 2, 2015, CiCi's Home, San Antonio, Texas: With jet lag still in her bones, CiCi stood by her coffee niche for her morning elixir. Jon's hand shook as he held his cup. He said he had slept well because he had a plan, but to CiCi's eyes, he appeared even more tired than he was the night before. CiCi decided it was her duty as friend extraordinaire to distract him and lift his spirits. Her tales from the Pacific might do the trick—she had to try something. "Did I tell you about the outdoor showers with hot and cold running water?" She headed toward her bedroom to gather her purse and phone to go with Jon to his kidney doc.

"Yes."

"What about the boars that snorted around my tent at night?"

"Yes, that too."

"The Leather and Leis group who held a retreat there?" She peeked out her bedroom door to be sure he was listening and not playing on his phone.

"The group with whips and handcuffs? Yes, several times on the phone." But that detail made Jon smile. He nudged her into the garage. "You're sure you want to do this?"

"Again? You're a broken record. I already told you I knew I'd do this someday when Val donated her kidney. It seems obvious that people would donate their extra organ. I read the memoir of a woman who went to a clinic and offered to anyone in need, like donating blood. It's called non-directed donation."

"Would you do that?" he asked as he held her door open.

"I still have both kidneys, don't I?" She climbed into the passenger's seat and waited for him. "Yeah, I'm not that altruistic, but there are those who are. I heard about a bank employee who offered his kidney because of a poster he saw in a hallway at that bank. The sick man's wife worked there and took a chance with the advertisement. The donor had never met either of them, just saw the poster." She wondered to herself why bodies had two kidneys if they only needed one. There must have been a reason during the original design process. This was not something to ponder with Jon.

"I'm not that person."

"Me neither. There are people who see a Facebook plea who sign up. A tourist at Disney World got his transplant because he wore a t-shirt that said he needed a kidney, type O, and included his phone number. A stranger took a picture and posted it. Voila. He got a donor. There was an elderly woman in England who donated because she said she would not be needing both of hers. I don't know how many years that eighty-year-old kidney would give, but a year would allow someone to see a grandchild graduate from high school or watch a loved one reach a milestone. What's a year or two worth?"

Jon held his seatbelt as if he couldn't figure out how it worked. "What if we aren't a match?"

"Then we keep looking."

CiCi had insisted that she go with him to this nephrology appointment. She wanted to hear what the doc had to say. Jon was brilliant, but CiCi had grown wary of his claims of medical knowledge from his one full year of medical school. He was prone to frequent self-diagnoses. Although, she reminded herself, he knew that the antibiotic he took the previous year was wrong but could not convince the doctors. Several doctors had been certain they needed to get rid of his urinary tract infection. When that didn't work, they went for a prostate infection. He told the docs he knew his own body and knew something was not right. Turned out he got an inflamed kidney that started failing. Steroids started to clear the inflammation but set off blood pressure and sugar issues. The kidney was in trouble.

At the doctor's office, they learned Jon's nephrologist served on the transplant panel at Santa Maria Hospital. When CiCi told him she would donate, the doc started taking active notes.

Then she revealed she had had breast cancer, setting the conversation on pause. She added it had been nineteen years since her diagnosis, and she had had no chemo. "It was just a little thingie," she stressed.

Dr. DiLiberto admitted he could not see how CiCi would be any different from people never diagnosed if there had been no recurrence in nineteen years. He told them to go to the transplant clinic at the hospital and start the process. It was worth a try.

The doctor explained that with living donors, surgery was scheduled at the donor's convenience, not like the rush that occurred with deceased donors. When asked about her time frame, CiCi told him, "Before Jon becomes too critical to survive." She added she had a trip to China already paid for and scuba diving in the Caribbean the next spring.

He wrote in his notes "transplant in October 2015."

It all sounded so possible, if she were an acceptable match.

As they made their way back to the car, CiCi admitted to Jon she had been concerned her cancer bit would interfere, but Dr. DiLiberto didn't seem bothered by it. The cancer had been her motivator to improve her circumstances in the past and would do so again.

Her little house was a 1990 HUD repo in need of serious love that she picked up after her divorce. About two years after she moved in, paint started peeling off. The neighbors told her the house had caught fire while vacant. That explained so much. She had wondered why one kitchen cabinet was light wood and the rest dark. The contractor had painted the cabinet exteriors white but not the interiors. The cabinet fronts were even assorted designs.

And there was soot underneath each shelf. The cleaners had wiped the shelf tops and sides but not underneath. She guessed they counted on her not to look up inside. They guessed correctly—she didn't notice until she was placing the shelf paper. Sitting at home recovering from cancer surgery forced her to look at her home more carefully.

CiCi's inattention to details drove Jon nuts. She assumed all would be right in the world while Jon told her not everyone wanted to hold hands and enjoy milk and cookies with her. Had she paid attention to details when she offered her kidney? Was she glossing over the bad stuff again? Was she cruel to tease Jon with a donation without remembering she was a cancer survivor? It was only a moment's delay, but she didn't say anything after she remembered. Freud would jump on the subconscious froo froo. She had Googled live donation after cancer and found that survivors of skin cancers could donate but not the breast (or organ) cancers. But DiLiberto set a surgery date.

Her round of that teeny bit of breast cancer was supposed to teach her to take charge whenever she could. It worked to make her fix her fixer upper. The peeling paint required thick texture that she finger painted all over the main rooms. She researched all textures, and, being a Gemini and unable to pick just one, she gave each of the smaller rooms unique patterns. The texture process reminded her of her years in theatre constructing sets and wiring lights. The house became her stage. She tiled floors and bathrooms, removed walls, created arches. She was class favorite at Home Depot and thrived on her daring DIY projects. With more paint on herself than on the walls, she would tell her teenaged daughter, "Everything can be fixed." The wiring for a ceiling fan—piece of cake. Black to black and white to white, read the directions. And then she got the Internet with Google and YouTube.

Of course, when Jon moved in, he set about fixing her fixes. The light in her study niche that used to be the old closet was not

41

right—she had tied into a kitchen light by mistake, so the kitchen light had to be on to work the study lights. Not dangerous, just inconvenient. Jon fixed it first thing. Then he added vanity lights and a wall-mounted ironing board to her spectacular DIY closet/dressing room.

CiCi's house symbolized her with its awkward corners and misplaced tiles, but with all its flaws, it was her. And Jon had spent the last few years fixing her. She got things started, and he finished them. She pushed her donation concerns to the back of her mind. The two of them could design, build, and fix anything—they could fix this kidney thing.

As Jon drove to the transplant clinic, CiCi Googled away and filled him in. "They have paired donation, too. That's something I would do. I knew about it but forgot. If I don't match you but match someone on the waiting list who has a donor who matches you, they switch us up. They do the surgeries at the same time, and everyone wins. Cool."

He tilted his head side to side, stretching his neck. "There was a TV show about a hospital that did an eight-way transplant. Do you think that's just fiction?"

"It says here there are now domino pairings where three transplants happen because a non-directed person donates to A, A's donor goes to B, B's donor goes to C. Whoa! That chain could go on forever."

"I wonder how often that actually happens?"

CiCi looked up from her phone for a moment. "More and more now. They completed a chain of thirty-five transplants and seventy surgeries. The first donor in the chain said she had a spare kidney they could give to anyone, and it dominoed from there. Starting that chain means she saved thirty-five people."

He looked at her for longer than he should have taken his eyes from the road, but no harm done. "In that TV show, one donor wanted to back out. That would be a bummer if you got to the hospital, had eight transplants, or thirty-five, all set up, and a donor backs out midway. That one donor takes out all the remaining transplants."

"How did the show end?"

Jon rolled his eyes at her and faked a yawn. "It's TV. Of course, the donor recommitted. Everyone went home happily ever after."

The hum of the car engine could barely be heard over the hum of the brains riding in the car. CiCi added, "They try hard to be sure there is no coercion. The donor must do this with no pressure, and they may change their mind even rolling down the hall to anesthesia."

"That's good."

Jon wasn't himself. She had to tell him to stop for a car in front of them at a stoplight. Another time he stopped for a green light. Fortunately, no one else was on the road. He even weaved a little and slowed down and sped up, like he was drunk. CiCi hoped it was because he was thinking about the donor trees and not because of his illness. She quit Googling to help him concentrate. It was so odd for Jon, who drove a car like he would pilot a plane. She should have offered to drive, but her driving made Mr. Perfect nuts. He always claimed seasickness because she gripped the steering wheel and constantly adjusted. Her driving, though, was nothing like this.

As they rounded the corner to pull into the parking lot at Santa Maria, CiCi pointed at a small group of protesters blocking the front of the clinic entrance. "What in the world? Once when I was teaching at Salk High School, the animal rights activists protested. They had foam frog hats and were upset because the anatomy classes dissected preserved frogs and cats."

"Listen. This protest is against organ donation."

The chant was simple: "No more transplants."

Jon called the protesters travesties of fanatics because the signs posted words like *Criminal*, *Evil*, and *Monsters*.

"I see the signs," said CiCi. "But why would anyone protest transplants? The foam frog heads wanted to make their point and be on the news. Our sweet nerds were thrilled to have some real excitement. The only time Salk was in the news was when a student got an award for academic achievement, which was all the time, so boring."

Jon told her the people in that school needed a life. She needed a life. Too many stories about schools.

CiCi frowned at him—she and kid stories were one, a package deal.

He looked again at the protest. "These people are blocking the clinic door."

CiCi promised nothing would happen. "They want to be heard. Besides, this is a Catholic hospital—it must be okay with God to transplant organs. Park the car."

Over the chants from the group, a lone protester with a different sign and a brochure in his hand approached CiCi. "Are you going in there?" This protester was timid, whispering.

"Yes, we are," she whispered back.

"Please read this appeal about living donors—there is a website. It's not just about the risk of death. If donation is so safe, why don't more kidney doctors have just one kidney?" His sign said *Donors with Complications*.

CiCi smiled at him, placing the literature in her folder.

Spying the conversation, one of the loud demonstrators broke from the march to shout at Jon. "Those people in there are ghouls. They let people die and then take parts from the dead. Abomination!"

Jon was ready. CiCi recognized the jaw tension. In an argument, he could be so precise that it left the opponent smothered. "If they simply *let* people die, there would not be a seven-year waiting list. Besides, we're using a living donor. No dead bodies here, and certainly not for a ghoul's dinner."

"No, no, not dinner. Are you sick?" The poor guy gasped and stammered, then saw Jon's smirk. "You're worse. You're interfering with God's will."

Jon had more to say, but his argument went without ears because the annoying protester had marched back to his group, and the timid guy had slipped back to the sidewalk. The small group of one appeared melancholy separated from the larger, more boisterous group. CiCi thought it odd but did not have the where-with-all to ponder it in that moment.

Always the gentleman, Jon walked around the car to escort CiCi. "I canvassed the signs for the name of an organization. But no one is claiming the protest. I assume these are Christian Scientists or something." They had watched detective shows with cops saving children suffering from appendicitis when the parents did not believe in medical intervention.

He asked a protester, "Is it against God's will that a mere mortal invented the air conditioning you live in or the car you drive? Do you ever see a doctor for any illness?"

"This is creating life from something that had died." The man whined as he waved his sign in Jon's face.

A woman came up to help her friend. "If the deceased is buried without all its parts, it will not be whole in heaven. We worry about their souls."

This woman looked to CiCi as if she would cry. CiCi couldn't decide if the demonstration was because one marcher had lost an argument about a close family member's Do Not Resuscitate orders or if it was about religious views of death. "Donors have free choice," CiCi said.

"They know not what they do," the woman responded.

Jon was bored—CiCi wondered how he had lasted this long. He pulled CiCi closer. "Time to move on."

As Jon and CiCi squeezed their way through the crowd, someone accidentally hit him with his sign. Jon raised his arms to shield his face, but the group misunderstood his move of self-defense and mobbed him. Fortunately, a priest walked by on his way out of the main hospital entrance and intervened. Security arrived at that same time. Jon and CiCi ran inside the clinic as the police dragged away two protesters who had turned on the priest.

"Just want to be heard?" Jon asked CiCi once they were inside the building.

"I don't get it. What could be wrong with giving life?"

"Somebody somewhere got misinformation and rallied a bunch of other people who knew even less. They found their cause. It amazes me how quickly that can happen with social networking."

CiCi pointed down the hall to the entrance to the clinic. "Please don't start up on the evils of social stuff again. Didn't I just tell you about the Facebook pleas bringing in living donors?"

"Do you have any information in that Google brain of yours that says how often that happens?"

"Okay, so there are lots of stories of strangers donating, but I haven't seen one from Facebook other than the Disney guy. But spreading the stories should count and getting the message out to friends and then friends of friends can't be bad. Besides, we met online, so you can't judge social media."

Chapter 7

December 28, 2004, Phuket Island, Thailand: The next morning, after eating a boxed Thai breakfast of noodles and fruit donated by locals, Eva, Marco, and Charles hopped a ride on a truck heading to the *wat* via Phuket International Hospital. With hotels full of displaced tourists and Thai medical relief personnel, the owners of low-end hostels housed other volunteers and families who had lost their homes. Hilmi had offered to put up the three Americans at his place, but his home was already wall to wall packed with fellow shop owners from the beach. Since the new friends wanted to stay together, they chose the tent camps.

On the way to the hospital, Charles pointed down the road to Patong Beach. "That guy's using a big ass elephant to move shit."

The driver told them the man and his elephant had been logging trees in the North around Chiang Mai. When the animal and his owner aged, they moved to Phuket for an easier, more comfortable life. Since the majestic creatures are the national animal of Thailand, with their touch considered a blessing, rides along the beach meant lucrative business for the owner. When the tsunami drawback started, a girl had just climbed into the seat. That animal's instinct was to escape, so it took off, girl and all. The mom and owner chased after them, so all four made it to higher land. "That elephant is a hero."

Eva sobbed into Marco's shoulder. "They're safe?" she asked. "My friends? It must be them. But the dad? They gave up so much to get a transplant and then to have him drowned by an ocean."

The driver said he didn't know any names, but if the man was in the hotel, there was not much hope for him.

The four of them watched the man and beast work to clear refuse to find victims before driving on.

The Wall of Love outside Phuket International Hospital grew bigger. Literally a wall, family members posted pictures of the missing, praying they were in some kind person's home, or a hospital, or walking around the island in an amnesic state.

There were ten hospitals in the six affected districts. The Thai government mobilized medical personnel from around the country at once, but the hospitals still strained with the load. Phuket International Hospital had a hundred fifty beds, all full. There were gurneys and benches filled with patients in the corridors, outpatient rooms, and every inch of space. Bangkok Hospital Phuket and Vachira Hospital were in the same shape.

Within two trips the day before, the process had become routine. Marco and Charles recorded each corpse with a name—if known—the date and time the body was received, and the name of the hospital. Then they piled the bodies into the truck to take to Eva's temple. Eva would greet them, saying, "We will get them home." It became difficult to find a proper place to lay them without stacking, which Eva forbade.

But this was a new morning and the first trip of the day, so Eva made the hospital run with the guys. There were no bodies at this hospital—everyone had made it through the surgeries. In addition, to the relief of all, electricity was coming on around the disaster area.

They headed on to Vachira, and when their truck passed the rear entrance to the hospital, Charles leaned toward Marco and pointed to stacks of supply pallets. Each pallet was marked *Tsunami Relief.* "I wonder what each of those pallets is worth."

"What?" asked Marco.

"My cash washed out to sea with my belongings, and I don't have a credit card. You?" asked Charles.

Marco conceded the same.

Charles returned to the value of the pallets. "We're at the mercy of the volunteer camps right now. Dude, we lost everything. How are we going to eat after they quit feeding us?"

"Are you talking about stealing medical supplies and selling them? What would Eva say?" Marco whispered.

Charles didn't bother to whisper. "She's not even listening. Look at her staring off at the sea like a lovesick puppy. She's not my mother. Besides, don't think of it as stealing. Call it recompense for our services."

Eva still looked off toward the sea.

Marco clenched his jaw and looked down to the ground, away from Charles. "Really? These people suffered the most outrageous tragedy, and you want to get paid back for saving lives? Look at them. The Thais have lost entire families, yet they help everyone else, including the tourists. Including us."

"I didn't realize you were such a hu-man-i-tar-i-an." Charles held out each syllable.

Marco picked up his head and stared into Charles's eyes. "I'm not, but right is right, and this idea ain't right. And every movie I've seen with a Thai prison doesn't look good."

"Okay, but we have to bring in money. We don't have Eva's sweet personality to get us babysitter positions."

"No," said Eva, "I don't do babies." She had been listening, after all. "And you are an idiotic selfish ass, Charles. Do you really think you could approach someone to sell those supplies and not be questioned about how you got them? You're dumber than I thought."

Charles stuck out his chin like a defiant child. "Look, Eva, we can't survive without work visas here. The schools need caretakers for the babies with missing parents. You can do that. But us?"

Marco picked at his nails and looked down.

When they climbed out of the truck to head into the hospital, they bumped into the kid. His toothy grin shocked them.

"I find Grandmother!" the kid exclaimed. "She here helping other old people."

"No shit?" said Charles.

"No shit," mimicked the kid.

"What about the rest of your family?" Marco asked.

The smile dimmed. "They gone. Grandmother say all gone. Dr. Ethan say, too. They all gone." Then the smile came back. "But I have Grandma. Now I help others to find Grandmother or Auntie or Brother."

"How do you keep going?" Marco asked. "You're what, ten years old?"

"I have twelve years. I hear people say Earth punish us. They say they nothing now. I have Grandmother. I not alone."

They shook hands man to man, and the kid took off to help an old man through the door.

"Wait!" called Charles. "What's your name?"

"Chati. You?"

"Charles. This is Marco, and Eva's over there talking to that doc."

"Cool. Laters," Chati said. Twelve years old going on thirty.

While Eva completed paperwork, the guys loaded the truck with bloating bodies that leaked and even exploded. One of the American Aid workers gave Charles a bar of Irish Spring soap to sniff to offset the smells, but it didn't work because the bacteria that cause odors replicate in the nostrils within a short time. The odor seeped through face masks and into their mouths and throats to where they could taste it. The rescuers would retch for the rest of their lives at the memories of the stench.

Back at the *wat*, Eva supervised cleaning, bagging, and tagging each personal item and photographed them with the body. As she posted the photographs on a huge board for families to view, she saw Charles pocketing a wedding ring. But when she asked about it, he acted insulted and said he wiped it off on his pants and returned it.

Finally, the evening organizer told them to leave, to get rest.

As they trudged past the notice board on their way to the camp shuttle, a young woman broke into tears. She found her missing sister—she saw the shirt they had bought at Patong Beach Boutique the day before in a photo on the board. It was one of those terrible yet wonderful moments. Her sister was dead, but she had been found. At least this family would have closure. Eva had photographed that one.

Chapter 8

July 2, 2015, Santa Maria Transplant Hospital, San Antonio, Texas:

Once inside the clinic, all was calm, nothing like the parking lot, yet clearly a busy place. Too busy. That told CiCi too many people needed organ transplants. Everything appeared clinical, with four rows of typical waiting room chairs upholstered in their brown cushioned vinyl seats and an occasional end table strategically spaced. Lone people stared vacantly at the mounted television while pairs of people talked quietly. Perhaps the pairs were the patient and a support friend, but hopefully they were patients with their living donors like Jon and CiCi. The two friends headed to the receptionist, who couldn't have been more bored with her job as she handed Jon a stack of forms, so many forms.

CiCi asked about forms for living donors.

Another receptionist rushed over. "Are you here to donate to someone specific, or are you offering non-directed donation to anyone who needs the kidney?"

When CiCi said she planned to donate to the man sitting in the first row and starting on forms, the woman's excitement left. "You can't fill out anything until he has been accepted as a viable candidate."

"Rude," thought CiCi. She took in the signage around the room. *Number 1 Hospital for Liver Transplants in America* said one. *Living Donor Program for Livers, Kidneys, and Pancreas Here* said another. And on the wall next to her, *Risks for Live Donors in Kidney Transplants.*

Jon watched her study the third sign. "That sign got your attention?"

"Nothing new. I already read that stuff."

"Not stuff," Jon corrected. "Real. Are you sure about this?"

"If I said I could get hit by a truck when I walk on the sidewalk, would it satisfy you?"

"Not so much."

"Figured. Let's get on with this," said CiCi. This was about getting Jon on a transplant list. Period. He had to become eligible before there was any point in pursuing the living donor part.

While Jon finished the forms and played his phone game, CiCi chatted with others in the waiting room. Jon often teased her about how she could talk to whoever was near as if they'd been friends forever. She would become lifelong buddies with someone in line at the grocery store, acting as if they were having meaningful conversations. In fairness, however, CiCi found herself often embarrassed at restaurants because Jon would insert humor into other people's conversations. Their *brother/sister* nit picking was constant but harmless.

"So, were you early enough to miss the protesters out front?" CiCi asked the woman next to her.

"Oh no, I got to walk right through the middle of them. I have no idea who they were."

CiCi said she had looked around for identification but couldn't find any. It was a puzzle to her that anyone would protest transplants. Maybe it was a religious group, but that didn't seem likely. Transplants had been around since the fifties. CiCi remembered hearing about them as a child.

As if reading CiCi's mind, her seat neighbor said, "I know the Catholics support transplants. We're Catholic, so the first thing we did when I became ill was to check it out with the Church. Did you know Pope Benedict the Sixteenth had a donor card from the nineteen seventies?"

"Cool!" CiCi liked that such a powerful voice endorsed the transplants.

"There's a poster with him over there."

CiCi followed her finger to see a poster picturing the Pope. Above his head was a statement with his signature: "It's a profound act of love."

"Yeah," said her neighbor, "but when he became Pope, he could no longer donate. As Pope, when he died, his body became property of the Church and had to stay whole for burial."

CiCi frowned but kept her thoughts to herself. If it's good for the pauper, it should be good for the king. Or did she have that backward? She had read that statistically Catholics were the least likely to register on their driver's licenses.

Again, the woman read her mind. "The Vatican considers transplants morally and ethically acceptable."

CiCi looked again at the poster and smiled. "They must—this is a Catholic hospital. Maybe it's best the Pope doesn't donate. I don't know about needing the body intact thing for a Pope, but how would anyone decide who would receive a part of the Pope's body? Whoa. What a rush. What if you found out your kidney was from the Supreme Pontiff? Would it go to your head? Or would you fret over not being worthy?"

"Interesting. I like you. My name is Esther."

"CiCi. Why are you here?"

"I moved from Colorado with my daughter who helps care for me. That means I need to register with a new transplant clinic."

CiCi was aghast. "You have to start over on the waiting list?"

"No, no. I'm still in my place with UNOS, but I do have to register with the local region."

Just as CiCi and Esther became gal pals, all were called into the conference room for their Kidney Transplants 101 class. They each took turns introducing themselves and their purpose for being there. There was a brother/sister team with the sister planning to donate to her brother, but the rest of the participants were alone, just getting on the it-might-happen-in-seven-years list.

Some patients had been on dialysis for years already when they decided on the transplant—others were searching for answers. Jon and a ragged-looking woman were the only patients there who had not yet started dialysis. He had learned that transplants with no dialysis had a higher success rate, one more reason he was determined not to dialyze.

The ragged-looking woman said nothing more than her name. Her lips trembled and her eyes reddened with tears, but the fierceness in her stare kept others from asking her anything further.

Jon pointed out to CiCi there was no one there to donate "just cuz." CiCi frowned at him—she did that a lot.

They learned how the United Network for Organ Sharing (UNOS) worked. Recently, the organization had revised how to prioritize transplants. CiCi realized these people decided who would live and who would not. How does one decide who gets left behind? Most of the country had a wait time of three to five years, but the San Antonio region was seven years, if lucky. They didn't go into why. For some reason, Houston was only three years, but patients could sign up in only one region at a time. The problem with Jon going to Houston was that the recipient had to be there within three hours of the notice. Driving from San Antonio would take three and a half hours for Jon, if not rush hour, and not counting the time needed to grab a ready bag and find parking.

With a private plane now out of the question, he reminded CiCi about his own plane soaring over the country so gracefully, efficiently, and quickly. Moving to Houston was out—he could not afford to live on his own anymore. And with his health failing, he would need CiCi's help. Jon was an only child of only children and was on his own in his elder years. He would not ask his stepdaughter and her family in the Northwest to take care of him. At CiCi's, he gave back through cooking, light construction, and honey-dos that she called *Jonny-dos*.

Jon whispered to CiCi like he knew what she was thinking. "Even if I could move to Houston, that's three years too long. I don't have three years."

"Dialysis could…" CiCi knew not to finish.

Next on the agenda was the good news for those who were on dialysis—the rules had changed and gave years of credit backdated to when they first dialyzed. She saw Esther's face light up— irrelevant info for Jon, but it meant something to Esther.

"In Colorado, I would only have to wait three years—here it's so long," Esther whispered to CiCi. "At least I get credit for my two years on dialysis."

Transplant 101 continued with the qualification factors and then listed how heart conditions, obesity, smoking, and substance abuse could disqualify someone.

CiCi could read the faces of two patients attending. They were overweight. "These people have probably dealt with weight issues all their lives," CiCi whispered to Esther. "If they could have controlled it all along, they might not be diabetic and on dialysis." Then she reminded herself that there are multiple reasons kidneys fail, and it was wrong of her to assume they were diabetic and wrong to assume diabetes was due to weight. Jon wasn't diabetic anymore and not overweight, yet here he sat. His blood sugar had been under control for at least fifteen years.

Jon persisted with the wait list discrepancies. "I'm seventy. In three years, I could have heart issues. You heard the disqualifiers."

It was true the recipient had to have acceptable cardiovascular function to survive the surgery and the stress of post-op. CiCi thought he was a bit dramatic because she had read about elderly recipients. However, his father had died from heart issues, so she kept quiet.

The money lesson sparked interest from everyone. Medicare covered transplant costs for eligible patients. It also covered about eighty percent of the anti-rejection medications. But then came the clincher—not all employer-based insurance covered transplants the same. All End-Stage Kidney patients were Medicare eligible, but Medicare was secondary to Group Health Plans, and the rest got too confusing for CiCi to follow. It would take a good insurance counselor to weed through it. Jon's Medicare would take care of him for the rest of his life, but CiCi thought about her hair stylist's sister. Medicare covered her while on dialysis, but, after a transplant and because she was still young, she would have Medicare for only two years after surgery. Then what? CiCi's heart broke. Could this be why she turned down the transplant? How fair was that? Old folks could get transplants without too much of a financial drain, but the young ones with families depending on them had to fret. At least pre-existing conditions would not make them uninsurable, but CiCi thought about proposals in Congress to do away with the *Affordable Care Act*. She hoped whatever Congress did would have a pre-existing conditions allowance, and not just for kidneys. CiCi, herself, couldn't change employment years earlier because of the pre-existing breast cancer thing. There was insurance to cover her cancer if she moved, but the price was astronomical. She knew what it was like to be stuck. She would not be sixty-five for three more years, so she made a note to herself to get a letter assuring insurability from her current carrier, but what about younger people like her daughter?

"You can do this," CiCi whispered to Jon. "You don't have to run away to Thailand."

Jon wasn't as optimistic. "I still need a donor and can't wait seven years for a deceased one."

Timing was perfect. The nurse brought up how to get a living donor. She mentioned letters to friends, posters, Facebook, church prayers. The list went on. When she asked if there were any hopeful living donors in the room, CiCi and the sister raised their hands. CiCi felt like she was in elementary school: *pick me, pick me.*

"Great," said the nurse. "We'll get your information while your recipients get their blood tests. But first, how do you know each other?"

CiCi and Jon told their story about meeting via *PairForLife.com* and becoming devoted friends. They knew their chance for being a kidney match was slim, but they had the same A-negative blood type, so that was a start.

The nurse looked around the room at each patient and raised her arms as if preaching to a congregation. "You never know. There's something about chemical attractions. We have had several husband/wife matches." Then she focused on CiCi and Jon. "You two ended up best friends, so maybe the chemistry is there." Then she went back to preaching to her room. "Also, there is paired sharing. We can talk about that later. For now, I will take the living donors with me to talk in the next room."

"Well, all righty then," CiCi told Jon. "We're rockin' and rollin' now." With that, she said goodbye to Esther, wishing her well, and squeezed Jon's hand as he headed for his blood draw and urine sample.

CiCi and the sister began Intro to Living Donation 201. They learned about a three-in-ten-thousand risk of death. It sounded great until CiCi realized that was one in thirty-three hundred, which was the size of a high school where she had taught for a few years. That school no longer felt so big. But the optimist took charge again right away. Yes, she could get high blood pressure as she aged, but, even without donation, most people's blood pressure increased with age (except CiCi's parents', which bode well for CiCi). There would be a scar—no sweat. Scars meant life had happened. The surgery would be performed laparoscopically— three little slices and one about two inches long, no fears for potential bikini lines if CiCi ever wore another bikini. Both she and the sister laughed about the bikini concern.

The nurse continued through the risks list: infection, hernia, damaging another organ while going for the kidney, blood clots, and other typical surgery risks. Internal scar tissue sometimes caused pain in later years. Of course, there was the risk of the donors facing their own kidney failure if something damaged the only one left. They would get a priority status with UNOS if that happened, though not a move to the head of the line, as many assumed. It was a risk worth pause, but she learned that kidneys generally both decline together unless cancer or injury took place.

Having one was as good as having two. CiCi thought about that quiet little man at the protest.

The donors learned they would have a team set up just for them. Clinics tried to avoid coercion by not allowing any crossover between the donor's and the recipient's care. That sounded like a good thing.

Then the two potential donors separated for interviews.

As soon as the nurse started CiCi's medical history, with cancer the second item on the list, the interview was over.

"But it was nineteen years ago. I didn't do chemo," CiCi pleaded. "Jon's nephrologist said nineteen years means I am like any other prospective donor."

The poor nurse. She learned about CiCi's tenacity and headed off to bring in the head honcho. CiCi explained she had Dr. DiLiberto's approval, and he was one of Santa Maria's transplant committee doctors.

Dr. Head Honcho was clear. "No." He explained it was for her own health that the ruling was in place. If she were to get cancer again, it would be difficult for her to do chemo on just one kidney.

"But," said CiCi, "any donor could develop cancer later in life and might need chemo. If I had donated at age forty-two, no one would have known that at age forty-three I would have breast cancer. Besides, I didn't have chemo then. I'm just like any other potential donor."

"But you *did* have cancer, and we know that. The answer is unequivocally no."

She met up with Jon as he was returning from the lab.

The fire in her face told him they had turned her down. "You know, you don't do rejection well."

"They have their protocol," she mocked.

"I don't like this place much, anyway. Too many patients."

Chapter 9

January 2005, Phuket, Thailand:
Business had slowed down for Eva, for which she thanked her list of holy names who served her so well in the wave. So many families, however, had still not found their loved ones, and so many of the loved ones in Eva's care had not yet been found by their families. She looked at the man Marco was processing—the poor person had decomposed so much they only guessed he was a man because of his clothing. She had smelled dead animals before, but this was different. A doctor kindly gave her Vicks to spread under her nose.

At that moment, she pondered Charles's proposal at the hospital to steal and sell the medical supplies. She was grateful Chati walked up when he did, or she would have made a public mess out of telling Charles what she thought of his idea. But he was right. Their usefulness lessened each day, so time to think about her next move. The room she had rented was gone, and so was the manager's hotel, so he might not need a tutor for his son for a while. But there was no way she would steal medical supplies.

"Dude!" Charles exploded into the *wat*. "I was talking to a reporter out there. Not a single person died on one of the Andaman Islands."

Eva looked up from her corpse of the minute. "And?"

"They're all fishermen. When they felt the quake, they headed out to sea where the wave was a big hump and waited until after it crashed."

"That's probably what their ancestors did. Not like us gullible tourists who ran out to watch the spectacular event," replied Marco.

Charles added that there was no earthquake to feel in Phuket, so it wasn't their fault they were stupid.

"I repeat, and?" Eva finished logging in the remains of a young woman and moved to another shrouded body, hoping there was something there to help her with her task. Bodies were deteriorating rapidly now.

"I'm no Good Samaritan," Charles said. "I need to be paid. Besides, the Thais have enough volunteers. It's the new year, time to take charge of my life."

Eva stared at him. Take charge of his life? Who was this person? This didn't sound much like Charles. He must have been listening to a motivational tape or something.

Charles acted like the reporter had sought him out for the job. "The tsunami covered some of those islands. I—we—can work in construction. For hire. The government couldn't possibly look closely at visas at a time like this."

"So, what makes you think they'll hire you?" asked Eva.

"If the wave wiped over the island, and these were poor fishermen, the homes were complete losses. Everyone is still alive. They'll rebuild, and without building codes."

Eva reached across her makeshift table and pinched Charles on the cheek. "So? What? Are you planning to get paid in fish?"

Charles swatted her hand away, made a face, and told her he had a job lined up in Bangkok to pay his way to the islands. No more death.

Marco finally agreed with Charles. He told Eva he admired the Thais, but he had had enough, too. He had overheard a doctor at the hospital say the American doctors were leaving. If the docs were leaving, why not him? He wouldn't go to the islands, but he would work with Charles in Bangkok. He couldn't go home yet.

61

Even though the guys didn't ask Eva to join them, she said she needed to stay in Phuket longer. She loved it there.

Back at the tent that afternoon, Eva watched Charles and Marco pack their few belongings into their new backpacks that she was certain had belonged to someone who no longer needed them. She knew it would be unlikely for Americans with no special skill to work for money in Bangkok and wondered if Marco knew that, too. She also knew they could never admit they would finance their way to the islands by selling jewelry taken from the dead. They never took the only form of jewelry ID—they weren't evil—she knew they just took extra stuff, thinking it would be easy to claim it had been lost in the chaos. She knew, but she said nothing.

Eva didn't understand why Marco had bonded with Charles so tightly. She had named that bond *the brotherhood of the white van*. Why couldn't Charles follow Marco instead of Marco following Charles? Charles had a plan and was on the move, and Marco went along for the ride.

As the white van brotherhood headed out in an unexplained rush, Charles looked back toward the tent. "Hey Eva, what happens when you get scared half to death … twice?"

"What?"

"Don't know—saw it in a fortune cookie. Cheers."

And they were gone.

****

The guys were relieved Eva chose not to go—there was a halo about her that irritated them, particularly Charles.

The itinerary changed before they got to the end of the road. Charles had never planned to go to Bangkok. Charles guided them away from the highway to the city center and headed to the remains of the shipyard. Since Marco didn't know how to get to Bangkok, much less how to sell the jewelry, he stuck with Charles and soon discovered Charles had not even looked at a map for this decision to head into the ocean.

Chaos still pervaded what remained of the port of Phuket. The only active ships were anchored at sea with tenders transporting essential personnel. Clearing debris and unloading supplies was the only business.

Charles marched toward some activity around one of the tenders.

Marco, following two paces behind Charles, grabbed Charles's shoulder to stop him. "What are we doing?" Obviously, there were no flights or ferries yet into the Andaman Islands because of the tsunami damage.

Slapping Marco's hand off his shoulder, Charles stopped so suddenly that Marco ran into him. "The reporter outside the *wat* gave me the names of the three English-speaking boat captains he had interviewed and the names of their ships."

"Are you going to walk up and ask willy-nilly if we can hitch a ride? We aren't hitchhiking across America here."

Charles turned to face the boats anchored in the bay. "No, we aren't going willy-nilly hitchhiking. We negotiate. I know what I'm doing. These captains will only be in port getting supplies until tomorrow. Come or don't come." And he headed down the street.

Marco followed.

When Charles approached the first captain about steerage and work, the sailor laughed heartily at the naïve Americans and started to walk off, but he turned and handed Marco a map. He suggested they know where they were going before jumping onto a boat. The Andaman Islands were near Thailand but belonged to India, which was across the Andaman Sea and the Bay of Bengal. They should check the Indian visa laws. Then he looked fiercely at Charles and called him a fool. The question of payment didn't come up.

Charles learned quickly and approached the second captain with a plan to work while on board and then volunteer aid once they got to the islands. This captain sized up Marco's muscular stance

63

and agreed to take him but said Charles didn't have the strength. Marco politely declined.

Charles, born for business, took "No" as a learning opportunity. It helped that the third captain they found needed money from the diamond engagement rings Charles showed him. Once on board, the captain assigned them to a gray-haired crew member, four and a half feet tall, whose shoulders bulged from years of pulling ropes and hauling fully loaded trunks up and down gangplanks. He said his name was George, the name he took during his English classes.

The captain walked away, and George grumbled at Marco and Charles as he steered them toward a tiny galley with two gas burners, an old stainless-steel sink that didn't know it was *stainless*, and a small pile of pots and pans. "The captain, he think I like talk with Americans because I take English class. Americans are vultures. But it is what it is. A famous thing you say, no?" He didn't wait for an answer. "You cook? Cook quit yesterday."

Marco said he used to help at his aunt's taco café but didn't know much about cooking fish.

George slapped him on the back. "You learn. You read Thai? We have Thai cookbooks." He growled a frightening pirate sounding laugh, including the "arrr." Then he turned to Charles. "You, skinny man, you will do what this guy say. You wash pots and pans until they shiny. And you keep head pretty and neat."

Charles threw his backpack on the small wobbly table, making it rock. He didn't try to stop the tip, but it survived the fall. "Marco doesn't tell me what to do."

"He do now."

Charles turned away from George to glare at Marco, then turned to George. "What is this about my head?"

George laughed the pirate laugh again. "Not you head. You stupid? We go up to fresh air now and check head out now."

Just before the base of the companionway, George pointed to the head. He didn't need to point, though. The smell from the toilet was distinct.

Marco put a friendly arm around Charles. "It's not as bad as the bodies."

Charles shoved Marco's arm away and stormed up the stairs.

Marco smiled and stepped out into the fresh air to stand beside Charles and stared out at sea. The boat had already traveled out of Phuket and was heading to sea. George came up behind him and pushed Marco's shoulder just enough to make him grab the nearest railing. "Do you wonder," he asked, "we throw you and skinny friend overboard once we go deep water? I think have you money. You be tasty chum for fish we catch for dinner." Marco tried to laugh, to play the joke, but his throat dried up. All he could do was cough.

Charles bounced around, looking for help. The other sailors weren't paying any attention.

George howled. "Don't mess you pants. We nowhere clean them." He put his arm around Marco's shoulder and whispered so Charles could not hear. "Not worry. We merchants, not pirates. But Charles not you friend."

The first day passed. Marco surprised himself with his first dinner. It was a simple pan-fried fish the crew caught that afternoon. They, at least, had gutted the fish and prepared it for Marco to use. George gave him cooking tips while grabbing some coffee in the galley. From George, Marco learned there were over three hundred islands in the archipelago, and over two thousand people died. Charles's story was about only one island, but tribal history did teach them to head to sea after a quake, which saved lives. Charles wanted a way to make money fast, but George straightened him out. Many islands were off limits to outsiders. The captain said their course headed five days through the Bay of Bengal to Sri Lanka, a better fit for them. In fact, their vessel was taking supplies for the tsunami victims there before heading to the southern ports in India. He said an estimated 30,000 people died in Sri Lanka. Because of the tragedy, the Sri Lankan Civil War was on hold, but the rebels made it impossible to get those supplies to the controlled areas.

The sound of war and rebels terrified Marco. That's why he didn't enlist in the military at home, and here they would deal with more death. Needing to go somewhere, the islands a no-go and Sri Lanka not appealing, Charles negotiated steerage to Chennai on the coast of southern India where the captain said much tsunami aid was needed. Their short trip to the Andaman Islands ended up ten days to India.

Later, while eating the curried snapper caught that day, Marco snarled his words at Charles. "We'll still work among the dead."

Charles rolled up his fist, but at the last minute hit the table instead of Marco. "Dude, we can make our way to New Delhi and figure it out then. We still have jewelry to sell. India has a low cost of living. We can stay there with little money. And a lot of them speak English."

Marco wasn't sure about living on a serious budget in New Delhi. Again, movies came to mind. He liked Thailand and only left with Charles because he thought there was a plan.

Charles sulked for the rest of the voyage. Not liking him much, Marco let him simmer. He even considered dumping Charles, but knowing no one else, his situation felt hopeless. Charles was dangerous, but not as dangerous as being alone.

****

Finally in the waters off southern India, the captain sent them ashore in a dinghy near the small fishing village of Sippikulam. This way, they avoided the port authority at Tuticorin and the passport issues, which would have resulted in an expensive embarrassment for the captain (and their arrest, Marco pointed out to Charles). He gave them written instructions asking a friend to house them for the night and to help them find their way to Chennai.

Since Sippikulam was primarily a flat beach, few structures remained. But, fortunately for the locals, the island of Sri Lanka had blocked some of the fury from the wave. As planned, the busy recovery efforts on the shore disguised the Americans' arrival. Charles showed the instructions to the first person he saw. The man couldn't read; however, Charles's botched pronunciation of the contact's name earned a laugh and a finger pointing to a large man only twenty feet away.

The big guy made a quick cell phone call and escorted them to his shack where they cleaned up as much as possible in a barrel of fresh water. Another phone call and an hour later had them drinking in a cramped, smoky dive with their new host, a most likable little man in an expensive western suit who spoke superb English. A suit in this place with no air conditioning, not even a fan—Marco wondered why the pretense. Charles, however, caught on at once and explained that the two Americans were on a life adventure before becoming serious about their careers. His father was a wealthy stockbroker in Chicago, and Marco's family owned a huge hotel chain in the southern U.S.

Marco choked, spitting out his beer.

Their host introduced himself as Ori—he was a financial adviser with businesses growing faster than imaginable. Charles said he had a good imagination.

Ori smiled. He lowered his voice and spoke only to Charles.

Conversations from locals at tables around them—also in whispers with an occasional burst of laughter—added to the conspiratorial air. Thick grease laden smoke and dim light didn't comfort Marco's nerves any, either.

Charles appeared comfortable in the dark back-room atmosphere, and he didn't even protest that this guy kept calling him Charlie. He leaned over to Marco and apologized for being such a jerk on the ship. "Ori filled me in on his business. We have our golden ride here. Ori made me realize we missed the opportunity of a lifetime in Thailand. We're good-looking, charismatic young men. With the connections we made helping the tsunami victims, we could have set ourselves up as brokers to bring Americans to Thailand for transplants. The villagers lost everything and will be desperate to make ends meet."

Ori excused himself to play a vintage jukebox. It had old forty-five rpm records of American rock and roll sung in what Charles said was Hindi but learned later was Tamil.

Marco didn't care about the music, but at least the noise covered what Charles was saying. Marco whispered, "Selling organs is against the law everywhere."

"It is, but who's looking? Everyone knows Thailand is the go-to place for transplant tourism."

Something that sounded like the Beach Boys chanting *Good Vibrations* blasted through the voices.

"I think their new laws make that not true anymore. Besides, what do you know about it? Just what connections are you talking about?"

"Shit, Marco. Are you Eva now? You aren't so perfect. You got here using jewelry stolen from dead people."

Marco winced. "Bastard. Besides, we aren't in Thailand anymore, or haven't you noticed? We are, like, on another planet."

"So now we're name calling. This place is desperate to bring in money—we don't have to be in Thailand. And this guy is an entrepreneur." With that, he bought a round of drinks and proposed a toast to new endeavors. "I like India," he announced to all in the bar. "I think I might stay awhile."

Most present did not speak English, but they knew they were getting drinks. Ori grinned so big his mustache reached to his eyes.

That night, they stayed at Ori's home, a palatial estate high on a hill overlooking the water. They watched the cleanup crews at work on the debris from the wave that was not a wave, more like a gigantic explosive inflation of the sea. A hurriedly built new fishing dock moored the few boats returning to life.

****

The next day, Ori helped them get passports. Charles was all smiles. Marco wasn't smiling, but he was relieved—passports meant maybe he wouldn't end up in an Indian prison. Then the three entrepreneurs were off to the Tuticorin Airport to fly to Chennai for "the business opportunity of a lifetime."

It was convenient to have Ori along to guide them and to translate, but Marco wondered just what that boat captain had written in his message to this man. Or what Charles had agreed to without Marco's knowledge. His skin crawled. He kept seeing the dead bodies from the temple as he fondled the jewelry in his pockets. He also saw Charles's white van saving him when his roof disintegrated.

"Thank you for doing so much for us. You didn't have to." Marco tried for more insight into this golden ride.

"It is no problem, my friend. We are conducting business. Business is always worthwhile. I hope you enjoy our flight."

On the plane, Charles asked Ori about the effects of the tsunami on the area and how much business they would find. Ori told them statistics depended on who was counting—authorities estimated over 10,000 people died in India. Many bodies remained unclaimed. Since bodies were in these guys' realm of recent expertise, they knew that meant a mass grave.

It was not the dead that mattered in their new line of work. The counts were not yet in, but an estimated 70,000 refugees were to be displaced miles from the fishing piers into resettlement areas in the territory Marco and Charles would cover.

Ori said, "Farmlands hit by the wave will never be useful again because of saline pollution. And fishing boats and piers were destroyed. These are poor people, so how can they rebuild?"

The people had lived a life wound around religion, the sea, tides, the moon, and fish. The ruined land meant idle lives for these victims and little hope for honest income.

"And we can solve that for them?" Marco couldn't stop his sarcasm. He thought about his ride on the roof crashing up the street in Patong. It was not just the dead who got caught in currents. Sitting here on a plane to God knows where, he was the living dead and caught in Charles's wake. This man Ori presented a pious tone, but Marco understood the true motivation as he begrudgingly accepted his contract with the devil.

Ori faced Marco directly, using his hands for emphasis as if making a public speech. "Their piers, their boats, their way of life is gone. But you will help." He placed his finger on Marco's chest. "They see themselves as nobodies. And the women? The women in India are modest. Some were found nude because their clothing had come off in the tangles of the debris. We think too many women chose to drown rather than consciously expose themselves. Those who survived suffer nightmares and shame."

Marco visualized his own mother and sister in this life. Charles kept talking, but Marco stayed in his thoughts.

"Shame and poverty breed desperation," said Ori.

Marco turned to Charles for assurance but found none.

"Gentlemen," Ori said, "we are humanitarians. We will help these people help themselves. And now we have arrived."

****

A driver dressed in a traditional sari met them at Chennai International in a luxurious black limousine. She offered vodka tonics with a squeeze of lime to refresh them before meeting Carrie Breun at the Hilton Chennai.

Over dinner, Ori guided Charles and Marco delicately through conversations with Ms. Breun. Ori masterfully tamed Charles and emboldened Marco. There was no negotiating—Ms. Breun ran a firmly established kidney brokerage out of Los Angeles, reaching across the world. That she could find a place for Charles and Marco in that business was an honor not to be questioned.

In no time, the young Americans were finding Indian donors for kidney transplant recipients from the U.S., Israel, and England. Charles had seen himself as the broker when toasting to entrepreneurship in that bar in Sippikulam, but he soon learned the wealthy Indians already had an established brokerage system with no space for a youngster from Chicago. Charles and Marco's job description sounded more like scavengers than brokers.

Ms. Breun had worked in this system since transplant tourism first started twenty years earlier, making herself indispensable with multinational organ recipient connections. Her foot had already pushed itself well into the door. Hell, not only the door, the entire castle. With his vision of grandeur vanished, Charles embraced his new business. Marco, not so much, but at least he wasn't in an Indian prison.

Over time, the two returned to Thailand several times to complete tours for Ms. Breun, but the government there made it increasingly difficult to use Thais as donors. Tourists had to come with a family donor and documentation attesting to the relationship. Part of what Charles and Marco did under Ori's guidance and Ms. Breun's orders was to create that needed familial documentation for recruited *cousin* donors from Brazil, Pakistan, and Myanmar. Finding donors within the vast population of Chennai and using the Indian hospitals and surgeons, though illegal, made India much more suitable for their purposes than Thailand.

Years passed—neither of them talked about Eva or *the kid*.

Chapter 10

July 2, 2015, CTMRI, San Antonio, Texas:
When Dr. Alexandra Segel opened the door to her building at the Institute, she stopped as she always did to take in a deep breath. Most people thought it was her delay tactic before facing the stress of her work. They were wrong. She loved this place with its pure white walls, white tile, bright light, stainless steel everything. It was a cliché research lab, which was part of the draw—it was predictable. She and Maura had talked about sharing a house during their early career days, but they decided it would have to be a duplex. Maura was all about color—she called it *warm*. Alex supposed that made her preference for white the opposite, but it wasn't *cool*. No, not *cool*—it was clean, not busy. It was like the time she visited the Missouri Ozarks in August. Texas air was hot and syrupy. Like reds and oranges. The Ozarks air was warm halter top weather, but it was clean and crisp. Like white. Like her lab. As she stood now at the main door and took in her ceremonial cleansing breath—as Maura would call it—the clean and crisp *white* air penetrated all the way to her toes.

Within two steps, she heard him yelling. So much for *clean and crisp*, she told herself. Walls muffled the conversation allowing only the words *temperature* and *time* to pass through.

And then she heard, "You dumbass piece of shit! You ruined us!"

Her lab assistant walked by and rolled his eyes.

"What's happening?" Alex's eyes asked back.

"Too bad for that kid. He's just an intern. Doctor South's been reaming him about losing the volunteer's kidney and IPS cells because he didn't check the temperature when he arrived after his class this morning. Dr. South found it while you were out. Hope the kid doesn't quit. He just needs to grow up." Her assistant continued his journey out the door, cigarettes and cell phone in his hand.

"Wait! The kidney?" Too late, the man was out of range. Alex knew the kid, Stanley, a timid little guy not even out of college, working as a summer intern. Dr. South often berated interns and chastised any doctors who dared challenge his judgement, so Dr. Segel chose not to intervene and headed toward her own office.

Like so many others Alex had met in medical research, Dr. South could be terribly overbearing. No, that would be a serious understatement—they were flat out assholes and did all they could to stress the interns. Other doctors admonished Alex for being too soft. She supposed *assholeness* had to be *modus operandi* to sort out the best of the best, but she found that idea hard to buy into—she thought it only sorted the most persistent of the persistent. At any rate, the interns did impossible feats for a chance at a slot on the permanent staff after graduation.

These kids had to be top in their classes just to enter the facility. When she thought about it, only the top of the top high schools got into the top research universities. Then only the top of the top universities got into the top medical programs, so these were the valedictorians of the valedictorians of the valedictorians. This kid had come from Salk High School, the local medical careers magnet school, and had wanted to work in medicine his entire life. More concerned about a good grade than being right, he had trouble learning when to stand his ground. Too bad. He was extraordinarily talented.

Alex tried to recall what she had heard on a meditation site. (Maura had signed her up in her not-so-subtle manner to counsel.) It was something about OCR or OPR or some such acronym, sounded like co-dependence stuff. Step one in becoming a full-fledged *suckerunderling* (Maura's word) was allowing wrong to happen for fear of loss of, say, prestige, or a job. South knew how to find his *suckers*, and Maura told Alex she was one of them.

"Fine, Maura," she said to herself. For now, however, she needed to get to her office to check reports.

The flashing light caught her attention at once. The temperature on the vault for THE kidney said "OFF," but a quick scan of the record showed forty-three degrees for five hours. In Fahrenheit, that would be like a fever of 109 plus! That kidney always had to be at body temperature. In essence, the incubator had malfunctioned, and the intern let it have a fever, burning the scaffold and all the attached cells.

"Damn. Really? He couldn't burn test cells? Damn, damn, damn!" The impact hit her. She was a fool to feel sorry for him. "Idiot!" She had attended a CTMRI upper level staff meeting that morning and then coffee with Maura. She should have looked herself, but she relied on her team to do their jobs. Swatting her stapler off the desk, she caught herself before knocking the microscope over.

Separated from the lab by a glass wall, she saw her team. And they saw her. Respectfully, they turned back to work. Needing privacy to think, she reached for the button to make the glass opaque. But she stopped her hand. She looked over the lab and watched her crew working with vials of blood, centrifuges, atomic force microscopes, slides, all those things that shout "lab" at visitors. It wasn't the stuff of a lab that grabbed her heartstrings. What Alex saw were three of her five scientists (her one assistant was outside smoking cigarettes again, and the intern was in South's purgatory) who stood by those instruments hour after hour, squinting their eyes and furrowing their brows as they performed test after test, searching. Searching. Searching. It didn't count if the cell regeneration happened only once. Watching these three at work now, she decided they must not have heard about the kidney yet, or they were so good at their jobs that they knew to push on.

Her team was one of the best in the nation working with regenerative medicine. They specifically were trying to rebuild a kidney with induced pluripotent stem (IPS) cells from a damaged organ donated by a kidney disease patient. What could be so difficult? They had successfully remodeled pig kidneys—lucky oinkers. And now they had decellularized deceased human kidneys down to a basic scaffold just like they did with the pigs to provide something to shape the new cells. Alex had tried to explain the work to Maura many times, but her best explanation was to refer to the human manipulation process as miracle work. Alex told herself this was warmth. Maura could have all the color she wanted, but this was life.

Embryonic cells became whatever was needed to perform whatever function. They were all a fetus had, yet somehow those cells became a baby with all its parts. In 1962, Scottish researchers cloned Dolly the sheep, ground-breaking news. They made an entire animal, but a kidney patient didn't need an entire person, just a kidney. In 2006, Shinya Yamanaka of Japan discovered how to reprogram adult mouse skin cells to revert to their embryonic state, bringing about IPS cells. He used gene editing technology to add only four genes, and all the switched off genes turned on: hearts, lungs, eyes, all of them.

A decade passed, and Alex's team was now deliberately manipulating their reprogrammed cells by urging IPS cells developed from the patient's skin to become kidney cells. They were not creating babies (though Alex assumed labs somewhere in the world were trying to do just that)—they were trying to save the lives of people already in the world. Dialysis was never the permanent answer. For now, people with failed kidneys relied on transplants for their best hope of quality life. But the immunosuppressant medications needed with transplanted organs had side effects ranging from headaches, to tremors, to glaucoma, along with vulnerability to every cold virus out there. It was a lengthy list. Besides, the transplant world could not maintain a supply of donors.

Studying how carefully her team entered details into their computers, Alex reached for the button again to seclude herself. She turned to her stainless-steel desk and stared at the latest lab report she had provided for the foundation (i.e., the Senator). She had hoped it was an illusion yesterday, but there it was again, in black and white. The deceased human test kidney did not filter enough blood per minute, causing oxygen issues in the cells. The kidney needed more blood to reach each cell, but, when the techs increased the volume, the flow exploded the cells. Even if they still had Estes's kidney, they were not ready to risk implantation if deceased kidneys were blowing up.

Then she picked up the report given to the Senator—the one she had mentioned to Maura at coffee, Dr. South's version. She didn't want to look at it.

Being the right size compared to human organs and performing the proper functions made pigs natural test subjects for her team. Extensive research from the 1990s already existed that explored using the animals as donors in human kidney transplants. Pig transplants faced two major setbacks besides the creep factor of putting animal parts into a human. First, scientists discovered carbohydrates covered pig kidneys and caused human antibodies to attack them fiercely. Gene editing, however, allowed research farms to make the animals without carbohydrates. Baboons survived with modified pig kidneys, so why not humans?

The second reason was the stuff of post-apocalyptic novels. In 1998, a team found that genes for retroviruses thrived in pigs but avoided detection. The fear of monster retroviruses killing off humanity brought the pig transplants to a halt.

Alex's team began their remodeling studies with these creatures, knowing the goal was human kidneys. About the time South's team decellularized human kidneys, the evolution of CRISPR/Cas9 allowed advanced gene editing to end the retrovirus issue and reopened research for using genetically altered pig organs for human transplants. China was well on its way in this field. Alex wished them luck—in the U.S., animal rights and GMO activists would have a heyday with that research.

Stirring the imaginary sugar in her coffee, she thought their explosion problem was because they removed too much when decellularizing the human organs, causing a weakness in the remaining scaffold. Maybe luck and not skill made their volunteer's kidney work. Then again, maybe it was because they were building on kidneys from deceased human donors. The pigs were living, and Mr. Estes was living. It was too bad they could not conduct research with living humans like labs did in the 1950s. Mr. Estes's value was irreplaceable. She decided to meet with her team to discuss the deceased versus living aspect.

If the research, the team, and the remodeled kidney were to survive, they had to beat the pig-to-human transplants being studied in China and the artificial implants from the West Coast group. Alex had been telling Maura about West Coast again, knowing kidney talk rated alongside plain rice cakes for Maura's interest inventory. Dr. South's human trials had to happen, and soon. He had been ranting about it for months. He told the NIH, in writing, that everything was going according to schedule and that human clinical trials could begin soon.

When Alex looked again at the reports still in her hands, she saw the discrepancy. The reported success statistics came from their pig models used in their trials. It worked for the pigs, but they now had moved on to human cadaveric models. She frowned and decided not to think about it right then.

Closing her eyes, Alex visualized her wonderful team in the adjacent room working to the best of their abilities. They needed more help and more funds to buy more equipment to explore more variables. South's concept had to do it all, not just replace dialysis—people died on dialysis. Their kidney would be the whole enchilada and make the hated dialysis diet a thing of the past.

Alex took a deep breath. Kidneys are perfect. She must have thought mighty big of herself to imagine she could duplicate such a wonder. It might have been better to focus on making transplants more practical like the other team at the Institute.

Maura's voice tickled her head. "Get over yourself." Maura would tell her to get to work.

The figures on the report to the Senate committee must have been a careless error, Alex decided. She would ask Dr. South about it when he was in a better mood. He must have been tired and looked at the old pig chart instead of the current human one when reporting their progress.

She hit the window button again to see her team busy at work. They, at least, weren't wasting their day wondering about incorrect reports and burned kidneys.

Chapter 11

anuary 2008, Oliver Tambo International Airport, Johannesburg, South Africa:

The nineteen hours on three planes from Bangkok to Johannesburg allowed Eva to cycle through excitement, sorrow, guilt, joy, love, fear, more guilt, more excitement. As she reminisced about her nine years in Thailand, the tsunami remained her strongest memory—so much pain, yet so much courage and love at the same time.

Thinking about the three babies she had delivered in the little villages, however, still made her catch her breath and brought tears. She had never seen herself taking care of children, but necessity dictated she needed a job. Thailand had strict rules for working foreigners—she could not replace a Thai. She could, though, teach kindergarten in English. To Eva's surprise, she enjoyed children.

By far, most women in Thailand gave birth in hospitals, but remote rural communities occasionally relied on midwives when there was no time to go to the hospital. For the first delivery, Eva was teaching English to the midwife's five-year-old son when the woman asked Eva to help translate for an American woman volunteering in a local village. Eva agreed.

The American, unaware of her pregnancy, had escaped an abusive husband and moved to Thailand to live affordably. When their visas expired, most American expats left the country for a few hours and started their time again. But pregnant, this woman feared traveling that far. Since she had overstayed her visa by weeks, she avoided the hospital when her contractions started.

Giving up one's home to live undocumented in a foreign country wasn't a light choice, but it seemed this woman's only way. And now she was in serious legal jeopardy—Thai immigration prisons were fearsome places. First, she would have her baby and then solve the visa problem. Eva never learned of the woman's outcome.

Eva's second delivery was more planned, and she felt honored to assist the midwife. However, the third delivery, a total surprise, was the midwife's own baby who announced his presence a little early. The midwife talked her through everything, but it was Eva who received the baby.

Now following her nine-hour layover in Bangkok, leaving Suvarnabhumi Airport after so many years took the wind out of her. She had identified the dead, saved lives, enriched lives, and brought lives into the world. What could be next? Four years had passed while she continued to help tsunami victims, and bodies still needed identification at the Phuket morgue. She could spend the rest of her life there and never solve that problem. Many were from Myanmar, where the families were too poor to repatriate them. She wondered if her own body would go home to Texas if she died. She let her parents know her location once a year, but they never acknowledged her notes.

Before she knew it, she was on Kenyan Airlines from Nairobi to Johannesburg to join up with an HIV AIDS awareness program that was turning the tide on the spread of this terrible disease in Botswana. She had learned about the program from Dr. Smith, an American guest doctor who periodically helped with kidney transplants in Phuket. It seemed odd the Thais needed guest doctors when they ran amazing medical tourism facilities, but he said bringing in American doctors helped the credibility of their programs with the American patients. She had met him a couple of weeks earlier while helping with a tsunami victim's years-delayed identification. He seemed like a genuine, caring physician. She trusted him.

As she peered out the plane's window, she watched the lush green of central Africa turn to desert mountains. The Oliver Tambo International Airport in Johannesburg claimed to be the busiest airport in all of Africa. Since everything she owned fit in her carry-on and one large handbag, Eva didn't need to wait for her baggage. She owned two sun dresses, one pair of light cotton pants, two blouses, a sarong to cover her during temple visits, three sets of undies, and one change of shoes. She lived comfortably if she stayed in warm climates. It had been years since she experienced wintry weather, so she would buy a jacket for winter in Botswana. To think of June and July as winter boggled her mind.

She looked around the crowd for the greeter from the HIV program who would take her to their satellite site in Gaborone at the border between South Africa and Botswana. The brochure had said arriving at Johannesburg's airport was easier than flying directly to Gaborone, and Eva didn't question the advice. Called Hope in Victory, the program's brochure was impressive. Dr. Smith had set up a position for her.

The airport was as busy as the brochure claimed. She had prepared to save money every way possible and bit into her peanut butter sandwiches from her backpack. Large cranes and scaffolding sprawled everywhere, and posters bragged of the magnificent renovations underway for the 2010 FIFA events. South Africa would be ready for them, but not yet. However, for now, she savored her tasty peanut butter—fine restaurants and the future of the rail did not interest Eva since the Hope people would take care of food and transportation.

After an hour of locals assuring her terrible traffic plagued Johannesburg, she asked someone with a cell phone to call the number from the brochure. Not a working number. Fighting fear and tears, she sat on a bench to think. This was a reputable organization doing good for the world, and an American doctor had arranged everything for her. Surely, they would be along soon.

Charity organizations often cut budgets, so maybe the office phone had to go.

Exhausted, her despair took hold. She wanted a shower. Signs mentioned showers at Rennies Lounge that cost little for access, but she feared for her money situation now. She used all her cash from her jobs in Phuket for the plane fare. She still had money from her so-called college fund but avoided using it.

And what if the Hope in Victory people showed up while she showered?

Chapter 12

July 2, 2015, Santa Maria Hospital, San Antonio, Texas:

"So now what?" CiCi wondered. The lobby had lost its charm. CiCi decided even the picture of the Pope with his admirable message looked dull.

Jon was quiet as they exited the clinic. There were still a dozen protesters, but they no longer shouted with the fervor they had earlier—it was more like bored children who could not let Mom have the last word. They looked sad to CiCi until she remembered they had attacked Jon. As they walked toward the car, she reminded herself to look at the brochure soon, but not in Jon's presence.

Jon broke his silence. "See that thirty-something woman standing by the wall? The scraggly one? She was in the conference room where they held the introductory lesson."

Facial recognition was always hard for CiCi. She relied on voice and body movement to identify people. Jon made fun of her inability to recognize movie stars, but she didn't care about stars. "I don't know," CiCi said. "You tell me."

Jon said, "I think she introduced herself as Belva or Melba, or something like that."

"She looks confused. Should we offer to help her?"

"No, she looks like she knows how to get around on her own, a street woman. I'll bet money she came in to use the restroom and pretended to be a patient to get fruit and bagels. I'm tired."

CiCi studied her companion—his entire body sagged, and he had shrunk two inches under the disappointment. "Let's take the afternoon off and go for some sushi."

"That's something I won't be able to eat after a transplant, so I guess I need to fill up now." He quickened his steps. Eating sushi and raw oysters always turned his mood around, and the restaurant owner would have a delightful story to distract him from his illness.

Dooziesushi was a small mom-and-pop place with about six little tables and a counter in a strip mall near home. It was a fun international event for dinner. Al, the owner, was from China, his wife from Thailand, and his help from Vietnam. Not one Japanese person in a place that sold only sushi. To top it off, music came from a clock radio and ranged from classic rock to French café. No Japanese anything other than the sash tied around Al's forehead, yet Al offered the best sushi in town. The place had become Jon's hangout when CiCi traveled. Ignoring table service, they always sat at the sushi bar, so Jon and Al talked while Al worked. This night, however, Al had taken the night off, leaving Jon to fret over his future depleted immune system and raw oyster-induced bacterial infections.

Whenever oysters were in season, Jon bought a three-dozen bag at the grocery store once a week. While he salivated just thinking about oysters on the half shell, CiCi gagged at the smell, always had, something about eating a couple of dozen when she was only seven and throwing up for hours. Her brother rescued her by walking to the corner convenience store and coming home with Pepto Bismol. Through the years, her brother told everyone it wasn't that dramatic, but CiCi would not allow oysters, even in tiny bits for Thanksgiving dressing and gravy.

"You know, if I had money, I'd just go to Thailand."

CiCi cut him off. "So you have said. You know if you got caught, you'd go to jail."

"They would have to catch me in the act," he grumbled back.

"I just don't think it's all that easy, and Thai jails are not happy places. There must be more to it. What would you do for follow-up care?"

"People do it all the time," he snapped.

"I already looked it up in case you robbed a bank. Medicare would not cover your post-op needs unless you do it in the only Medicare-certified hospital in Mexico, and you would need a family connection with the donor. So there."

He smiled—she knew him so well. "If I robbed a bank, I would take enough to cover post-op. So there."

"I'm certain the penitentiary would take diligent care of you. Did you know I had a big FBI warning sign cross my screen while I searched illegal markets?"

"I'm sure Dr. DiLiberto will speak for your cause when they haul you off."

CiCi was pleased with herself—at least she got him to smile a bit.

****

Once they were home, Jon headed to bed for a nap. He tired easily these days but still seemed healthy. It was hard to listen to him talk about dying. Not that he moped and appealed to sympathy—his was hard-facts talk. CiCi was in a quandary. She had already paid for an expensive two-week tour to China that her friend Catalina had talked her into months before her camp-out in Hawaii. She had used sick-day payout money she got from her school district at retirement. It had all sounded grand, so grand that she talked another friend into being her roommate since Catalina had someone else. But the tour was due to leave the next week, and now she agonized over leaving Jon alone in the house—he had to ask her to open his water bottles these days. Jon wasn't a family member, so she didn't think trip insurance would refund her if she canceled. And Ruthie would be stuck without a roommate. But this kidney thing meant life or death.

Other than tiring so easily, Jon seemed fine. Worry and depression explained some of the fatigue. And the prostate issues that began before she left for Hawaii lingered despite the antibiotics, causing him to get up several times in the night for bladder matters. Clearly, the kidneys were still filtering something. She would speak with his doctor about leaving him alone. She knew if she spoke to Jon, he would tell her to go. He would never want her to alter her lifestyle for him. Alter her body, yes, her lifestyle, no.

Picking up her phone to start another relentless Google search to figure out why the protesters were at the clinic, CiCi called Val, who taught Human Geography and World Religions at Salk. She was a brilliant teacher. And she had her own experience with a kidney transplant. CiCi had not talked with her in years other than helping with the history fair. This would be great. She wondered if Val ran into any opposition with her donation.

****

"You honor me," said Val over a glass of wine at Thursday's Child. Thursday's was not the best place to talk, too noisy—but it was all CiCi could think of when Val said she had time right then but would be busy the rest of the week.

It was CiCi who should have felt honored. She admired Val's travels and wisdom from her days as an international flight attendant before the airline went out of business. Val was part of CiCi's motivation to see as much of the world as possible. CiCi knew her own body was aging, and traveling would get complicated once arthritis set in, so she planned to get it all in right away. Retirement was great.

"Before we start on the protesters and religion, did you have any second thoughts after you donated?" CiCi pulled out the information the man at the protest had given her. He grieved so deeply that she couldn't dismiss him.

Val shook her head. "It was the right choice for me. And I've had no personal difficulties because of it."

CiCi recalled Val telling her it was the Elliott brothers of the San Antonio Spurs who inspired her to give. Sean Elliott's kidney failed because of an all-too-common kidney disease. In 1999, his brother gave him his spare, which allowed Sean to return to basketball. CiCi thought it'd be nice to let Noel Elliott know the influence he had, but she suspected all the media attention through the years was a pretty good hint. Transplant statistics showed an increase in living donation went up 16 percent because of Noel's deed.

Val continued. "But you need to do your research. Look at the message from that man. His wife donated to a stranger who rejected and died just a year later. His wife now has so much pain from internal scar tissue that she can't function as a mother to her own children. She's young and has a lifetime to deal with this."

"So, you don't recommend it?"

"This is a personal decision. I have no regrets and am grateful I could give a young girl and her family more years together. Would I have done it if I had dependent children? I don't know. Complications are rare. Do your research."

CiCi smiled and took one of Val's hands. "You would run into a burning house to save someone—it's who you are. I'll perform due diligence. Now, why would there be such a shortage of deceased kidneys for transplantation? Why do we need living donors? Teach me. What would instigate protests?"

"People fear what they don't understand; then they make the source of the fear into something evil. Once it becomes evil, it gets confused with religion, even if the religion makes no claim for it."

"But I read nineteen people in America die every day while waiting for a kidney transplant. Where is the fear coming from? Wouldn't they be more afraid of the disease than the solution?"

"CiCi," Val said, "my guess is that those protesters were voicing the fears that many people hide."

CiCi waited—she knew Val would have more to offer.

Val sipped her wine, taking time to form her answer. "If I knew the source of the fear, I'd have solved the transplant issue. You could have donated your spare years ago but didn't. Why not?"

"Because I thought I might need it for someone close to me, but I marked my driver's license. Is it fear or just apathy?"

"Laziness, apathy, fear, ignorance? I mean, how hard is it to mark a driver's license? Yet people don't get around to it. They stand in line to renew the license and can't take an extra second to mark a box? Even laziness wouldn't account for that."

Val twirled her glass a bit and caught the light glowing through it. "France passed a law making all citizens automatic organ donors when deceased unless the individuals specifically place themselves on the refusal register. That takes care of the laziness and apathy part. It's inconvenient to opt-out and makes them feel selfish unless they have a sound reason. The French government hopes this will solve the problem. Critics don't think it will make much difference."

A server approached to see if they would like a basket of chips or some egg rolls. Both women waved him away.

CiCi leaned back in her seat to get comfortable but then pulled forward again because there was more to learn. "Sounds like a refusal registry is worth a try, but what could be a sound reason to oppose transplants? I've been looking. It looks like all the major religions support organ donation."

Val clarified, "It's the cultures, not the religions per se. The Japanese Shinto, for example, don't have a mandate against transplants, but they don't support the idea of brain death. They also have strong considerations about honoring what the ancestors gave them—their bodies. Westerners think the Shinto are concerned that the dead body is impure and dangerous. If they allowed injury, even as organ donation, they would interfere with the *itai*."

"*Itai?*" CiCi questioned.

"The connection between the deceased and those who mourn for the person. But *itai* is the West's explanation as to why the Japanese have a low rate of organ donation. Japanese scholars say deceased donor organ procurement can only take place after full circulatory death. Volunteering as a living donor is acceptable, but culturally they don't see altruism as we do. The gift requires something in return." Val paused and began again. "Culture studies require far more than a night with a drink in hand."

"Are there Shinto in San Antonio who would organize a protest?" CiCi asked, not understanding *itai* at all.

Val considered the question. "Probably not. We have Buddhist temples but no Shinto that I know of. Besides, protesting doesn't really fit."

They talked more about religions and beliefs about the afterlife. CiCi and Jon were so different from each other. He was a confirmed atheist—one died, and that was that. He would have agreed with Beowulf's heroic morality idea that promoted slaying dragons and performing great deeds so the bards would sing the legends. That was his eternity—the stuff of legends.

CiCi agreed Jon's concept was possible, but she believed everything was possible. Jon became intrigued with her dating profile because she mentioned she was a Texas Druid and posted a picture of the mini-Stonehenge surrounded by Texas bluebonnets in a cow pasture near Center Point—Texas, not England. The Druid part wasn't true—she thought *Druid* sounded fun but knew little about it. Nonetheless, Jon was impressed a Texan knew what a Druid was. She thought he was nuts. Anyone who loved the King Arthur tales knew Merlin was a Druid.

To CiCi, all was possible. Her mother always set out a Nativity scene at Christmas, but she also set out a Star of David, a coconut, and an ugly Aztec idol she had picked up in Mexico. Her mom joked she wanted to cover all bases. Then she would go into her speech about December twenty-fifth being a winter festival period used by the Romans to coax the heathen Anglo-Saxon Druids into Christianity. CiCi's cousin had traced their ancestry to the Viking invasion in England, and, though Vikings weren't Druids, CiCi decided she was close enough to claim wanna-be Druid.

CiCi brought her thoughts back to Thursday's Child and wine with her friend. Val was sure the protesters were not Christian Scientists. During her own transplant planning, a Christian Science friend explained her church believed primarily in spiritual healing, but organ and tissue donations were individual choices. If a church member needed a kidney and, if even with prayer, was certain to die, the church would support a transplant.

"So, what about the Jehovah's Witness?" asked CiCi. "TV doctor shows often have big drama over taking custody of a child because the parents refuse transfusions or appendectomies and so forth."

"That's a little over-simplified. They don't allow the exchange of blood, which was wise before blood typing came into play. If there is no blood exchange, they would allow it."

CiCi texted a friend who had been a transplant nurse before switching to teaching clinical classes at Salk. Thrilled to get a quick response, CiCi relayed the message to Val. "Kidney transplants involve only about a tablespoon of blood loss, so no transfusions. And all blood is removed from the donor kidney because as soon as blood is exposed to air, it clots."

Val nodded. "I'm sure the surgeons are very careful about that, but I didn't realize it was so little blood."

"So where did the protest come from?"

"The idea of what happens after death is such a fearful puzzle."

This was probably the best explanation CiCi could get. It was time to let it go. "True. 'What dreams may come when we have shuffled off this mortal coil, must give us pause' and all that.

Shakespeare and even *Star Trek* mention the 'Undiscovered Country.'"

"Leave it to the retired English teacher," said Val with her wine glass held up to toast English teachers.

CiCi returned the toast. "Maybe it was a combined protest group who didn't even understand each other's reasons. Most shouted about interfering with God's will, but one guy mentioned doctors not saving people so they could harvest the organs for profit. And there was the quiet man whose wife suffered so much, and her recipient didn't even survive."

The two decided the mysteries of the mind, body, and soul were too much to solve in one night and agreed organ transplants topped the lists of medical science wonders, right up there just under the discovery of penicillin.

CiCi once again thanked Val for squeezing her in at the last moment. "Do you remember that kid we had at Salk who did his independent study as a campaign to promote organ donation?"

"Yeah, he was a great kid and had connections. He raised twenty thousand dollars at one city wide talent show. I hear he's now in business on Wall Street, so I'm thinking his donation campaign is on his back burner now."

CiCi grew pensive. "You never know. I found him on Facebook a few years ago. I should write him and tell him I'm thinking about him. He was such a super high school kid. I think that project was more than just a grade for him."

Val held up her empty glass. "To great kids. And on that note, I need to head home. Good luck with your answers."

As they parted, Val called after her. "CiCi, I think the protests were deeper. Who decides life and death?"

****

91

Once home, CiCi did a recap of what Val had said for Jon's benefit. He wasn't impressed. Jon announced he'd had enough kidney shit for a day and turned on the TV, wrapped himself in a blanket and watched *Kitchen Wars* through his eyelids.

Chapter 13

January 2008, Oliver Tambo International Airport, Johannesburg, South Africa:

Eva studied the walkways at the airport, hoping that somehow the Hope in Victory people would suddenly appear. When she saw two men walking toward her, she thought they were an apparition. "No way!"

"Eva!"

"Marco? Charles?" Eva squealed with delight as the *white van brotherhood* headed toward her. They had disappointed her when they left Thailand, but helping the dead wasn't for everyone. Eva told them about the births in Thailand and how she loved her time there, but she was excited to start a new adventure with Hope in Victory. That was until she found herself all alone in the airport.

"We know of that place," Charles said. "It's a shed with a computer. It got busted for narcotics a few days ago."

In that moment, all of Eva's energy fizzed out of her.

The guys filled her in on their time in India. They were worried when the captain told them the Andaman Islands and Sri Lanka were not good choices. But when he set them up with the host who set them up with Carrie Breun, everything turned around for them.

"We help people get urgent transplants and help the poor at the same time," explained Marco. "We find donors from various parts of the world who match American patients. Ms. Breun negotiates the exchange of money and the return of the patients to the States."

"That can't be right. It can't be legal. I know Thailand requires donors to be blood relatives. I'm sure it's like that everywhere."

"Look, Eva," said Charles, "you always worry about laws. Your friend in Thailand? The one with the elephant that saved them from the tsunami? Did she ever mention anything about that hero who flew from America with them?"

Eva recalled the friend coming to the *wat* when she could not find her husband. No, she never asked about the donor.

Charles expected her silence. "She would have if she knew that donor as a friend or family member. She would have been so grateful that she wouldn't stop talking about that person, or searching."

Marco said, "We're concerned about what's fair."

Charles took over again. "Those laws screw both parties. With the money the donors receive, they can buy themselves out of debts and dangerous living circumstances. We're fuckin' heroes. Even your precious Thailand uses the Burmese immigrants for their kidneys."

"Myanmarese, not Burmese," she corrected.

"Whatever. Thais know it helps the poor illegals get back on their feet and serves the rich Americans at the same time. They can't say it publicly because rich governments have something up their asses trying to sound almighty and humane."

"Join us," interrupted Marco. "We could use a woman's touch. We just got back from recruiting a donor in Manaus, Brazil, who we brought to Johannesburg. This case was tough and took two months of interviews and blood tests, but we found a great match for a young woman from New Orleans. Our clinic in Manaus keeps a list of volunteers and their basic blood work."

Charles tapped his hands against his pants, stood up, sat back down, and stood up again. "Usually, we pick someone from the list, do a little last-minute blood work to look for underlying factors. Two days max, most of the time."

"And then?" asked Eva.

Marco answered. "We escort the donor to Johannesburg to meet the recipient who someone else brings. They learn about each other so they can sound like family."

"Like pretending to know a fiancé to get married to get a green card?" Eva was interested.

"Sort of. Anyway, they have the transplant, we give the donor a ticket to get back home, and we're done." Charles was practically dancing by now. "We travel, run our own lives, and help people. It's a win-win, Eva. Are you with us? We have to…"

Eva stopped him. "You don't escort the donor home?" She paused. No reply. "What's in it for the donor?"

"Two thousand U.S. dollars upfront and three thousand after the operation. In their home countries, that's enough for them to pay off debts, or move to a new house, or get medical care for a loved one," Marco explained. "Charles is prancing around because we need to get on our way to the Delta in Botswana. We're starting a new clinic there. A guide is meeting us in Gaborone and will stay with us during business hours. At our new clinic, we'll recruit the donors and bring them here or to Durban. Great hospitals here, by the way."

Charles added, "It's a long trip, but during that time, we help the donor with relationship questions so that if an authority asks, they can sound credible. Our guide translates when needed, in case you're wondering."

The guys continued their pitch, and they were convincing. They would help the poor, and Eva had to work. Eva had believed in *signs* since getting to Thailand. These guys were surely a sign today. And she was originally heading to Botswana, so part of her plan worked.

"Hope in Victory, my ass," she said. "I have to do something since I can't live in the airport. I'm not saying I'll do this, but can I go with you for now and figure out something?" It was illegal, but Charles was right—this arrangement happened in Thailand with the right connections.

When they got to Gaborone, the three sat around a wobbly table at a cafe and reminisced. It felt right to be together again.

Then Marco turned serious. "Eva, organ transplants don't really exist in Botswana. They don't even have an organ bank for legal transplants. The government has talked about it, but it hasn't happened. They see it as cost prohibitive."

Charles leaned so closely to Eva's face that his hot breath stung her eyes. "So, you must keep your mouth shut about your business. Watch that warm social shit you do with the locals. It's more than illegal—it's a shunned practice in the Delta. They barely support blood donation."

Marco gathered the napkins and took them to the trash bin next to their table. "Don't worry—we know how to work this. That's part of why we'll be successful. It will be beyond the government's imagination that we do this. Besides, the transplant is in South Africa. We don't even exchange money inside Botswana."

Eva stared at them, face frozen.

Marco sat down and tried again. "We'll teach them to save lives with a donor list of their own once they see transplants work safely."

Saving lives, this part was good, so Eva relaxed.

Since the day was half gone, they would spend the night at a partner's place in Gaborone at the Botswana border, then continue to the Okavango Delta. Eva convinced them to let her find out what had happened to Hope in Victory—the guys agreed that she should see for herself that it was a con operation.

****

Still uncommitted to the cause, Eva rode with them during the second day past the Pans—the flats made of salt-covered mud. The vastness both magnified and minimized Eva's place in the world—she was riding in a jeep through a *National Geographic* documentary. The rainy season made river crossings dangerous, but they were in luck for this journey. Heat coupled with intense humidity weighed heavily, but these travelers thrived in humidity and heat. Besides, the nights were magically pleasant.

As they approached the Delta, Eva's dreams from watching *Discovery Channel* as a child came true. A dazzle of zebras blended into a canvas of stripes, and a matriarch paraded her herd of elephants across the road, stopping the jeep for over thirty minutes. A mere human had best not tell elephants to move. Unimaginable birds graced the scene with red and blue *painted* faces, bulging eyes, beaks of all shapes. Non-flight ostriches stood tall in the bushes, able to kill lions and shred a human in moments. The driver made sure his passengers stayed covered in mosquito repellent and gave Eva a long-sleeved shirt, explaining that malaria was a concern in Botswana. For humans, the mosquito was the deadliest animal on earth. Finally arriving, they took residence at a tiny shack on the Delta side of Maun near the smaller villages and set about learning the ways of the land.

****

Maun was a good-sized city, about 50,000 population, with shopping centers and all the conveniences of a modern city, yet it was still called a village in Botswana. As the safari tourism capital of the continent, there was a nice international airport, so Eva asked why they didn't fly. The guys explained they weren't sure about their visas, so they drove to avoid the airport immigration center. Eva knew Americans didn't need visas in Botswana—that was one thing Dr. Smith told her in Phuket, but maybe another lie. The destination and sponsoring organization she declared with her passport were now incorrect, so it was better she didn't fly, after all. Besides, she decided, the drive allowed her to learn more about Botswana. And she liked the driver, a friendly, cheerful man. He told her his name was Baruti, meaning one who teaches. In her travels, she loved the pride people had in their names. *Baruti* seemed the perfect name to her.

The Okavango Delta was a massive inland delta where the Okavango River came to a dead-end in the middle of the country. Eva rejoiced at the cacophony of bird twitters, frog croaks, bat clicks, squirrel chatter, monkey screams, hippo grunts, and elephant trumpets. Baruti often sang along.

Without ever overtly agreeing to work with Marco and Charles, Eva found herself sucked in. The threesome visited family huts near the swampland by using *mokoros,* gliding two or three inches above the surface through tall stands of papyrus and reeds, and masses of water lily blooms. When dealing with the tourists, guides used fiberglass versions, but the three Americans were working and not touring, so Baruti had arranged for the old, authentic boats. With only an ax, the locals carved their special canoes from one piece of a Bonoto tree trunk, no need for classy fiberglass boats here where everything moved slowly and cautiously. The boatman stood in the back and pushed them along using a pole. Eva transported herself to the mangroves of Phuket. Her memory listened to her friend singing in Thai. The jungle and the desert, so different yet so similar. When the sun peered through the trees with elephants walking near the shore, it was hard to remember she was working.

Older documentaries back home referred to the nomad tribes as *Bushmen*, but Baruti told Eva they didn't like it when outsiders used that term. Baruti explained that though most contemporary books referred to them as *San*, tribal names like *Khoisan* or the Click name *!Kung San* were better. Eva tried to learn tribal names. Marco and Charles didn't bother—they didn't want to know the people.

The rainy season passed into dry, cooler days. The flood cycle coming down from the Angolan Highlands peaked during the lowland's dry season when the surrounding area was thirsty, bringing large herds to the Delta. Once a favorite domain for foreign hunters, the current reserves protected the wildlife with the more humane hobby of photo safaris. Ever present, Baruti safeguarded his naïve travelers from potential wildlife dangers. He also guarded Eva from curious men.

After the mountain floods, the land dried again, sending the herds off to find water until the next floods brought them back. Days were lovely, but Eva had to buy a coat for the nights when temperatures got close to freezing, her first coat since leaving Texas.

Recruitment floundered. It may have had two steps forward, but then they took three steps back. Wealthy foreign corporations owned the lodges and held the management level positions. Locals worked as underpaid guides and grunt workers. And HIV took so many lives. Poverty levels in the Delta were the highest of all of Botswana. A few thousand U.S. dollars could relieve someone of major debts.

Money would have helped, but not at the cost of human dignity. The Botswana resisted the concept of removing a body part, and the *Khoisan* would have nothing to do with such an inhuman act. The little success the team had was due to how quickly Eva learned Setswana. It wasn't the local dialect, but since she greeted people with a friendly *dumela rra* for men or *dumela mma* for women, tensions dropped. The simple fact she recognized the difference made for an icebreaker. From there, they'd conduct business in simplified English.

Baruti's efforts guided the conversations, but the act of translation mired the process. Although English was the official language in Botswana and spoken in larger cities like Gaborone, and Setswana was the national language, there were over twenty dialects in the outer villages and little English. With Baruti's help, Eva learned bits of the *Khoisan* people's Click languages that had sounds within words like *tsk-tsk*, tongue pops, and throat sounds. When linguists wrote the words, they used *!* and other symbols for the unique sounds.

The clinic's outward appearance was a hut in which a group of young sociologists studied the impact of tourism on the people of the Delta. There was not even a name for this group. The so-called clinic's true purpose was to interview for donor candidates and test for blood type—all significant testing and surgeries were done in Johannesburg or Durban in South Africa. Kidney donation was so publicly abhorrent that no one on the team of four openly admitted why they were there, nor did any candidates who agreed to further testing. The donor candidates became a secret society not even known to each other. Eva wondered why the recruiting team wasn't chased away, but Charles said money talked. The tribes had entered the developed world along with Maun, acquiring tastes for *things* and the traps that came with them. Tourism paid well, but not for the villagers.

With Eva's superpower for casual conversation, they visited huts and asked questions about how lives had changed with the rise of tourism. That led to how the greedy corporations did not meet promises about access to good medical care, which led to talks about kidney disease. Slowly the conversation moved from the villagers' own kidney disease risks to how they could help others. Finally, through Baruti's translations, the team introduced the idea that villagers could help themselves financially by selling their spare kidney.

Communities developed around the safari camps. The kidney clinic would help the ones in need, then move on to the next community. The latest move was to a cluster of ten homes near Matsaudi/Sakapane, a village of about three hundred fifty people who worked in the safari trades in the nearby reserves. The locals made their own palm wine, a common practice, which required burning off the brush from around the palm trees. One night, the fire raged out of control and headed straight for the camp where the Americans recruited. Stupefied by the speed of the spread and the tremendous noise, Eva stared at the flames as they sucked the oxygen out of the air. Baruti found her unconscious and hauled her to safety.

During the chaos, Charles and Marco disappeared, so Eva wavered between fear for her friends and betrayal for once again being left alone. For ten days, the blaze roared on with the wind blowing it in a circle back to the compound where they had set up the clinic. Finally, a heavy rain ended the fire. Eva gazed across the panorama of burned grass and dead wood. The palms lived, but suffered, as did the families of the fifteen people who died.

When villagers found two charred bodies at the remains of the clinic, Eva and Baruti were certain her missing companions had died in the fire. But two days later, Baruti approached Eva with news. "A villager told me he had heard the *sociologist* men thought you and I died. They headed south to Kang to help people in the Kalahari Desert. I need to work, Miss Eva, so I will take you there to find Marco and Charles."

"You know, Baruti, I never asked them for the contact information to reach Carrie Breun. Why am I so stupid?"

"Not stupid, Miss Eva. You trust. You trust the world and the people in it."

Once again, Eva found herself stranded in a foreign country. Chasing Marco and Charles was all she had.

Chapter 14

July 9, 2015, True Care Renal Center, San Antonio, Texas:

CiCi had been sitting in the car for at least five minutes, just sitting. She should have been at home packing for China, not sitting in a hot car in July in Texas in the parking lot of True Care Renal Center. She usually waited until the last minute for packing, but things happened suddenly these days, so she might lose that last-minute time, which was why she shouldn't have been going to China, but Jon insisted she go. When she left the house that morning, Jon had stretched out in his recliner for his mid-morning nap number two. Not able to let go of his refusal to dialyze, she ran to the car when Val called to tell her a friend was at his dialysis treatment and looking forward to her visit.

The reception desk was unattended, so CiCi followed the sign to the treatment room. She had looked on YouTube at various dialysis videos during her quest to understand Jon's attitude, so there were no surprises when she opened a door into a spacious room with a huge central desk covered in computers and papers. No one manned that desk, either. Patients occupied large institution-blue recliners with tray tables, each separated by machines. Some formed a square to look at each other, while several lined the wall. Every seat was filled.

Six people in scrubs and masks circled one chair, each busily adding medications to an IV bag or tapping a monitor or calling on a cell phone. All the other patients except one watched. The exception was sleeping and missing the entire show. Finally, a patient saw CiCi standing at the entry and got a nurse's attention.

"Please remain in the lobby. We will be right with you," the nurse said.

But CiCi stayed by the door, pretending not to hear.

Moments later, everyone went back to their stations as if nothing unusual had occurred. Val's friend had been the center of attention—his blood pressure had dropped, so he passed out. When the attending doctor gave him saline, he came around, but not all was good in his world. Though not an everyday occurrence at the center, CiCi learned his event was common enough that business moved on with little excitement. Saul tried to be friendly, but he didn't feel well. He asked if she could come back another time. CiCi explained she was heading to China but would be back in two weeks.

Saul's neighbor overheard the conversation and offered to talk. He introduced himself as Nahn and was part of the group with the chairs facing each other. Soon, his entire group chimed in. The *walls*, the *squares* called them, were more private or busy with work on their laptops. Some kept full employment and families and needed these hours for virtual work, sleep, or time alone. Most of the *squares* were older and wanted the time to socialize since their real lives were isolated. The sleeper kept sleeping.

"So what happened to Saul is common?" CiCi asked.

Estelle, an older woman, the clinic matriarch, answered. "Low blood pressure requires constant monitoring." She pointed to the pressure cuff on her arm. CiCi thought it was to watch for high blood pressure, not low. Her own low blood pressure was a sign of pride to her.

Estelle caught her confused look. "It can cause our fistula to collapse, which means a big emergency because it's all about blood going out and blood going back in. No fistula, no flow."

"Fistula?" asked CiCi.

"Too much to go into, but the quick explanation is they connected a vein and an artery for the two needles." She pointed to her leg. "Blood goes out through one, filters over there in the machine, then back into me through the other one." She looked at her machine. "I call it Harold. Harold and his ancestors have been my friends for twenty years."

"Twenty? But I thought…"

"You thought correctly." Saul jumped in. Val told her that Saul took every opportunity to teach about his disease. Here he was, still not feeling well and yet unable to hold back. "We're lucky to get five, maybe ten, years. Estelle, here, has obeyed the rules and defied the odds, which is why we all call her Mother Essie."

CiCi studied Estelle's face. Her eyes told of both joy and fury. "No transplant, Estelle?"

"Not yet. Rare blood type, they tell me. But back to the blood pressure."

CiCi noticed she turned the topic away from transplants. Did she know why the hair stylist's sister never accepted her transplant offers? There had to be more story here.

Mother Essie said, "They take out our blood. Sometimes our bodies take notice of the missing volume and start moving liquids out of tissues. Pressure drops because the volume is wrong. Over the long-term, low-pressure events can lead to strokes, heart issues, and unconsciousness. But if my fistula clots, I don't get my blood back. Harold can't do his job. Then I don't finish the treatment and can have unfiltered blood or too much fluid."

"What can you do?"

Saul said, "They lay us back with feet higher than the heart and give us saline. That's what they were doing with me. If that doesn't work, we're off to a hospital. I'll be making a doctor's visit to check me out."

"I've had my fistula collapse three times." Estelle showed CiCi the two long scars in her arms from earlier fistulae. "It's all about diet, fluids, and medication control. When they put in a new one, they must go to the other arm. When we run out of arm space, they go to thighs."

104

A young kid at the wall nearby took up the question. He wasn't more than fifteen. He waved his cuffed arm, his phone glowing in his hand. "They put this cuff on our good arm, so it checks, like, twelve times. Every time I get a high score going on my game, I have to hold still for the cuff to do its thing. It sucks."

CiCi already knew why the cuff had to be on the good arm— they had to avoid pressure on the fistula. What would they do with her since she couldn't have any blood draws or even blood pressure cuffs on her right arm because they took lymph nodes from that underarm when checking for breast cancer cells? She only had one arm for medical needs.

Tessa, the woman in the chair next to her, whispered to CiCi that the kid had suffered from a severe infection that led to his kidney failure.

"I see you whispering about me." The kid looked up from his phone. "I got sick, and Mom couldn't take off work to take me to the doctor. Whatever. Now I get to ride a bus here to the center three times a week because I'm not old enough to dialyze myself at home, and my mom works two jobs. So sad story. But I have a cousin who says he will give me one of his kidneys. No more ropes to hold me down." Then he was back on his phone.

CiCi knew teens and understood they already had emotional swings, but with the added kidney stress, this kid was having trouble. She admired the kid's optimism. She turned back to Saul. "But I read that the anti-rejection medicines can have horrible side effects."

"Dialysis has horrible side effects," Saul said. "Transplants let us go about our business."

"And finish a freakin' video game," yelled the kid.

That kid was missing school, friends, and the ability to rebel, so no wonder he hated this place. Jon, however, would not accept hallucinations and shaky hands known to go with the anti-rejection meds. And his eyesight might diminish. Tinkering with his remote-control planes might have to go, and then what would he do?

Would he remain happy with the transplant? Or would she be donating for nothing?

The *squares* talked about the diet requirements—deep down, CiCi understood why Jon resisted that with so much passion, but these people were doing okay. They were waiting for transplants, but it was more—they wanted to watch kids and grandkids grow up. One patient wanted her new grandchild to be old enough to remember her. Another was writing a novel and wanted time to see it published—if he got a transplant, all the better, because then he would write a sequel. One woman had started a new business just before her diagnosis. She had employees depending on her, some even tested to be living donors for her. She was buying time to keep things going for these people who needed her. CiCi looked around the center, at the nurses and technicians walking the floor checking and rechecking, at the machines humming with the red *snakes* hooking the patients to the machines, at Estelle hooked up to *Harold*.

"Why the name *Harold?*" CiCi asked Estelle.

"Harold was the kindest, gentlest man I ever knew, so the machine that is saving my life is Harold. This one is Harold the Eighth. I get sentimental every time they replace him."

Jon did not have their circumstances. He had step-grandkids, but distance and lack of money meant he rarely visited them and assumed they would not miss him much if he were gone.

"Why don't you do home dialysis?" CiCi asked. "I read it was more convenient and filtered better."

"Yes and no," said Nahn. "I tried home dialysis first. It sounded great because I was around my family more and still went to work. But I couldn't do much with the kids because I was on the machine. They didn't like it. Then I tried peritoneal dialysis to filter all night in my sleep, but I kept getting infections and didn't last long on that. So many enormous boxes. Every month, supplies arrived that would fill two of our bedrooms. Moving around in our bedroom became a dance routine because of the machine, and the boxes got stored in the kids' rooms."

Estelle rolled her head from side to side with her eyes closed, as if in a dream. "It's not just the boxes—they're a nightmare to navigate around, but also someone has to hook you up and take you off. I'm old and live alone, but I'm not so old that I want a caretaker. Besides, these people in this room are my social life. I love them." Mother Essie blew each of them a kiss and got kisses back.

CiCi thought home dialysis could work for Jon. She could hook him up and watch his vitals. He could watch his shows or sleep through the dialysis and have the evening for himself. It would mean she couldn't travel anymore, so he wouldn't like that. They got along better when she was gone a lot.

The group then pointed out through their own specific examples that with dialysis they would go for their treatment and leave exhausted that entire day, feel good the next day, and then feel terrible again.

There were more diet tales. One guy said he always ate ham sandwiches the day of dialysis because his treatment removed excess salt. "Ham sandwiches are my favorite food, but I have to time them right."

His name was Arthur, but CiCi would forever remember him as the *ham on rye* guy. She was a fries kinda gal and would hate to lose that food choice. Jon may have been right about the restricted diet.

CiCi had a list of questions that might as well have come from a middle school journalism student—she never got them out of her bag. The *squares* offered more than her questions ever touched. "I read that the average life of a transplanted kidney is five to ten years, which sounds about like dialysis."

Mother Essie said, "Once in a while, kidneys fail immediately after transplant, and some last thirty, even forty years. I've been coming here long enough to see people come in to wait for their third transplant. From this chair, transplants mean nothing lost and everything to gain." Estelle peeked over at Harold to check her progress, then turned back to CiCi. "Why are you really visiting us today? What is it you need to know?"

CiCi had been hiding this question from herself. It probably didn't matter since the clinic had turned her away because of her bout with breast cancer. She could continue to hide from the truth. But these people opened up to her, and they faced tougher questions than hers every day. "I offered to give my kidney to my best friend. It's a long story, but he has refused dialysis. I want to know why he would give up without trying."

"And for you to donate, you risk your future and your life?" asked Saul.

"Yeah. Why would Jon be so willing for me to take a risk when he won't fight for his own life with dialysis?"

Mother Essie said, "You need to ask him. We can't help with that one. Many are not in these chairs anymore because they decided not to continue."

They spoke about grandkids and much lighter topics, such as her trip to China. CiCi thanked them for their honesty and headed to the door.

From the wall, the kid yelled out, "I am not my disease!"

CiCi looked back at him. He had that face of teen youth she loved so much during her years of teaching: determination, obstinance, and joy enveloped in uncertainty. She wanted to hug him, but she settled on a fist bump.

Time to pack.

Chapter 15

July 2008, Kang, Botswana:
Baruti threw his satchel into the back of the jeep and checked the caps on the gas tanks stored there. "Miss Eva, I cannot find them anywhere. No sociologists or kidney men have been in Kang."

"Now what? What will I do now?" Eva caught herself biting her fingernails again, not much nail left. Sticking her hands under her legs, she squeezed every muscle in her body, even that little one between the ear and the cheekbone. When she relaxed them, her urge to cry disappeared. A friend in Thailand taught her that trick.

Baruti walked to her door. "I must work. I cannot stay here, and I cannot take you back to Maun. There is nothing there for you."

"I have nowhere to go."

"I can drive you to the U.S. Embassy in Gaborone. From there you could go home to America."

"My parents don't want me, and I don't have the money to fly home on my own. I have money to help with gas and food for now, but not plane fare." Shaking her head didn't convince her, but she'd denied her parents' stolen money for so many years the thought of dipping into it terrified her more than staying in a new country. Besides, it was best the locals thought she was as poor as they were. She was a survivor—she survived a tsunami and a fire. This? This setback meant nothing.

"You cannot stay here. Your money will disappear." Baruti leaned over her door and looked her in the eyes. "And I must go home. I must get a job with a safari group." He then walked around to his side, climbed over the door, and plopped himself into the driver's seat, his way of saying he was in charge.

During one of her runs to South Africa with a donor, Eva got a residence permit to remain in Botswana. She liked the villagers, and they liked her—they had sipped tea. "I can teach English to the villagers."

"But you do not speak local dialects."

"A friend in Thailand taught English as a foreign language in Indonesia for years. She taught the children of embassy diplomats from across the world, and one year she had children from thirty-nine languages. She spoke only English."

Baruti placed both hands on the steering wheel and turned his gaze straight forward. "Eva, the San of the Kalahari are sometimes eager for tourism, but most resent tourists. It is dangerous for you."

"How do you know?"

"I am San."

Of course. Baruti moved so fluidly among everyone that Eva had made him universal in her mind. Not so much assumed, she never questioned it. She heard villagers call him a name with the clicks in it, but she thought it was a term of friendship. She liked that *Baruti* meant teacher and stuck with that. Scolding herself for insensitivity, she frowned. Why didn't she learn his real name?

"You do not know us. My own people do not trust me anymore because I work with tourists. You are right—English helps guides and trackers, but it is not popular. People outside the large cities fear change and secretly resent outsiders."

"How did you learn English?"

Baruti took his time, like he was searching for a winning reply that would divert her direction. Finally, he sighed. "From someone like you. But you must not recruit kidney donors. If you will teach English, do not let it be known you were ever here to take advantage of donors."

"Take advantage? No, I've been helping them." Eva sat speechless for a moment. Did Baruti see her that way? She had never formally agreed to help Marco and Charles. Was that because she saw the recruiting that way, too, and couldn't admit it as she rode along in the *mokoros*?

Baruti wouldn't look at her. "Marco and Charles taught you well." After the silence stifled them, he turned to Eva with tears in his eyes. "I betrayed my people. I was glad when the kidney men disappeared. You are not Marco and Charles. I trust you."

"Thank you, but why did you join them to begin with if you dislike them so much?"

"I was foolish. I wanted things, things tribal life could not give me. And I was hungry. There is much about our lives you cannot understand." Baruti lowered his chin to his chest, shallow breaths his only movement. After quiet thought, he finally lifted his face toward her and, with sad eyes, formed a plan. "I will take you north again to my cousin's family in Ghanzi. It is only three hours to drive. My uncle speaks a little English, and the town is bigger than Kang, with more possibilities for you. My cousin and his wife run a school—maybe they can use your help."

"How can I thank you?"

"While you are there, I want you to talk with the people who sold their kidneys. My cousin has helped them—no one else will talk with them."

Eva nodded, and they headed to a gas station.

Baruti filled the spare gas cans while Eva picked up snacks at a shack next door and refilled water bottles. She had counted only three service stations on the drive south from Maun and had heard horror stories of people stranded with car trouble and of collisions with the donkeys along the road. She knew to prepare for days in a desert, even if the drive should be only three hours.

The return north denied Eva the excitement she'd felt during other journeys with Baruti. It surprised her to notice the dull nothing in the landscape. Before, the vastness awed her; now it looked dry and dead, no trees, just scrubby bushes. She knew it was the dry season, unlike her first venture to the Delta months earlier when rains threatened dangerous floods on the roads. While riding south two days earlier, she was so eager to find Marco and Charles to either hug them or punch them—she was not yet sure which—that she hadn't noticed how the Kalahari of the dry season exaggerated her own West Texas terrain.

This time, to keep Baruti from seeing her tears, she looked off to the side. The landscape along the Trans Kalahari Highway took her thoughts to home. Her eyes saw the scrubby dry bushes over parched land during her drive to California where she sold her car and took off to Thailand. During the fall of 1998, Central Texas had a record-breaking flood. But by her August 1999 trip, the entire Southwest U.S. experienced a severe drought. In the Kalahari, the rainy season would return to this scrubby place and bring water and life. Why hadn't she noticed that when she had been so eager not to be in her parents' grip that she found a land so much like home?

But then, Texas held no herds of elephants.

****

Finally settled with Baruti's family, Eva made herself useful to earn room and board. Ghanzi was a booming farming community that supplied most of the beef for Botswana to export to the European Union. With a new shopping center, cafes, and broadband Internet at the post office, Eva met the locals. Hanging around the post office Internet using her host's laptop, she saw more of what Baruti warned. The *Khoisan* resisted change. When the government set up the Central Kalahari Game Reserve in the name of preservation, officials moved the tribes to resettlement camps near Ghanzi. Given five cattle or goats, these hunters and gatherers were expected to farm.

The Botswana officials knew failure was imminent. The nomads learned to rely on government handouts and to abuse alcohol. Eva had heard comparable stories of Native Americans during her own upbringing. Botswana acted in the name of sustainability for endangered species, but, in the early 1990s, diamonds were found. Saving endangered species by digging mines? Not a fit in Eva's mind. With desperation overwhelming the San way of life, the temptation to sell a kidney was understandable.

Feeling like a CIA operative, Eva did as Baruti asked and met donors in covert meetings. Never sure if Baruti had told his cousin what she did in Maun, she kept the sociology cover. She said she had stumbled across donors while working with Baruti and wanted to learn more of their plight so that she could help others. The locals enjoyed gossip, and secrets spread out of control in no time. But not this secret. No one wanted to claim knowledge of an organ sale. Knowing seemed to bring bad luck.

Sales had sounded good to the donors when they agreed, but there was no help later. They couldn't admit even to their families what they'd done to bring money home. Some believed their ancestors turned against them. Others explained the scars as wounds from animals while in the Bush. Recovery time was impossible, for most returned to work too soon. If there were complications or infection, they were on their own. But mostly the isolation disturbed them. When they suddenly had money, neighbors accused them of thefts. Spouses doubted them. In no time, the money disappeared, and they were worse off than before the surgery. And alone. Marco and Charles did well for themselves to leave when they did. Once donors returned in such sad mental states, the kidney team would be chased out with fire. Bitterness tightened Eva's throat.

The desert pulled on her soul. It was easy to see an existence of power far beyond human controls. Activity, effort, intention clashed with the natural rhythm. She remembered a travel ad description: "Kalahari—a sharp, staccato phrase, in an otherwise andante movement." Survival in the Bush was a piercing shrill, slightly out of pitch, note against a dirge. No, not a dirge—dirges mourned the dead—the desert lived. It was more like *Close Encounters of the Third Kind* when the humans played their tinny keyboard with the spaceship blasting in heavy, sticky bass.

Eva was grateful she lived in a village with running water—in the Bush, they had to haul water from cattle posts miles away to have more than a few sips at any one time. A forty-four gallon drum full of water weighed four hundred pounds. Human needs required effort in a land that refused to move. For just a cup of coffee, she would first have to collect firewood. Often after visiting the San communities, tourists spoke of young boys starting their cooking fires by rubbing sticks. Eva thought this may have been a show for the tourists, but her hosts told her otherwise. The desert was so hot and dry it was as if the *Master Chef* had rendered the land to the quintessence of nature. The slow rhythm of the Kalahari allowed Eva to absorb an aura of patience emanating from the earth, a constant reminder, a caress, to be still.

Eva whispered gratitude to Baruti daily.

****

The seasons changed again. By late October, the heat intensified with the rains soon starting. The humidity on the rise reminded Eva of a summer in Houston, but without air conditioning. She wondered if she would ever get accustomed to her upside-down life where January was hot and wet while in June she froze at night. Sometimes she walked into the desert to clear her head, never forgetting Baruti's survival lessons on deadly snakes and dangerous wild animals. Silence overwhelmed thought—not even insects chirped. Heat rippled across the sand—she had thought that was something cameras did to images. Old Hollywood cowboy movies showed it when the lost cowboy dying of thirst staggered across the Pecos Mountains, with rattlesnakes shaking behind a nearby rock and a mirage of water drawing the man forward. That was Hollywood. In the Kalahari, venomous puff adders replaced rattlesnakes. In the silence, Eva listened to herself.

During one of her desert epiphanies, Eva grappled with the effect transplant tourism had on the people she wanted to help. In the cafe, she'd read a magazine article introducing an anthropologist's latest theory involving the San of the Kalahari. DNA tests revealed modern-day San came from fourteen ancestral populations as much as 200,000 years ago. And from these ethnic groups, the theory proposed 150 Africans ventured north to populate the rest of the world via the Red Sea. Kalahari's peaceful nomads carried with them the DNA of the original humans. Eva's heart ripped apart. Baruti was right. What had she done? She meant to do good, but she was just another White Imperialist thinking she knew better than those who lived there since the beginning.

****

Her hosts had done enough—it was time to move on. She thanked Baruti's cousin who arranged her way to Gaborone, where she agreed to teach English at a Baptist church until she earned money for a flight to somewhere. As the cousin helped her gather her few belongings, he gave her a note from Baruti.

My dear Miss Eva, I hope you find the peace you need. I pray you will not need this, but I knew how to contact Ms. Breun. Forgive me. I did not know where your friends went, but I had a contact in Kang. Think hard. I sold my soul to the devil when I helped the kidney men. But it is not mine to judge you. Your work, whatever it may be, is not yet finished. Baruti.

115

Eva stared at the phone number and address in Los Angeles burning into her soul. Baruti had known. He wasn't heading to a safari—he was with the kidney brokers. Should she cry or laugh? Feeling his sad eyes pierce her thoughts, she thanked Baruti for his faith in her and cursed Carrie Breun while tearing the paper into shreds.

****

Life with the church in Gaborone filled an emptiness in Eva, but the pastor let her know this was only a one-year assignment. She'd never been a religious person, never taken time for church during her childhood. In Thailand, however, she'd learned from the young Buddhist monks about living in harmony. This church persuaded gently by modeling, no judgments. She liked it.

The year passed quickly, and it was time to focus on her next career. By May, with the dry season's arrival, she had found an affiliate of Hands Helping Physicians, a reputable group helping doctors in struggling countries. Impressed with her kidney transplant knowledge, they signed her up with a team to aid transplants in Tabriz, Iran, where it was legal to sell a kidney through government-controlled centers. Kidney transplants saved lives, but at whose expense and whose benefit? This sounded perfect. Controlled meant proper follow-up care and no exploitation. It was only fair that the donors should benefit from their sacrifice.

Chapter 16

Juty 10, 2015, Dr. Alex Segel's Lab at CTMRI, San Antonio, Texas:

"So, if it worked for the pig kidney, it should work for humans." Yameekah, one of Dr. Alexandra Segel's favorite lab techs, showed her results to Dr. Segel, not that she had a choice since Alex was looking over her shoulder. Everything networked live from the lab to Alex's tablet and desk computer—she could monitor from anywhere in the world if she wanted, but Alex preferred old-fashioned direct contact with her team.

Segel's other favorite tech, Jennifer, joined in. The truth was that Alex had only the two techs, but if there were more, these two would be her favorites. Though still in their early thirties, the two techs had spent so many years together in the lab that their minds had merged, melded more than old married couples' minds. When Alex discovered this, she named them after Lewis Carrol's *Looking Glass* twins, Tweedledee and Tweedledum. Even when they disagreed, they did so in agreement.

The two techs told her in near unison, "The pigs are happily producing all the hormones they need for happy hearts, and filtration is nearly perfect." They did a prissy little pig dance accompanied by oinks.

Alex put on her serious boss face. "Ya'll have fun, but don't be so giddy when Dr. South comes by. He's feeling the pressure from the Senator right now."

"Why not just tell the guy what happened and use his other kidney as the scaffold? He's already on dialysis."

"It's not that easy. He's so fragile he won't make it through the extra surgery. Besides, the Senator will see us as careless. How do we reconcile that? We cannot tell the family. And you guys promised not to tell anyone. This is too important."

The two women avoided her eyes—there was no argument to win.

If only it were that simple. "And what about the months it took us to grow and adjust the IPS cells on the first kidney? Dr. South's presentation at last year's World Stem Cell Summit right here in San Antonio predicted our human trials would begin last month, and Senator Estes was the guest of honor because of her work in gaining Congressional financial backing."

"We get it. No piggy dances." They chimed in together. It didn't matter which one was speaking—they had one mind. Sometimes they took turns with words to form entire sentences. "But really, what went wrong with this human test? We did the protocol, and the colonies looked perfect." And then Tweedledee and Tweedledum were silent.

There had to be more. These two never stopped talking suddenly. Alex waited, but they stayed mum.

Yameekah finally broke the silence. "Our current problem is the deceased versus living kidney issue. I think that's why the seeding doesn't initiate."

Alex could tell there was something far deeper bothering these two. "And?"

"The death bit, but it can't be the length of time the kidney is out-of-body," Tweedledee pointed out.

Dr. Segel responded, "True. Our entire team has discussed this so many times but seems to get nowhere. Transplant statistics show living donor kidneys last years longer than deceased donor kidneys, but deceased organs do work."

118

That feeling of something unsaid lingered.

Jennifer said, "Our test we just completed was with a brain-dead patient kept on life support until we harvested. No time out-of-body issue."

"I always wondered about that time-out-of-body thing, anyway," Yameekah added. "They send living donor kidneys from California to New York. That flight keeps the kidney out of a body longer than when a patient receives a transplant from someone who died in the same city."

The other Tweedle picked up a specimen slide and studied it. "That doesn't seem relevant here. Regardless, life support or not, our test subject was dead." She dropped the slide in the biohazard trash. "And seeding failed."

"Besides, we always failed with seeding when we used the deceased pigs from the farm, and they are minutes from life, but we win with living pigs. There's something about *life*." Tweedledee and Tweedledum took turns with the words to make one answer and delivered the last line as a chorus.

They had to have rehearsed this. Alex loved these two. "Indeed, there is something about *life*."

Again, they filled in for each other to make a sentence. "You know, like that movie *21 Grams*. When the spirit leaves the body, there goes twenty-one grams of weight. It must be those missing grams that make the IPS cells stick and grow."

"And survive," said Alex. "So, you are saying pigs have spirits?"

"Have we weighed a pig at death?"

This time, they all got silent, a pregnant pause moment. Spirit in science?

Breaking the silence, Tweedledee and Tweedledum simultaneously changed the topic, each giving three or four words. "Sooo, we think we corrected the problem with the fibrosis. We found a gene that didn't switch off. You'll see on our next run. Tell the IPS guys to be ready to seed and watch these little guys self-organize to all the right places."

119

These two techs made Alex smile and, for just a moment, forget the massive problems their remodeled kidney project faced. She thought back to Dr. South screaming at the intern the previous week. South had every right to his anger. In weeks, not months or years, the remodeled kidney would have been in place, but that was now moot. It was not every day that an elderly man with failed kidneys volunteered to be a guinea pig.

Only cadaveric kidneys were approved for human research. Bodies donated to science were corpses, which was great for the early studies, but returning the kidney to the corpse to see it urinate could never happen. That required life. Occasionally, though, they received organs from patients who were organ donors on life support. These rare organs had been deemed nonviable for transplant. Alex thought to herself that it would be interesting to be able to return a remodeled kidney to that same brain-dead patient while kept on life support to see if the body urinated. She wouldn't need the senator's dad, but no one had volunteered for that.

Since South's group had done so well with living pig kidneys, the National Institute of Health accepted the only way to explore the potential of this phenomenal approach was with a living person. It helped that the volunteer's support was his daughter, Senator Estes. NIH approved this one patient, and they emphasized *one*, to be fast-tracked. The biotechnology division at NIH delayed the trial as long as possible, but now the man had only months to live and was not even healthy enough for the transplant list. There was a good chance he would die in surgery. He knew all this but said he was ninety-one years old—for him, breathing was a risk.

The young intern destroyed hope with one careless oversight. Funding the research depended on hope for the senator's dad, so everyone swore secrecy about the incident, even the intern. He got to keep his job so he would be grateful and not go public.

With that loss in her mind, Alex moved across the lab to where Dr. Sarah Wang was manipulating a synthetic elastic polymer cooked up by the chem lab. "Dr. Segel," the older woman said without even looking up, "I think this will do the job."

"That's good." Afraid to get excited about any good news right now, Alex forced her voice to sound as if this were normal, everyday information. "It will allow us to transplant the kidney much earlier into the protocol."

Dr. Segel had developed the remodeling concept, and the Tweedles, Dee and Dum, cast their magic spell to make it so. Now Dr. Wang helped to shape the blobs. In a fetus, the stem cells shaped themselves properly into three dimensions, but in the lab, the bean shape would sometimes get lumpy and even break off while first forming.

Alex knew they had to push forward, even without their precious scaffold. They had to keep testing innovative ideas, so, when the opportunity came again, they would be ready. Alex told Dr. Wang, "Your polymer coating will hold the shape while the fragile cells finish forming." This was great news—Alex paused to savor the moment. "The elasticity will allow the stretch needed with growth."

"The patient would still need dialysis for a while," Dr. Wang said.

"But if we show growth and potential?"

"And if the polymer dissolves over time, so be it. By then, the cells will have fully matured and will hold their form without it." Doctor Sarah Wang had a matronly grandmother appearance as she carefully coated the red blob in her hand. That blob was already a lost cause but good enough to assess the liquidity of the polymer. "And it's adhering perfectly."

At that moment, Alex quit listening and stared out the window into the hallway. Dr. South stood there speaking with Kamini, the bioengineer/computer expert who recently joined the team. Her last name was Balasubramanium, but it was so difficult to say, even the well-traveled Dr. South didn't attempt it. Kamini had briefly worked in China as a software engineer at a lab using CRISPR/Cas9 to splice the PERV virus from pigs bred for human transplants. That program was well underway, so she headed to California to the West Coast lab to contribute to the software engineering needed for the artificial kidney there. That artificial kidney was almost ready for human trials when South stole Kamini away from them.

Dr. South convinced Kamini that using the patient's own kidney and own IPS cells would be the best solution. West Coast primarily worked with a computer engineer at Southern Wisconsin University. Kamini performed as a computer translator—as she called it—for the West Coast doctors if distance interfered with explanations, a job that bored her. She wanted more involvement with development and admitted to Dr. South her work there was about done. Alex conceded Kamini was a gold mine since she had now worked with three different approaches toward solving the kidney issue. Their remodeled kidney would be the right one.

But Kamini was not the object of Alex's gaze. Alex's mind drifted into a silent monologue. Dr. South really was good-looking. He had it all. His family was not particularly wealthy, but he didn't struggle to pay back medical school loans like she did.

Dr. Wang coughed. "He's drop dead gorgeous and athletic. Too bad I'm not thirty years younger."

Alex came back to reality. "Sorry Sarah." She felt her face burn from being caught in her daydream. "Yes, the polymer coating is a perfect solution." Alex felt like her grandmother had admonished her for PDA. She hadn't experienced that since the elderly biology teacher caught her kissing a boy behind the science building in high school and made her write an essay titled *Public Displays of Affection: Why They Must Not Happen on Campus*.

Dr. Wang teased this effect she had on Alex, loving the opportunity to perform foster grandparenting. Privately, they referred to each other as Grandmama and Granddaughter.

Ignoring Alex's return to reality, Grandmama Sarah continued her review of *Dr. Hottie*. "He attended the best private high school, which helped him obtain full scholarships through undergraduate school."

Alex had never considered Sarah's life outside the lab. "How do you know this?"

"Oh, honey, back in my prime, I served on the admissions committee at Rice University when he applied for pre-med. Of course, we accepted him when we discovered charisma, intelligence, and sincerity packaged up in an eighteen-year-old. And now he has his specialty in nephrology and surgery. He's performed kidney transplants all over the world—too many to count—but he decided he could better solve the kidney disease issue by inventing this remodeled version. Now he's directing major research that will change the lives of thousands of Americans who need a second chance. I think Rice did well." Grandmama beamed with pride.

"Indeed." Only Grandmama Sarah would call her honey. "What brought you here?" Alex knew Dr. Wang commanded enthusiastic respect in the lab—she had worked with the WHO, the CDC, and the NIH. She had most of the alphabet in her resume. Coming here must have seemed tame—Alex wondered what CTMRI had offered her. Dr. Wang specifically asked to work in the lab with the techs—she didn't want an office. Alex decided their research took Sarah back to her days as a research professor at MIT. Alex laughed to herself. More letters.

"He brought me." She gazed in Dr. South's direction and draped her arm over Alex's shoulder, another move only Dr. Wang would try. "I got wind of his proof of concept through some screening I was doing with NIH and decided I wanted to be a part of it. I was tired of paper pushing. Watch this one—he will do whatever is necessary to see this project succeed, Alex."

"I need to get myself back to work." Alex, once again, wondered how she deserved her place on such a magnificent team.

123

She headed back into her office, closed off the viewing glass into her lab, and stared out the door into the hallway. Kamini had moved on, but South was still there. How did he do it? He even somehow had time to go on adventure trips that took him around the world scuba diving and white-water rafting. In fact, his trip the previous year was to India to dive the Andaman and Nicobar Islands between India and Thailand. Someone told her he'd already been to Thailand several times, so he wanted to try some place different. He wrote off the trips by doing volunteer medical service in countries where poverty increased the number of kidney disease patients beyond that in the U.S. How did someone with his classic charm stay single?

Dr. South saw her staring and smiled.

Alex smiled back.

Chapter 17

July 10, 2015, CiCi's Home, San Antonio, Texas:
Jon woke early with new enthusiasm. The nights belonged to CiCi, but the mornings were his. That was one reason they shared the house so well. That, and her travels, gave him time to himself. Refreshed and ready to find himself a donor, he set to work.

First, he needed to explain his situation to his stepdaughter, Kelly, whom he had raised from when she started school. After first chewing him out for not telling her earlier, she offered to donate, but that wouldn't happen. That clarity came to him during the night. He'd had a glorious life, and he wasn't about to let her take that risk. Besides, as his stepdaughter, the chances of a match were slim. She fussed with him, but he said she may need that kidney someday for her children.

Kelly called her husband, Bryce, who called Jon right away to offer. Most dads in Jon's experience doubted the marriage choices of their children, but this guy had always been A++ in Jon's book. Again, Jon turned down the offer. The overture came from Bryce's heart, but, again, Jon said the grandkids might need that kidney someday. He didn't reveal his inner thoughts—his son-in-law was a police officer—he could need his own spare kidney someday.

He decided he would not allow CiCi's niece to donate for the same reasons as his stepdaughter. And not CiCi's daughter—if something went wrong, CiCi would kill him. He would allow CiCi, however, to donate because she was already in her sixties, and most American transplant institutes wouldn't consider living donors after sixty-five because of age-related illnesses. If Kambri were to need a kidney, CiCi would age out soon.

The offers from the kids sparked his enthusiasm to reach out further. He still had not told his lifelong friends living in other parts of the U.S. about his health, so he decided it was time. It was a tough task writing about his diagnosis and that he wanted more than their sympathies. Tact required him to keep it short, but the request was immense. Working all morning in his cubbyhole of an office, he had the email ready for proofreading by the time CiCi woke up. That was CiCi's job. Jon cooked; CiCi edited. It worked for both.

Finally, emerging from her bedroom, rubbing her eyes, and inhaling the steam from her coffee Jon had placed in her hand, CiCi found Jon in drive mode.

"Sit down." He pulled out a chair at the dining table. "I need you to proofread this before I send it out." He handed her the print-out of the email. "It can't hurt to ask."

CiCi grabbed a red pen from the kitchen drawer and set to work. "You've been a busy boy this morning." She hadn't even had her morning yogurt—coffee would have to do for now.

"There's more," Jon said. "I want to call University Hills. They also have a transplant center. I'm going to get them to commit to screening you before I get excited and go there in person. I don't want to give blood and fill out forms if they won't even look at a cancer survivor."

Even in CiCi's groggy morning state, she noticed he was asking for help from friends and would inconvenience her with blood tests when he had not even registered to see if he was eligible. That was one of his major personality changes. During his days in business, he would have asked nothing of others without first performing his own due diligence. That seemed only fair. She decided being told one is dying turns focus inward. That seemed fair as well.

"Can I wake up first?"

But there was no stopping him. Jon wasn't the most patient of people—he had little tolerance for bullshit, like unnecessary blood tests.

While CiCi had her trusty red pen at work on the email, Jon called University Hills Hospital. With his super salesperson persuasion, he convinced Kiera to talk with CiCi and handed her the phone.

"But he doesn't care about a cancer cell being passed to him." She argued with the phone, waving it around and frowning into the screen. "He's seventy and dying." She paused to listen, then started again. "Did I tell you the part about he is dying?"

She saw Jon eavesdropping and wincing at her sarcasm.

"Nineteen fifty-three ... nineteen years ago ... pretty fit for my age ... one hundred sixty-three pounds."

The answers continued for fifteen minutes.

Finally, CiCi ended the call and returned the phone to Jon. "Kiera completed the donor survey and conceded to giving it to the committee before they have you do blood tests. She promised to get back to us after the committee meets." She picked up her red pen to finish her first task. "We missed the meeting today, and they don't meet again for two weeks. But she promised to let us know."

"Two weeks?" Jon fondled the phone, looking like he was going to call her back, but instead gave CiCi a rare kiss on the cheek. "That works. We should know something when you get back from China. I'll send out the emails to see if anyone else is able or willing to donate."

"In the meantime," CiCi said, "you need to register."

****

That afternoon, on the way to a late lunch with her girlfriends Catalina and Ruthie to talk last minute plans for China, CiCi heard a public radio report explaining that stem cell therapies would be available in, hopefully, twenty-five years. Too late for Jon. He was in the garage tinkering when she left, and the radio was on out there. Jon had to have heard the report, so no need for her to mention it.

When she returned home, Jon was on the phone with his old buddy in California. She heard, "No, no, I understand … No, I understand. Yeah, me, too."

As the evening progressed, he got more phone calls. All cared and worried for him. All wished they could donate, but all had physical factors that eliminated them at once: diabetes, heart disease, high blood pressure, auto-immune conditions, age. This was the problem with older living donors. Since Jon was seventy, most of his friends were over sixty-five. His ex-wife had offered, but she was unemployed and without insurance—it wouldn't be a good idea for her to donate. CiCi and Jon had already learned the transplant clinics disqualified donors without insurance just in case something else came up during testing. CiCi figured those *something elses* would come up at some point even without trying to donate. At least this way, the individual would know. She supposed ignorance was bliss when there was no insurance.

After one of his many naps for the day, Jon announced he was going to bed early. CiCi noticed in the last week Jon surrendered more easily to lethargy and grew sallower—no, grayer—each day. It wasn't so much lethargy—he always did stuff around the house, even mowed the yard, but he did it more slowly and needed more naps. The gray tinted his skin, but not his mood. She admired Jon's tenacity and was grateful he never moped. It had to be difficult for him.

So, Jon headed to bed, and CiCi started packing her last-minute stuff for the plane. China had seemed like such a great idea when she and her girlfriend planned it a year earlier. It all sounded good when she paid deposits while living in her tent at Kalani in Hawaii. The rover life captivated her fantasy, no routine life for the newly retired schoolteacher. Now she wasn't so sure. What if he slept the entire two weeks and didn't look after himself? Or worse?

Reviewing the contents already packed in the suitcase, making sure she had her sarong for places that didn't approve of shorts or knees, and zipping her passport into her handbag, she worried. Her daughter and niece lived close by and promised to check on Jon daily to be sure he got up and about, so he had assured her he would be fine.

CiCi was a night owl and loved her quiet time to ponder and watch *death and dismemberment* TV shows after Jon shuffled to bed. Her friends would pick her up early to go to the airport. With Jon in bed with the birds, she had time to herself and could still get a good night's sleep. Tonight's show was an old rerun involving *Gypsies* who kidnapped a little girl to be the future wife of their son. Times had changed since the premier of this show—CiCi knew *gypsy* was no longer acceptable to refer to the Roma community, but the traveler theme fit for the night's TV viewing as she finished packing.

Val had told her at Friday's that the Romani religion didn't favor organ donation. CiCi didn't realize Romani was a religion—she thought it was a culture. There wasn't a formal Roma resolution against transplants, but their concept of the afterlife required the body to be intact. They believed that for one year after death, the soul retraced its steps and kept a physical shape. That idea fascinated CiCi, that she would revisit her life. She hoped the soul would be objective—she and her daughter remembered events so differently. Memory played vexing tricks. At any rate, missing body parts were not desired for the Romani culture.

While watching the show, she Googled *Romani*. About 20,000 Romani Americans lived in Texas, mostly in Houston and Fort Worth, but a surprising number lived around San Antonio. Over centuries, they had migrated from India into Eastern Europe as resistance to the rise of Islam, with many ending up as slaves in what is now Romania until 1864. When they were freed, they had no country of their own—or housing or schooling—and were easily identified because they were the first people of color in Europe. They first arrived in the Americas with Christopher Columbus in the 1490s. Early Brits thought they originated in Egypt, calling them *Gypsies*, and during the colonial period, Britain shipped their *Roma problem* as slaves to the southern plantations. CiCi couldn't find anything about how they left the plantations. Were they freed along with the Black people during the Civil War?

When Hollywood came along, they became branded as *bad people*. Although the United Kingdom included *Gypsy or Traveler* as a protected ethnicity, Roma or Gypsy was not an ethnic classification in U.S. census surveys. She wondered about her own classes. How many Romani children had she taught? During her certification classes to teach English as a Second Language, her group of six teachers presented research on education in India. The other five thought it was silly to study India because they didn't have Indian students. She told them her students from northern India had last names such as Aurora and Vora, Spanish sounding. The group met again the next week and reported they had several Indian students they had assumed were Hispanic. Had CiCi done that with her Romani students? Their children attended public school looking Hispanic or Indian or Native American. The teachers didn't know differently in her day. Then the poor Romani kids read stories in their schoolbooks teaching that *they* were thieves.

When she looked up from her research, the show was ending. The FBI had saved the little girl from the *Travelers*. CiCi didn't mind missing the show—she had seen it at least twice before. The TV was background noise for her.

She decided the protesters were not Roma and reminded herself never to presume. Val was right—the protesters resulted from fake news from nowhere.

Unlike CiCi's wild, disjointed fantasy brain, Jon was a non-fiction buff. She informed him at least her shows were fiction with controllable plots that allowed the good guys to win. He watched *Maury* and *Steve Wilkos* in the mornings with actual people saying ugly things about spouses and family members. At least her *Criminal Minds* and *Law and Order: Special Victims Unit* taught people not to do that stuff, and without profanity. Do the crime and do the time.

With the timid protester's brochure about donors with complications tucked into her study-while-flying pocket of her carry-on bag, she let her mind return to her burning questions. Why would Jon expect so much of her when he no longer expected it of himself? When talking about transplants, he claimed a good thing about the anti-rejection meds was that he could quit taking them if he found the side effects too tough to accept. Would he simply give up because the medicines made him feel crappy? Would he disrespect her gift so easily? Jon had told her years earlier that she was too easy, that she would give away everything she had. If she could fold herself into her suitcases, she could hide from these questions. The questions wouldn't matter, anyway. With Santa Maria declaring such a final "No" because of the cancer, there wasn't much room for hope in University Hills either.

Chapter 18

May 2009, Tabriz, Iran:
How could she be so naïve? Only when Eva was in the taxi speaking with her guide did she figure out her error, and now she was scolding herself. While interviewing in Gaborone, she only heard the word *hands* in the organization's name. Par for Eva, she had verified nothing—the decision to go had to happen. They paid for the flight. Now here she stood.

Back in Johannesburg's airport waiting to fly to Tabriz, she learned how to wrap her sarong around her hair and neck. She had planned to buy a beautiful scarf once she got to Iran, but her sarong had served her well for over a decade—it would work for the time being. Then she bought a below-the-butt length long-sleeved baggy shirt from a fellow passenger to cover her blouse and pants. She couldn't even approach the gate without it. Airline personnel and flight attendants checked often, offering tricks of the trade to keep items in place. As she disembarked the plane, an attendant reminded her she had check points and passport guards who would also inspect. Eva looked over her clothing, excited that it wasn't the black cover sack she had seen in movies. This was doable.

While trying to find her contact at baggage claim, as she was told to do, she nearly missed her chaperone because she was looking for the word *physicians*.

"You cannot read? I have been standing here holding this sign for a long time." Her chaperone chastised her as if she were a child.

It turned out they were not Hands Helping Physicians—they called themselves Doctors Join Hands, the DJH.

Her chaperone held the rear passenger door for Eva to enter the cab and got into the front seat with the driver. She had passed all scrutiny and now rode with her chaperone to the hospital to learn what her life held next.

"I will be with you to help you adjust to our ways." His exaggerated sigh caught Eva off-guard—he didn't like her without even knowing her.

Driving through the city with the windows open brought Eva out of her funk. The cool weather surprised her, not even seventy degrees, so, no, she wouldn't die from heat stroke in the extra apparel. She had lived in Celsius countries for half her life but still favored Fahrenheit. Old habits. Her concept of the Middle East was heat, desert, and sand—a common error, a mental transfer of the Egyptian pictures from high school geography. She knew better. She had assumed Botswana was hot and dry all the time prior to living there. Between Tabriz's buildings, she could see green mountains on both sides. The city was higher in the mountains than she realized, and impressive, much larger than she expected and with so many skyscrapers. History class taught her Iran was the cradle of civilization with the Silk Road and the Mongols, but this looked modern.

The driver announced their arrival, the first thing he said since she got into the car. As he opened her door for her to get out of the car, he handed her a business card. "In case you need a taxi."

****

Eva approached the receptionist at the Tabriz hospital, which looked nice enough. The man at the desk told Eva to follow him for a quick tour of the facilities.

While walking, he spoke with well-rehearsed English. "In the 1990s, Iran became the only country in the world where selling a

133

kidney was legal. This revolutionary state-regulated system prevented abuse of the poor. By 1999, the kidney transplant waiting list for Iranians disappeared. All needs had been met. Iranians needing kidneys got them rather than dying in wait."

Eva noticed he strutted down the hallways. She supposed he had a good reason to be proud.

They walked past one of the recovery rooms where a happy Iranian patient was speaking with his doctor. *Note to self*, thought Eva, *get a course in Persian right away*, proud that she knew Iranians spoke Persian instead of Arabic. Large patient rooms had all the amenities and equipment of modern hospitals. Vigilant staff watched live feeds of the patients from a central desk.

The receptionist continued strutting as he made his introduction. "Our proactive government prevented transplant tourism that used Iranian kidneys. Now foreign recipients in Iran must share the nationality of their donors." Eva's experience with South Africa's illegal market had taught her about wealthy Americans, Israelis, and Europeans who bought kidneys with no regard for the donors. They pretended to have familial connections, but only a fool believed them. The arrangement in Iran sounded perfect. She was thirty, she told herself, time to settle in and make peace with her future. It would all work out—it had to.

From the next room came an American accent. A woman asked to go home. The receptionist pointed out that this woman had brought her cousin from America. "She wanted to compensate her relative for saving her from a long waiting list. America would not allow compensation. Besides, she saved a great deal of time and money by doing the transplant here."

"Don't the States restrict travel here?" Eva asked her guide. She felt the blood rush to her face as soon as she asked the question. Here she stood—in a hospital in Iran.

He moved on as if she never spoke. "We also have an Israeli woman, and the man in surgery is British. We have an excellent reputation worldwide."

Eva assumed there were more Iranians in other rooms. Someone designed the tour to impress her global understanding.

Next, they entered the observation deck for the operating room (OR), which looked more impressive than any Eva had seen on TV shows. She'd recruited donors from Botswana to send to Johannesburg and learned the stories from her host in Gaborone, but she had never seen the actual procedure. Watching a transplant up close thrilled her—she saw both surgery theaters from the observation room. So little blood. And on the monitors, she could see what the laparoscopes showed the surgeons. Right in front of her eyes was the kidney. Timing was everything. The surgeons didn't start the recipient's incision until the kidney was removed from the donor. It all flowed from one cut to the next—from one body to the next. She asked the receptionist about follow-up for the donors.

He put on his best used car sales persona, complete with brilliant white teeth. "They get excellent care—they never complain. But foreign donors return to their respective countries—we do not control care there."

As they approached the doors to go back to the lobby, Eva heard familiar voices. It had to be her imagination, but, no, her ears did not deceive.

"Eva? It's you!? You're finally here!" shouted Charles in his not-so-hospital-quiet voice.

Marco looked like he was about to hug her but stopped suddenly. "We thought you died in the fire."

Eva turned away to collapse into a nearby chair. Her vision for her future vanished and left her gasping for air. Marco and Charles waved off the receptionist and escorted Eva into a private conference room.

135

****

"You deserted me in Botswana to make it on my own. Baruti saved my life. Where were you? We searched for you forever. Baruti took me to Kang because some villagers said you headed that way."

"Eva," they pleaded together.

Then Charles took over the conversation. "We searched everywhere for you. One local took us to a tent filled with burned bodies. A woman with a ring like yours was so burned we couldn't tell who she was. We decided it was like Phuket. You know—identify the accessories."

"This ring? You dumb asses. I bought this at the market in Maun—there were a hundred just like it. You know—mass marketing." While mocking Charles, she wondered how often that misidentification happened after the tsunami.

Marco put his arm around Eva's shoulder, but she brushed it off to walk away.

Marco pleaded with her. "Sit down with us and talk. We're all alive and here. Doctors Join Hands is a wonderful organization saving the lives of people every day."

"I'm such an idiot. Until I got into the taxi, I thought it was Hands Helping Physicians, a proper organization."

"We are real," Charles said. "It's us, Eva. Carrie Breun set this up to help in Iran."

"Carrie Breun? What is it you do here?" She needed to spit.

Marco looked at Charles as if appealing for help. Finding none, he looked down at his folded hands. "Look, after the fire in Maun, we decided recruiting in the Delta wasn't a good idea, so we moved on to Kang. But it turns out the locals dislike foreigners."

Eva smiled to herself. When they asked her what she was doing after they left, she told them she taught English to the villagers. Wasted ears, though—they didn't catch her sarcasm.

Charles took over as usual. "About ten years ago, the Iranian government figured out foreigners got the stronger, better matches from Iranian donors because they could pay more. From then on, people had to have kidney donors from their own nationality. These days Iranian kidneys can only go to Iranians."

"Yes, so the receptionist said."

Charles explained foreign surgeries brought in more money to the hospitals than the Iranian government and even the wealthy Iranians paid. Hospitals struggled for money. "We help the hospitals work around the rules. We unbind their hands, so to speak."

When DJH began in Iran, Carrie Breun sent the two recruiters all over Brazil to find *relatives* and arrange matching nationality documents. No one said anything, a blind eye sort of thing.

"But it wasn't enough." Charles explained further. "Plenty of Iranian locals begged to take part, and falsifying local papers rather than bringing donors internationally made the transplant much easier. These hospitals didn't complain about our process."

Experience told Eva the Iranian people would be the ones to suffer. She stared at Charles and Marco for only a second and walked out of the clinic. She felt a little sorry for Marco and Charles. As gullible as Eva was, illegal activity involving recipients from the West in Iran sounded like a bad idea.

Chapter 19

July 24, 2015, CiCi's Home, San Antonio, Texas: The return flight from China arrived mid-morning. Since Jon wasn't driving more than a couple of miles to the grocery these days, CiCi rode home from the airport with Catalina and her husband, Jerry. Jon let CiCi know before she left China that *the girls* had vacated. There was a standing travel joke between them about taking down the poles and hustling the strippers out before she got home. Even seriously ill, he kept his humor. He had emailed daily to tell her he was coping fine and enjoying the time without her nagging. Although he didn't say it, she knew he was also checking to be sure she was safe, and not just because she had a spare kidney.

Jerry brought in the suitcase without asking so Jon wouldn't have to accept the help. Men know.

Since Jon said nothing about word from Kiera at University Hills regarding the transplant, CiCi didn't bring it up. No news was either no news or sad news, so it would be best to let Jon tell her in his own time. She moved into trip babble mode to pretend there was nothing unusual. Her Facebook page chronicled her journey, but Jon refused to have anything to do with social media, so she had sent him selected photos and commentary daily. Now she felt obliged to give him the moment by moment—at least it filled the silence of waiting for news about the transplant.

The Great Wall had been impressive, with gorgeous views of the country, but really? Mongols couldn't climb over it with a bit of persistence and loss of life? Hundreds of thousands of Chinese lost their lives building it. But it was impressive. CiCi wondered if it walled people out or kept them in. Walls and fences were often built to perform both functions: Bush's fence along the Mexico border, the Berlin Wall, the Ice Wall in *Game of Thrones,* personal walls around failing kidneys.

She told Jon about her trips to Tiananmen Square, the Terra Cotta Warriors, the silk factory, the acrobat performance, the beautiful cruise down the Chang Jiang with all the excursions up the tributaries for a taste of Chinese culture (well-crafted and choreographed by the Chinese government). Shanghai in the night fog, with the massive apartment complexes towering over the streets, made her think of the very dark scenes in the old movie *Blade Runner.*

Her favorite excursion was the panda display in Chongqing. While volunteering at Kalani on Hawaii, she'd befriended a young Chinese man who'd just completed his university degree in Canada. He came to the retreat center to gain U.S. experience before heading home. CiCi laughed about working in paradise and thinking it was a U.S. experience.

When CiCi left for China, it so happened Samson had just returned to his home in Chengdu to begin his career. They met up at the Chengdu Zoo. While watching the amazing pandas, CiCi got to show off her Chinese protégé to her friends, and Samson got to show off his American teacher to his parents. Friends crossing paths in distant lands delighted CiCi—it had happened to her several times. Her path with Samson was perfect.

Jon remained quiet and politely listened to her adventures. He had gone to Hong Kong for his dad on business when he was a young man, but he hadn't been to mainland China. CiCi treasured the times when she saw things he had not—he had done so much in his life. He hadn't ridden an elephant bareback like she did in Thailand, so that was one for CiCi. Never mind that he pulled out the ancient movie projector and showed her films of his ten-year-old self meeting the King of Siam while his dad conducted business in Bangkok. Who still had movie projectors, anyway? Jon, of course. Every time she decided he was filling her with con stories,

139

he supplied proof. "He had not zip-lined upside down through the Costa Rican Rainforest," she told herself.

"So now we are down to your souvenir," CiCi announced.

"Okay, let's have it."

Souvenirs for Jon baffled CiCi. He either already had it, had one and had given it away, would like something she couldn't afford, or had nowhere to put it. While in Beijing, the group visited a government tea house. Many times, the salespeople reminded them they should buy government guaranteed products. The Government made sure the product was what they claimed and purity was true. CiCi heard the word *purity* so often she wondered if they were trying to convince themselves. This young woman was good at her sales as she guided the group of eight Americans skillfully and efficiently through their tasting of eight teas. She told them what to expect with flavors and how they helped medicinally. CiCi had found her souvenir.

"I bought you tea."

"Tea? I'm so thrilled."

The sarcasm didn't faze CiCi in the least. "Ginseng Oolong is for good kidney function." She tried a Chinese accent but admittedly sounded stupid. "The girl said to drink it four times a day."

"Let's try it."

Surprised, CiCi jumped up to hand him his other gift. She was certain he would laugh at her, say thank you, and never try it. He was not a tea man.

"I got you this tea steeping cup to go with it." She added the hot water. "Look! The dragon turns into the Great Wall!" CiCi exaggerated the fun fact of the magic teacup, hoping to at least have a moment of smile with the souvenir.

He played along with oohs and aahs. "This is quite tasty." He asked for another.

About an hour later, he startled CiCi, saying he thought the tea did something for him, that he felt good. CiCi joked that the

Chinese government must have given her not-so-pure tea laced with narcotics, but Jon was happy, so she was thrilled.

It had been a long flight, so Jon took another cup of tea and recommended they both get a good rest.

****

The next morning, CiCi woke up to the coffee grinder and the smell of coffee. Jon made himself tea and left the coffee for her. "Gotta tell my docs about this stuff. It works. It may not fix the kidneys, but I feel good." He Googled Ginseng Oolong and found it known for boosting energy.

"All righty then. I was going for desperate gift and struck pay dirt. Cool."

They sat in silence, a challenging task for CiCi. Finally, she burst out, "And what about Kiera and University Hills?"

"Not a word yet." Salesmanship filtered every aspect of Jon's life, even while sick. "In business we say no call is a good thing—it means they have not said 'No.'"

Like in a *Twilight Zone* episode with mind-readers, CiCi's phone buzzed. She went into immediate squeak mode, the voice that took over her body when she couldn't control the conversation. She knew it was happening, even felt sorry for Kiera on the other end, but did not stop.

"Really? No one knows if they have cancer starting in their bodies. You take donors in their sixties—any of them could have a cancer cell floating around. I have been nineteen years with no recurrence."

Kiera could not say a word—CiCi charged on. "If I'd donated when I was forty-two, we wouldn't have known that the *in situ* ductile breast cancer was there. *In situ*, in position, never left home, not invasive."

There was no time to come up for air—she kept on.

141

"Besides, the other hospital said they were worried about me, and now you say you're worried about him. I don't think either hospital knows—you're just grabbing at straws."

And then there was the pause.

CiCi calmed down. "I know you're just the messenger. I know you're sorry, but not as sorry as we are." With that, CiCi put down the phone.

Jon spent the day drinking hot Ginseng Oolong tea and watching dysfunctional family morning shows. *Jerry Springer* was the hit today.

CiCi saw a defeated man and added *defeated* next to *sick* on her list of what Jon didn't do well. Tomorrow, they would chat again about dialysis.

Chapter 20

May 2009, Tabriz, Iran:
The warm breeze felt wonderful against Eva's neck until her body warned her it wasn't fully covered. Re-wrapping the sarong/scarf over her shoulders, Eva returned her attention to her escape. Not releasing her passport to the hospital receptionist, as he had requested, may have topped her luck list. Instead, she handed him a photocopy she had brought with her from Botswana, a tip she learned early in Thailand. But here she was in a foreign country with nowhere to go, again.

Walking around unchaperoned instigated Eva's first lesson in Iranian culture. She exited the hospital—alone and caught up in her frustration. No—anger. No—anguish. A member of the fashion morality approached her, shouting in Persian. Not only was she unaccompanied, when she covered her neck, she allowed the sarong/*hijab* to slip off her hair. While waiting outside for his next fare, the taxi driver heard the ruckus and ran to her side, tugging her wrap to remind her to fix it. He then assured the man he was her chaperone, that his wife would host her. None of this was true, but it sounded convincing. The driver explained Eva had just arrived in Iran and spoke only English—he would insure she learned the ways of the people within the day. He told Eva to show the cleric her plane ticket and her stamped visa. The man grumbled something and walked away. Then, in English, the driver translated for Eva what he'd said.

The enforcer turned back to them and spoke in English, accented as it was. "People cry when we approach them, but when we let them go, nothing changes. I am doing the divine. I answer to virtue."

It took a strong nudge from the driver for Eva to move her feet toward the car. "My name is Kourosh Abbasi," he said. "I understand how hard it is to sort your way in a new country. I attended university in England and had to learn to navigate a new world. But England was not an enemy nation to my homeland. You have more to consider than I."

"Thank you so much. What would I have done if you weren't there? Um, I'm Eva."

"Yes, I overheard your guide on the way from the airport. You would have gone to the jail. So why are you alone outside the hospital?"

Eva shook. Why was she sitting in a taxi in Iran with no one, no things, no help other than a few thousand dollars she still had from home? Her visa specified thirty days as a *student*. The hospital in Tabriz was to work something out with the government for her to stay longer. Not a student and not an employee, she was in trouble. As Mr. Abbasi pointed out, Iran was on the list of the United States' bad guys. Her own country could turn on her. And here she was in a car with a stranger. At least he spoke English.

"You're terrified. Please, let me apologize. I had hoped you would laugh at the jail remark—I forgot you have probably only heard about extremists in Iran. That man was a busybody volunteer—he is not a cleric or a police officer. And the police rarely bother foreigners if they correct their clothing, but the culture in Tabriz does follow proper *hijab*." He gave a nervous laugh, the laugh someone gives when he knows he made a social blunder. "As for unescorted women, you would have been fine if the fashion morality enforcer had anything better to do."

She relaxed. It was her turn to make the nervous social blunder laugh.

"Now," Kourosh said, "where can I take you?"

Eva fumbled for words. Her dry mouth couldn't shape the sounds. Noises came out as stutters and coughs.

The driver remained parked until he feared he would draw attention. Then he drove forward, giving her time to sort out her business. He started talking, which relieved the mental vacuum forming in the car. He told her his wife was the counselor at the Tabriz *anjoman*.

The word *counselor* sounded good to Eva, but she didn't know what an *anjoman* was. Not wanting to look even more vulnerable to her new host, she just nodded.

His monologue then turned to the big question. "What happened with your guide and the Doctors Join Hands?"

"Hands?" Her voice returned. "Hands? I thought they were Hands Helping Physicians!" She cried and sobbed incoherent sentences about South Africa and Hope in Victory. "Nowhere to go. Can't go home." Then she spoke broken thoughts about Botswana and Marco and Charles and Baruti. Then the name Carrie Breun.

Kourosh's eyebrows almost lifted off the top of his head. "Carrie Breun? You know Carrie Breun?"

Not sure how to interpret Kourosh's agitation, Eva shook again and fell silent. Did he work with Carrie Breun, too? If she spoke poorly of Ms. Breun, he might turn her over to the police for having no purpose in Iran. If she spoke favorably, he might include her with illegal kidney transplants.

It didn't matter—Kourosh cut off her thoughts. "Carrie Breun is evil. She preys on the poor to benefit her wealthy Americans. Are you with her?"

He enunciated *Americans* so sharply Eva thought the word could break the front windshield. What if he hated Americans? It wasn't her fault. "No, it was a misunderstanding. You're right. She's evil. She doesn't care about the donors. She only wants more donors. That's why I was in front of the hospital alone. I just found out that Doctors Join Hands was her organization. I thought she was helping the villagers in Botswana, but after I left her and spoke with the people, I realized what was happening. I came here to get away from the illegal market. Then they showed up here." Eva couldn't catch her breath. She grabbed her chest and doubled over.

Finally out of traffic, Kourosh pulled the car off the road and opened the backseat door. Every alarm Eva could muster went off: alone, strange country, man at her car door.

"You're having a panic attack." He told her to unbutton her top cover to allow air. "You're safe. Breathe, Eva. I will take you to my wife. Azara can help you."

Eva tried meditation breaths—she had to take control. It worked, so he left her lying on the seat and drove on. She would survive this—she always survived. "What is an *anjoman*?"

"This is what we call our offices where counselors match kidney patients with living donors. My wife counsels the donors."

"Donors get paid here, right?"

"Yes, my wife negotiates that and makes sure the donor is selling without pressure from anyone. She will help you figure out where to go next."

Eva overheard Kourosh make a cell phone call to his wife that started as an argument that turned into soft words. When he ended the call and said his wife agreed, no questions asked, Eva hoped the argument wasn't about her.

Kourosh pointed off the road to an old building with a blue entrance. "The Blue Mosque."

"I thought the Blue Mosque was in Istanbul."

"Ours came first, built in fourteen sixty-five. Used to be brilliant blue all over, but an earthquake two hundred fifty years ago did this to it. We have been restoring it for a long time. For now, only the *iwan* tiles are blue. And the interior—the Shah's tomb—is repaired. Maybe we can take you inside someday."

Grateful for the distraction, Eva studied the building. Florida's St. Augustine wasn't even that old. The mosque made an infant out of the Alamo.

Kourosh distracted his anxious passenger with local trivia. He told her the term *Middle East* was correct since they were the center of the Ancient Civilizations of Europe, Asia, and Africa. The Ancients in the region welcomed all religions, and, in fact, the Constitution still protected minority religions if they didn't try to convert Muslims. These days a Muslim converting to another faith could face death. Eva wondered how so much freedom could have reversed itself so drastically. *Handmaid's Tale* seemed impossible when her friends made her read it—couldn't happen, she told them. She thought she should read it again.

They rode in silence. As soon as they arrived, Azara rushed to the car and hugged Eva. After imagining Kourosh's wife in a red *handmaid's* cloak but predicting the black *chador* common in Iranian women, Eva laughed with relief. No red or black on this woman.

In her forties, Azara's smile glowed, surrounded by her simple hijab. "You poor dear."

Eva could not resist snuggling into her embrace. She had gone through so many frightening experiences, but there were always kind people waiting to help her.

Once inside the door, Kourosh excused himself, saying he needed to make money. The office buzzed with ten nervous men and women sitting on uncomfortable benches. A receptionist spoke with an elderly gentleman. Azara explained he was asking about his turn, and then Azara guided Eva to her desk, which caused even more chatter from those waiting. Eva assumed her sudden priority upset them.

"Tell me a little about yourself." Azara approached Eva directly and with an interviewer's tone, a switch from the warm embrace next to the car. "Do you speak Azeri? Do you know anyone in Iran other than that horrendous DJH group?"

"I don't really know them," Eva jumped in. "I had helped with kidney donation in Botswana and thought I was helping people." Eva gave a brief review of her time in Maun with Marco and

147

Charles, the fire, Baruti and his family, and her epiphany in the desert where she understood how she harmed the very people she wanted to help. She suddenly stopped herself and noticed Azara's kind face. How rude. She hadn't answered Azara's question. "I'm sorry. What is Azeri? I confused it with your name, but that doesn't even make sense. Don't Iranians speak Persian? No, I don't speak Azeri, but I pick up conversational language quickly. I got by in Botswana within two months."

Good at her job, Azara made Eva comfortable. "Simple mistake. Most Iranians are Persian and speak Persian. You may have heard it called Farsi, which is a dialect of Persian. Tabriz is special with a long history as part of Azerbaijan. The Azeri Iranians kept that heritage but love Iran. Azerbaijani is our language. We say Azeri to shorten it."

"So, the hospital and the man who yelled at me?"

"Most likely Azeri. Do you know anything about Iran?"

Eva had to confess she knew only what she had heard in America in the 1990s: women with no rights and owned by their husbands, men with multiple wives, women covered in black, and religious fanatics. Both women laughed.

"Why would you ever come here?" Azara had a musical laugh. Then more seriously, "I am my husband's only wife. I have my career. And though I follow proper *hijab*, I am not covered in a big black sack."

"I figured I knew little when I saw a woman drive a taxi alone. I thought women couldn't drive."

"You seem to have confused us with Saudi Arabia." She paused. "Extremists in our rural areas might live that way, and Tehran can be strict. Women still marry young by Western standards, but most of today's girls go to the university and have careers."

"To be honest, I was desperate for a charity organization to hire me to get on with my life after Botswana, so when that group showed up in Gaborone, I went for it."

148

There was Azara's welcoming smile again. "Khoda knows best."

"Khoda?"

"*Khoda* is the Persian word for God. *Allah* is Arabic. Oh, and *Tanri* is Azeri, but is used to mean multiple deities and not the one and only." Language lesson over, Azara returned to the problem at hand. "Kourosh said you figured out about the fraud DJH as soon as you got here. We suspected Carrie Breun was involved. We have seen no doctors—it should be called Thieves Join Hands. In Iran, we buy kidneys from living donors, but it is nothing like what Ms. Breun is doing. We work to match donors with recipients just as they do in America, but we offer the donor money—I don't know the conversion, thousands in U.S. dollars—for housing, food, and living essentials to thank them for their sacrifice. The government guarantees the base amount, and the rest is negotiated and paid by the recipient or charities. It's our job to help with the charity part. Our organization is not a broker or dealer, and we are under scrutiny of the Organization for Iranian Organ Transplants."

Eva looked at an information sheet in her hand describing all that, but it was in Azeri and Persian—she could see differences but didn't know which was which. She looked up at Azara and understood Kourosh's pride in her work.

"Although our focus is on recipients, I counsel donors to be sure they haven't been pressured and that the sacrifice will help the family. It would be wrong if their lives would be no different the next year except with one less kidney."

This hit home to Eva. So many of their donors in Botswana were worse off after the donation than when they started the process. Iran provided follow-up care for them, unlike what was happening with Carrie Breun's group.

"When we first began sales, the hospitals filled with Saudis, Israelis, Brits, and Americans. Our own people lost out to the wealthy foreign patients. Our government made it illegal in 1992 for Iranian kidneys to go to foreign recipients. Now, foreign patients must bring a relative of their own nationality to receive a transplant here."

All suddenly cleared up for Eva. "And that is where Carrie Breun comes in. The minute I saw Marco and Charles at the Tabriz hospital, I knew something wasn't right."

"Carrie Breun and her associates caused a wonderful transplant unit in Tehran to shut down just last year. Iran enforces the foreign recipient policies. They were caught. Well, not Ms. Breun, but the unit was caught. Your friends are taking a dangerous road, and their work could end this for all of us."

"Not my friends," corrected Eva. "How can I help?" Eva felt guilty about her couple of hours with DJH and assumed stuff like that would eventually cause Iran to ban all foreign transplants, with or without their own donors.

They talked for another hour. Since Eva didn't see Iranian donors at the hospital, there was nothing she could do for now. Later, she could become part of a sting, but she'd already blown her cover.

"What about Islam? Aren't Muslims strict about things like blood and transplants?"

"My dear," Azara laughed, "Persia has always been strong in science. Look where we are on the world map—the bridge for East with West. Persians began the concept of university hospitals long before the West, modeling for future doctors. While the medieval Christian hospitals performed surgeries with dirty hands, Islamic hospitals used alcohol and other antiseptics on contaminated areas. Smallpox and leprosy and tuberculosis? Contagious and required quarantine. We taught America how to vaccinate against smallpox. We also used opium for pain relief during surgeries and tooth extractions. The medieval Christians thought disease was a punishment from God, but the Persians recognized it as another problem to be solved. And so it is with kidney transplants."

The speech appeared well-rehearsed, obviously an enthusiastic topic for Azara since she had more to say. "Iran is modern. We even allow third party donors for *in vitro* fertilization."

The last bit blew away many of Eva's preconceptions of Iranian women. "So, no problem with being whole after death and stuff?"

Both women laughed again.

"Okay, the clerics took issue with using cadavers for kidneys, but eventually said it was acceptable if the organs saved lives. Living donors aren't a concern."

Eva was a little uncomfortable risking a living person's life over violating a dead one, but even U.S. doctors suggested patients find living donors—the kidneys lasted longer.

Azara clarified. "Shi'a clerics sometimes take issue with a male and female kidney match or a non-Muslim and Muslim match. But in a country with a ninety-eight percent Muslim population, that is not a concern. The Jewish rabbis faced similar decisions. I'm told some orthodox sects adamantly oppose deceased organ donation, yet Israel as a state supports it. I imagine the Vatican faced this, too, in the beginning." She frowned and added that the Saudi Wahhabis were harsh. "Perhaps that was why Saudis were coming to Iran for transplants before the law changed."

"But what about the *selling* part?"

"The Qur'an looks favorably at those who help themselves by helping others."

"I learned in Thailand that it's okay to take pleasure in helping others." Eva looked back at her conversations with the many Buddhist monks. "There was something from the Dalai Lama that said a good deed is still a good deed, even if it improves the self. Something like that."

"Smart man, that Dalai Lama."

Eva learned both Kourosh and Azara had gone to universities in England, which explained their wonderful command of English. Though an arranged marriage, they had met at the university on their own terms and had had a long, loving marriage. The family was from central Iran, around Tehran and Isfahan. Kourosh moved them to Tabriz for his job where he taught English full-time at Tabriz University. The taxi business on the side gave them a little extra money. He claimed he enjoyed airport runs the most because he often chanced upon interesting people. He planned to author a book someday, or screenplays for movies.

Talking with Azara comforted Eva—she might find a place to belong for now. Azara told Eva it would surprise her how many Iranians speak English—it worked well for business with all Europeans. Eva told her that was true in Thailand, too, and relayed the story of the tsunami and how she met Marco and Charles. Azara closed her eyes with the wonder of Eva's tale.

Azara had gained her degree in sociology. When their first son faced kidney failure, she felt the living donor program calling her. "Most of the people working at the *anjomans* are volunteers who were donors or recipients themselves. I have one of the few paid positions."

Azara finally addressed the obvious. "Eva, why can't you go home?"

"May I leave it with I can't?"

After a moment of thought, Azara changed the subject. "I need to make a phone call in Persian. Please excuse me."

When she finished the call, Azara told Eva she could clean the house, babysit, and teach English to the children of Kourosh's cousin who managed the *anjoman* on the outskirts of Isfahan. She could share a room with the oldest daughter until they figured out something better. All the Abbasi men were kind gentlemen—she would find safety there. The four children were ages three to fifteen, so Eva would be a substantial contribution. If she agreed, she could take on other students in the community. It turned out Kourosh and Azara had already planned a visit to Isfahan the next week, so the ten-hour drive would give them time to talk.

"You will like Isfahan. It is *the Pearl of Persia*. We call it *half the world* because centuries ago it was where the markets from the East met the markets from the West, that bridge I mentioned. There are two *anjomans* in Isfahan, but one is depressing. Our cousin's *anjoman* is the good one and extremely busy. Your care for the children will allow Zenda to dedicate more time to her career."

Were they passing her off to someone else? Had she offended them? Eva's insecurities attacked her at once. Pulling her sarong around her like a security blanket and remembering Azara's warm hug when they first met, she decided optimism outweighed fear. Grabbing at hope was all she could do. "But what about my visa? The hospital staff was supposed to fix it after I got here. It says I'm a student for thirty days."

"Oh, I wasn't thinking." Azara picked up the phone and made another call, leaving Eva to wonder. This time, it was Azara's family who could help. Her brother was the captain of police in Tehran. He would give her help with the proper documents. Tehran was just a couple of hours out of the way, and Azara had wanted to visit her brother for months. An overnight at her brother's would do the trick.

So, it was all set. Azara took Eva's hand. "Khoda, Allah, God knows best."

Chapter 21

August 7, 2015, Alex's Lab at CTMRI, San Antonio, Texas:

Dr. Ethan South stood at Dr. Segal's door to find her alone in the lab, yelling at her phone.

Alex paced around her desk, picked up papers to look at and put them back down, but never turned toward her door. "I know, Kamini, I know, dammit. ... Yes, we did the protocol just like the computer formula told us. ... Yes, I'll think of something for you to input to fix it. We need those cells. I'll get the team to brainstorm what chemical we need for the stimulant. Then it's in your hands to get the algorithm." She slammed her cell phone onto the table as if it were an old-style landline. "Well, that ought to shut her up."

Dr. South studied her a moment longer. She was a talented researcher, always diligent, precise, too much so. Right now, Dr. South needed her not to be so observant and correct. "Whoa! I didn't do it. Please say that was not because of something I did." He peeked his head into the doorway, pretending to cringe.

"What? Oh, Dr. South. No, that was for Kamini. Not really, it was for me. I haven't found the information she needs to complete the formula for that one hormone secretion. Those cells aren't specializing just yet."

He strolled up to Alex and ever so gently placed his hand on her shoulder. "You'll get it, of that I'm certain." He had that special effect on women and used it well. He assumed Alex had dreams of love and family now that her career flourished. "You need to get out more, hang with friends. Get out of this lab."

Alex slumped onto a nearby stool. "Sure, I'll just call someone from my extensive list of people dying to go barhopping with me."

Just as he suspected, Dr. Segel didn't have a social life. How could she when she was always working? Which, he reminded himself, was why he was visiting her at this moment with a hand on her shoulder. He had seen her studying the reports again, the ones he had sent to the foundation. "How about your coffee shop friend?"

"Maura? You've met Maura?"

"That's her name? I've seen you two at the cafeteria."

Alex sat up. "Maura has an even smaller list of barhopping buddies than I have."

"Where does she work that she casually meets you for lunch so often?" They'd been working together for years now, but he really knew nothing about this mousy underling of his. He rubbed his hand over the top of her shoulder and massaged her neck. Nice body. He wondered why he hadn't noticed before. Probably her age—she had to be in her mid-thirties.

"That feels good," Alex said. "It's been a tough day with the dance of the test tubes. I think I'm already getting old lady shoulders." Her body swayed with the neck rub. "Oh, yes, uh, Maura. She works in Human Resources. She's the one who verifies applicants for positions in this lab."

He pulled his hand off her shoulder and stepped back to return to a professional distance. "HR, huh? I don't recall Maura's name from my earlier requests for personnel. I thought I knew everyone there."

"It's the perfect place for her. She loves helping people and sees it as her way of improving the world."

South decided the Maura woman wouldn't know he was married since he didn't put it on any of his paperwork at HR. He could pursue wooing Dr. Segel without concern. "Well, good for her. Everyone needs to find their niche—and yours, dear Doctor, is on this team."

Dr. South liked his personal life. His wife was a simpleton. Her parents were delighted someone would marry her, even though it was just for their money. They set up a huge bank account as a wedding present—her early inheritance. They desperately wanted an heir. Well, that would not happen—he had taken care of that business years earlier.

"So why don't you go home? Everyone else has," he said.

Alex leaned back on her work counter and smiled before turning back to her microscope. "Not everyone. You're here."

"I'm only here to pick up some paperwork I want to take home." He wondered, again, why he'd never noticed her as more than one of the lab rats—she had a sexy smile. He stepped up and rubbed her shoulders some more and leaned over her as if to see what she'd been working on.

Alex turned to face him. They were so close she had to lean back on the counter to keep her lips off his as she spoke. "Now what has you so concerned that you would work on it this late at night, even if you are doing it at home?"

"That damn deadline. I want to go over my notes again before I try tomorrow to convince Senator Estes to give us more time." He paused. "You must be hungry. Would you like to join me for dinner? Perhaps help me prepare?" He saw the alarm women get when they receive unexpected proposals. "At a restaurant, of course."

"A restaurant? Good idea. I have protocols from the lab that might help you with the Senator tomorrow." Alex tidied up around her microscope and shut down her computer. She hung up her white coat as he, so gallantly, opened the door to escort her out of the building. There was no time to change clothes. This man was wearing a Canali chalk line suit, rich slate gray. She had her frumpy loose skirt, not even an A-line business look, and knit pullover, comfy for long hours in the lab. At least he didn't have a tie. She hoped he meant they would go to a place like Chili's.

"Shall we ride in my car? I can bring you back here to the parking lot to pick up yours after dinner." Dr. South pressed his hand to the small of her back and guided her.

Alex sucked in a breath when she saw her boss's car, then pretended a little stumble to cover her reaction. His hand was right there, ready to catch her. This was not a car—this was a chariot of fire. To call it red would be an insult, as this was anywhere from cardinal red to rich Cabernet depending on the shadows, and the shiniest gloss Alex had ever seen. And gold wheel rims. Thank God they walked up from the rear where she saw *Tesla* written on the trunk. She didn't know one car from another once she left the rank of her basic Toyota. "A Tesla? Nice." She forced her voice to sound like she rode in one every day.

He smiled.

When he opened the door for her to slide in, she gasped again. This time, she didn't bother to hide it. The interior was the most exquisite experience of her life, or so it seemed now. Nothing was too good for this man. The creamy tan interior felt like she folded into a toasted marshmallow. No, that would imply rough, crusty edges—there was nothing rough or crusty about these seats. Embossed on the steering wheel in gold was *T Sportline*. A sickening feeling told her this car would not be sitting in a Chili's parking lot.

"Bonahan's has opened a second restaurant here in the medical center that I've been wanting to try."

San Antonio had developed a second *downtown* with its own skyline. Comprising many hospitals, labs, and office complexes towering over the rolling hills, it became the pride of the city. It also housed the university medical school. All the locals knew exactly where the med center was.

South reached down by Alex's thigh and checked her seatbelt. "It won't have the beautiful downtown Riverwalk balcony, but I hear it's quite nice."

Alex knew Bonahan's had four dollar signs in *DiningWishes.com*. "I'm not dressed for elegance. Besides, don't you need a reservation?"

"You look beautiful. They're in the med center, so they can't expect people to come from work in cocktail dresses. As for reservations, I never have a problem with that at restaurants around here."

It was a quick ride, for which awe-stricken Alex was grateful. They pulled up to the valet, who helped Alex out of the car. She wanted to roll herself into a little ball when she saw her feet step onto the pavement. No heels, flats had always been the shoes to wear in a lab. Yes, a pair of black heels would reside in her office starting tomorrow.

As the maître d' immediately seated them at a quiet table in a corner, Alex wondered when her companion had time to put on his tie. How did she miss that?

"A bottle of Chateau Rothschild." Not a request, Dr. South *notified* the waiter of his wishes.

Overwhelmed, Alex didn't notice he never asked her if she preferred a red or a white. Since she preferred red, the question was moot.

They toasted to the remodeled kidney and vowed to get out of the office earlier each night, the old work to live rather than live to work motto.

"Think back," said Dr. South, "we originally tried to inject kidneys with multipotent skin cells, hoping to assist a kidney in repairing itself."

Alex smiled. "We and twenty-five other labs. It sounded so simple." He was preaching to the choir here—she had led that effort. They tried it in monkeys, but it added more kidney in all the wrong places rather than fixing the damaged parts. This guy with gorgeous, built shoulders had difficulty with small talk on a date. No, not a date. She scolded herself and reminded herself they were there on business. Thus, the business talk. She had to get around to talking about those reports that were the pigs' tests instead of the human tests. Soon. She would get to them soon. Instead, she said, "And there was the kidney that wouldn't stop growing."

"We thought we were in the nineteen fifties sci-fi movie *The Blob.*"

It was nice to laugh, so needed.

Dr. South's voice grew serious again. "That's why we turned to stripping the monkey's own damaged kidney and growing his own cells on it. Which was your idea. Brilliant."

"Thanks." She swirled her wine around the way she had seen connoisseurs do in movies. "It made sense to get rid of the damage, start fresh, and avoid the next horror film."

Tipping his wine glass towards Alex, he continued the compliment. "To your brilliance and to renewed life."

"No sacrificial donors and zero rejection." Alex tapped her glass against his. She thought she would swoon. Recognition from Ethan South meant more to her than pay raises any day.

The waiter approached with menus and started to describe the evening's recommendation when Dr. South interrupted. "We won't be needing these. We'll start with risotto and truffle for an appetizer and the lobster thermidor with asparagus spears for the entrée. I don't believe we will require dessert, but check back later."

Alex was shocked. He hadn't asked if she even liked lobster or if she were allergic to shellfish or anything. But then, she loved lobster, and she wasn't allergic to anything, so no harm done. And lobster thermidor? Who would question that? She had never been to such a fine restaurant before—best she leave it to him to order. Still, she wondered what the other menu items were. She would peek online later. The present issue was figuring out how to eat with the correct utensil. She remembered her women's club sponsor in high school saying silverware from the outside first. Here she was, a research doctor who made a great salary but gawked at a luxury car and didn't know how to present herself properly at a fine restaurant. She wasn't starring in *Pretty Woman,* but, then, Dr. South could give Richard Gere a run for his money. For one, he was just as handsome and younger. She vowed to study her *Emily Post*.

They talked more about how far the team had advanced since their first vision of saving so many people. And with a permanent cure, not just a treatment. Then silence. She knew she should offer a topic, but the only thing she wanted to say involved the discrepancies in the reports, and she didn't want to say that just then.

"Al Gore and Orrin Hatch." Dr. South said the names, no explanation, no context.

Puzzled but relieved he had broken the silence, she went with her gut. "Who sponsored the National Organ Transplant Act of Nineteen Eighty-Four?"

"Smart Lady." Dr. South leaned over to refill Alex's wineglass and handed it to her. "Wishful thinking for $600: *Brain dead* donor program." He whispered in her ear like this silliness was pillow talk.

It was stuff they both knew, but somehow his whisper was the sexiest sound she had heard in a long time, so she would play along. Alex whispered back in his ear. "How did NOTA plan to get donors for transplants?" She let her voice go deep and breathy. "And, still, we don't have enough donors."

They sat in silence, barely breathing. The reports yelled at her— it had been a month—but it was such a lovely night.

Again, it was Dr. South who broke the spell. "Job security for us." He then tapped her glass.

As they sipped, he described the wine with words like finesse, cherries, smoke, damp earth, and cigar wrapper. It was clearly time for Alex to loosen her spending practices to learn more about drinking earth and cigar wrappers. This Rothschild was an orgasm in a bottle. The lobster thermidor, though, stood up well with it. Red wine with lobster? She wouldn't have guessed.

When they finished dinner, Dr. South moved to the seat next to Alex and poured still more wine. "Enough of this. Tell me about yourself. You must do something outside of the lab."

Alex giggled. The hunk of a doc showed interest in her non-life life. "I do yoga when Maura forces me."

"Maura forces you? I would enjoy watching that."

"What? Watch Maura force me?"

"Yes, that. I heard you go after Kamini."

"Kamini's easy. Maura does guilt trips on me."

While they chatted about Alex's life, Ethan's hand was busy caressing her thigh, occasionally slipping up her skirt just teasingly.

Alex soaked up the attention. "When we were kids, she made me go back to the carnival ticket booth because they gave me a dollar too much change." She heard her speech slurring. She knew it was time to end this.

Ethan squeezed her thigh. "You were going to keep it? It's a good thing she saved you from such sin."

"You're making fun of me. But you don't understand—Maura's tough." She moaned.

"And yet you still meet for coffee." His deep voice mesmerized her.

The waiter offered dessert or a coffee.

Dr. South winked at Alex. "No. Everything has been most satisfactory."

Alex thought a coffee would be nice, yet once again, he didn't ask. Anyway, the smile and the wink were better than a coffee. She also smiled to herself when she realized he was so interested in her they never even talked about his concerns for the next day's agenda. This was a date, after all. He would figure out what to tell the Senator. He always did.

Alex staggered as they stepped out the door. Ethan grinned. They decided she would not return to work in the lab, so he called her an Uber to get home—she could Uber back to work in the morning. Ending the evening with first a sweet kiss on the cheek,

161

then a passionate mouth to mouth, Alex silently told Maura she didn't have the right moment to ask about the reports. When the taxi arrived—far too quickly, Alex lamented—he walked her to the curb.

Chapter 22

August 7, 2015, CiCi's Home, San Antonio, Texas:
CiCi's government approved Chinese tea became Jon's safety rope. Whether it helped him or was a placebo didn't matter—it gave him something to do for his situation. He took a thermos of his special brew every time he and CiCi went out the door. More than once, he had her turn the car around when he left his thermos while visiting friends. If others reached for it, they were taking their lives in their hands. One time, he and CiCi took an outing for two days in the Texas Hill Country to volunteer during the bourbon bottling at Garrison Brother's distillery. (It took CiCi years to convince Jon that Texas had award-winning bourbon, but, once he finally tasted it, he was all in). Holding onto his thermos like his life depended on it, he persevered on his feet (and a stool) the entire day—no nap until he got home that evening.

But the tea could not do more than give him energy boosts. The mornings became vital to Jon because that was all he could count on. His first nap happened before noon, with naps two and three coming two hours apart. CiCi's solo time at night grew as Jon started going to bed earlier and earlier. August pushed on and still no plan. When CiCi mentioned dialysis since their second hospital, University Hills, had turned them down, Jon bit off her head. He tried to remain upbeat, but that topic was off-limits. She vowed never to mention it again.

"Grab your keys," Jon announced. "We're going to Central Texas Medical Research Institute."

CiCi had left him alone in his office that morning, doing whatever it was he did for hours. It was usually tied to viewing model airplane videos and practicing his piloting skills on a virtual app. He programmed his remote control for the flight simulations to say, "Oh shit," every time he crashed a virtual plane. She called it his plane porn. When no profanity came from his office, she assumed he was having a good day at the *airfield*.

This morning, though, he'd been researching transplant centers again. She knew there was a third one, but, when she mentioned it before, he was too discouraged to discuss it. "I didn't want to say anything out loud this time until I got confirmation they would see us." His making his thermos of tea cued CiCi to get a move on. "The director of transplants has agreed to listen to your speech about the nineteen years bit. You know, the one you berated University Hills with?"

"Do I at least have time to change clothes? I've been working in the yard all morning. I just came inside." CiCi headed into her room.

"Don't want to rush you, but I want to get there before he heads to lunch and changes his mind. I'll be in the car."

He loaded up a large bag of cookies for the doctor's office. Jon had been on one of his baking binges early that morning—CiCi awoke to vanilla and chocolate wafting from the oven and under her door. It took all her willpower to resist the mouthwatering biscuits of sin, otherwise she would be three hundred pounds. After he moved in, she had to convince herself she no longer loved cookies. It worked unless he made the peanut butter ones—for those, nothing worked.

Baking cookies was Jon's happy dance, or his stress dance, or his frustrated dance. It was all the same language: cookies. He had had no diabetic symptoms since his gastric bypass—cookies did not cause his kidneys to fail. In fact, cookies were often his go-to sugar when he would go hypoglycemic. CiCi should have known he was working on the Central Texas transplant group when he danced around the kitchen this morning. Grabbing her keys and a cookie for herself, she headed out.

****

No protesters. That was a relief, but that same bedraggled woman from the *Kidney 101* lesson at the first clinic they had interviewed was standing by the water fountain. This was a small clinic, not the factory ambiance CiCi experienced before. Business must've been booming because excuse-our-dust signs hung all around the several remodeling projects.

On the way up the elevator, CiCi pointed out cookies were not the best thing to take to a transplant clinic when so many people needed transplants because of kidney disease due to diabetes. Jon reminded her she knew so little about how the world worked. CiCi knew enough to know it was pointless to battle with him. Exiting the elevator to a hallway of draped plastic and rolls of carpet required the token right-or-left dance, bumping into each other before Jon spun CiCi around to find suite 310.

Once again, CiCi was wrong. The receptionist squealed with delight and took the cookies to the break room. Those cookies were consumed before Jon and CiCi even saw the nurse. They didn't get in to see the doctor right away like Jon had hoped—they had to go through the *Kidney Transplant 101* introduction with all the other potential patients like they did at the first hospital.

"This time, though, they already know I had cancer." She saw him fidget. "You told them, right?"

"Yes, I told them everything. And they reminded me I should look for other donors because cancer may not be the only reason you might not work out."

They went over transplant definitions, statistics about living versus deceased transplants, the national UNOS database, and how

165

to find a donor. When asked if anyone had a living donor in mind, CiCi waved her arm like an excited first grader. The kind nurse smiled and started her talk about paired matches and multi-paired matches—old news to CiCi.

From the intro, the presenter guided CiCi to the doctor's office for an interview. Nobody spent wasted dollars on that space. The doc's desk looked about like the one CiCi had used as a public-school teacher, but without the stacks of papers. She liked that— put the money in the service, not the decorations. Dr. Halabi had to be a great dad. He was a teddy bear man that made CiCi want to snuggle up in his arms. Of course, she didn't, but still, she wanted to. And he listened. She could tell he had no agenda prior to their meeting—he was going to give her a chance. Give Jon a chance.

They talked for an hour.

Finally, he put down his tablet, sat back with his hands in his lap, and said, "You learned the risks during the introduction. Do you still want to pursue this?"

CiCi told him about her friend Val, who had donated to a cousin so many years ago. She told him about students who had been kidney recipients while in her class. He said he was considering her appeal, that he had never accepted a cancer survivor before. She said she understood, and then she gave him her speech about how anyone could have cancer cells running around. This time, she delivered the message gently, with reason and without emotion.

"I make no promises," Dr. Halabi said. "I plan to conference with other transplant nephrologists from around the country. Living donor transplants require two patients, not a patient and extra organ. This transplant must be good for both of you."

"You have kind eyes, Doctor." Those eyes let her see into his soul. "I know you will make the right decision."

The cookies must have worked. The doctor instructed the phlebotomist, Minnie, to draw CiCi's blood for preliminary testing.

Lark, CiCi's appointed personal nurse, gave her a DVD and a notebook about what donation involved for the donor. Nothing from the donor could be shared with the recipient, and CiCi and Jon's respective nurses were sworn to secrecy. That felt good, even though she knew there wasn't much secrecy when sharing a home.

Walking back to the reception area, she caught Jon's eyes. They could read each other's thoughts. "Maybe?"

Next step. Wait.

Chapter 23

2009-2010, The Abbasi Home, Isfahan, Iran:
Running into the house at quarterback speed each day as school ended became the norm for the Abbasi children. There to receive them at the goal line stood Eva with arms out, ready for the tackle. Thanks to her taxi driver and his wife in Tabriz, she had found a home with the extended Abassi family in Isfahan. Eva introduced the kids to frozen yogurt grapes. Her mom used to freeze grapes in the summer, making little popsicles. Eva added her touch by dropping them into yogurt and freezing them into special treats. The kids adored her.

Snack over, they all pulled cushions off the chairs and plopped onto the floor for their English lessons. Eva created fun games and crafts. Once in the house, per *Baba* and *Maman's* orders, the children spoke only English to Eva. In turn, they helped Eva speak only Persian to adults in the house and community. In no time at all, Eva conversed with neighbors who so admired the Abbasi children's progress that they bartered services with Eva to tutor their children as well. As school let out for the summer, the children looked forward to something to do with their days. The neighborhood women took her to shop and along on family visits to other parts of Iran that were not very curious about her citizenship. Sometimes she claimed she was Canadian because it was easier.

Unable to receive pay because of her visa status, the community saw to it that Eva had everything she needed. They collectively pitched in for a doctor's care when she got a serious bacterial infection in a cut on her knee. Eva longed for free arms and hair, and she knew at some point she would have to find another home, but for now, life was working out rather well.

When the school year began again in September, and Eva's days emptied, Zenda Abbasi approached Eva. "You've been doing an excellent job with the children, but I can see you know how to do much more."

"Are you telling me it's time to leave?" She'd hoped she would have at least a year with the Abbasis. Besides, she loved this family, especially the children.

"No. Quite the contrary. We want you to do more." Zenda took both of Eva's hands in hers. "If it would not be too much burden, that is."

Surprised, Eva hugged Zenda. The Abbasis had saved her life and supported her every need, yet they feared they would burden her. How had she been so lucky to happen across the right taxi driver? Then she realized Kourosh enjoyed making the airport runs but despised Carrie Breun. Suspicious, he had placed himself there to check on the workings of the DJH. "Of course. What can I do?"

"You said you worked with kidney sellers before and learned of abuses. In our clinic, we must focus on recipients, that's clear. But we want to be sure we protect our donors. Would you help us with screenings?"

"My Persian isn't that good yet."

"You'll have people around who can translate. Your experiences will help us see red flags, I think you call them."

Unable to sit in her seat any longer but refraining from jumping up and down with excitement, Eva walked to the children's bookshelf, pretending to tidy it a bit. "But what about the language lessons?"

"That's why I mentioned a burden. We still want you to tutor the children. And we know you benefit from the neighbors' donations, so we don't want to take that away. The *anjoman* cannot pay you because of your visa, and most people there are volunteers, but I think you will enjoy it."

****

Working at the *anjoman* exposed more questions for Eva—little scabs peeled away, allowing more worries. Bartering over the price of a kidney demeaned both recipient and donor. Just how valuable was life and how sacrificial was the donation? In Botswana, prices were final and always favored the broker. In Iran, the clerics set up organ donation as a mutual exchange of gifts, given unconditionally and enforced by law. Enforceable gifts reminded Eva of the oxymoron examples from school: jumbo shrimp, a devout atheist. How did one enforce a gift? What was the fair exchange for the impoverished donor? For the impoverished recipient? With both struggling to survive, were the gifts predatory? Miserly? Reasonable? Recipients could accept deceased donations for free, but that required waiting while on dialysis, starting death. Besides, most clients did not even know about cadaver options. Best she didn't think about it—let the scabs grow back.

With paid donations legal, she didn't need to caution the donor about discretion or secrets or fear of fines or jail. All involved seemed content with how the donation process worked for them. Eva recalled a story from Tabriz about a recipient who, in gratitude, offered to give his daughter to his seller. Eva was shocked and repulsed. Women were not chattel passed off as barter. She told herself it was just an expression like Americans joke about giving someone their first-born child. Surely, he didn't mean it. But, she learned, occasionally the recipient married the donor. Still unsure of how Iranian marriages were arranged and dowries determined, Eva sensed deep down the kidney trade went beyond the government standard. Even in Iran, government oversight could not check all negotiations occurring outside the *anjoman* doors.

Each district in Iran developed its own guidelines for donor compensation. As Eva suspected, even a government program still left room for negotiation, and those who could pay more won. Other *anjomans* presented different views from that of Zenda's— Eva was grateful she was with the Abbasi family. So were her sellers. Zenda's team worked hard to help the donor. Eva learned some places followed the practice of government-subsidized altruism precisely. Recipients first had to wait six months for a cadaver donation. The sellers had to pretend their sole purpose was to help the recipient. They had to sign an oath that they wanted only the government money. They couldn't admit to any further money passing hands. But everyone knew the going rate for a kidney there ranged from four to six times the established allotment.

"That strict policy leads to lies, which lead to disappointment for both parties," lamented Zenda.

"I'll bet that happens sometimes in the U.S. I wonder if anyone checks the donor's bank account," added Eva.

"Without the *anjoman* overseeing the negotiations, the seller might take a deposit and disappear, or the recipient might not pay the balance. No contract—no bounds."

"I heard stories like that in Botswana."

This *anjoman* kept everything transparent. The entire staff worked to help the donor succeed after the surgery and to make sure the recipient received a healthy kidney.

Zenda was going over old ground with Eva during these talks, but she continued the lectures. "It will do no good if the donor receives a payment that isn't enough to help and returns to debt."

Eva soaked up the attention and agreed with most of what Zenda preached because her own world travels had taught her as much. "Clients don't always understand this debt issue and fear they'll never find a suitable donor. Here, at least, there are more donors than recipients." The ladies performed these back-and-forth sessions daily.

Eva had her own stories to contribute. "The other day I walked close to a hospital and saw graffiti on walls and posters with people's blood type and their phone number."

Zenda flinched and looked away from Eva. "We try to contact them to present an organized list to recipients. They think they will bypass the *anjoman* oversight, but they must go through us to get the surgery scheduled. We can guide them through their decisions. People like your Carrie Breun…"

"Not MY Carrie Breun," interrupted Eva.

"Fair enough, not yours. People like Ms. Breun try to usurp that and harm not just us but, also, the excellent work Hands Helping Physicians does by infringing on their name. Authorities already chased the pariahs out of Tabriz, but there's always someone to replace them."

Desperation drove so many people to plead to be picked. Everywhere in the world, the problem wasn't that an organ market existed—the problem was that poverty existed. No person should have to sell a kidney to pay a child's hospital bill or to get married. Eva thought the Iranian government smart to devise a plan to address unemployment, kidney disease, and organ shortages all in one. The deal could still exploit the poor, but at least they got a chance, a better deal than the team offered in Botswana.

"You're pensive, Eva. Do you wonder about your two friends?"

Surprised by the question, Eva quickly brought her mind back to Zenda. "Marco and Charles? No. I don't care what happened to them. While I was naming the dead from the Boxing Day tsunami, I spent time around Thai hospitals. I know they offered some questionable medical tourism. I overheard a husband hiss anger at the U.S. system. He asked what he was supposed to do—just watch his wife die? With his wife not doing well on dialysis and no U.S.

kidney available, Thailand became their only possibility." Eva still grieved about her friend whom the elephant had rescued. Did they sell everything to have her husband washed away? "The rich got kidneys, and the poor watched their loved ones die."

Eva turned both hands over to make small bowls. Sometimes she desperately wished to redo everything the right way, but a ninety-year-old Thai shop owner had taught her well about the difference between wishes and shits—only one would fill her hands. She emptied the air from her hands and picked up a folder to give her hands something to do. "That's why I thought I was helping in Botswana."

"But it was illegal." Zenda made it sound so clear cut, so idiotically obvious.

"Yes, but it's done. Then Baruti's family showed me what happened to the donors. I mean, kidney trade is not a thing in Botswana. Why were we even there?" Baruti's letter stung her memory. "Why do we think it is so bad to receive money for such a gift when donors are taking risks? There is no price that can pay for it, anyway. Why can't the sellers be honored?"

"That is the reason we see our kidney sellers as donors and not sellers. They are gifters."

Work at the *anjoman* consumed three days a week, leaving Eva a sense of purpose with time to join other women at the markets. During the evenings, she continued tutoring the neighborhood children in English. The mountain elevation kept the summer temperature tame when she arrived in May, but as the months passed, days grew pleasantly cool while nights would freeze a person in no time. Fortunately, the neighborhood women dressed her appropriately for winter.

With Zenda's efforts well-known all over the province, mentioning her name over the phone to a charitable organization made money appear. When they needed a trip into the rural areas, Zenda cleared Eva's day to go with her. Zenda drove in town, but her husband, Saeed, drove for longer trips. Though bitterly cold, the winter drives thrilled Eva most. A thin layer of snow covered the ground in a land with only four inches of precipitation a year. Growing up in Dallas, Eva had seen a little snow, but Thailand and Botswana erased any such images. The white over the raw brown of the desert turned her world into a winter wonderland. These trips were as close to family as Eva had ever experienced.

Though hesitant at first, the clients at the *anjoman* warmed to the American, patiently speaking with Eva while using a translator's help. Eva found her confidence with the language developing quickly as she heard story after story from sellers of all ages, both male and female. She wrote what she heard using her own English phonics to form words as they sounded to her. Within months, she had collected enough stories for a short book she wanted to title *Spare Parts*.

It wasn't just the matching and the payments from the government and the recipients—Eva appreciated the way this *anjoman* did more than transplants. A widowed mother with three young children was desperate to bring money into her home. She and her husband had been struggling with money problems their entire married life. She came from Tehran and moved to Isfahan for love. The families of both the husband and the wife had arranged other marriages, but these two defied obligations and married on their own. The cliché Romeo and Juliet story cost the young couple everything because neither family would have anything to do with them. When her husband died in a work accident, no one stepped up to help the young mother.

Eva turned this one over to Zenda, knowing the kidney sale was a temporary stopgap and not the woman's best option. It wouldn't solve her financial problems for long and would leave her short a kidney. Zenda agreed and set to work on her phone. Within an hour, a local mosque organized a fund to help with rent and clothing. Another group found a food source, and yet another organization found her a job with an adoption agency that would pay her twice what she earned cleaning houses. Far better than selling the kidney, the *anjoman* solved this problem.

Counselors at other clinics would have said, "It's not my job."

Celebrating spring required weeks of major house cleaning both at the Abbasi home and the *anjoman*. In fact, the entire country busied itself with *Nowruz*, which that year would be at 9:02 PM March 20. Far more than popping fireworks, the Persian New Year meant cleaning away the previous year and starting anew, a clean slate. Eva decided that was much better than the Gregorian New Year in the dead of winter. Spring meant new life. New life meant shopping for new clothes, and the ladies of the neighborhood made sure Eva had them.

Daily, Eva and the children tended the *haft-seen*, a decorated flat tray they would later float down a river. This tradition reminded Eva somewhat of the Day of the Dead altars they made in Spanish classes back home in Texas but with living grass, dried fruit, spices, and the rest of the seven required elements. The Abbasis added a little home-made papier mâché kidney to symbolize renewed life.

Zenda loved stars and butterflies, so, under Eva's guidance, the children covered the house with decorations. After three weeks of beating the giant Persian rugs clean, scrubbing tiles until they glistened, preparing food, and forming the *haft-seen* to symbolize fresh growth for the upcoming year, the celebration began. Thirteen days of Abbasi festivity.

The four-day work holiday meant family time, so they started with a road trip to Tehran to visit Saeed's grandmother. The children paraded home-to-home banging on pots with spoons until they got treats, like Halloween but without costumes, and noisier. Food festivals took place nightly, but the first feast centered on greens and herbs to emphasize the celebration of renewal.

On the thirteenth day of celebration, all of Iran went on picnics. It was bad luck to stay home, so the family, including Eva, headed into the mountains to find the perfect flowing stream to send off their little barge of new life.

As they pushed it into the water, Saeed, as patriarch, spoke to his family. "This celebration is one of hope, new life, and possibilities, a tradition surviving three thousand years of wars, famines, and plagues." Then he turned to Eva. "This isn't religious—it's about the challenging work of cleaning out the old to uncover our true selves and to start fresh. With that effort done, we can go forward."

Celebrations over and public holidays at an end, spring moved toward summer. At the *anjoman*, Eva noticed young men enthusiastically signed up to donate, even if not destitute. Because others would benefit more from the money, they were often turned down. When Eva asked about this, Zenda explained young men were eager to open businesses or get married.

"Also," Zenda whispered so as not to embarrass the young man in front of them, "donors are exempt from the two-year Iranian military commitment."

Stories poured in. One man sought to sell his kidney to pay for an eye operation for his daughter who was born with crossed eyes. Now that she was three years old, her parents wanted to help her but couldn't find the money for the surgery. They could make it otherwise—they needed just this one thing. The *anjoman* verified the story and investigated the home. Indeed, this kidney donation would improve that family's circumstances, and there was a recipient willing to pay four times the government money on top of the government's stipend. Eva quickly calculated in her head about six thousand U.S. dollars in the exchange rates at that time. A match. Deal done. The transplant and the girl's eye surgery happened on the same day at the same hospital to make it easier for the mother to care for both at once.

Drug addicts could no longer donate. Zenda explained this was not clear when the program began, so the addicts poured in. "It is not that they are dirty and socially unacceptable, although mostly true—we can't count on them to show up for appointments." Addicts were unhealthy and poor patients in terms of their follow-up care, thus not fitting the *anjoman's* policy to help those who would benefit. "Now every client at this *anjoman* has to take drug screening tests."

Zenda didn't need to justify this to Eva. These were hard-core addicts—Eva could recognize them as soon as they walked into the clinic.

Pinching herself to remember that Azara's police captain brother in Tehran couldn't forge paperwork forever, Eva needed to think about where she would go next. For now, though, the children loved her, and her work was valued.

Zenda put the phone down with such force that everyone in the office looked up. "Eva, I need to speak with you."

Bewildered, Eva excused herself from her current interview and slipped over to Zenda's desk. "Did I do something wrong?"

"Carrie Breun and company are back in town."

There it was. Bubble burst. Sticky hot lava filled with sulfur had just poured all over Eva.

Chapter 24

August 8, 2015, CTMRI, San Antonio, Texas: The line for coffee was long, and Alex was tired. The guy in front of her forgot a tray and had everyone in the line pass a message down to send him one. A tray? He was just getting two coffees. In Alex's truck-stop waitressing days, she carried seven coffee cups without a tray. Ah, those were the days, such talent wasted on ungrateful grumps during the graveyard shift who left such measly tips and smiled big while doing it.

Finally at the cash register, she saw Maura's hand wave fiercely from her table. Usually, Alex was the first one to arrive—Maura always had that one more phone call she had to make. Alex then checked herself, wondering why that tray-less guy sent her into such a downer. Thoughts of the great evening the night before had her quickening her steps and smiling again.

"And good day to you, too," said Maura as Alex dropped into her seat. "Just coffee? No lunch?"

"No, I had a nut bar a bit ago in the lab. I was famished. Now I'm full."

Maura coughed. "Really? A nut bar made you full? Puleeze."

Alex instinctively brushed her hands over her tummy to be sure it was still flat. "Girlish figure and all that stuff."

"You look exhausted."

"I had a late night, that's all." Alex couldn't hide a coy smile.

"Exhausted, but happy?" Maura squealed. "Alexandra Segel, you have a man in your life!"

"Shhhh! Hush! You'll jinx me. It's way, way too early to think such a thing. And before you ask, no, we did not do *it*."

"Whatever." Maura kicked under the table, tapping Alex on the shin.

"Ow!" Alex faked horrific pain, then set about picking at her nails. "No, really, Maura, it was nothing."

Maura switched topics. "So, hey, congrats on the new hire. Nan will be the perfect nurse to add to the team."

"New hire?"

"Nan? Doctor South told HR he likes to get out of the lab to perform surgeries to keep current, so he requested an Operating Room nurse. His budget had the room for it, and Nan likes to play with research along with her work in the OR, so, voila, a perfect match. She's friends with Lark over at the living donor facility. You know, keeping it in the family sort of thing."

Maura was all bubbles and smiles about this, but Alex was lost. Why didn't Ethan say anything to her at dinner? Yes, she had a right to call him by his first name after that lovely dinner. This Nan person might not work directly with her, so not her concern.

"You didn't know?" Maura said. "I thought you would since you were involved with everything else about the research team."

As Alex watched Maura panic because it was a definite protocol no-no for her to reveal new hires, she replayed her memory of her time with Ethan the night before. It wasn't the new hire that bothered her—Ethan had sounded like he didn't know Maura worked in HR.

The silence drove Maura to plead. "Oh Alex, please don't say anything. You must act completely surprised when Doctor South introduces Nan."

"Not to worry. Now I have a pinkie swear on you."

They did their official elaborate pinkie swear from high school that looked like one of those high fives kids do: a clap, a wave over the head, two pats on the heart, and finally the pinkie hook.

"Now, back to what's important," Maura said. "When did you have time to meet someone?"

"It's just a guy. Really, nothing." Alex flipped her hair and wiggled her shoulder to get Maura to notice her dress. Normally frumpy, today work-efficient Alex wore a form-fitted dress. This was a test to see if someone would zoom in on the discreet ruching at just the right spot to add more to Alex's teeny breasts. Would Ethan notice?

"Wait? What's with the sexy dress?" Maura passed the test and pursued more information about her bestie's new love. Then halted. Fun was over. "It must be someone in the Institute, thus the dress at work. Don't tell me. We're done for today. I want to keep my job." She raised her coffee cup. "To our youths, our beauty, and our extremely high intellect."

Before they separated, Alex had to ask one more question. "Did you ever meet with Doctor South personally? About Nan?"

"No, Nan's application was managed through paperwork and budget committee stuff. I never even signed a paper." She stood up and put her chair back under the table. "Alex? Pinkie swear?"

"Pinkie swear. And to be clear, we do not *play* with research."

On the way back to the lab, Alex decided Maura was mistaken about Nan. Maura seldom made mistakes about people, but there was a Dr. Ethan Smith in another department. Who would have thought there would be two Ethans? It was such an unusual name, but it did sound classy and sophisticated, and this was the world of doctors. That had to be it. Dr. Smith managed a different study and, also, did surgeries along with his research. Dr. South once said people sometimes mixed them up because the outline of *Smith* is the same shape as the outline of *South,* a mind trick. Yes, that had to be it.

Chapter 25

May 2010, Zenda's Clinic, Isfahan, Iran:
The Iranian government boasted that they had conquered the kidney transplant waiting list, but, after a year in Isfahan and hearing stories from other provinces, Eva knew money talked in all languages. Many kidney disease patients didn't qualify for the list because lack of money or proximity to doctors delayed treatment, making them too ill for a transplant. Unknown non-patients died because they didn't get to doctors for a diagnosis. Despite the *anjoman's* efforts, a recipient had to have money for the privilege of life. Nothing new there.

With a surplus of potential donors in Iran, it wasn't always the donors who were exploited. The clerics classified organs as non-commodities, but reality trumped *The Gift*. Commodities always relied on supply and demand. The legal sales created a bidding war for the best bang for the buck. Sometimes the donors regretted selling at a low price when they found out they could have made more money, but sometimes the recipients suffered because it was "pay up or die." The government paid the base price, but who paid the negotiated price? The *anjoman* reached out to charity organizations if the recipient met financial qualifications, but other districts didn't try as hard as this one in Isfahan.

As for the continuous health of the donors, follow-up faced difficulties. Even with the legal status, social stigma drove donors into hiding, not wanting family or employers to know they had been so desperate. The nature of their desperation meant they often moved, so following them as years passed was impossible. Thus, no one had complete statistics on continued health or living conditions. Eva ran across unofficial polls that estimated seventy-five percent of the donors wished they had not volunteered. Could Iran claim a win?

Iran's system was far from perfect, but Eva remained convinced exploitation of the poor occurred less commonly than in other countries. This had been consuming Eva's thoughts when Zenda announced that Carrie Breun's organization was back in Iran. Her heart froze.

"Eva? Eva? Did you hear me?" Zenda grabbed Eva's arm and pulled her into the office where others would not hear them.

Feeling that tightness in her chest that she had had in the taxi with Kourosh a year earlier, Eva struggled for air. "I thought Carrie Breun's people had to leave the country."

"They did, but they returned. Profiteers are profiteers. They'll reach into the guts of anyone vulnerable."

"How can Americans work here? Won't they be obvious?"

Zenda stood tall and pointed to Eva. "You work here."

"True, but I'm here with your blessing. Am I not? And Azara's police brother in Tehran." Where was this going? Should she stay in the confined room or run?

"That is the problem," said Zenda. "Ehsan called. Your name came up while discussing Ms. Breun. He must be careful to protect his paperwork at the police station. Ms. Breun's client this time is an American."

Eva found her breath. Anger strengthened her. "But foreigners can't receive Iranian transplants."

"Yes, on paper, that's correct. But officials are sometimes vulnerable to bribes. And sometimes the doctors accept the bribes."

Determined not to cry, Eva shook her head to hide her tears from Zenda. "Why my name?" Eva was crumbling while Zenda stood firm, stoic. Eva chided herself for thinking she was part of this family. Of course, she was an outsider. Of course, she had only herself—that's how her life worked. And, of course, Zenda had to look after her own family.

Zenda walked over to a very small window as if looking for police to show up any minute. "This arrangement was only temporary until you figured out your next destination. It's been a year. We can't risk our family—Ehsan must destroy your paper trail to protect himself. We've arranged to take you to the airport. Eva, where will you go?"

Terror struck. Nowhere. Eva choked back her tears and forced herself to focus. She could go back to Thailand. She had friends there, but her positions in those homes disappeared over two years ago. Besides, she liked the Abbasis. And loved their children.

"Thailand. I will return to Phuket, I guess. Until I can think of something else."

"Why not go home to the States?"

"I can't. I have no way to live there."

Zenda took her hand. "Thailand it is. Do you still have your savings for a ticket?"

"Yes." Zenda was the only person who knew she had a little money, the only person she trusted with that information. The dam burst. No longer able to hold back, Eva rubbed her sleeve over her face.

Zenda wrapped her in her arms for a moment and then, just as Eva had seen her do with her children, she held Eva's shoulders tightly while pushing her back, her eyes kind but firm. "Go! Pack at once! You must leave now. Saeed will take you on the motorcycle to Qom to meet Azara's brother. Then Ehsan will drive you in his police car to Tehran International. He can help with the visa into Thailand."

****

The motorcycle hummed as it bounced over holes in the pavement, mixing the pleasure of the fresh air with Eva's dislike for dust and her abject dread for her future. She gave the children everything she had acquired during her stay with the Abbasis and took only a large backpack and layers of clothes. Covered even more than usual so as not to draw any attention, Eva welcomed the occasional moment when the wind blew her manteau open. The bike's vibration numbed her against yet another loss. She had put her only family—and her friends at the *anjoman*—in danger.

For three hours, she tried to empty her mind by focusing on the vibration of the bike. Trying not to be paranoid, she noticed a sedan following them. Of course, it was following—there was only one major highway to get them from Isfahan to Tehran. Besides, why would anyone be after her? Leaving the country was the difficulty. She blocked out the sedan with images of her friends in Thailand. But Thailand led her thoughts to the tsunami and to Marco and Charles.

Eva had grown to love the desolate land beyond Isfahan's lush fruit farms. Beauty lived in the desert here as it did in Ghanzi. The harsh land removed the busy-ness of cities and forests. Only true survivors made it in the desert.

The sedan followed closer and closer. She saw Saeed constantly check his rear view mirror. The only vehicles on the road, the motorcycle and the sedan sped past dry gullies. After the next curve, the sedan pulled beside them. From the passenger seat, Charles looked her straight in the eyes. Eva's scream disappeared into the roar of the motorcycle. Eva leaned forward to see the driver—an older man with a matted beard. The car pushed against the bike.

The last thing she heard was Charles yelling "No!" over the sound of the bike flying off the pavement and rolling down the hill into the gully.

****

"Eva?"

Eva opened her eyes too fast at first. The light hurt. Her head hurt. Her entire body hurt. Machines beeped. This was a hospital room. A woman in white leaned over her.

"Eva?" the nurse said to her in a near whisper. "Eva, I am a friend. You must listen."

"Saeed?" asked Eva, panicking.

"Eva, you must listen. You must not ask for the Abbasis. They cannot know you. I am a friend, but they cannot know you. Ehsan has fixed your papers for now—you should already be in Thailand. But you are here, in the hospital in Qod. Do you understand?" The nurse was comforting, yet somehow terrifying.

Eva nodded.

"You were in an accident. A family found you in the gully."

Eva was awake now, and so was her pain.

"Saeed Abbasi is dead." The nurse bowed her head and closed her eyes, her voice so quiet. Eva pretended for a moment she did not hear.

Eva gasped and moaned. She focused on her tremendous physical pain for relief.

"Eva, you have broken your left femur, two ribs, four fingers, your collarbone. Your spleen was damaged, but the doctors stitched it. And we had to remove one kidney to save your life."

"What?" She looked up past the nurse to the window in her door. Looking at her sadly was Marco.

Chapter 26

August 21, 2015, CiCi's Home, San Antonio, Texas:

CiCi checked her phone again and sucked in a huge breath. It had been two weeks since she met the staff at CTMRI. Was she nuts? Did she mean it when she said she would do it? She'd had cancer—now Central Texas was really going to consider her as an acceptable donor. She could always say no, but then what about Jon? Did she mean it when she told herself so many years ago that she admired Val for her donation and hoped she would do the same if the opportunity arose? She could just pretend Central Texas never called back.

"Jon!" CiCi shouted from her room to his back bedroom before she finished her thought. "Julissa from CTMRI just scheduled a time for me to meet with the social worker and the donor advocate. They have an opening today." Silence from the back room. She had to shout it all again, this time walking toward him. "Jon! I got a call back. I'm going to the Institute now!" Still silence. "I hear you puttering around in there. What are you doing?"

What she didn't know was that he struggled with her same doubts, his thoughts and night visions swirling into endless holes: Did she mean it? Was she out of her mind? Questions played in never-ending loops. He'd appreciated her offer but had accepted his fate. Death wouldn't be so bad after the amazing life he'd led. Slow death tied to a machine was not for him. He appreciated Central Texas was playing along and pretending to be interested, but now they had taken it to the next level. It didn't matter because he and CiCi wouldn't be a match, anyway. "Let me change my clothes," Jon finally answered.

"Not you. Me. I'm the one going. Don't you see? You wanted them to check me out before you go through any more testing just to be told no. They agreed. No one else would do that. We have found our place. These people care and will stretch a little." And CiCi was gone.

****

All was peaceful when she arrived. This was a good place. The elevators had lost their shiny finished walls to backer board to prepare for the remodeling. Giving renewed life to the place seemed symbolic somehow. She exited with the right-or-left dance and found her door.

"Hey, Julissa, correct?" CiCi checked—she was so bad at matching names with faces, always had been. It wasn't just recognizing stars on television—she used to fear the start of each school year because she knew she would forget students' names from the previous year and then have those same kids again in the next level class. Even worse, she wouldn't get them in a class and would have to know their names in the hallway. One year, a beautiful young lady showed up in CiCi's junior level English class. The girl kept saying, "I'm Michelle," as if that should have meant something to CiCi. After about three weeks, it occurred to CiCi that this *Michelle* was her own daughter's playmate from elementary school. No way. This girl was gorgeous. Her daughter's nine-year-old friend was skinny with big ears and couldn't keep her shorts squared on her hips. Amazing things happen to little girls over seven years.

But CiCi got this one right—it was Julissa. The receptionist was a perfect match for her role: welcoming, smiling magnificently, laughing at the patients' dumb jokes. And she was nice enough to not ask about the baked goods CiCi neglected to bring. Short, fluffy hair, middle-aged, and nurturing, she was the person who made insecure patients relax.

Before CiCi could sit down with a cup of thick coffee that smelled like it had been on the burner for days, Brianna introduced herself as CiCi's social worker and collected her for their first interview. She looked young for someone involved in life and death decisions.

While they headed down the hall, open doors revealed no one screening that day. The exam rooms were tiny spaces, smaller than most CiCi had visited. They had the stock exam table with one rolling chair for the doctor. The obligatory sink and antiseptic gel dominated the room with nothing else for decor, not even posters on the wall, consistent with Dr. Halabi's office at her earlier visit. CiCi guessed not much happened there other than palpations and blood pressure checks. The real exams would be sent out. How odd that she hadn't noticed these other rooms before—she had only seen Dr. Halabi's compassionate eyes. Need to know, perhaps?

It turned out Brianna's interview space was even smaller, but she had decorated it with cheerful posters promoting the *Share Your Spare* theme. Even a little vase with carnations sat on the table. Brianna settled CiCi into her designated spot and claimed her own seat near the exit. This young, petite Brianna person was one of those tiny-but-mighty folks who could see through bullshit and get business done.

CiCi was thrilled. "Well, good. Let's do this."

"Is your name Cornelia Dorothea Clawson-Dawson?" Brianna suppressed a giggle, but CiCi saw it and smiled.

"Yes. I blame my name for all my flaws. In third grade, my loving mother called me Cori Dori in front of my friends, and, well, a small town and all that—such a painful memory." CiCi placed her hand on her forehead and dropped her head, dramatizing great pain.

Briana laughed.

"The story gets worse. I had to run away to the university to escape my haunting name. A literature professor called me by my initials, C.C. I liked it, so I kept it. But then I married Todd Dawson."

By then Brianna was slapping the table. "You poor thing."

"Yep, that made me Cori Dori Clawson-Dawson."

"And you live with Jon Deaux? Jon Doe? Really?" Brianna composed herself and apologized, but CiCi was laughing as hard as she was. "So, you are divorced? I have to ask because I have to verify home stability."

CiCi was impressed. Brianna had slipped in those personal questions as casual conversation. "Yes, after Todd revisited his youthful stud muffin ways, we divorced, but I kept his name. I had my hands in public schools, dance studios, and theaters—and *Soap and Shit*. That's what I called my various multilevel marketing enterprises."

Brianna took notes. "My mom did *Soap and Shit*, too. She made enough to send me to college and start her retirement."

"Not me—I kept giving the stuff away. But my daughter's last name is Dawson, so I still hyphenate." CiCi decided Jon was right—her brain was a cosmic commode of random thoughts—she had strayed from the question. "Don't ever change your name if you marry. Wait, are you married?"

Brianna shook her head. "So how did you meet Jon?"

"*PairForLife.com*."

Brianna had that tell-me-more-girlfriend look.

CiCi explained she had worried about bringing strange men into her young daughter's life, so she worked—and worked and worked—and skipped dating. Didn't make any money to proclaim, but she was a role model for hard work and perseverance to her daughter. Like kids ever notice. But when her precious Kambri headed three hours away to university, she realized she needed her own life. She hadn't dated for thirty years and couldn't figure out how to start, so she gave *PairForLife.com* a try. She told Brianna about Jon's profile with the rooster and the donkey and that he actually called himself Jon Doe, spelled *d o e*.

"Aha, but it's *d e a u x*, correct?"

"Pronounced doe, unless you wrinkle up your nose and push your tongue up on the sides of your teeth. It's a French thing."

As soon as Brianna could control herself again, she dove into the real questions. That other stuff was just a warm-up. So many questions. Did CiCi understand what was involved? Did she have a compliant attitude toward supporting her own health? Did she have a dedicated support system? Did she have a history of psychological or psycho-pathological issues? Brianna's skill at getting CiCi to do the talking and elaborating didn't go unnoticed—though Jon would point out it took little skill for that. In this chatter, Brianna listened for consistency and observed behavioral traits for any deception. This was fine with CiCi. She liked the young woman—they would be BFFs by the end of the interview. As CiCi's very own social worker, Brianna couldn't speak with Jon about anything to do with the transplant. In fact, she couldn't even speak with Jon's social worker about CiCi. The donor and recipient concerns were separate.

"This is better for you," Brianna explained. "We don't want you to feel pressured. You can change your mind at any time. We will just tell Jon that the donor is not viable."

CiCi decided that could work well only if the two did not live together. Of course, Jon wouldn't pressure her, but watching him grow sicker would say enough.

Brianna next ushered CiCi into the conference room to speak with Mr. Horowitz, the donor advocate. This was a huge space with a table big enough to make tough decisions. But it was a sterile, unfriendly place—Brianna's closet-sized cubby hole was much more comfortable. Mr. Horowitz had his own checklist. Interestingly, he wasn't an employee of the transplant hospital—he taught history at a local university. As a firm believer in living kidney donation, he did this advocacy gig once a month. Kidney disease had struck his grandmother, a brother, and one of his children. Grandma had had polycystic kidney disease (PKD), and the brother had diabetes issues. The brother found a living donor and had been living with that kidney for twenty-plus years. Mr. Horowitz's child, though, took after Grandma. At age twelve, her kidneys were still functioning enough, but doctors were certain her condition was progressing rapidly, requiring a transplant in her early adult years. Mr. Horowitz invested one day a month at the clinic hoping to build good mojo for when his family needed it.

The interview with Mr. Horowitz covered the same areas as Brianna's, but, in this interview, he declared himself CiCi's advocate. If she had any concerns going forward or felt pressured, she was to call him. CiCi took his card and assured him all was well at *Kidneys R CiCi*. Besides, she told herself, she wouldn't be acceptable because of the cancer thing.

"The cancer thing?" CiCi asked Brianna when she saw her at Julissa's desk.

Brianna replied, "Dr. Halabi is communicating with a panel of nephrologists from all around the U.S. You're an unusual case because you had no chemo and you're twenty years clear. In the meantime, we'll keep evaluating and moving forward." Brianna moved CiCi back out into the reception area.

"So, the cancer could still eliminate me?"

"It could."

"It's just that the *PairForLife.com* thing bringing about our friendship and the fact we are both A negative blood types seems like such fun coincidences that there must be more to our story."

"A negative? You could be my donor!" And there she was again, that woman Jon and CiCi saw at Santa Maria Hospital, the woman who looked like a bedraggled homeless person who Jon decided was there for the free hors d'oeuvres. Jon thought her name was Belva or something.

CiCi smiled. "Well, hello again, Belva."

Julissa stepped away from the reception counter and toward the strange woman. "She already has a recipient—that's why she's here."

"No!" the woman shouted. "It's a sign. She is donating to an old guy who won't live long enough to appreciate her gift. And the name is Eva, not Belva."

Julissa coaxed her closer to the door without her noticing. "There's much more to being a match than blood type, Eva."

CiCi admired Julissa's skill once again.

Eva yelled back into the room as Julissa pressed her into the exit. "I did not sell my kidney. I was in an accident in Iran. The doctors had to remove it to save my life."

Julissa replied, "I'm just the messenger. I can set up another appointment with Dr. Halabi for you."

Eva grabbed at her stomach as if she had a sudden pain. "Jeez! Don't be a condescending bitch. I'm not stupid. But you are. The Iranians are smart and allow people to sell kidneys legally, but I did not. Besides, foreigners can't buy or sell kidneys in Iran anymore. Couldn't have sold mine." She stormed out the door, pounding the wall as she left. "The tyranny of the gift. Look it up."

CiCi froze.

Julissa did what she did so well running the front desk: she apologized for the disruption and worked to return the peace and quiet to the room.

"What? No, no problem," said CiCi. Then she looked at Brianna. "They can sell their kidneys in Iran?" She saw Brianna's face cloud over. "Wait, no. I don't want anything for mine. I'm just intrigued that they even do transplants in Iran. Any issues with blood mixing?"

"No, the Muslims endorse kidney transplants."

CiCi reached for her phone to Google Iranian kidney transplants. "Of course, I feel ridiculous now. I know so little."

"If you're really interested, read Fry-Revere's book *Kidney Sellers*. I just got back from a conference, and she was a guest speaker. It's an easy read and interesting."

"Tyranny?"

Brianna shrugged her shoulders.

Chapter 27

August 21, 2015, CTMRI—Alex's Lab, San Antonio, Texas:

Alex arrived at Dr. South's office just as Kamini approached from the other direction with one of those I-would-rather-not-be-smiling smiles.

"Nan is quite the looker," Kamini said.

"Nan?"

"Yeah, there, standing beside South," said Kamini.

"Nan? Here? Why?" After Maura had spilled the beans about the new hire, Alex decided that Maura had definitely mistaken South's name. That Smith/South thing was real. When she first started her career at CTMRI, she told her parents she was working for Ethan Smith. It was one of her assistants who questioned her about it. So embarrassed. She didn't even know the name of her boss.

"She's the recent addition to the team he's going to introduce at the meeting. Didn't you get the memo?" Kamini bumped shoulders with Alex as if they were now best buddies ready to face off against the new girl.

"I've been a little distracted." Seven weeks—yes, she was counting the weeks—and those reports still niggled at her somewhere between her ear and her eyebrow, right where her headache was. She couldn't make herself ask about the reports, and she had seen no other issues, but then, there wasn't much to report without a kidney scaffold.

Now, Nan stood at South's door greeting people. Alex had no email from South that mentioned any new hire. So why the secrecy? She supposed it didn't really matter—she just felt a little betrayed.

"Good, the rest of the team has arrived," Dr. South proclaimed. "As I was saying, we received a sudden gift from the hospital. Please let me introduce Nnee Ndaba, Nurse Extraordinaire. We call her Nan. Nan was my surgical nurse when I first performed transplants. When CTMRI offered her to us without even considering the budget, I grabbed her. She'll be assisting as we head into our human trials, which is the other part of today's meeting."

Alex felt genuinely surprised because she had heard from Maura that this was completely planned and budgeted by South, just without Alex's input. She had to stop herself from glaring as Nan gracefully moved around the room.

Kamini pulled her shoulders back and tilted her head to look sideways at Alex, clearly pleased she knew something the almighty second in command did not. "You really weren't in the loop about this?" She yanked the top off her lipstick to freshen her appearance, still looking at Alex. "I hate she's so gorgeous. There goes any chance I might have at winning the doctor's attention."

That brought Alex around. Kamini was interested in the boss, too. To make matters worse, Kamini was right—Nan was stunning.

"Just kidding—I have better things to do than grovel for a man. But she is so tall and slender, I might become a lesbian."

Alex knew too much about Kamini's reputation to believe that. "I choose to call her skinny."

For the first time since Kamini joined the team, Alex felt a friendship with the woman, who in her own right was lovely, a little short, but exotic. Nan was as tall as Dr. South, model tall, and with legs that could win a sprint with grace and ease. Then her body smoothly transitioned into delicate curves on her lean figure. What wouldn't Alex and Kamini envy? Even her hair was perfect Senegalese twists tied into a knot on top. Spectacularly sophisticated.

"I'll bet her neck hurts by the end of each day." Kamini rubbed her neck in empathy.

Alex coughed her coffee through her nose. "Ouch, you made me snort."

Both women laughed.

"Something I missed?" Ethan was standing right behind them.

"Not a thing," said Alex while the two ladies' eyes dared each other to speak up.

They headed toward Nurse Nan to make a personal welcome and overheard her talking with the techs. "Yes, my parents came here from a small village in southern Africa before I was born. Life was so difficult. A family here in San Antonio worked with churches to help desperate families. I was born here, attended school here, and now only travel to Botswana every few years to check on my remaining family there."

Alex was aware of a large Nigerian organization in San Antonio, but not Botswanan. "She certainly knows how to work a crowd. The story is well rehearsed," Alex whispered to Kamini.

"Or it's simply true. Some people have tough stories."

Alex decided it was time to re-evaluate her attitude toward Kamini—perhaps there was more backstory deserving respect.

As Alex and Kamini solidified their bond against the new girl, Nan started revealing small tales from her career, along with young Ethan South stories. She and Ethan had met during his first rotation in medical school. She had just started nursing at the same hospital and worked on the floor where he made his debut in the medical world. He saw blood and fainted. She caught him and covered for him with a flimsy explanation to his supervising doctor. "We now have a private ritual every time he makes his first surgical cut. It's a little drop of his head and shoulders for a nanosecond—then he sets to work. Have you seen it?"

Soon all were laughing, with her laugh being the heartiest. She would laugh at the inanest jokes. Alex decided it must come from all the years of nursing where she had pretended with each patient that it was the first time she had heard old man flirtations or poop jokes. She certainly was good at it. If she was as good a nurse as she was a socializer, South had made an excellent choice.

Chapter 28

August 21, 2015, CTMRI, San Antonio, Texas: Draping her work sweater over the hook in her locker, Amethyst once again questioned her ability to change the world, a daily routine these days. She'd only been working in transplants for three years and learned the hard way that few candidates get a transplant. As Brianna's counterpart, she worked with the recipients. Jon had been to the clinic only once, but she liked him—a funny guy, always had smart-alecky remarks about everything, but the fun type of smart remark. She was eager to hear how the interview with CiCi went, knowing that Brianna took the confidentiality part of her career seriously and would never tell. It didn't matter, anyway, because CiCi's cancer thing was a done deal. She was curious why Dr. Halabi had moved forward, but Halabi was about what was right for the patient, so there was the *maybe*.

Amethyst yanked off her sweater and called out to Brianna. "It's been a long day. Let's get out of here and soak up the sunshine before we become office icicles."

Brianna gave her the thumbs up.

Amethyst led Brianna and Julissa to the elevator door. "I tell myself every day I'm lucky to work in this amazing …"

The three had worked together since Amethyst's arrival but still did the awkward elevator silence. They caught themselves doing it during their first trip down together. From then on, they talked and, mid-sentence, went silent the moment they stepped through the elevator doors, almost holding their breath until the door reopened. Once freed, the chatter started mid-sentence where they had left off. Others along for the ride looked at them curiously, saying nothing to these peculiar scrub creatures of the third floor. It wasn't a deliberate decision to make it their ceremonial end-of-day ritual, but there they were in a full elevator holding their breath mid-sentence, not saying a word.

Arriving on the ground floor this day, they all breathed at once. "…but freezing clinic." Amethyst finished her tirade while the other two hustled her out the front doors.

"Sunshine, yes!" Amethyst threw her arms up toward the sky.

Julissa pulled Amethyst's arms down. "August in Texas is more than sunshine—it's like that CERN experiment where it got to nine point nine trillion degrees." The others stared as Julissa explained she used that bit of trivia in a novel she wrote. "Isn't that Eva over there on the curb?" Julissa asked before anyone could question her about what *CERN* was. "Quick, go around."

"Too late," Brianna said. "She's distressed. Be nice."

Eva sat huddled over herself. She'd been crying and wringing her shirt into a wrinkled blob. "You know," she said to them, "I'm a survivor."

The other three were speechless. Amethyst scolded herself about how it was her job to know what to say, but she had nothing. All she could do was ask where Eva had parked.

"Car?" Eva jerked her head up and launched an assault. "No car! I'm at the mercy of the shit-ass bus company, but I have no money for the ride."

All three women opened their purses—Brianna even offered to drive her home. But there was no *home*.

Eva shrank and curled herself back into an insignificant ball. "I'm not really a disaster. I've done important things in my life. Just having trouble right now."

The women acknowledged her situation with perfunctory nods. Then Julissa asked if she had family in town who could help.

Wrong question—between sobs and gulps of air, she told them her parents disowned her when she left to volunteer around the world.

"No way," said Julissa. "How could someone be against doing charitable stuff? That can't be bad, can it?"

"I was supposed to be a lawyer. I had all the top private schooling in Dallas, AP exam tutors, SAT tutors, you name it. No scrimping on their investment in me."

The acid in Eva's words didn't stop Julissa. "Sounds great. I wish I could do that for my kids."

The two social workers winced at Julissa's blunder and remained silent as Eva talked.

"Um, yeah, just grand. After my bachelor's at UT, I couldn't face more fucking school and the fucking LSAT and fucking forever debt to my fucking parents. Besides, I wasn't an exceptional student and wouldn't have been accepted. Fucking Baylor Law School was the only place my parents would consider because that's where they fucking went."

Her parents, she told the women, were a husband-and-wife law firm and had grand visions of adding their daughter. She was an only child and their only hope. "So, I said, 'Fuck it,' and took off. I had heard about volunteering around the world and decided time away would be good for me."

She'd used Yahoo to search volunteer web sites. There weren't many—the Internet was still new in 1999. Her friends thought she was cool and techie. Her parents called her a stupid fool. She found umbrella organizations where she had to pay for her flight and just a little each week to the host family in developing countries where she would work for free. For that she needed money, so she forged her parents' names on checks and took twenty thousand dollars from her law school fund.

"I was going to pay it back when I could. Besides, it was for my education—world travel would be educational. I'd read up. I knew what I was doing."

Minutes had gone by, so the ladies brushed off the dirt on the curb and joined Eva.

"Forgery is a serious crime," Brianna said, finally breaking the story. "Did they press charges?"

"No, but they've never spoken to me since."

"Nothing?" asked Julissa.

"I know what you're thinking. They aren't dead. I see news about them now and then. I send them letters at least once a year to tell them where I am. If they wanted to see me, they could find me." Eva cried again but stifled her tears quickly.

She told them about living in southern Thailand in 2004 and how she survived the tsunami. And the identification of the dead. Then the babies. Then her Hope in Victory snafu and Botswana and the fire. She mentioned tutoring English. Finally, she talked about Doctors Join Hands in Iran where she ran into Marco and Charles again, and the wonderful Abbasi family who helped her avoid them. She talked endlessly about the *anjomans* and their excellent work. There were bumps along the way, she admitted, but she'd trusted the Universe to take care of her. She had had an amazing life, until it wasn't. She did so many more good deeds than if she had stayed to be a lawyer in her parents' firm.

The story continued as a jumbled mess, but she managed to reveal the essence: that she had to flee Iran for her freedom and that Mr. Abbasi had been driving the motorcycle to help her escape.

"We were nearly to Qod. It wasn't an accident, though. Someone deliberately ran us off the road." She began sobbing again. "He had been my friend, but he tried to kill me."

"Mr. Abbasi?" interrupted Julissa.

"No. Aren't you listening? Charles. But I didn't die. I don't die! And I won't die now. I can't. My work is not done."

No one spoke.

"I had to use the last of my money to pay my hospital bill. I didn't sell my kidney—I had to pay the hospital after they removed it. It was a lifesaving surgery. But I knew I was okay and could live on one kidney. I had taught that to others. I knew all about it."

"So, what happened to the remaining kidney?" asked Julissa.

Amethyst had known about Eva's drug addiction. Eva's doctor, who volunteered at a free clinic, had forwarded test results to Dr. Halabi for a second opinion. When her remaining kidney started failing, Eva admitted to that doctor that she'd been an IV cocaine abuser. She couldn't hide the tracks.

Sitting on the curb, Eva told the ladies since she didn't have any caregivers in Iran to help her after the accident, the doctors encouraged her to continue the opioids for a couple of weeks to keep her functionally pain-free. The opiates worked well, and, no, she wasn't at once addicted. Cocaine came later.

During her interviews with Amethyst, Eva insisted she was clean—she hadn't used since France. Amethyst explained to her that recovering addicts could receive transplants. It was her homelessness and inability to ensure her follow-up care that was the final straw against eligibility, but Eva refused to acknowledge that. Amethyst had kept all that information confidential, but she didn't know all the backstory because Eva was too proud during the interview to give details.

"The second kidney was courtesy of my Italian hero."

The ladies moved a bit, adjusting their positions on the hard curb, but said nothing. At least they were in the shade.

"My nephrectomy was healing nicely, but I had broken my leg and collarbone and other little bones. I couldn't go back to the *anjoman*. They were like my family, but I'd already put them at risk because of my two-second association with DJH. And because of me, Saeed was dead. How could I ever look at the Abbasi family again?"

"So, where does the Italian hero come in?" asked Julissa.

Eva spoke so quietly, wistfully, such a change. "He was a fellow traveler who was in the hospital while I was there. Appendicitis. He told me I could live with him at his place in Italy in return for housekeeping, just until I could find something else. He even paid my plane fare."

Julissa said that was nice of him.

"Yeah, we fell in love. Put it in one of your romance novels. I did cocaine with him to show him my trust. It felt good, like the opiates I had in Iran after my accident. Then we injected it, and I was hooked. Here's a fun fact since we are having such a fun evening. Did you know in 1887 the surgeon general announced that cocaine was a non-addictive remedy for depression?"

No one laughed.

Brianna said illegal drugs rarely cause kidney damage.

Eva sobbed back, "I know this. We dealt with addicts trying to donate at the *anjoman*. Cocaine, however, constricts blood flow, a big deal for kidneys. Leave it to me to be exceptional."

Brianna asked if they could call someone to pick her up. Eva said no and asked, again, if they'd been listening. She shouted she was all alone.

Amethyst offered to call the police to help her go to a shelter, but Eva panicked and became aggressive again. "I won't die. I don't die. Not this way."

There was nothing more the ladies could do. Eva was a survivor and would find her way back to wherever she stayed. On their way to their respective cars, Amethyst told them she had arranged for Eva to start dialysis as a Medicare kidney disability patient, but she had to have a residence. Eva hadn't followed through. The women decided they would investigate housing for her the next day. They were social workers—this was what they did for a living.

As they left, Eva flipped her finger at them.

Chapter 29

September 8, 2015, CTMRI, San Antonio, Texas:

Amir bumped into Dr. Segel as she headed for the common room of the Institute. The building housed labs working on different initiatives. Designers for the common room intended to encourage the sharing that medical researchers should idealistically, optimistically, even naively, but at least ethically, provide. The nature of professional exchange was why the concept of patents and copyright on medical advances was such a controversy. Who owned the DNA sequence or the blood within a sample drawn from a patient? Did the patient? The lab? The institution? Ownership of ideas when trying to improve the human condition seemed counterproductive, but power corrupts, and absolute power corrupts absolutely.

Amir and Segel's bump was not a rhetorical bump—Amir was racing down the hall while looking at a file of papers when he crashed into the back of her. Of course, she had coffee in her hands—that was her trademark. Quick reflexes sent him sideways, so it was Amir who hit the floor.

"Dr. Segel! Oh no! I'm so sorry." Poor Amir used his own sleeve to wipe Dr. Segel's coffee off her foot.

"Amir, it's okay. Cheap patent leather, see? My well-known coffee spills dictate I wear patent leather."

Pulling himself up, he sheepishly grinned at her. Amir worked for Doctor Sandra Jimenez's research team that was studying a different approach to solving the shortage of kidneys issue. The Institute believed in professional exchange, but there were limits—

they would never have competition for the same approach within the same building.

Dr. Jimenez proposed the artificial and remodeled kidneys were fantasies and that the only genuine hope, other than curing the actual kidneys before they completely failed, was to make transplants easier and without rejection issues. She proposed tweaking the donor kidney's antigens to make the organ appear to the recipient's body as the original. Matching would no longer be an issue, and there would be no need for expensive lifelong anti-rejection drugs that had so many side effects. Currently, even with the wonder drugs of Prograf and Cellcept, the best matches eventually faced chronic rejection over years, requiring another transplant. Although support groups reported forty-year-old transplants, the average expectancy for a living donor organ was fifteen years. The recipient's immune system wore out the donated kidney—certainly better than no transplant but far from an ultimate goal for a young recipient.

Dr. Segel had crossed paths with Amir several times during his months at the Institute and always found him pleasant and eager. He had quickly introduced himself and explained he learned of her work through the Institute's scuttlebutt. Certain he had placed himself so he would deliberately cross her path, she thought he might be infatuated with her. However, he was a young med student working part-time in Jimenez's lab for both money and experience, so she decided it was a schoolboy crush he would get over, or he just wanted to learn everything. Careful not to reveal any proprietary research, the two often enjoyed their encounters on a purely intellectual level.

She looked at Amir with coffee all over his sleeve and appreciated his awkwardness even more.

During these meetings, they talked about organ rejection, antigens, and specifically HLA antigens. They discussed how people had proteins that coated their cells that their own body learned as its own, like wearing colors in team sports to figure out who was on what side. A kidney recipient's immune system learned to attack antigens that didn't belong to it. Babies had their mother's immunities for about six to twelve months while their own system developed. After that, even a mother's kidney might not be a good match; after all, the father donated half the genes. Only identical twins would be perfect matches. Corneal transplants rarely faced rejection because there was no blood supply involved. Kidneys, however, were all about the blood.

Like South, Dr. Jimenez wanted the total function of the kidney, complete with hormone production. Where South's team was trying to make a remodeled kidney from the recipient's own cells, Jimenez's team was trying to make donor kidneys completely compatible. Jimenez acknowledged the superior benefits to what South was attempting—after all, her method still needed donors—but felt it was years away, if ever. She recognized the immediate crisis.

Using CRISPR/Cas9 and her own witch's brew of enzymes, IPS cells, and blood, Dr. Jimenez planned to adjust factors from the donor's cells so the recipient would not recognize them and attack them, like camouflaging the other team's colors. She called this adjustment process mutarsanguicellation. With living donors, the technicians could have blood samples and IPS cells from both the recipient and the donor well before the surgery to decide what needed tweaking. Jimenez's team tried to use Renal Progenitor cells instead of the KMS cells Segel used. No one really understood how the two kidney specialist cells worked. The plan was to have everything prepared ahead of the surgery. Then, when the kidney was removed, they would make the tweaks to the donor kidney in about forty-five minutes and place it into the recipient well within the time constraints for success. There would be no rejection.

Dr. South resented this research. The effort was absurd in his mind and took valuable funds from his project. Even if the research worked, and that would be a big *if*, there would still be the shortage of donors.

Dr. Segel imagined South's rants in her mind while she spoke with Amir during their brief encounters. *What does Jimenez hope to accomplish? What would they solve other than to make the current dire situation still bad? They still risk the lives of living donors. The remodeled kidney is the only way to do this.* South would then continue his rampage toward the pharmaceutical industry, blasting away at how Jimenez would face the same blocks that he faced with them. *They're only interested in the bottom profit line. With no rejection drugs, Big Pharma would lose out.*

Alex never treated Amir like a competitor—she was genuinely interested in his success. And she loved numbers and statistics. The world was tidy with numbers, chaos theory and all.

Amir loved that, too. This day was Amir's perfect day. This day, he had rushed down that hallway, hoping to run into Dr. Segel— well, not actually run into her—but he wanted to share the good news. Amir knew not to reveal any of the methodology—there were proprietary issues involved. He knew he mustn't even hint at success.

As Dr. Segel walked off, he could not contain himself. "We did it. Mutarsanguicellation worked!"

Chapter 30

September 8, 2015, CiCi's Home, San Antonio, Texas:

CiCi read an article about a recipient who went from not-approved-for-transplant to recipient within twenty-four hours; however, that was a unique circumstance involving a suddenly deceased relative. For CiCi and Jon, another two weeks dragged by. Body aches went along with kidney disease, and though he never mentioned them, CiCi watched him wince more and more often. While in Hawaii, she had learned how to perform *lomi lomi* massages and now helped Jon with the horrible cramps. *Lomi lomi* was good stuff. It was only a three-day class and designed just for her *ohana*, so Jon was the only person to benefit from this knowledge. As she tidied up around the house, she contemplated this morning's massage—with each session, she felt less and less muscle in his legs. But that wasn't all. Jon's taste buds were gone, his appetite vanished, and the fatigue took his breath away. Man cannot live on massages alone.

CiCi's attempt at housework to fill time until her appointment that afternoon did little for her spirits. Nothing was simple after age sixty, and, one more time, CiCi's age caused the need for extra effort. All the funny birthday cards about old age she'd sent her sister one year came back to haunt her. It was easy to laugh when she was fifty-five and her sister turned sixty-five. Since she was now sixty-three, a cancer survivor, and experiencing a bit of osteopenia, yet one more thing made life more difficult than it needed to be. The transplant doc wanted another bone density test and a consultation with an oncologist to speak with CiCi about treatment options should she get cancer again while having only one kidney. In the meantime, the doctor had created his network of nephrologists from around the United States to brainstorm the possibility of using a cancer survivor. CTMRI seemed to be trying to help.

Loaded with a bag of Jon's cookies, CiCi found her way into the clinic, which Jon would say was a major accomplishment. Her right-left boogie spins always sent her the wrong direction any time she came off an elevator, fodder for Jon's sarcasm. This time was no different.

Julissa's face lit up when she saw the cookies. "What kind are these?"

"Oatmeal raisin with macadamia nuts."

"I might put them in the break room, or I might forget and leave them in my purse." Julissa laughed like it was the greatest joke ever. "Let me call Lark to tell her you're here. As your personal nurse, she will be the one to escort you and answer surgery-related questions."

On their way to one of the exam rooms, CiCi overheard Brianna tell Amethyst that when she got home the other day, she noticed the garage door opener was missing.

"Weird," Brianna said. "No big deal, cheap to replace, but why?"

Amethyst told her she must have dropped it somewhere.

"But it's usually clipped to my visor. I'm getting batty these days. I can't find my new running shoes I keep in the back seat."

"Check the freezer." Amethyst laughed. "The other day I was putting away my scissors and later found them by the milk in the refrigerator."

CiCi interrupted. "I didn't mean to eavesdrop. You should change the remote to your garage. Someone could have taken your garage door opener and now has the key to your house."

Brianna shrugged. "Not an issue because there's nothing worth stealing in my little house."

"Maybe so, but I've heard about people who keep the remote in their car in their driveway, and burglars break into the car and then have access to the home." The ladies didn't say anymore, but CiCi could see their minds react.

Lark did her blood pressure cuff and stethoscope magic and then apologized for the extra trip. CiCi studied her face. She could tell Lark liked her job and wondered if she had ever had a patient go sour. It had to be traumatic to invest so much energy into a patient and then lose the battle. How would she, herself, feel about Jon if they turned out not to match, and she had to watch him die?

Lark explained about the calcium test and collecting urine for twenty-four hours. CiCi had already had bone density tests, but Dr. Halabi wanted a more thorough and current version with her endocrinologist's signature of approval for donation. Armed with paperwork for labs, CiCi headed back to the lobby. She could hear Eva through the door since the woman didn't practice her indoor voice.

"Oh my, Eva's here again," CiCi said to Lark before opening the door. "Is there a back way out?"

"Ah, I heard you met during your last visit. This has been an ongoing drama for a while."

CiCi sighed—she sighed a lot these last few months. "It's like she knows I'm here. Does she sit at your entrance and wait to see if I'll show up?"

"I hope not. That would be such a waste."

"She's at clinics every time I go."

Lark put CiCi's chart on the counter for Julissa to file. "Coincidence, I'm certain. She's been here when you're not. Would you rather wait here in the hall until she leaves?"

CiCi spied a nearby chair beside the little cubbyhole where the blood draws happened. "Just until the coast is clear." She still heard Eva's voice from the lobby.

****

Eva wasn't one to give up—she pled her case again with the four women captured in their attempt to resolve her predicament. "Okay, yes, I had a drug problem. There, are you happy? The first step is to acknowledge the addiction. But I'll be dead before I can complete all twelve steps. I did *not* sell my kidney."

Brianna put her hand on Eva's shoulder, but Eva pulled away. "We told you before it's not your addiction—it's your instability that disqualifies you. Amethyst found you a half-way house and got you food stamps that will take effect as soon as you list that house as your permanent address."

"I can do this. I kicked the addiction." Eva started in again, as if Brianna had never spoken. "When I was in Italy, I knew I had to leave Gino or die." And then she said, as if reading their minds, "He was selling me to get our drugs. So, I found a group in France who would pay me to teach English. I stole train fare from Gino and freakin' cold turkeyed."

"On your own?" Julissa had been taking notes. "You're amazing. I want to write a story about you."

Eva knocked the pen out of Julissa's hand. "I'll write my own story. And yeah, I did it alone. But I relapsed. And they kicked me out."

Lark asked, "What brought you to San Antonio?"

"I used to Facebook an old volunteer friend from Thailand whenever we both had computer access. She lived here and said I could come any time. The only thing I knew to do was to sell drugs in France to pay my airfare. I cold-turkeyed again because I needed every penny." And then with sudden horror in her eyes, "Could the withdrawals have ruined my kidney?"

Lark frowned. "No, I don't think the withdrawals did it—you were young and strong." She told her about medical articles regarding addiction and kidney issues. There wasn't evidence tying the two together. Eva would have to have been one-in-a-million cases when cocaine constricted blood flow enough to have damaged a kidney, but, since she only had one kidney, maybe that did it. As for the withdrawal causing undue stress on her kidneys, probably not. Maybe she simply got kidney disease.

"So, what happened when you got here?" Julissa asked, with no pen this time.

"I went to my friend's address, but she had died a month before."

Amethyst asked, "You didn't call her before you left?"

When Eva reminded them she and her friend were volunteers and had no phones, Amethyst whispered to her colleagues that, more than likely, she didn't want to know if her friend was still there. She was desperate for her plan to work. Then Amethyst moved to end the conversation. Part of being a social worker for a transplant center was guiding ineligible patients out of the clinic.

Eva spun around away from Amethyst. "I know people who can help me buy a kidney. I want a legal transplant. I want to be right again. But I know people."

Amethyst stepped back. "It's not that easy, even if you know people."

"Sure it is. My work in Botswana wasn't all tutoring. Marco and Charles and me, we found donors who would sell their kidneys to rich Americans and Europeans."

"But that's illegal." Julissa reached for her pen again.

Eva turned to her and glared into her eyes. "But it's done. Charles and Marco know Carrie Breun in Los Angeles who brokers deals."

Brianna slammed her clipboard onto the wooden chair arm. "But you aren't a rich American."

"I don't want to, but I'll sell drugs again. I live around addicts— someone will tell me how to connect."

Lark informed her there's a fifty thousand dollar fine and five years in prison if caught in illegal kidney sales, but Eva kept going, ignoring Lark. "So, sick people can't buy a kidney, but doctors and

211

hospitals can sure as hell send a bill for the transplants. That's paying for a kidney."

No one responded.

"I repeat," declared Eva, "people do it all the time. And I wouldn't do it in the U.S., so the U.S. won't catch me."

Lark tried again to reason with her. "Medicare doesn't cover post-op or medications for kidney transplants performed outside the United States. So, how do you plan to keep that kidney alive?"

That did it. Eva's will finally broke. This wasn't Iran. She had worked the donor end for medical tourists with little thought toward the recipients' post-surgery. With no answer, she picked up her bag and walked out the door. As she left, Julissa grabbed the bag of cookies and added a note for Eva. Everyone agreed she needed cookies more than they did.

Outside, Eva was going to throw the cookies in the trash but stopped to look at the note.

Call me. Julissa.

And there was the phone number. Laughing deliriously, she pulled the bag open, grabbed the biggest cookie, and ate. No bus today. No money. The weather was pleasant, so she would sleep in the greenway a few blocks over. Dinner tonight would be cookies and a bottle of water that she picked up as she left the clinic.

Chapter 31

September 9, 2015, Bus 604, San Antonio, Texas: Dressed in her normal frumpy jeans, a tattered long sleeve shirt, and a nice pair of running shoes, Eva entered VIA bus 604, hauling with her a bucket of cleaning products she had borrowed from the shelter. What was she thinking? Who used a city bus for a get-away car? But what else could she do? If she *borrowed* a car, she would add to a list of crimes. She always took pride in trying to do the right thing, and stealing a car was theft—no way around that. And it wasn't like anyone would loan her a car, anyway.

No, this would work out fine. It could be normal for a housekeeper to ride a bus, and no one would have license tags or anything to help with ID. She'd appear as a simple dirty-blondish white woman about medium height. Mid-thirties. That would describe ten percent of San Antonio. And there was an old wide-brimmed sun hat hanging down over her eyes. Fair white women needed to protect their faces from the sun. Yes, she would walk tiredly the two blocks down the street from the stop straight to Brianna's house and look like all was as it should be.

Brianna was at work, but often housekeepers went to empty homes while the owner worked. And she and Brianna had talked about pets when the women were trying to calm her down once. So, no dog to bark or bite.

She walked up to the garage door, letting the bucket tip over to spill out the products. That way any snooping neighbors would see cleaning products. A mop would have been a nice addition, but she couldn't see how to sneak one out of the shelter, and she sure as hell couldn't afford to buy one. Mops, brooms, and vacuum cleaners should be supplied by the owner. The cleaning products would be, too, but she needed props. She was careful to keep her face toward the garage door.

The door opened with the remote. Good deal. Fortunately, Brianna hadn't gotten around to changing the pins to her door yet. Eva laughed to herself, mumbling aloud and mimicking Brianna. "To do list: lock car. And find missing remote. Tomorrow." There was no alarm to the house, either. That was probably on Brianna's other list, the someday list.

Gathering up her bucket, she entered purposefully. Not sure what she wanted to find in the house, her gut told her she would find something useful to persuade CiCi to give her the kidney. Brianna was CiCi's social worker, not her confessor, so that something was a mystery. With time to figure it out before Brianna got home, she decided she might as well relax in the air conditioning. It would look suspicious if the housekeeper left in ten minutes.

The house had only two bedrooms, one bathroom, and an open kitchen/dining area. The living room was small, cozy. A starter home from the 'eighties. "The yard is pleasant—too bad she doesn't have a dog to play in it," Eva said to herself, aloud. She decided she was talking to herself way too much these days—she was too young for that shit. "I will talk to things instead," she told the wall.

The second bedroom was Brianna's office with papers cluttered in small piles. It would be a dream come true if there was something she could use for leverage. "No," she told the desk, "Not leverage. Persuasion."

Donning her cleaning gloves to avoid fingerprints, she looked through the papers, making sure everything was in the same order and stacked as they were when she got there. There was nothing from work. This very industrious Brianna was going for a PhD in social work. It struck Eva as humorous that the topic dealt with non-military related PTSD in homeless women. "That's why the nosey bitch was so interested in my story that day out on the curb. I thought she cared. I'm her lab rat," she told herself. "And there I go, talking to myself again."

Finding nothing to help her in the office, she headed to the living room. It was a tidy little place with an inviting sofa. Feeling the pull of such an invite, Eva made herself comfortable. Gray dust clumped on the blades of the ceiling fan, but everything else was spotless. Her heart pounded briefly. What if the old guy across the street saw a real housekeeper come in earlier? She decided it was too late to fret over such things now, so she stretched out.

As she reached back, she felt something hard behind the throw pillow. "No way," she told the sofa. "A day planner?" Eva thought she was the only person left in America who didn't have life planned on a smart phone. Gino bought her a cell phone in Italy, but she had to leave that behind and never found money for another one, much less a smart one with a monthly planner. And here was Brianna, up-and-coming in her career, with a classic, hard copy day planner. But why leave it at home?

On the end table lay an old phone—not the flip style but may as well have been—and beside it was a box for a new phone. Mystery solved. Brianna, behind in the cellular world, had been sitting on the couch entering information from the address book and calendar. When she finished, she left the planner that ended up lost behind the pillow.

"Well, Ms. B, what is in here that I could use?" she asked the planner. The top page was the week's calendar. Brianna was one of those who took the previous week and placed it at the back, prioritizing the current week. "How very efficient of her. Well, good for her." This stung. Nothing in Eva's life was good. "Nosy social worker, she can get to me without even being here." She knew it wasn't Brianna, though. Her sting came from losing her home in Iran. She missed the Abbasi family and hoped they were doing well, no thanks to her.

She looked back at the calendar. "Well, shit." The calendar showed Brianna would get off at 2:00. There was no doctor's appointment or anything scheduled, so Eva could not count on Brianna staying away. She needed to find it—whatever *it* was—and get out of there to catch the bus before 2:20.

No matter how many times she flipped through pages, there was nothing to see other than patient appointments. CiCi's appointment the next week was there, so Eva made a mental note for later. Only the address section remained, listed alphabetically by last names. Not knowing CiCi's full name, she flipped through the addresses page by page, predicting CiCi would have something like *Zett*. But it didn't take long after all. CiCi was CiCi Clawson-Dawson with Cornelia Dorothea beside it in parentheses. "What a name."

She found a pen and a scrap of paper in the office, wrote the address, and replaced everything as it had been. She had been there only about thirty minutes and knew she needed to be there at least an hour to appear believable, so she went back to the couch to sit in comfort. Something else useful might come to her; although, she couldn't imagine what that could be. She didn't even know what she would do with the address.

Not used to air conditioning, she wrapped Brianna's little throw blanket around her shoulders and curled up on the sofa, hoping for something, anything, to help her approach CiCi about the kidney. She woke up with a start and found it almost 2:00. "Damn!" It was the clock's turn for verbal abuse. She gathered her cleaning items and bucket and headed for the garage. Remembering the planner, she headed back to the sofa and slipped it behind the pillow, smoothing the sofa cushion. Then she took her stuff and left.

Eva decided she would leave the garage door opener on the pavement near Brianna's car the next time she was at the clinic. She had noticed the car parked in the same spot when she was casing it earlier. She looked at her new running shoes—they must have been extras Brianna was going to drop at Goodwill. Eva saved her the trip.

Bucket in hand, the *housekeeper* caught the 604 to go back to her shelter. On the way, she realized she still had the blanket around her neck, so she put it in her shoulder bag to get it back to Brianna somehow. That would be tricky. Once at the shelter, she placed all the supplies, even the gloves, back where they belonged. She explained to the storage closet, "I'm not a thief."

That night an idea struck—she could kidnap CiCi. She only needed quiet time with her to convince her it would be better to donate her kidney to young Eva than to old Jon, who would not have long to use it. CiCi would understand since this was for her own good. It tickled her fancy that she could go down in infamy as the criminal with the get-away bus.

Chapter 32

September 10, 2015, CTMRI, San Antonio, Texas:

The lab rats had cleared out an hour before Alex stopped for the day. Scrolling through her computer looking at files and then closing them again so many times her mouse hand cramped, she didn't even know what she was looking for. She did know that the Nan thing was bugging her, but she dared not admit why, not even to herself. The files wouldn't tell her, but scrolling through them should have provided a distraction. It didn't work. Dinner with Ethan was lovely, but then nothing. Since then, only shoulder rubs and smiles. She hated that, and men did it all the time. *He's not that into you if …* just sexual teasing from a male superior.

"Knock, knock." As if reading her mind, Ethan called from her door. She told herself not to turn around—to look totally absorbed in her computer. She grabbed a document she could pretend to scrutinize in case he walked into her office, which he did. And he shut the door.

"What on earth are you focused on?" he asked.

"Oh, just checking through some stats—you know how I love stats." Her heart pounded. She hoped the air in her voice would not give her away. It did.

He leaned over her shoulder, peeking at her paperwork. She had even found a scrap paper with old notes on it, so her efforts looked authentic if he didn't look too closely. He didn't. She felt his breath on her neck, and there was his royal $2000 Clive Christian men's cologne: woody and exotic. The brand meant nothing to her, but she prized the *woody and exotic* part, for it seeped into her core. She got up from the safety of her chair to walk to the work counter across the room to tinker with her nanomapping microscope. She picked up a slide to add to her cover story.

Again, South walked up behind her to look over her shoulder. As she peered into the microscope, the only thing she saw was a vision of Ethan with his trousers off. Damn him. He reached both arms around her, conveniently moving the slide into a better position for her. The vision in the microscope suddenly became hot porn.

She lifted her head to ask him where he'd been and realized he was unbuttoning her blouse. Here? In the office? He apologized for taking so long to get back to her—he had had too many distractions this last month. Month? Yes, a month. He'd ignored her for a month. Yet she couldn't make herself stop him from undressing her. He was the boss, so she wouldn't get into trouble—that would fall on him, and she was a consenting adult. This was the most excited she had ever been. She returned to watching *porn* through her microscope.

Should she slow him down? She was grateful her lab coat was across the room on the rack. One less thing to take off. What was she thinking?

"A front snap?" questioned Ethan, nibbling on her ear. "That's a delightful treat, certainly convenient."

She felt the cool air as he opened her bra.

He turned her around, kissing her gently down her neck. Alex had yet to say anything since lying about checking stats. Her own stats were skyrocketing right now. Alex let her head fall back.

He was leaning against her as he purred to her. "You're lovely."

Alex couldn't speak.

"Don't answer."

His breath intoxicated her.

"I have to meet with one of our financial backers tonight, but soon, Alex, I'll fix you a wonderful dinner at my place."

And with that, he put her clothes back in order and excused himself.

Chapter 33

September 10, 2015, Bus 606, San Antonio, Texas:
What a beautiful morning for a bus ride: sky blue skies, not too hot, muted sun behind just a few clouds. *Sky-blue skies,* Eva noted that her talent for descriptions matched the quality of her mode of transportation. "Thank you again, Brianna, for your non-tech savviness. What a wonderful day for truth," she whispered to the clouds in the *sky-blue sky.* The bus fare was a donation from a guy who tossed a couple of dollars to her while she was sitting on a sidewalk. Nice guy. There was no plan—Eva would wing it, just as she had most of her life. "Flexibility, yes," she told the sidewalk. "It's all about flexibility."

The trip was easy—a tiny walk to the 606, ride about thirty-five minutes with a short delay at the bus hub, then a little walk through CiCi's neighborhood. The homes were far humbler than Eva had expected. Standing in CiCi's empty driveway, she realized the glitch. CiCi wasn't home. Eva knew she wouldn't be at the clinic with Jon because Brianna had written in her planner to make certain CiCi would not be there. CiCi was supposed to be home— the plan required that. But there was no plan—flexibility, yes. There was a security sign in the yard, so Eva could not wait inside. It was mid-morning in a working neighborhood—hopefully, no one would notice what she was up to. There was only one car in the driveway three houses up the road.

Eva found the bench on the front porch and pretended she belonged there. She, herself, didn't know what she was up to, but that would come. She just needed a little quiet time with CiCi.

That's all she needed. She would make her understand the tyranny of the gift. If CiCi gave her kidney to Jon, he would be forever indebted to her. Eva had learned about this burden of indefinite indebtedness just before she left the Abassis. It could become unbearable. How would he ever repay her, look her in the face every day? That was one reason the Iranian government paid the donor. If the recipient and the donor agreed on a payment, then the debt ended, or so they thought. If CiCi gave the kidney to Eva, she would never have to see her again. They could all move on with their lives.

Seeing CiCi's car coming around the corner two blocks down, Eva hid behind the big brown garbage can. Then the plan came together. There was a small pile of cut one-by-four scraps someone had used to repair the fence and not yet cleaned up. She tried a practice swing. Another sign.

Then she saw the old man across the street sitting on his front porch. She dropped the wood and pretended to tidy up the pile. Still looking. Time to go. CiCi's car left the stop sign at the end of the block and headed home. Eva, still hidden by the trash can, hurried across the neighbor's yard and then ambled to the bus stop, trying to look like she belonged there.

****

As CiCi parked and reached for her packages, she looked straight into Eva's eyes just before she jumped into the bus. Wanting to know what that homeless woman who coveted her kidney was doing in her neighborhood, she followed her. It wouldn't be difficult since CiCi had ridden the 606 enough times to know the route by heart.

Eva didn't go to a homeless shelter. She didn't go anywhere recognizable as a home. At the medical center hub, she walked three blocks to an overgrown field. CiCi knew that field well—it

221

supplied part of the parking at Salk High School. She knew, also, that there was thick underbrush and often questionable drug activity in that underbrush. The city talked of clean-up, but no action had happened in the twenty years CiCi worked at the school. Once, a body showed up in the bushes near the students' cars, so parents quickly found other places for the kids to leave their vehicles.

CiCi let Eva get down a scrappy trail before she parked her car along the side of the road. "Stealth," she told herself. "Deer hunter silence." But despite her care, she snapped a twig as she came up to a dilapidated old shack. The sound from the twig brought Eva out the back and around to surprise CiCi from behind.

"What are you doing following me? This is my home!" Eva's eyes were wide. She held a broken baseball bat in both hands as if she were about to hit a home run.

After a slight scream, CiCi turned to face her. She wanted to ask why Eva was at her house, but the baseball bat and fear sucked away any sound she could make.

"Get inside. You can't be seen." Eva shook the bat at CiCi. "No, wait. I need rope." Jumping up and down in delight while still threatening CiCi with the bat, she commanded CiCi inside again. "I have just the thing." She handed CiCi two frayed bungee cords. "I got these babies in Thailand—they held my suitcase closed for years." She pulled a new blanket out of her shoulder bag, one of her treasures from Brianna's house. "Tie up your feet and hands. If you try anything, I'll hit you with this bat." She threw the blanket at CiCi's feet.

"You want me to use bungee cords?" CiCi relaxed a little. This might be easy. Watching Eva's eyes dart all over the room with such fierceness they almost crossed, CiCi obeyed. She spread the blanket and sat to wrap her ankles—not too tight—just enough to look convincing. "I don't think I can tie my own wrists."

"Of course you can't. I'm not stupid. Put your hands behind you."

CiCi put her hands at her back, then twisted to grab the bat from Eva's hands when Eva hit her, hard. "I told you not to try anything."

Now everything about Eva evoked danger. With her head throbbing, fear settled in CiCi's gut—CiCi did as told. Eva tied the bungees tightly, but there was still a little stretch in the worn-out cords. CiCi asked herself what she had gotten into. Jon would be furious with her.

Suddenly Eva wrapped CiCi's mouth shut with dirty socks tied together. "I can't have you yelling." She added a blindfold made of who knows what. CiCi listened as Eva left the shed. She had to escape. Working at her wrists, she was almost free when Eva came back in.

"I'm so sorry about the gross sock." Eva apologized to the bewildered CiCi, even rubbed her head.

She sounded so calm, scary calm.

"Oh yeah, and sorry for the bump on the head. It'll all be okay. You'll see."

Chapter 34

September 10, 2015, CTMRI, San Antonio, Texas:

Behind the closed, locked door and shut blinds of South's office, Nurse Nan and Dr. South conferred. The building was silent for the night—Alex was nowhere around to see Nan enter.

Nan gave Ethan a kiss on the check. "So, what are you up to now, dear Dr. Ethan?" Nurse Nan knew all about Ethan's philandering—she had personal experience. During her turn, he didn't hide his marriage and took her to classy hotels. She was part of his lesson in learning the need for discretion, but he was young and teachable. They still got together occasionally just for kicks, or when he needed her nursing skills for something.

Ethan gave her that *Who me?* look.

Nan stroked his cheek with the back of her hand. "Your beautiful jawbone is much nicer without that stubble you're sporting these days. I like a clean shave." Ethan had been clenching that jawbone lately—she needed to relax it for him. "I saw the sweet Doctor Alex eyeing your every move, and I don't think she likes me much." Her height was perfect, eye-to-eye with Ethan's face.

"Oh, you think she's jealous of you? Play nice. She's the best lab queen imaginable, and she's what'll make this remodeled kidney come true." Ethan returned the stroke on her cheek and continued teasingly down her neck. "I need her help."

They enjoyed each other a moment longer. Then Ethan signaled to a chair for Nan and pulled a second chair next to her for himself.

Nan accepted the cue—she expected nothing from him but a role in the adventure. Always candid with each other, she supported him, no matter what he needed. Right now, he needed her nursing skills and her willingness to bend the law.

"I need a living kidney donor."

"Is that all?" Nan lived on the edge. Part of the reward when working with Ethan was that he would take her along on his mission trips where she enjoyed white water rafting, diving with sharks, and whatever else he had planned. And there was the sex. Yes, the sex made the trips particularly special. "Where shall we go? My connections in South Africa are slim right now."

Ethan frowned. "That's too bad—South Africa would have been nice."

"Can I know why you need this kidney?" she asked. "Does it have to do with the donation that intern fried?"

"You heard about that, did you?"

Nan leaned forward and whispered. "Your secret's still safe with the world. I'm just that good at digging up dirt." Then, rocking back in her chair, she caught his eyes again and scolded him. "That was a shame. Careless of the kid. But careless of your team to allow an intern to do any work that would jeopardize everything."

"I own that. Watching timers is way down the chain of command, but this one screwed us bad. What's done is done. Now I need to solve it. I need another kidney." He presented his case as if he were ordering a car part.

Nan didn't blink, no moment for thought. "I loved India last year. And the bungalow next to the beach was phenomenal."

"It was good, but all above ground. I have never found a good connection for the type of kidney deal I need now. Are you sure you lost South Africa? Botswana?" He took her hands and all but pleaded with his eyes.

Nan kept hold of his hands but looked away. She adored those eyes and could easily get sucked in too quickly. Only she could get that look from him—hurt, pleading, sweet. For Ethan's life outside

225

of Nan, those eyes sparkled with control, manipulation, desire. She wanted passionately to help him. A donor from Botswana would never happen, not these days. Her connection in Gaborone had disappeared years earlier, something about a scandal involving a fire north of the Kalahari around the Delta. She had met the men involved but never learned their controller's name from the States. The men vanished right away. Besides, Botswana was home—she had vowed to herself never to test the laws at home. And South Africa had tightened up its watch on transplants.

She might hook them up with someone in Nigeria, she thought. Neither she nor Ethan enjoyed the illegal organ market. For one, it came with grave consequences if caught. For another, it was distasteful to them. Whenever Ethan performed an illegal transplant, the money supported his research to create the remodeled kidney. The magnificent car and all the grand living came out of his wife's inheritance. He didn't use the illegal money for his own desires. Nan joined him because she wanted to ride the wave Ethan created. They both knew an artificial kidney that truly worked well would end the kidney market, and they were for that. Ethan's concept was the best answer, but he had to beat the pig and the artificial kidneys to the market to survive. They would do what they needed for the greater good, along with a push toward Ethan's legacy.

Ethan and Nan purposely did this kind of work outside the U.S. There was internet lore of victims waking up in New York hotels in a tub of ice and notes on stools beside them saying get to a hospital fast because their kidneys were gone. And there were stories of corruptible funeral directors. As horrifying as that sounded, it didn't really work that way. One could remove a kidney and risk the donor, but what would be done with the kidney? One doesn't just pop a kidney into a body in a hotel room—there would need to be a hospital with an operating room ready for the recipient. With no donor, there would be questions, paper trails, post-op considerations.

Organ trafficking within the U.S. was either well-hidden or rare enough to evade the law. The first case with actual conviction was in 2009, a kidney broker named Levy Izhak Rosenbaum, aka *Matchmaker*. He was a Brooklyn rabbi who matched Israeli donors and then brought them to the U.S. for wealthy recipients. The courts convicted some surgeons but never stated which hospitals were used. Rosenbaum said it was easy to fool hospitals into believing the act was entirely through altruism. The rabbi, though, charged $160,000 for an organ.

Rosenbaum said, "One reason it was so expensive was because you have to *shmear* all the time." It took money to pay Israeli doctors, prepare visas, and offer care for the donors while in the U.S. The donor would receive $10,000 funneled through a *charity*. The Israeli police and officials claimed ignorance of the Israeli role in it. Ethan and Nan had discussed the irony of wealthy Israelis traveling to countries like South Africa and Pakistan to buy kidneys when Israel's own impoverished citizens sold kidneys to the Americans. Crossing borders helped hide the activity.

The European Union had a case around that same time. The authorities closed Medicus Clinic in Prestina, Kosovo, and convicted five men of organized crime, people trafficking, and grievous bodily harm. These doctors lured poor donors from Turkey, Russia, Moldova, and Kazakhstan with assurances of up to 15,000 euro for their kidneys. Most of the rich recipients came from Israel. At the time Nan learned of the case, Lutfi Dervishi and his son had gone into hiding and didn't serve their sentences. Interpol still wanted Moshe Harel from Israel and Dr. Yusuf Sonmez of Turkey. Nan thought she heard something recently on National Public Radio that Sonmez was believed to be in the Netherlands, but maybe she just saw it on the Internet.

Wherever there was poverty, there was an entrepreneur ready to exploit, but not all procured kidneys came from willing victims. War often brought about unwilling donors, especially those wars with undisciplined soldiers. There were questions about elements of the Kosovo Liberation Army in 1999. The Chinese were known to harvest kidneys from prisoners of conscience. Sometimes a so-called prisoner patient would have surgery for a sickness they didn't really have and not even realize the kidney was gone.

When the organs of a human body could total over $700,000, corruption thrived. A single kidney alone could bring in $30,000 with the right buyer. Of course, the recipient would pay at least five times that because of other expenses, and the donor would be lucky to receive $4000, if still alive.

As most investigators into the world of underground organs knew, the traffic for these organs journeyed from south to north and from the poor to the rich. And, yes, dark to light, but mostly poor to rich. Once, visa control prevented traffickers from bringing potential donors from Moldova. The donors were desperately poor, dressed in rags and even malnourished, yet they were going to New York City as tourists?

When asked why rich recipients didn't ask a loved one to donate a kidney, they would say they didn't want to put their loved ones through such difficulty. They would say it was far better to buy the kidney from someone they didn't know and didn't really care about afterward. Dehumanizing the very human organ made that piece of a person into a commodity.

Nan had convinced Ethan over the years that it was best to move around. A kidney clinic in Prestina, Kosovo, failed because those doctors had practiced in the same location for two years. Airport officials in Prestina detained a Turkish donor because he was clearly suffering pain from the donation. Authorities then collected data from over eighty witnesses and thirty transplants that led to the Prestina clinic. If she and Ethan moved around, there wouldn't be so many opportunities for locals to give them away. Of course, they would be vulnerable to unknown brokers and hospitals. Still, she insisted, it was best to travel the world.

Hanging around the San Antonio CTMRI clinic and getting to know everyone while expecting her position with Ethan, Nan had cozied up to Julissa. As the clinic receptionist, Julissa was privy to gossip and wanted to share. During one conversation, Julissa mentioned a woman named Eva who had a history with the kidney donors overseas and who now desperately needed a kidney herself. Nan thought there might be something there Ethan could use.

"How do you plan to use this kidney you need so badly?" Nan saw Ethan's mind spinning. He would save his project at all costs.

"I'm not sure yet."

Nan had done enough thinking for the night as she became conscious of Ethan caressing her in all those tender places that made collaborating with him so worthwhile. She seductively slipped off her scrubs and proceeded to undress Ethan. It would be a nice evening.

Chapter 35

September 10, 2015, A Shed in San Antonio, Texas:

Eva removed the sock and blindfold. With one finger over her mouth warning CiCi to stay quiet, she used her other hand to rub the base of CiCi's head where she had hit her earlier. CiCi tried to adjust and sit up, but her hands were still bound. She winced at the bright light. Her mind shrieked in fear. Then Eva leaned into her line of sight.

"What the hell? Eva?"

"I'm so, so, so sorry about the bump on your head. You were going to leave. I needed to talk with you, but you were always with someone else. Then, outside, a minute ago, I realized you had solved my problem."

CiCi's brain gushed with questions. "What? How? You kidnapped me!"

"Kidnap? You came here, may I remind you. I just want quiet time alone with you. Besides, I won't ransom you or anything."

"Really? Taking me without my permission? Almost knocking me unconscious? What do you want?" CiCi tried to sit. "You tied me up."

"Technically, you tied up your own feet." Eva laughed at her own joke. "The blindfold was a dumb idea—you walked here, so you know the location. It seemed like the right thing to do, though. We shall call this a *non-kidnapping.*"

CiCi looked around, trying to get her bearings. This place was a dump and reeked of cats.

Eva studied her. "I saw you following my bus. I used to sleep here until Amethyst got me into the shelter. This was perfect.

Thank you. I was going to take you from your house, but that old fart across the street saw me."

"Eva, it's not too late. I'm not really hurt, at least as far as I can tell all bound up like this. And I didn't pay attention while following you, so I don't know where I am." She lied. "You could just let me go." CiCi tried to reason with her while working at the bungees behind her back. "My wrists are getting sore—can you at least loosen them?"

Eva lost control. "I'll bet you think life is neat and tidy. Your friend got sick and needs a kidney, so you say, 'Oh, I'll just give him one of mine. I don't need it.' You'll just get some tests, and they'll unzip you, take your kidney, zip you back up, and then zip it into your friend. All will be hunky dory."

"Is this about you wanting me to donate to you? What makes you think my kidney will do you any good? I had cancer twenty years ago—the clinic isn't even sure they will use me for Jon. Hell, Eva, we don't even know if I'm a match for Jon yet."

Then she looked around and decided she was not in a position to argue. The entire Medical Center had been farms fifty years earlier. This must have been part of a barn, filled with stuff—that's the only word CiCi could come up with for the collection of old toasters, bed frames, an old suitcase, and a blender off to the side. Eva smelled of desperation. She did, at least, supply a blanket for the flooring—if it could be called *flooring*—for them to sit on.

Eva frantically worked at CiCi's phone to get the unlock pattern. CiCi could help, but her hands were tied. She had to laugh at her personal joke and complimented herself on being old-fashioned, no facial recognition or even fingerprint security for her phone.

"Ha!" Eva blurted. "Wouldn't it be nice if scientists could make each of us a clone to keep in storage somewhere until we needed it for an organ or tissue?"

Noting the bitter sarcasm in Eva's voice, CiCi went with the conversation. "Right, like that old movie *The Island?* That one where the clones figured out the world beyond their walls wasn't really contaminated, so they escaped."

"Yeah, I saw it in Italy at an English language movie place. They learned they were cloned for modifications as needed by their sponsors. Yeah, well, it turned out the clones were human." At first excited by the conversation, Eva became uncontrollably angry and threw CiCi's cell phone across the room. "But donors aren't clones. I saw what brokers did to donors."

Eva paced around the floor like a caged animal, a walk CiCi had seen once before. One of her students couldn't sit still in class—restlessness became knee bouncing and obvious fidgeting. Then came the caged tiger walk. CiCi sent the young lady to the school counselor and later learned she suffered PTSD from an assault at her bus stop that morning.

"Eva, what did you see?"

Eva started with fragments that led into rambling, but eventually CiCi pieced together the story. She told CiCi how beautiful Thailand was until the Boxing Day Tsunami changed everything. She told her about meeting Marco and Charles and how they seemed like good friends, but she was sure she saw Charles pocket a dead woman's jewelry. Eva rattled something like, "Who would do that?" Then the guys left, and life was good, then Botswana and something about a fire, then Baruti and the truth. And something about Charles and Marco again. She kept weeping. "I thought I was helping."

CiCi recalled the earlier conflict in the clinic. She'd heard about Charles and Marco through the door. The bits she gathered from that episode with the fragments Eva gave this time sent a chill through CiCi.

Then Eva pulled CiCi's face so close to hers that spittle flew into CiCi's eyes as she told horror story after horror story from Botswana. "Everyone profits but the donor. That's true here, too, you know. Hey, did you know genetic testing showed we all descended from the people of the Kalahari Desert?"

By then, both women were crying. "Charles and Marco ... they ... evil." Words choked her as she tried to make CiCi understand. "I was so happy when I was in Iran because there Zenda and I tried to help the donors make good choices." When Eva talked about Iran, her pacing picked up again and her thoughts rambled even more erratically.

CiCi knew little about Iran, just what she heard in American news, which was not usually favorable. She once had a student from Iran who had escaped with her mother and brother in a jeep with rifle bullets aimed at them, just like Sally Field in *Not Without My Daughter*. The brother was at the age for military draft, and the girl was to be married at thirteen. Her mother decided to break that family tradition. The girl, a magnificent student, caught up her English language skills in one year. CiCi loved that girl. But that was CiCi's knowledge of Iran. Eva's words were of beauty and goodness and loving mixed with extreme weather and covered hair.

The more Eva talked, the faster she walked and the tighter the circles became.

CiCi had freed her hands, but Eva still held tight to the bat, so she kept her hands behind her. She thought back to what she had overheard in the clinic. "Eva, what's your last name?"

"Davenport. Who cares?"

"Of *the* Davenports?"

"Yeah, 'Tis I," Eva replied with a snob look complete with pinkie in the air.

CiCi couldn't imagine how bad home had to be to give up everything and become a street urchin with kidney disease. She studied the bungees still on her feet. If she were to escape, she would need to get to her feet. And her old hips didn't let her move like she used to. "I had no idea."

"CiCi, you know nothing. I'm going to save all three of us."

"Eva, how? How can you do that? This is crazy." CiCi tried to stay as calm as possible.

"If you donate to a person you cherish, you will regret it the rest of your life. And he will, too."

"If I don't donate, he won't have much life left for either of us to notice. And then I'll regret it as long as I live. I need you to help me understand. How is tying me up going to help all three of us?"

"I'm getting there." Eva's mood swings had become so extreme CiCi gasped. Eva continued her story. "One afternoon, after I'd been working in Iran almost a year, a middle-aged man looking radiantly healthy pushed his way to the front reception desk and demanded to speak with the head counselor." Eva took a deep breath. "He spoke too fast for me to follow, but later Zenda filled in the missing parts for me. Zenda was calm the whole time he yelled at her." Eva stopped and studied CiCi. Then she said with suspicion in her voice, "Like you are now."

As Eva resumed circling, CiCi did her best to fill in the missing information. "Okay, Eva, I'm listening."

"So, this guy kept saying that the *anjoman* ruined his life. I was near the door and thought I should run to the next office to get help, but Zenda knew what she was doing. She said what you just said." Mid-circle, Eva stooped to tie and retie her new sneakers. The bow refused to sit evenly, frustrating her into a flurry of tugs and loops. "Zenda told that poor man, 'I need you to help me understand.' She meant it, CiCi. Do you?" Then Eva scratched a scab on her arm until it bled.

"I do now, Eva. Right now, you scare me. Is there more to our scene here? Where is this going? Are you going to hurt me?"

"Now, why would I do that? I need your kidney. If I hurt you, well, duh."

CiCi was decidedly too old to sit on a floor in one position. "Please continue the story." Relieved to know her life wasn't in immediate danger, she shivered and wondered how Eva planned to get her kidney.

Eva said the poor man cried that it was all too good to be true. The *anjoman* allowed his cousin to sell him the kidney. "This is where you need to pay close attention, CiCi," scolded Eva when she noticed CiCi looking around.

Eva continued. "This man—I never learned his name, so call him Feroz—said he gave his cousin so much money, five times the government offer, just as they had agreed. Zenda said that she remembered it. The counselors at the *anjoman* thought it had been a miracle that a non-sibling relative who matched lived with Feroz. It made it very convenient. Feroz then started yelling again that no one knew anything."

"What went wrong?"

"He said his cousin watched every move he made. He watched him drink water and kept count of the glasses. Feroz told him he drank at work, but the cousin wanted proof. He constantly corrected Feroz's wife to be sure meat was thoroughly cooked and vegetables well washed. Oh, and he ran off any little dogs in case they had bacteria or fungus Feroz might get. Every morning and night, he asked if Feroz had taken his medicines. There was no respect for this man's space anymore. The cousin thought he owned him and didn't trust Feroz with his gift."

CiCi recalled when a colleague saved her from choking on a gooey nacho thirty years earlier. Her mother said some cultures believe saving a person denies that person's destiny. The hero becomes responsible for that person for the rest of his or her life. Maybe Feroz's cousin believed that way. Maybe it wasn't lack of trust but a matter of obligation for him to ensure Feroz's new destiny.

"This is so sad," CiCi said.

"Did they tell you about this?"

CiCi closed her eyes. No, they didn't tell her everything. Those first days in the clinics seemed like a year ago but had been only a month. Not that it would change her mind, she made herself a mental note to Google this behavior. If she got home. "Eva, I don't think this is going to be a problem for Jon and me."

"You think you're so different? You're better? When Zenda offered to speak with the cousin, Feroz said it wouldn't help. He pleaded with her to be sure only strangers donate kidneys. It's too hard to do it with those who are around so much. The donor was Feroz's favorite cousin, his friend. After the transplant, he didn't want to see him."

They sat without talking for a moment, no more pacing or shoe tying.

Then Eva added, "Even if the cousin did nothing to irritate him, Feroz said he still would have felt greedy for taking such a prize from him. *The Tyranny of the Gift*—it's real—there's a name for it."

"You mentioned it once at the clinic."

"And did you Google it?"

"No."

"Figures. 'Cause you're ignorant. What will Jon do if something happens to you? How will he bear it?"

"Eva, I know my risks."

"That's what Zenda pointed out. The *anjoman* made sure they knew the risks. But they did not tell him about this."

Eva rubbed her eyes and pried at her lids. The dark circles underneath them exaggerated a need for sleep. "What about your daughter?"

"My daughter knows this is entirely my decision."

"Is it? Is it entirely your decision? The Iranians say mutual exchange avoids that unspoken pressure."

"That's not happening here."

"Really? You never donated to someone you didn't know. You didn't go on a website and say, 'Hmmm, I think I'll give my kidney away today.' How do you sit around and let a dear friend or a family member die when you could do something about it, even if a risk to you?"

CiCi had to admit that with family or friendships that fine line between altruism and the covert call to sacrifice blurred, but she was certain that wasn't the case between Jon and herself. "Firemen run into fires."

"That's your answer? That's their job. They have e-quip-ment."

Eva's voice reminded CiCi of teens when they smart off to each other. She elongated each syllable and made the *e* screech. Eva was no teen.

The two talked reasonably from there on. Eva agreed the ability to save lives through transplants was just short of a miracle. CiCi agreed there could be sub-conscious coercion. Yes, it might be hard to let go. CiCi mentioned the Netherlands' recent plan she heard about on the radio. They wouldn't compensate with money, but they offered medical insurance for life and covered all costs related to the transplant, along with sick leave, job guarantees, and other benefits. No worries about elective surgery coverage or lack of insurance. That sounded reasonable to Eva, but she wanted to know why a donor couldn't benefit financially—everyone else did: doctors, hospitals, labs, pharmaceuticals, PR agents. In the end, she remained firm that undisclosed donation was the only possibility. If that were the case, CiCi thought, even with financial rewards, there would be very few living donors.

"Let's call it a brutal miracle," CiCi said.

Eva nodded and returned to her story of Feroz. She said he had reached a point of tears and told Zenda, "With a stranger, you pay, and it is done." How would an outsider know what happened behind the walls of a family? Feroz's story could happen even in the U.S., even with the social worker, the donor advocate, the doctors constantly verifying there was no coercion. The pressure afterward, the guilt. "And you need to listen!" Eva growled at her. "Feroz admitted it was the gift of life. He didn't deny that. But he would rather have been dead than live like that."

"So, what happened?"

"Feroz strangled his cousin while he slept and then plunged a knife into his own heart."

Silence.

Finally, CiCi said, "You kept mentioning Charles and Marco. Where are they now?"

Eva collapsed without answering. "The Thais are right about karma. I just need to accept I'm dead. I won't bother you anymore." Then she pulled out a knife.

CiCi gasped—this time she brought her hands in front, huddling into a ball.

Eva threw the knife through the chest of a rat that ran past CiCi's toes. Then she cut CiCi's feet free with the bloody blade. "Go on. I knew your hands were free." She threw CiCi's keys to her and let her go.

The sun was about to set.

As CiCi walked out of the shed, Eva called after her, "CiCi! What happens if you get scared half to death … twice?"

CiCi kept walking, ignoring Eva's hysterical laughter.

Chapter 36

September 10, 2015, Chennai, Tamil Nadu, India:
Carrie Breun hadn't been to Chennai since the boys worked in Botswana. It seemed ages ago. She knew it was condescending for her to refer to Marco and Charles as boys, but even in their thirties, they didn't deserve the title of men. She had worked to get them out of scrapes too many times. Alas, they were handy and eager, so she kept them.

Carrie's British grandfather Derek served in the Royal Army in India and told tremendous stories. Her grandmother learned to cook the foods of Tamil Nadu before they returned to England because Da-daddy D desired it. They had servants for their every need and lived high on a hill with a spectacular breeze blowing nonstop off the Bay of Bengal, conveniently not downwind of the city. Sometimes the heat wore on Na-nanny. But, even in his hot, stiff English uniform, Da-daddy D loved the colony.

Carrie took in the city's view and strolled down memory lane. Madras. That's what Da-daddy called it. She never grew accustomed to calling it Chennai, even though it had regained its local name twenty years earlier. Most of the population was Tamil, with a strong minority of Telugu. Linguists said no such word as *chennai* existed in Tamil, that it came from Telugu. Da-daddy D knew well the Tamil/Telugu struggles for recognition. Many in the city wanted to change the name back to Madras, the name they had known for three hundred years. Slogans, memes, and articles floated through the Internet that claimed, "Chennai is a City, but Madras is an Emotion." Carrie wasn't the only one troubled with the new name.

Years earlier, she had decided if she ever had to leave California, Madras was where she would head. She had money hidden around the world, so she could live well with all the servants she wanted. But it wasn't just the comfortable life—the city called to her. It was the Portuguese who first discovered the Tamil merchants in 1522 and built the port São Tomé. The British established Fort St. George in 1639 for the English East India Company. Villages expanded around the fort, making Madras the first modern city in India. The city's heritage of merchants drew Carrie—she was, after all, a merchant. Touching the walls of Fort St. George, her grandfather's favorite place, took priority every visit. She thrilled at the sight of the tall spires standing over the tomb of St. Thomas, who was thought to have brought Christ's lessons to gatherers at nearby caves and mounts during the first century AD. In those days, Madras—or Chennai—wasn't a city, just a gathering of souls. Not religious, not even spiritual, Carrie respected history, and she respected St. Thomas's tenacity—or audacity—to assert his truth to others who saw things differently.

The colors of Madras made her happy. Well over a thousand years old, the Hindu temples with their colored carvings of sacred cows alongside gods and goddesses challenged the splendor of any peacock's feather. The striking white ISKCON (Hare Krishna) temple built after the millennium contrasted dramatically with the kaleidoscope effect of the much older temples. At night, colored lights for Darshan painted the ISKCON with electric blues, pinks, and purples—breath-taking.

Travel blogs mentioned overwhelming sights, sounds, and smells. It was true. The smells required adjustment. It was an overcrowded city with inadequate sewage drainage, so one needed to get past the acrid stink of urine, far worse than what a city girl experienced on her first trip to a dairy farm. But once Carrie turned that off in her mind, she smelled musk from the ancient rivers and cardamom from the spicy street food. Near the temples, rose and jasmine welcomed visitors, an excellent perfume to cover an otherwise disgusting stench. Within the busy-ness and noise, the people were gracious, overtly kind. She was no fool—she knew to practice common safety protocols for women traveling alone. She didn't like calling people to share her whereabouts like most women did, so she hired two burly escorts to accompany her. Yet, Chennai—or Madras—presented her indescribable comfort.

For over twenty years, the kidney sales in Chennai had rewarded Ms. Breun well. The slums of the Vilivakkam neighborhood generated kidney business, gaining the nickname Kidneyvakkam. Poverty was the breeder. The tsunami brought more—the sellers were desperate. Carrie Breun negotiated no kidney brokerage herself. If something went wrong, she wanted no direct lineage to the deal. She visited sites to observe, to inspect hospitals and hotels, to estimate potential, and to refine what percentage of any negotiation was a true value. She was more than a merchant.

In Tsunami Nagar, a settlement on the outskirts of Chennai, slums had always perched next to the wealthy. The tsunami didn't create this juxtaposition—it merely added to the existing deep, culturally ingrained environment of the *haves* and the *have-nots*. The caste system of birthright—legally gone—still penetrated Chennai, more noticeably there than in other parts of India. Rising technology with call centers created a way out of the slums, but only if schools survived and if children got to them. Cruise ships offered dream jobs requiring long hours, seven days a week, and at least nine months at sea. But those jobs were in high demand, and competition was tough. With the tsunami, those who had survived by day-to-day fishing and farming lost everything. Poverty begat more poverty.

Carrie didn't condemn them for their poverty. How many Americans could go three months without a paycheck? In America, credit cards morph into vampires once the paycheck disappears. Lose the car, can't get to work; can't get to work, can't buy a car or pay for the bus fare, if there is a bus. Add a doctor visit or two? Recovery is a struggle often relying on family members who can't always help. Medicaid? Welfare? Social food pantries? And that is in America. The slums of Chennai grew exponentially, so no condemnation, only an opportunity for organ business.

The ruling body for the state of Tamil Nadu wanted to abolish slums and devised plans for a slum-free Chennai by 2013, then 2017, then 2023. They even had a board for it: the Tamil Nadu Slum Clearance Board, created by the Tamil Nadu Slum Areas Act of 1971. 1971: forty-four years. Their task was to remove slums and to offer livable hygienic housing. Still, in little more than a decade, the number of slums grew by half. The 2004 Indian Ocean tsunami was part of that. After the disaster, the government moved survivors to land south of the city with promises of better accommodations soon. With broken promises, Tsunami Nagar was born. *Nagar* meant *town* in Hindi, so Tsunami Town was intended to be more than a resettlement location—the word *town* implied homes with city services.

Even though her business profited, Carrie felt pain for these people. Resettlement areas existed on low-lying flood-prone marsh land and where the salt from the tsunami ruined farmland. Fishermen were ten miles or more inland from their earlier livelihoods. These people had no money for bus fare, and walking took three hours each way. Nearly seventeen hundred families received single-room homes, which meant one room served as a living room, a bedroom, and a kitchen. Multiple families shared toilets and bathing facilities. The men gave up fishing and preoccupied themselves with alcohol and beating their wives. In some slums, children walked two to four miles to get to the nearest corporation school, yet there might be six state-owned wine shops within half that distance. Ms. Breun mused over how the fishermen were moved so far from the shore in the name of safety, yet the Chennai coastline exploded with luxury high-rise housing and resorts. A desalination plant even appeared. Conveniently, the government forgot the tsunami's message.

The women of Tsunami Nagar longed for work. For a while, they could work for a non-profit, non-government organization that developed a waste disposal system. The NGO trained the women—gave them protective gloves, aprons, and masks—and set them to sorting organic waste from the rest of the trash. It was efficient and cleaned up the community. The organization then sold organic waste to farmers as compost. The women contributed something useful and felt good about their work. In 2012, that came to a halt—no more money, no more waste efficiency. Garbage piled up around the homes. The women described their days to Carrie during her reconnaissance visits—wake up, pass time, go to bed. There were no prospects for improvement.

Tsunami Nagar wasn't Ms. Breun's only source—the Chennai branch of her kidney trade had been growing for at least twenty years. The population of Chennai ranged anywhere from four to nine million, depending on who decided the metropolis's boundaries. Someone declared the poverty rate wasn't even ten percent, yet almost a third of the city's population lived in slums where people survived on less than a dollar a day.

Carrie admired skills in statistical representations. There were well over two thousand, and growing, shanty towns in the Chennai vicinity. Government could not just abolish slums—the people had to go somewhere. Claiming to clean the river for ecological purposes, the Tamil Nadu Housing Board demolished the shanty towns to build new but sub-standard tenements in the low-lying flatlands. The TNHB then filled defunct lakes to create land for new, high-end housing and shopping centers. The rains fell with no lakebeds to fill and, thus, no drainage, leaving the residents of those new flatland settlements standing in sewage water. And the poor stayed poor.

Carrie told her driver to take her to the airport—she was finished here for the moment. The *have-nots* of Kidneyvakkam and Tsunami Nagar still had one thing the *haves* needed.

Chapter 37

September 10, 2015, Salk High School Parking Lot, San Antonio, Texas: As the sun slipped down behind the trees, the orange light from the afterglow performed the cliché burst into CiCi's eyes. For years while teaching English at the health magnet school, she had watched the sun set through the window that looked over the very spot in the field where she stood now.

She studied the keys still in her hand. When did Eva take them? Then she looked back at Eva, a limp form of a body deflated over herself. Relieved, angry, sad, back to angry, and settling on relief and a throbbing head, CiCi knew she should go to a hospital.

Feeling giddy, she headed for the school. There still would be kids and teachers finishing their long days with extra-curricular this-*es* and thats. They would help. Then she realized she didn't want to tell anyone about Eva. To cover up for bursting into the school, she borrowed a student's phone to call Jon to apologize for being so late, saying she was fine and would explain later. Too shaken to drive home, she told him she had car problems and broke her phone, and could he please risk driving to get her?

****

"I don't know how it happened," she told Jon for the third time. "I pulled into the driveway and saw Eva getting into the bus, so I followed her. Next thing I knew, she had me tying myself up with bungees."

"I told you she was dangerous. Why on Earth would you follow her?" Jon snapped.

"Hey, don't get all pissy with me. I have a headache."

"But I told you." He stopped short. "And once again, why didn't you report it?"

"Yes, you were right, as always—Eva is dangerous." CiCi answered with as condescending a voice as she could muster. She ignored the police part as she rambled on with jokes about protecting his kidney from bungee ties. She could take him to the scene, but she doubted Eva would be there. She hoped Eva would be gone because she feared Jon would lose it.

****

Jon looked ill, and not kidney ill. "How did Eva find this place?"

"I hear the homeless have a network that even the police don't seem to hack. One stumbles across an access, tells the next who tells the next, and so on."

"The thought of anyone using a place like this for shelter makes me sick."

CiCi looked around with new purpose and could see the junk comprised an old table knocked over and a wooden box that could have been a chair. There was a pile of cardboard boxes. She originally thought the pile was just part of the junk, but it could have been bedding. She flashed for a moment to the beautiful children she met at her Bangkok friend's tiny school. They were the garbage dump kids. Her friend's school bathed them, gave them breakfast and lunch, and schooled them the best they could. For eight hours each day, the children were clean and healthy. Then she thought about the rat that ran past her foot that morning and shivered at the idea of sleeping there. Maybe the cat smell was a good thing, would discourage rats.

CiCi could see Jon's anger building. They were only friends, but there was never any doubt that Jon would protect her with his life.

It startled CiCi to realize she was doing the same for him with this kidney thing.

CiCi looked around her. She knew Eva would get medical care in jail, but she also knew Eva had been a free spirit since she left home. Irony coiled around Eva—someday it would strangle her. Eva was free to avoid her parents, but in that freedom, she kept confining herself. Even in Thailand, where she seemed to have been happiest, she had to fear her visa status. It took planning to be free, and how was that freedom? With that, CiCi's head started hurting again—she could only think of going home.

"I don't want her to go to jail," CiCi announced.

Jon turned and stared her down. "You need your head examined."

"I'll be fine. But she's a dying woman. A desperate, dying woman. I want a restraining order and mandated counseling for her. Can we do that?"

"Not without a report."

"She said she wouldn't bother me anymore, but I'll call Stan." She told Jon about the student who was assaulted at her school bus stop years earlier. Stan was the school police officer who helped that girl by having a chat with the guy at the bus stop. He had worked the Luby's Restaurant mass murder in Waco and then vice in Dallas. "He went into school policing because he wanted to make a difference before kids became lost causes. Retired now but still intimidating, I'm sure he'll convince her." CiCi rubbed the back of her head to check the knot. It was tolerable, no harm done. "You should have seen her when I left."

It was a plan she could live with. She could learn more about alternatives to jail before tomorrow. She had graduates who went into law—one of those *kids* could advise her.

****

Jon parked CiCi in the recliner and told her to stay there. Then he sat beside her. "Why were you getting groceries so early in the day? You're a vampire. You don't wake before noon."

CiCi loved her recliners. When they shopped for them four years back, they didn't realize the special benefit of the cup holder console between the seats. CiCi called it her *not-so-loveseat* sofa. When they reclined, the upright part of the console remained in place rather than reclining with the chairs, thus hiding CiCi and Jon from each other. Tonight, CiCi rocked back and pretended Jon wasn't there—she knew he wanted to call the police. He was right, though—normally she would still have been asleep when Eva showed up. And the bags weren't even groceries—they were her personal items that she didn't expect Jon to buy, like deodorant and shampoo, and her special choice in toilet tissue that Jon named Princess Ultra-Soft—he bought rough stuff that felt like sandpaper.

CiCi prescribed herself ice, Tylenol 3, and no exercise for a week. She twiddled her thumbs a bit, flipped through TV channels and then found the Amazon box Jon had left on the coffee table that day, not knowing CiCi was held captive in a cat den. She pulled at the tape, surprised it ripped off so easily. Amazon must have been saving on glue. It was her copy of *Kidney Sellers*, by Sigrid Fry-Revere, that Brianna had suggested. There were only three used copies available through Amazon's used books, so CiCi was thrilled with her slightly highlighted version, perfect for a recliner-ridden victim of a *non-kidnapping*.

Jon went about preparing a light dinner for them while CiCi flipped through her new book. Her headache wouldn't let her truly read, so she browsed and told Jon bits to enlighten him. "Fry-Revere talks about a man seeking a kidney donor through a dating site. The request wasn't on his profile, but he popped the donor question soon and offered ninety thousand dollars to an intern Fry-Revere knew. No way. Anyway, the author strongly guided the woman against it because, well, because it is against the law with major penalties."

Jon told her he thought their own story was far better.

CiCi smiled—he knew her so well. "The author described the kidney patient as corpse gray. They stayed in contact until he died."

"Am I corpse gray?"

"Yeah, you are. I hadn't thought much about it, but yeah, a bit haggard looking. This is the author who investigated kidney sales in Iran. She supports what Eva said and even mentions the tyranny of the gift."

"Do me a favor—don't mention Eva's name at dinner. Do you think you can come to the table?"

Over dinner, CiCi announced she was going to make herself a green cape with green awareness ribbons on it for the scuba club's Halloween party. She was going as the Caped Organ Crusader to promote awareness. Again, Jon told her she needed her head examined.

Just as CiCi took her last bite, the phone rang. It was Lark. "But?" asked CiCi. "When?" A moment later, she put down the phone and smiled at Jon.

"But?" asked Jon.

"We're a match." She paused a moment and then added, "I'm not pressing charges."

Chapter 38

September 11, 2015, Alex's Lab at CTMRI, San Antonio, Texas:

The day after Ethan's exploratory research under her blouse, Alex found sitting in her office attending to work troublesome. Dr. South came and went out of her lab just to torment her, or so it seemed. Once, when no one was looking, he bent down to pick up a little piece of paper near Alex's foot. On his way back up, he reached under her skirt. She jumped a little and giggled. Wanting to rip off his clothes right then, she, instead, settled for her own taunt. It was his turn to jump and giggle.

"Yeah," she purred to him, "men giggle." She could never admit this behavior to Maura.

"Tonight," he said, not asked.

She pulled her mind back to the present and turned her attention to her phone and the email from Kamini, who currently struggled with programming the team's recent discoveries. Since Alex's role fell directly under Dr. South in the hierarchy, Kamini approached Alex with problems rather than Dr. South to avoid South's short temper. For this one, however, Kamini would have to go to the boss.

Alex sat back and relished the wonder of their work. Stem cells in the fetus innately knew when and where to form an eyeball, or a heart, or a penis, or a vagina. Or make a tubule to filter blood. Occasionally mistakes happened in nature, but what a miracle those cells were. Now, Alex's team was working on their own miracle, and it was this artificial world that challenged the cells.

She visualized the stem cells as the hands of God, which morphed into the hands of Dr. South taking her clothes off. Alex decided she needed to see Ethan in his very private office—she would pay him back for the way he teased.

Through the closed door, Alex heard his familiar roar. "Dammit, Kamini, I already told you I can't afford to keep pissing around with this." It had to be about Kamini's earlier email. "Incompetence! How can it be so difficult to change one fucking algorithm?"

Moments of silence passed. Alex assumed Kamini was trying to explain how programming worked. That was never a good thing to do with Dr. Ethan South—he had no desire to be taught; he just wanted the work done. Perhaps, right now would not be the right time to see her man, so she headed back to her office and called Maura for lunch. She thought she might tell Maura about the flirtations, but not his name, and certainly she could never admit that she had let him unhook her bra in the office.

****

"And she's not around?" Maura asked Alex as they settled into a table away from the busy coffee center.

"No, the amazing Nurse Nan is *persona absentia*. We honestly have not seen the mystery woman other than that quick meet-and-greet." Alex stirred her non-existent sugar in her black coffee.

"This really has you bugged, but it's probably because her role doesn't directly involve the research team."

Alex caught herself leaning in toward Maura to be sure no one else heard her. "I don't think so. He told us Nan was a surprise gift from HR, but you told me he budgeted for her a while back."

"Okay, this whispering nonsense has me spooked. Forget Nefarious Nan. I want the scoop on Mystery Man. It's been a month. Is lover boy still around?"

Alex felt the blood rush to her face.

"Ha!" screamed Maura if a whisper could be screamed. "Spill it, Girlfriend."

"You said you didn't want to hear any more. You said you wanted to keep your job."

Maura waved her hand around as if erasing what she had said before and sat quietly with her eyes piercing Laura's mind.

With her face growing hot, Alex revealed the close body rubs and necking in the office but left it at the middle school level. She ended with an "and," then waved her hand as if to say, *and that's all.*

"Oh, no you don't, Dr. Alexandra Segel. You have more to tell me."

Before she knew it, Alex was telling everything, almost, and Maura was stamping her feet and clapping. And then Alex said *Ethan* instead of *he.*

"Wait! What? Ethan?" Maura's feet planted firmly on the ground, no more stomping and clapping. She pointed her finger at Alex, but the words did not come out. Finally, she stated more than asked, "Your mystery man is Dr. Ethan South?" This was Maura's great HR nightmare, and her best friend had brought it to her. "He's your boss." She separated each word, choking on *boss.*

"I am a consenting adult woman."

"Executives get fired for this."

"It can't be so wrong. He's not offering me any promotion or anything. Oh, Maura, leave it alone. I'm so happy."

"Yet." Maura obviously struggled to keep her voice calm. "End it."

"Stepping on my joy once again." Standing up and shoving her chair away from the table, Alex was not so calm. No one was close enough to hear her, but she felt eyes look her direction. "Come on, Maura," she heard herself whining. Maura was judgmental, but she was always right.

Taking a breath, Alex said she would be careful and pleaded with Maura to drop it. She promised to tell Dr. South they could not continue. Maura finally consented and pinkie swore to secrecy as Alex promised herself she would never tell Maura about any more of her romance adventures.

****

That evening after work, Ethan walked into Alex's office with papers in his hand. The lab had cleared out except for custodians. Earlier in the day, while they chatted at the coffee center near her lab, he reached past her for a mug, and she was sure he discovered the lacy bra with very thin lace deliberately worn under a very thin blouse. Finally, behind the closed and locked door, he peeled off Alex's blouse. His gaze headed directly to the lace. He was a fine surgeon, but it took his bumbling hands an eternity to maneuver the front clasp and throw the bra across the desk to join her discarded blouse.

Imitating moves she had seen on television, she pushed him into her over-sized office chair. The choreography in the shows worked much more gracefully. The rest of their clothing came off.

Maura certainly would not hear about the chair sex.

Without so much as a smile, he reminded her they had to appear professional at work, so they checked each other's attire and prepped to leave. Gathering papers to look like they had been discussing research matters, he returned to his charming ways. He softly caressed her hips and instructed, "No panties at work."

"As you wish." She tried to speak with her sexiest breathy voice, but the attempt fell flat. "Oh God," she said as she turned away so he couldn't see her blush. "I sound like a high school girl."

He grinned. "Skirts."

They walked out of the office and exited the building as if they were talking about their research. Alex's eyes went straight for the *chariot of fire* and then saw him searching for observers while they headed to his car. She told herself he was making sure they looked professional, no gossip for Maura's ears. He opened the door for her and helped her slide in. Silence. Awkward. Alex wished the old-style bench seats were popular again because she really wanted to sit close to him. Bucket seats were for old married people—the automobile industry missed the point.

They drove only a half-mile—it would have been a short romantic walk diagonally through the park from their lab to his condo. When the Tesla rolled up the slight hill to the entrance, the door attendant startled Alex, opening the door and gently guiding her out of the car as soon as the car came to a stop.

"Good evening," Ethan said as he bounced out, throwing the key at the valet, who had obviously practiced this routine several times. The massive carved glass door glided open like the doors to the Emerald City. Ethan escorted Alex through the lobby to the elevator.

"I'll take you on a tour later." He took Alex's hand and urged her forward. "I'm starved, so let's head on up."

Once in the elevator, the uniformed attendant pressed eighteen without asking. The brass on the elevator was so shiny Alex could check her hair and straighten her skirt with her reflection.

The door to his apartment was just a door, which seemed odd given all the glamor of the building.

"Welcome to my home," he said, breathing gently on her neck. "I must apologize for the lack of decor—it's the life of a bachelor who lives at work."

Alex smiled to herself—she knew Ethan was out the door well before she left each night, but bachelors had a reputation for stark furnishings. "Dinner? Shall we?"

They made an obligatory move toward the kitchen. Alex was the one who caused the distraction as she caressed his body. With no further delay, they headed to the bedroom instead. Tossing her on the bed, he began with kisses on her toes and headed up her thighs. After two hours of amazing sex, they blew off the kitchen and ordered pizza.

When their order arrived, Ethan spread a towel picnic style on the bed and slouched around it.

Savoring a mouthful of artichoke, spinach, and eggplant with white sauce on the perfectly crisp pizza from Girardo's Wood-Fired Pizza Palace, Alex needed to help her man focus. "We really need to work out a contingency plan to honor the Senator's deadline."

"Well, aren't you the mood breaker?" She did the hurt puppy look, so he corrected himself. "No, you're right. This is why I pay you."

"Uh, for the research. Let's be clear."

Ethan nearly choked. "Now," he said with his wine glass ready for a toast, "to the greater good."

"The greater good." Alex looked around the room and at her handsome knight—magic had entered her life.

Between bites of pizza, they reviewed the tremendous progress the team had made and how close they were to success. Alex remarked about the odd pillow talk, but Ethan told her kidneys were sexy. They come in pairs, and they look happily at each other their entire lives, until they don't. His charm worked, so they continued shop talk. Their concept had worked in mice, pigs, and even monkeys when they had living participants. However, remodeling deceased organs—no matter how fresh the source—failed. The stem cells occasionally seeded, but there was no growth; and within days, the renewed kidney did not just fail, it necrotized. Dead.

"Tweedledee and Tweedledum decided the deceased kidneys lost the grams of life's spirit," announced Alex.

"Come again?" asked Ethan. "Maybe we need to back off the wine, or sex, or both."

Forming her best pouty face, she slugged him in the arm. "Like the movie *21 Grams*. The Tweedles. You've met them. Jennifer and Yameekah?" She saw no recognition. "In my lab? I've told you about them." Nothing. "Anyway, the Tweedles decided there must be something about death that takes the stimulus from the IPS cells."

"Tweedledee and Tweedledum decided this?"

"Now you are being condescending."

"*C'est moi?*"

Alex wanted to slap him or kiss him or something, but she pressed on. "We need a living kidney."

"Had one. And it got away, thanks to incompetence."

Alex noticed with amazement Ethan had not added his usual expletive. "We may just have to tell our brave recipient," Alex conceded.

"And lose the Senator's support? That is her fucking father."

The expletive returned. "Perhaps another desperate transplant patient will take the risk." Alex wished she could rewind—she now sounded like Maura.

"Certainly. Desperate, old transplant patients are a dime a dozen." With a smirk and a pregnant pause, he squeezed his fist and released. "That will not solve the problem for the Senator's deadline. *Dead* line? Did I say that?"

Alex booed him, then took her own pregnant pause. "A living donor?"

"How would that help?"

"Sarah Wang's polymer coating holds the form while the kMS cells continue maturing. We already assume the recipient will need dialysis for a few days until the cells reach full maturity, just like with the pigs. She found she can also coat the blood vessels. We need to stall and do the real thing later. For now, we just need proof of concept. If we could find a donor with a close match, we could coat it with Sarah's polymer to keep his body from rejecting for just a little while. Buy some time."

"Use a faked remodel? Someone else's kidney and pretend it's the Senator's dad's?" Ethan pushed up onto his elbow and stared at her face.

The dismal talk depressed Alex. They couldn't possibly get the polymer on every surface. Were they accepting defeat? No, they were more determined than ever. Wine and more bedroom action helped to lighten her mood. Just as they reached complete exhaustion, Alex sat straight up. "Jimenez's team had success."

"So? Her idea is pointless. It would solve rejection, but it does not solve supply." Then Ethan caught on. "Tweak a donor kidney's antigens so that Estes's body thinks it is his own. How did you hear it worked? She has released no news yet."

"Amir let it slip the other day. They're not ready to go public, but it would solve our problem if—a big *if*—we got her cooperation. The process isn't ready for clinicals, so she would never consent."

"You're friendly with this Amir?"

"We talk in the hall. I think he's smitten with me because I say hello to him. He's a nice kid."

"Would he get you the research for us to duplicate?"

"No, I'm sure he's not that smitten. But what if we got it on our own?" Alex asked.

Ethan smothered her neck in kisses.

Alex was still plotting. "Of course, we would need a living donor, so we are back to square one, even if we get Jimenez's work."

Time was running out for them. They needed to show success, even if the old man died soon after—he already had a history of heart issues. If they just got a kidney into him that looked like the one they had removed, and if he lived a couple of weeks—or even a few days—with a functioning kidney. If.

"Leave the donor to me," Ethan said as he smothered her in kisses and fell asleep.

Amused that the handsome doctor snored offensively, Alex headed to the kitchen for a drink of ice water. She wondered if the others on the team would accept the faked kidney. As she opened the refrigerator, she decided the others wanted success as much as she did and would agree they needed to buy some time. In the refrigerator, the typical bachelor staples—a couple of six packs of beer and classy lunch meat—revealed Ethan's plan all along was to order out, no cooking by him. She smiled. A kidney switch was the only way. She felt herself get warm all over, grabbed her water, and headed back to wake up her super lover for more passion in the name of the greater good.

No, she would not tell Maura about sex in the office chair.

Chapter 39

September 15, 2015, Seattle, Washington:
Neither CiCi nor Jon practiced patience well. CiCi had dealt with the transplant complexities for only three months, and she knew Jon's experience with one delay after another took its toll—his body showed it. They matched, and the Institute had evaluated everything possible, but CiCi was sure they would find something else to delay her donation. She might have had an ingrown toenail ten years ago that would stop the transplant. But if they told her she was a match, then they meant to follow through.

"Relax," she told herself. She could hear Jon's voice in her head. "It is what it is."

Jon decided he needed to see his stepdaughter, Kelly, and her family in Washington state. If the transplant happened, he wanted to see them before such a significant surgery. If it didn't happen, he wanted to see them before he grew even weaker. Nurse Lark gave CiCi a tentative surgery date for the end of September, early October. She emphasized *tentative* but did say it wouldn't be earlier. CiCi decided that gave the clinic time to think of something else to disqualify her as a donor. She had made it past the cardiologist, the endocrinologist, the oncologist, the gynecologist, the gastroenterologist, the dermatologist, and the ophthalmologist. She wondered how many *ologists* were still out there and learned most donors didn't need so many. Jon said she judged unfairly since they had found all those areas of concern before telling them she was a match.

Whatever the reason for the delay, Jon had a couple of weeks to see his family. Both he and CiCi hesitated for him to fly alone, but they had never traveled together. Jon no longer had the funds to travel, but, in his day, he had slept in five-star hotels and ate what CiCi called white-linen-tablecloth food.

"I lived in a tent and ate nutrition bars," CiCi reminded him when they planned the trip. She feared he wouldn't enjoy traveling the way they could afford. Besides, too much time together would make them crazy.

They were great housemates but not of like travel minds. This trip to Washington, though, could work since they would stay at his daughter's home and only for a few days. The four grandkids were seven and younger. The youngest was only six weeks old and the reason his daughter hadn't been to see him in Texas. CiCi would love the kids, and Jon would be terrified. His daughter was eight when he married her mom—what did he know about rug rats? CiCi couldn't imagine hosting a dying man and his friend six weeks after a C-section. Kelly was Super Daughter.

CiCi had difficulty letting go of the time Jon passed out while they shopped for flooring. It was a low blood-sugar thing caused by his kidneys not doing their metabolic balances, easily fixed with a soft drink, but the event still scared CiCi. He even quit driving after that. There were three incidents within a month but nothing since. She believed him when he said he could tell something was coming and would eat. She stashed sugar candies in the cars, in her purse, in his bedroom, beside the couch, everywhere. There were a dozen orange juice sippy packs in the refrigerator. They both feared if he passed out in an airport during a layover, there would be ambulances and hospitals involved. She had to go with him to Washington.

Airplanes and the thought of airplanes took Jon to his happy place, always had. In his wealthy days, he owned his own Cessna 414 that seated seven passengers and the pilot in plush cream leather seats. He flew his family across the U.S. in his personal

259

plane. CiCi, on the other hand, delighted herself in cheap economy seats with a take-off to anywhere (the more layovers the better because there would be more take-offs). Jon was not so thrilled with the cattle call boarding into the tiny, uncomfortable seats of commercial airlines. This time, to CiCi's relief, he loaded up his Ginseng Oolong tea made with hot water from Starbucks and accepted his ride with grace.

Seattle was cold, at least to the thin-blooded Texans—the rest of the world would call it refreshing. Jon had always been the hot one at CiCi's house, turning the AC lower and freezing her into a throw blanket sausage. But after his kidneys failed, he lost so much muscle mass that cool temperatures affected him. The two never slept together at home, but his daughter's place was small, with only one guest room and one bed. CiCi joked about placing a bundling board in the bed. As they lay there the first night, fully dressed because they thought they were freezing, Jon shivered so badly his teeth clattered. CiCi gave up pretenses and threw herself on top of him, giving him her body heat. And that was how they spent the night, sound asleep.

Flying his entire adult life, Jon had accumulated over 8,000 piloting hours. CiCi didn't know if that was significant, but, when he announced it in front of other pilots—such as the astronaut he jockeyed with one afternoon—it impressed them. He could fly anything, except the space shuttle—the astronaut humbled Jon with that one. With his earlier diabetes and dependence on insulin, he lost his pilot's medical release for years, but regained it after his gastric bypass. The kidney thing took him out again—he knew not to bother scheduling his appointment for his annual flight physical.

Jon's bucket list had one item left. He wanted to introduce his seven-year-old grandchild, Nate, to the cockpit. Jon didn't tell him what they were going to do because he wanted to avoid fear. Since CiCi had never been in a private plane, she got to tag along. As they drove to the airport, Jon released a little information at a time to the boy. When they drove past a fire station, Nate announced he would rather see a fire truck than see planes.

CiCi gained new respect for Jon—his patience surprised her. Little by little, he and Nate ventured closer to the planes, first just watching helicopters land, then climbing around inside the little Cessna. Finally, Grandpa asked Number One Grandson if he wanted to taxi down the runway a little—he said nothing about taking off. Nate agreed that might be fun. CiCi kept quiet and buckled Nate and herself into the back seats. The headsets were a big thumbs up as far as the kid was concerned.

When Nate's parents agreed to let him fly with Grandpa, Jon arranged for an instructor to ride with them in a tiny Cessna four-seater. Super Pilot Jon—commercially licensed to fly helicopters, gliders, and airplanes, even instrument rated as a flight instructor—couldn't pilot this plane on his own. It would be deadly if Jon passed out in mid-air. All Nate knew was they were going to taxi. Then Grandpa suggested they fly just a little. That went well, so they went a little higher. Nate was sold. Planes were awesome. When Grandpa asked through the headset if Nate wanted to pilot, CiCi couldn't get the kid out of the seat belts fast enough. Nate climbed over CiCi and into Grandpa's lap before she could get the headset off him.

The kid did well. He paid attention to the lesson about how a gentle nudge moved the plane a lot. Nate asked Grandpa if he could go higher, so they did. This time, *gentle* didn't happen. The plane shot straight up for just a second until Grandpa got control again. CiCi lost her stomach and wondered if they would live to see a transplant. Grandpa Jon had a wonderful day, even if he had a pilot babysitter with him.

Other days involved family breakfasts and dinners Chef Jon wanted to make. As usual, Jon cooked great food and dirtied every pot and pan in the kitchen. CiCi and A++ son-in-law Bryce did the dishes. One night Kelly had a friend watch the kids while the four adults took a night for sushi. It seemed the proper thing to do—the Pacific coast required it. Remembering the forthcoming anti-rejection drugs he would take in order to keep the new kidney, Jon celebrated his last days with an immune system by eating three dozen raw oysters, along with Hamachi and other sushi favorites.

During CiCi's childhood, her parents often told a family story of gooey duck hunting. Not a duck, geoduck clams (pronounced *gooey duck*) ranged from two to eight pounds and flourished in the muck of Puget Sound in Washington state. Their snake-looking heads poked out of the sand, working as syphons in the murky water. The clams could live 150 years and were among the longest-living animals in the world. And these gentle creatures, looking like miniatures of Jabba the Hutt, were a culinary delicacy on the West Coast and in Japan. Because CiCi was a toddler, everyone in the family remembered the hunt but her. If it weren't for the family movies showing the hunters with shovels over their shoulders running across the cold, muddy sound to grab a clam by the neck, CiCi would have thought the tale was a snipe hunt. The syphon could stretch three feet, so one hunter held the neck while a partner dug as fast as possible to get under the body. The syphon was too big for the clam to retract into the shell, so once captured, it looked like a banana hanging out of the shell. No, much more phallic than a banana. As an adult, CiCi felt certain her mom loved the story so much because it defied her mother's stiff upbringing to run onto the sand to grab stretching *phalluses*.

One of CiCi's students went to Evergreen University in Washington, and surprise to CiCi, the mascot was the geoduck.

> *Go, Geoducks go,*
> *Through the mud and the sand,*
> *Let's go,*
> *Siphon high, squirt it out,*
> *Swivel all about,*
> *Let it all hang out ....*

The melody sounded more like an alma mater than a fight song, but with lyrics like that, who wouldn't fear the mighty geoduck? At least a geoduck sounded like a better mascot than the U.C. Santa Cruz banana slug.

Jon knew the story well and phoned all the sushi houses in Seattle to find one that had gooey duck on the menu, an expensive gesture of gratitude, no, love.

Bryce had never eaten sushi—raw seemed a ridiculous idea to him, but he did well. They did stop to buy the poor guy a fast-food hamburger on the way home. Jon had lived such a privileged life that exposing others to new experiences excited him as much as his own firsts. The Washington trip satisfied many of Jon's needs before he died.

CiCi watched as the week progressed. Their bedroom was upstairs. In the mornings, Jon was careful to bring down everything he needed for the day. The first day, he climbed upstairs to take his naps, but CiCi noticed he began spending his daytime naps in the downstairs recliners. The grandkids refrained from climbing on Grandpa while he slept through their youthful noise— Mom and Dad had done well with them. By the end of their stay, CiCi had to help Jon up the stairs for bed at night. He had no strength left, and his legs hurt. He didn't talk about it, but she knew. She massaged them before he slept for the night.

"Soon," she told him. It scared her when she realized she didn't know what *soon* would bring.

Chapter 40

September 21, 2015, CTMRI Lab, San Antonio, Texas:
During one of Ethan's daily panty checks in Alex's locked office, he and Alex decided to go forward with breaking into Jimenez's lab to photograph the hard copy research. Cell phones made that so easy, no need for a copy machine.

"You get Kamini to teach you how to hack Jimenez's files," suggested Alex, pulling him close. "She's so eager to please you, and she thinks you're disappointed in her work."

"Okay." Ethan grinned and then returned to his serious, strategic look. "Kamini had worked as part of the hospital's security camera engineering while we waited for salary approval."

Alex inhaled his Clive Christian cologne. How could he make office conspiracy sound sexy?

Ethan continued, "In the old days, Jimenez would have taken the work with her on her laptop each night, but now hospitals store everything on the server."

Each word seduced Alex as she played with his lab coat and sucked on each button delicately.

Lifting her chin and leading her away from the buttons heading down the coat, Ethan walked her through what they would need to pull this off. "Dr. Jimenez's computer will be a snap. I'm a computer hobbyist and know some programming here and there, but all we really need is Jimenez's password that is most likely written on a sticky note lying on her desk."

The hospital server was rated as safe, but in an era when hackers stole details of over one hundred million people in what authorities called security fraud on cyber steroids, no information was safe. Nine major banks and the Dow Jones were hacked. Then hackers exposed the Anthem Insurance health records for eighty million people. Ashley Madison's discreet adultery website led to suicides.

Ethan straightened his lab coat and looked away from Alex. "I will need help with the hospital's servers for surgical scheduling. Kamini will be perfect for that. Good catch, Dr. Alexandra."

Alex's job was to pump Amir some more to learn Jimenez's nightly work schedule and if they had duplicated their success. "It just so happens I'm already on that." Alex slipped Ethan's perfectly clean and starched lab coat off him. Ethan had been assisting in surgery that day, so he wore scrubs. Alex loved scrubs. "Amir is thrilled every time I pay attention to him," she said. "Anyway, he has a problem with honoring proprietary information." Scrubs had only a draw string holding them on.

"And…?" Ethan choked. He picked her up and took her to a cleared spot on her desk. She loved that she had Ethan begging. Victoria's Secret deserved a thank you note.

"They had a seventy-five percent success rate on every trial." She grinned as Ethan pulled back to stare at her, jaw hanging open. She gently guided him back to her. "And, drum roll please, Jimenez told her team they were all to go home early every day this week to celebrate. And they are taking half of the next week off—the lab will be closed. Jimenez is going to San Francisco to confer with a software guru about a minor change she wanted on the AFM for better CRISPR accuracy—that might improve that seventy-five percent. She'll be gone almost two weeks."

"Well, that'll work." It was time to stop talking and celebrate their plans.

When they finally slowed their breaths, Alex hugged him tightly against her, but she could see he was strategizing again. His mind was always working. "What's up?" She snuggled her face into the nape of his neck.

"If the old guy rejects, we'll make it look like a heart attack or a hospital infection. No one will question it. A little succinylcholine might work, doesn't leave much of a trace, or potassium chloride for a pulmonary embolism. Then he'll be cremated, as he has already requested."

Alex pushed away.

Ethan pulled her back. "They will never perform an autopsy on the old guy. Everyone at the hospital knows how fragile he already is, and, besides, they know how much we need him."

Alex let her arms fall limp beside her and squeezed her eyes shut. Getting caught was what he thought repulsed her? Not the murder? Breathing so fast she feared hyperventilating, she tried to stand, tried to walk away. But she froze.

Ethan grabbed her again just as the room swirled around her. "The man is going to die soon, anyway."

Alex understood this. He was on the fast-track medical trial approval because his life expectancy was short. Even the Senator realized that. Alex snuggled back into Ethan's body. She needed time to think clearly with so much happening so quickly. She noticed she hadn't made time for Maura recently. Might be a good thing.

****

Dr. South didn't make it to the office that next day. He left word there was a medical emergency involving a clinic overseas and that he would go there in the next few days to consult with the doctors. He needed this day in town to get things in order. First on the day's list was a call to Nan.

Since Ethan's first approach weeks earlier, Nan had been doing her homework, mining the clinic personnel for information in case something could be useful. Private information could do wonders to keep disgruntled people in line. Early in their friendship, Julissa told Nan about the day she sat on the curb with Brianna and

266

Amethyst while Eva poured out her story. And right after Nan's last visit with Ethan, Julissa mentioned Eva's bold statement that she "knew people." Acting innocent and intrigued by such a story, Nan asked if Julissa recalled names.

"Marco and Chris or Carl or Charles or some name starting with a *C*," answered Julissa.

"How does Eva plan to find these two guys?" she pressed.

"Hell, I don't know. She's an odd one. She talked about a woman named Carrie Brunn or Brown—I didn't believe any of it. That's all I know. I gave her my phone number. She never called."

Julissa appeared genuinely sad when she had no more to reveal. It was obvious to Nan this was a woman who thrived on drama. "But you said Brianna and Amethyst found her a place to live. Did they tell you where?" Nan was good at prying. She had the gossip whisper down pat and played the role perfectly.

"Yeah, I heard them talking about a shelter not too far from the clinic."

As Nurse Nan recounted the story to Ethan, she heard his car's road noise come to a stop. She had his full attention. Nan added that this had to be the Eva who *died* in the Maun fire that made the headlines in Gaborone years ago. Nan was certain Julissa would love to be part of the intrigue ahead, even if only for the value of more gossip. They would let her think they could get Eva a kidney.

This was the organizing Ethan needed to do this day. Now they needed to pick up Julissa, find the shelter, and hope Eva was still there. They would drive Nan's car since it was less pretentious than the doc's Tesla.

****

Eva had been sulking in her room ever since *Officer* Stan *ordered* her to stay away from CiCi. This time as she fumed, she hit her pillow until the seams burst and sent foam bits floating. Who did he think he was? He wasn't even a cop anymore. The bitch CiCi didn't need

267

to sic him on her. When she realized she couldn't save CiCi, she stayed away on her own. She had told herself she was desperate, but that wasn't an excuse. She was a good person, and good people don't non-kidnap.

When the house manager told her she had guests, Eva didn't want to leave her room, especially not to see Julissa. But as soon as Julissa introduced Dr. South as a nephrologist doing work in kidney research and transplants, Eva's mood turned around. She would meet with them.

Julissa had to get back to work, so Dr. South ordered an Uber for her. Nan whispered compliments to her for finding Eva and told her to say nothing to the others at the clinic because that might ruin Eva's chances for the transplant. The clinic wouldn't think favorably of Dr. South overriding their decision. Julissa promised to keep mum as she Ubered off.

With Julissa out of the way, the three headed to lunch at Denny's where they talked in a back booth, the doctor's treat, of course. As soon as Dr. South placed a twenty in her hand, the server was quick to allow privacy and serve only when called.

Holding Eva's hand and looking at her kindly, Dr. South began. "Eva, I think I can get you a healthy kidney."

Eva pulled her hand away at once as her eyes teared up. She didn't know whether to thank him or scorn him for a bad joke. "But how? Every clinic has turned me down. They think I sold my kidney. They know I'm a drug addict."

Dr. South sat quietly as she ranted about how she was misjudged.

"There's no transplant for me." She finally went silent.

He matched her silence with patience.

Eva heard dishes drop and a child crying from the other side of the restaurant. She bit off a fingernail and finally broke. "How? Why?"

"You're going to have to trust me," he said.

She bit at another nail, which she had already chewed down to the quick. There was something about the doctor's face, something familiar. He had that generic hot doctor look, but that wasn't it. She looked at Nan, who nodded reassuringly. Why Nan, who was a stranger, nodding *yes* would make it all right, Eva couldn't guess. But then, she had found sanctuary with other kind strangers in Botswana and in Iran, so why not? "Well, hell, what else can I do? I'm at the end."

"Eva, I can give you the kidney, but I need your help," Dr. South said.

And there it was, the catch, why they met at Denny's instead of a clinic. "What could I ever do for you?"

"I'm doing critical research to remodel damaged kidneys. That means I can remove a kidney, strip it to its bare minimum and then rebuild it with stem cells from the patient."

"Can't be done," Eva spat. This was all too good to be true.

"Let me explain."

Dr. South had a soothing voice. Nan reached over and rubbed Eva's shoulder lightly. Normally, Eva would have jerked away, but she wanted so badly for this to be true that she leaned into the caress, surprising herself. There was something about South, somewhere in her memories. She looked at him some more. Nothing.

Dr. South continued, "It can be done. We did it with mice, pigs, and monkeys. Humans are next, but I only have had deceased kidneys to work on and no way to implant the remodeled kidney into a living person." Dr. South looked at Eva in silence for a long moment. He rolled his head and started again. "We have a living patient volunteer, but we had an accident at the lab with his kidney. It was going very well until then."

"And what does this have to do with me?"

"You know people, people who can help me buy a kidney."

Startled at first, Eva then put it all together. In the clinic, she had announced to the world she had connections with the illegal market. Years ago in Botswana, when she read the note from Baruti, she vowed she would only need Carrie Breun's information if she were on her way to escort Ms. Breun to hell. She trembled— had that moment arrived? "That was a lot of talk," she told Dr. South. It was time to get up. Time to run. Now! But she didn't leave.

"Eva." It was Nan's turn to charm. "I know all about Charles, Marco, and Carrie Breun. I, too, had heard of them when I worked in Gaborone. My family is from Molepolole."

"That's close to Gaborone," said Eva quickly, like discovering an old friend. Then her suspicion returned. How did these people know so much about her, a nobody?

"Yes." Nan took a slow breath. "Eva, I heard the story of the fire in Maun. I was in Gaborone at the time, and a friend from Maun came to visit. I heard Marco and Charles left and continued their work in Brazil. The story was that you died in the fire. It is a miracle you're here now."

Eva bowed her head for just a moment of defeat and then sat up straight. "Miracle? Carrie Breun is an evil bitch. She preys on the poor."

Nan spoke with the care of a therapist. "Yes, she doesn't work with the finest outcomes—it's good that you saw what was happening and got out of it. Julissa has told us about your excellent work in Iran and how you care so deeply about the donors, something Ms. Breun didn't do."

Eva sat hypnotized, validated and terrified at the same time.

Nan continued. "We're trying to develop a technique that will bypass the illegal market completely and not put donors at risk ever again."

"Could this really happen?"

"Yes," answered Dr. South. "We are very close, but we need your help."

"What do you need?" asked Eva, scared but stronger now.

"We need two kidneys: one for our research to replace the one we lost in our lab accident, and one for you. We need to contact Carrie Breun."

Before Eva could bolt, Nan jumped in. "Eva, wait. We recognize you hate this woman. But think about it. If we succeed, we will put her out of business for good. You can help us do this. If we don't succeed, she'll continue to do as she has always done, and you'll be her victim. Am I correct it was men working for her that caused the accident that led to your condition now?"

Eva relaxed a little. "I'm not sure my information is even current."

"All we can do is try. Please write it on this notepad."

Eva wrote while silently cursing and thanking Baruti for leaving her the note about Carrie Breun. Dr. South and Nurse Nan hugged her and thanked her, reminding her of the good that would come of this.

Eva returned to the shelter with an extra order of food from Denny's and hugs of encouragement. Nan assured Eva they would be in touch as soon as they learned more.

This remodeled kidney thing needed to work out quickly because this deal would use up what Dr. South had left of his wife's inheritance. He always kept her finances separate from any of his shady work, but these were desperate times. Nan assured him Carrie Breun would know how to get a kidney to Texas in enough time to form the fake remodel for the old guy. They would have a little over twenty hours before the kidney would start declining. With the right private jets, it would make it. The kidney didn't have to last long—the volunteer was old—it just had to work. Nan told him Marco and Charles were legends in the illegal market. They would get the job done if Eva had the correct information.

****

It only took three calls to get to Ms. Breun. The first one went to a person who knew a person. Next came her secretary, and finally the boss. Dr. South assumed his bill would include three burner phones. Ms. Breun announced she was aware of Dr. South's work in clinics all over the world and would be happy to help him.

"How did you learn about me?" she asked.

It was safe to assume her minions from the two earlier calls had already told her, but Dr. South played along. "Eva. She said she and her two companions worked for you for a time."

"Eva? How is that little bitch?"

"She's dying—needs a kidney transplant."

Hysterical laughter mixed with most unprofessional profanity passed through the phone. "Why would I help her? She almost destroyed me in Iran."

"This call isn't for her. I promised her a transplant if she would help me get the one that I need for my patient. I don't intend to get her one."

"My kind of negotiator. Yes, we can do business. It turns out Marco and Charles are on their way to Chennai now."

That was a setback—Ethan had hoped the two recruiters were closer. India would surely stretch the limits of viability, might as well have a cadaver.

Ms. Breun informed him he was welcome to ask another broker. "Do you have one?" More laughter.

To avoid a paper trail, Dr. South flew round trip that night to California for arrangements with Ms. Breun and to deliver the blood samples from the volunteer for the transplant crossmatch. He agreed with Ms. Breun that it was unusual and risky to bring a kidney to the U.S. She required the patient fly to the donor's country, or at least for the two to meet up in India. He explained he couldn't provide the patient's name due to top security and that this especially important man was extremely frail. He wouldn't make it on such a journey. She said she felt honored to work with

Dr. Ethan South. It would cost more and would require private jets, but, yes, she could get the kidney to San Antonio.

They continued with their negotiations, talking more about his time constraints. He reiterated the patient's extremely frail status and his importance. Speeding the process would cost more, but she was sure they could accommodate. Urgency made India an even better location, as her contacts there kept an extensive database of potential donors eager to help. A couple of days later, he would have to fly to India to meet Marco and Charles to approve the donor and oversee the removal process.

Ethan's patience broke. "What the fuck? I must be in San Antonio to perform the recipient's surgery."

Carrie calmly and in a most condescending voice reminded him again that he was welcome to take his business elsewhere. He was asking her to send an illegally obtained organ to America—she wanted him to make sure it was the correct kidney. Besides, she refused to be the only person at risk in this.

"Hell, you'll be sitting pretty here in California. What's your risk?" She was a cool cucumber, but he saw her stiffen ever so slightly. He calmed himself down and accepted his position.

Then she added one more sting to his plans. The kidney could fly privately, but he would have to fly commercially to put distance between himself and the cargo. She did finally agree to his returning as soon as the patient was processed into the hospital— her Indian surgeon would remove the organ. This would further remove him from the scene, so good for all. By catching a flight a few hours earlier than the kidney, he would be back home in time for his precious contraband to arrive. She hoped he could sleep well on a plane—it would be a long flight.

Hesitating to add to the pressure, he asked for something more. He would also need Charles or Marco to overnight express blood samples from the donor-to-be before the surgery to have everything in proper order. With that, she lifted her eyebrows and glared a bit. He interpreted the gesture to mean he had insulted her blood-typing efforts, but Ms. Breun accepted the request. Dr. South wasn't surprised when Ms. Breun said she could do this, but it would cost more. They finalized their agreement—Charles would send the samples when money transferred.

Back on the plane to San Antonio, Dr. South reviewed the plan so far. India would work—it had to. South had been there recently during one of his volunteer trips. He belittled Jimenez's work publicly, but there was a little tickle that kept at him. During his last visit, he used cadaver kidneys to study his own version of antigen tweaking to avoid rejection. Using deceased kidneys in the U.S., Jimenez always dealt with a shortage, and always competition, and always money. In India, South had easy access to plentiful cadavers for research. His tweak never quite succeeded, though. Frustrating. Living donors were more difficult to get—that's where the brokers came in, and they protected that territory. Eva's connection was a gift.

He did worry that the research team in the lab would balk at using a fake kidney, so he had Nan sift through the team's backgrounds for leverage. As usual, Nan was ahead of him. The plan sounded so complex, but it had a logical flow chart in South's mind. This could work.

****

The plan was in motion. As soon as he returned from his meeting with Carrie Breun, South spoke with Kamini privately. All set to apply his cunning charm as a woman's dream come true, he changed strategies when he found her already devising her own means to save their project along with the wretched lives of the poor victimized donors in developing countries. He added bits of flattery about her work around the world, and when she heard about the faked kidney plan, she was in. Kamini decided not to teach him to hack into Jimenez's files—she would do it herself. And, yes, it would be a breeze to bypass the security cameras while he entered Jimenez's office, if still necessary. Kamini was his own dream come true, far easier than his high maintenance lab queen Alex. Once these ladies had broken into Jimenez's files—too bad he would not be there for that—he would remind them of their participation should they want out.

Chapter 41

September 23, 2015, Chennai, India:

"So leave!" yelled Charles.

"Grow up," Marco said. "You're almost forty years old."

This argument had begun as soon as the two men arrived at the Chennai airport. They had passed through the modern glass-walled facility to step outside when Charles took in a deep sniff of air. "Ah, the scent of urinals and generic Pine-sol." Then, laughing at a crippled beggar sitting on a filthy piece of carpet, he exclaimed, "Kidney Land! We're back!"

Marco was fed up with Charles's carelessness and inhumanity and had told him so. Whenever challenges faced them, as in Iran or the fire in Botswana, Charles blamed everyone else. Even Charles's language was *dude* immature. And pointing at disabled people and laughing was wrong in so many ways.

"Dude! I'm tired of your better-than-thou shit!" shouted Charles.

"I'm not better." Marco danced around in a circle, eager to get on with the assignment. "Man, we'll be middle-aged soon—we should own homes, have families."

"Quit whining." When Charles turned his back, Marco tackled him. "Oh, you want to fight?"

As they rolled around on the sidewalk, blocking the entrance, a crowd of locals gathered, laughing at the Americans. When Charles punched Marco in the face, members of the crowd placed bets. One older man then pulled them apart and, in perfect British English, reminded them the Indian jails are not happy places. "I take pride in this clean, very modern airport and am offended by your lunacy. You think you can come here and disrupt? You are idiots." He convinced the two travelers to shake hands and move toward the taxis.

Marco, pressing a dirty napkin against a cut, seethed while Charles, acting as if nothing had happened, hailed a ride. "Chase Park Hotel," he told the taxi driver.

The man stared at him, so Charles repeated the instruction slowly, as if the driver didn't understand. The driver frowned and put the taxi in gear.

Charles started laughing at him. "Did your rich American tipper vanish, dude? Were you thinking The Leela Palace at a hundred and eighty-five dollars a night would be a much better choice with its five stars and view of the water?" Chase Park was nineteen dollars a night.

"Really? Chase Park?" asked Marco.

"It'll do. It's cheap and has air conditioning."

Charles began pointing out more amenities, such as the fine coffee offered in their lobby, but Marco interrupted. "When the AC works."

"It's on Old Mahabalipuram Road. Where we need to work, may I remind you? The road got renamed to Rajiv Gandhi Salai. Sophisticated, don't you think?"

"Whatever." Marco picked at dirt from the scuffle. Charles had always made the decisions, and Marco let him.

Kidney sales had been against the law in India since 1994, but it didn't take the resourceful Indians long to get back into business. The 2004 tsunami offered tremendous potential since desperate victims did anything they could to pay the bills. Now and then, the legislature tightened enforcement to show power, but it never lasted long. One crackdown occurred in 2008 following an enormous scandal in Delhi that involved Dr. Kumar who had a transplant *hospital* in his basement where he had worked for seven years. Marco wondered who in their right mind would go to a basement for a major surgery. It was probably that basement sleaziness that shook up the feds. Ms. Breun always kept her entrepreneurs busy and knew when to move them. She somehow could see the 2008 crackdown coming and sent Charles and Marco to South Africa, Brazil, and Iran, twice crossing paths with Eva.

They hadn't seen Eva since that day in the hospital in Iran. The authorities almost caught them, but these guys were survivors. Iran was Carrie Breun's mistake—she was in way over her head there. From Iran they went to Brazil—they did their best work in tropical locations.

Recently, in 2014, the Indian government tried again to set up new rules emphasizing no sales and requiring close connections between donors and recipients. Charles and Marco had been in the procurement business for ten years and knew how to work around the systems in the world's organ baskets. They were back in the land of people begging to have kidneys removed and for so little money.

Once again, Chennai was safe for the *red* market. Marco had chanced upon Scott Carney's book with that title in a swap meet in Brazil. Carney was spot on—the market was *red*: blood, livers, lungs, ligaments, tissue. Marco considered himself a kidney specialist. Changing the paradigm of his career path was the beginning of the end for Marco. Sick of the business and Charles, Marco decided this was his last trip—it was time to go home.

Exhausted by their long flight from Brazil, they fell straight onto their beds.

No sooner did they fall asleep than the phone rang.

Charles groaned and shot the finger at the phone when he ended the call. "This job will be different. This time, the recipient will stay in the U.S." Information was a matter of need-to-know, and Marco and Charles didn't need to know much. "The kidney doc at the hospital here will give us basic crossmatch needs to run through our database. Breun said the blood samples will arrive this afternoon via private jet."

The recruiters needed to deliver a donor with type O blood and specific match requirements to the hospital in Chennai early the next day.

"No problem," Marco said. "We have an entire day to find the perfect match." His sarcasm sliced the air so sharply Charles winced.

The American surgeon would fly in to approve the donor—then Charles and Marco had to stick around long enough to be sure the doc accepted it. They would be off to Mumbai before the locals knew anything had occurred. Marco told himself he would be off to Texas, to home.

The next morning, with the sun shining into their room, the hotel looked good. The bed was sufficiently comfortable and the bathroom en suite, a pleasant treat considering other places they had stayed. And the price was right. They headed downstairs to the lobby for a local breakfast of *masala dosa* in the hotel restaurant—nothing like rice, lentils, potato, and curry leaves to start the day. Marco longed for breakfast tacos.

During breakfast, Marco turned on the laptop. "We have Wi-Fi in this grand resort. Why don't we call the doc and have him email the match info we need? No need for us to drive an hour to the hospital."

"Well, aren't you thinking this fine morning? Clever idea, old chap."

Marco couldn't decide if that was a compliment or sarcasm. He pulled out his cell phone and gave the doctor's receptionist his email information. Carrie Breun was ahead of them and had arranged the night before for the info to be in their morning email. Charles had known this and was messing with Marco's head for the hell of it. The guys finished breakfast and headed to the hot spot work center that was just a designated table in the lobby. It turned out the great Wi-Fi advertised on *Rooms-n-Shit.com* was only in the lobby. The email with the crossmatch info waited for them.

Charles and Marco had built a donor list from earlier years. Carrie Breun then had other recruiters add to it. Of course, the list was never current—people changed their minds or moved or got resettled by housing boards or died. But it was a starting place. With excellent coffee, they set to work, planning to have a donor selected shortly.

Not to be. After searching the database for an hour, footwork was the only way to get the job done. This wasn't UNOS, after all. The Chennai doc had sent suggested names along with the email, but, if they used his referrals, they wouldn't make as much money because of his finder's share. If they found no one, they made no money and would super piss off Carrie Breun.

"Look," said Marco as the two headed out, armed with blood typing kits for the tedious work of going door to door. They had planned to offer a few rupees if a local recruited someone who matched closely enough to take to the hospital for further testing. But one glance out the door told them no need. Overnight, word had spread that the kidney buyers were in town. Someone had recognized them from earlier trips. People, mostly women, had already lined up.

"Dammit! We can't be this obvious. We must go inside somewhere. If these people know, the police will, too. Not that they really care. But they might want a share of the profits."

The hotel manager heard Charles and offered his services. He invited them to use their room. He told the enthusiastic volunteers to disperse and return through the back, reminding everyone they could face seven years in jail for organ sales.

The hotel manager negotiated a financial agreement with the two recruiters, but he would deny knowing anything about business in the room. Conducting personal business was against hotel policy—it was written on the website.

The air-conditioned privacy of their room was much better than walking the streets. Marco sent word through the volunteers that they looked for type O blood with no HIV or other STDs and that hospital testing would confirm that. Along with lining up to donate kidneys, these sellers had been donating blood to supplement government subsidies and panhandling for years—they knew their status and whether to waste their day hoping.

With the remaining people, Marco pre-assessed groups of five, pretending to sit casually around the coffee bar while discreetly going over the surgery, post-op care, and potential complications. He then escorted candidates upstairs where Charles performed the blood typing and drew vials of blood for cross matching. Marco took histories, blood pressures, and weight. In Tsunami Nagar, underweight was more of a concern than obesity. Interviews moved efficiently. Marco then headed back down the stairs for the next group of five while Charles organized the vials and prepared them for the hospital lab.

To help with the language barrier, they had a questionnaire written in Tamil. Tamil Nadu was the only state in India that still resisted adopting Hindi as the national language, more bother for the guys. Of course, written questions only helped if the volunteer could read. The potential donors helped each other gather the information. Had they ever been refused as a donor because of medical reasons? Did they have someone to care for them after the surgery? Do they suffer from depression? There were twenty-five questions, most of which were gratuitous.

Only a few remained to be screened, but, at noon, they took a break. Even the donors paused for the lunch they had brought with them.

Marco stretched, eager for an end. "This is great for our database. But we need to get this blood to the lab for further matching."

"And your brilliance astounds me yet again." Charles's snarkiness never changed. "You take what we have so they can start, and I'll finish here."

"You know," said Marco, almost too soft to be heard, "we aren't just buying a kidney; we're buying a piece of a human being, a person with a story."

"Oooh, so right, Eva." All these years later, and Eva still seeped into their lives. "What's with you, man? I need to ask Carrie for a new partner. We are buying life. Our way of life—how's your savings account doing?"

Marco was already heading up the hill with no desire to respond. He wondered just what savings account Charles had since he spent everything. Marco had enough for a flight home and two months of rent money.

That was when the self-appointed mayor of Tsunami Nagar appeared. "Did you tell them the truth?" He shouted in English with his thick Indian accent, but good enough for Marco to get the gist. "Did you tell them about post-op infections? How about severe scarring? And weakness until they finally die? Did you tell the ladies their neighbors will forever wonder what else they will sell if they butcher their own body? How about the thieving recipients who do not bother paying the rest of the agreement?"

The hotel manager rushed a cup of tea to the old man. Marco quietly sat with him at the sidewalk table. "Yes, we talk with them about complications."

"Complications?" The old man's eyes swelled with tears. "My son sold his kidney to pay for surgery for his wife. They were so young and had a small baby. Now he has a huge scar across the side of his abdomen and is too weak to work."

"When did he do this surgery?"

"Four years ago. The thief never gave him the other half of his money after the surgery, so he did not have enough money for his wife. She died. He had to go back to work too early and now can't work at all. He has no energy. My son and grandson have nothing. They beg. I have no more to give them."

Marco wanted to cry with the old man. Instead, he told him that now they performed the surgeries laparoscopically, explaining that meant small incisions which allowed for faster, healthier healing. Follow-up care was the responsibility of the donor.

"Follow-up? There was no money. You never finished paying. There is an hour's bus ride to the kidney clinics. Do you tell them that?"

The hotel manager brought the old man another tea and consoled him, allowing Marco to slip away to deliver the vials of blood to the lab. As he rode off in the taxi, he formed his plan to go to the airport while Charles was sleeping. He needed this last assignment, couldn't quit now.

They didn't need to send the rest of the blood for immediate tests—the lab called Charles before the end of the day with the names of two suitable matches. They had a backup if the first choice didn't show. A win for all. At the American doctor's request, they had already sent the blood draws to the U.S. lab. Next, they waited for the American surgeon to get to the hospital.

"The timing has to reduce out-of-body time as much as possible for an eight AM surgery in the U.S.," the lab technician explained.

Charles said he didn't care about that part, not essential to his need-to-know requirements.

They could send the afternoon blood samples the next day to go ahead with tests to add the information to their database if they wanted to invest the money. Charles said the blood type and initial screening they already had from their own pre-assessments would suffice for now. Marco didn't care. This would be his last donor. He thought about transplant patients who waited years for a suitable donor, and here there were so many offers they found two matches within the day.

The volunteers went home to wait for another wealthy jackass.

Chapter 42

September 23, 2015, CTMRI Lab, San Antonio, Texas:
"What about Jimenez's lab? You can't leave now." Alex wanted to shriek—he couldn't drop this on her—not now. Everything relied on getting a kidney, but she'd assumed her knight in shining armor would be there for the break-in. "You want me to head this? I don't know how." And now she caught herself sounding desperate, whining like a child. She was no baby, but really? Breaking into Jimenez's lab? Without him?

Ethan pulled her close and kissed her so tenderly, then pulled her in even tighter. While moving down her neck, little kisses the entire time, he reminded her this was her idea, and wasn't their research going to save thousands of lives when they succeeded? He told her he believed in her, and he knew she believed in their research. They just needed to get over this one hurdle. All would be well.

"But you said Kamini found us everything we needed. I didn't think we still had to break in." There was that whine again. She hated when her voice controlled her. She told herself she wasn't whining; she was scared.

Ethan pulled away, just for a moment.

She saw it before he could control his façade—anger, impatience, condescension. Quickly recovering, he gently sucked on her earlobe and started to take her lab coat off. But she had seen it. She pulled her coat back onto her shoulders and stared him straight in the eyes. "What do I need to do?"

"Kamini got us all the procedures, but they have prepared vials of antigen stripping compound they use. We don't have time to develop our own. We need them. It would help to have photos of the setup, too. It would be great if we had Amir."

"Amir is not possible." She paused, waiting for an argument. Nothing. "All right, I'll do this, with Kamini's help." She had her head back up, had to appear strong. "Ha! I can't believe Jimenez professionally labeled that stuff *Witch's Brew*." When she looked down again, she saw she had buttoned her lab coat. "I'm guessing Kamini can get me in and out with no one knowing."

Ethan gave a confident nod. An embarrassed flush surged through her—he had known all along she would concede and had already arranged the security with Kamini. Such a sucker underling. She missed Maura's voice, her conscience. No, she had to stop thinking—she always sabotaged her relationships with men. This one believed in her.

Ethan patted her on the shoulder and then love-tapped her butt. "I'll need three days to get the kidney—you and Kamini will have to set up a lab at my apartment."

"Your apartment?" Alex hadn't considered that—of course, they couldn't do such a thing in the Institute.

He told Alex to tell Kamini she had been there once for a small party to cover why she knew so much about the place.

"Our lab has most of the instruments we'll need. You and Kamini will need to take some small equipment to the apartment— just slip them out discreetly. Who would question you, anyway? I think you can do autoclave work and the AFM stuff here at night. The apartment is so close you can go back and forth. You'll need to get three vials of *Witch's Brew* and one gelatin tray prepped with Jimenez's gel formulation, and they can't be seen in our lab." He texted her a list of items she would need from their own lab. "And be sure Jimenez's tray has a USB plug to connect to our computer to monitor temps."

She felt like she should eat the text when he finished. "We can order a complete used AFM system on eBay for a mere twenty thousand dollars." Alex joked, but as soon as she said it, she wished they would. It would cut down on the back and forth. "Can Julissa help? In case we need someone to stand guard?"

"Kamini will help—you just point to what you need. I have concerns about how much Julissa should know, if anything." He paused. The hum of the air conditioner blasted into the room, causing a note taped to Alex's computer to flick constantly. He ripped it off and pounded it onto her desk so hard he rubbed his hand afterwards. He then turned back to her. "I really need you, Alex. You can do this."

"Sure, set up an illegal lab with stolen equipment in your apartment. No problem. I will get the sterile field right while I'm at it." She wanted to scream, to slap him, but she kissed him on the cheek instead. "Just so long as you can extrapolate from Jimenez's notes and do the work."

With that, Ethan opened her office door to let himself out. "It would be great," he added, "if Amir would volunteer to join us."

****

Dr. Ethan South had to hurry off to Carrie Breun again for final arrangements and then to India. The future of the project relied on this. His legacy relied on this. It was all going to work out. He would get to the hospital in Chennai just in time for the nephrectomy. Since he was a renowned research doctor in both the U.S. and India, Kamini got him the required authority to have the blood samples sent back to the U.S. ahead of him. The kidney would find its way back on a private jet.

****

While Ethan was away, Kamini and Alex set to work. They prepared Dr. South's apartment, clearing counter space and tables for workspaces. Of course, that didn't take any effort since Ethan was a minimalist. There wasn't much more than a toaster and a couple of candles sitting out. Kamini had the same reaction as Alex did the first time she saw it. Alex had to act surprised, too, saying it didn't look so baren with all the people and drink glasses at the party. They laughed that he must have rented the dinnerware because there were only six water glasses and two wine glasses in the cabinet. There were paper plates, but not much in the way of utensils. She'd been there all night twice and never noticed anything other than the bare refrigerator. They had ordered pizza both times. Other than wine, Italian dressing, and parmesan, they didn't need much.

Ethan had been gone a full day, and Alex read texts asking about her panties and, of course, a follow-up message reminding her to delete those texts at once, which she most certainly did right after she turned warm all over. She assumed he sent them when he had layovers during the flight—it was exciting that he thought about her when he had to be exhausted.

Alex accepted that she would have to use the stolen files as a guide to prepare the donor samples when they arrived Saturday morning. That part was straight forward—she supposed Ethan knew that and knew she could manage it. Kamini would get her into Jimenez's lab once to use the X-ray irradiator—five minutes would do it. It was the irradiation that gave Jimenez the successful tweaks, but it was the irradiator that caused failures, too. She needed some of the compound, but just a drop, not vials. No one would know they had been in there. Kamini created loops for the video, so no camera would catch them. And with her *borrowed* admin access, she could remove all records of door entries into the labs. Alex would appear to be working in her lab or clocked out during this time.

287

The second break-in frightened Alex, the one when she and Kamini would transfer the equipment. The women made their plans for this to happen Saturday afternoon, two days before Ethan returned with the kidney. It would be the weekend, so Jimenez's team wouldn't be there to notice the missing equipment. The kidney would be back late Sunday night, a few hours before Ethan. They would perform the final tweak with the kidney as he prepped for surgery, and equipment would be back into the lab Monday morning before anyone got there. They would return it to a different spot that could be blamed on a poor little intern. That scapegoat might be Amir.

In the meantime, Alex spent Friday in her lab studying Jimenez's protocol. With thoughts of how their day of theft would work, she took a break from her regular day and closed herself off in her office. The lab swaddled her like a baby—Alex snuggled in the walls of her sanctuary. She needed time to think. Her heart raced one of those chest-pounding Edgar Allan Poe heartbeats so hard Alex was certain all those around heard it. That was absurd, of course, since she was alone in her office with the viewing window turned to opaque. Ethan had sound-proofed the offices for proprietary reasons—wouldn't want an underpaid technician selling trade secrets.

Sitting quietly, calming her heart rate as Maura had taught her, Alex focused on the bare, perfectly clean wall across from her desk. That was when she saw it, a chip in the plaster, creating a dark hollow. She looked away, telling herself it was nothing, but couldn't stop herself from returning to it. The spot had grown in that moment. Alex took her ruler to measure it. It was just a flaw in the paint—she knew it didn't grow, but she measured it and logged the dimensions anyway: 4 cm by 2.9 cm. She had to climb on a chair to get as precise as possible but still had to eyeball it just a little.

"Come on, Alex," she told herself, "you're losing it." She sat back down in her chair and flipped through papers. Distraction was what she needed. But her eyes returned to the spot. Why hadn't she noticed it before? It was always there, painted over from the previous year. There was a flaw in her perfectly white clinical wall, a little thing. The building was not collapsing, she hoped.

She confronted it. She told it there was no power in it—paint had smothered its life. "But why didn't the maintenance team fill you?"

Some flaws don't get fixed—they just get covered up, to show up later. Maura had told her to fix that reporting problem when she first noticed it, but all she did was help cover it up.

She stared at the spot for the rest of the afternoon.

Chapter 43

September 24, 2015, Chennai, India:
Finally on board his flight, Dr. Ethan South settled in for fifty hours of flying. Who did this for a living? Occupation choices puzzled him when he noticed a steward instead of a stewardess preparing his drink. Ah, for the good old days before they were called flight attendants. It didn't matter—he saw the stewardesses as he entered. They had to be in their forties. He ordered a top shelf Scotch whisky neat but was certain it would be whatever the cheap airline CEO bastards decided saved them the most money.

To return with the kidney on Breun's private jet would have been nice, but Ms. Breun was right—he dared not chance proximity with the organ, skipping customs and immigration. Even though his team had discussed not including Julissa, they were short hands, so Nan instructed her to retrieve the kidney from Breun's plane and escort it to the lab where Alex would start work.

Still, he didn't even get first class all the way. He left San Antonio at noon. That worked out well because it gave him time to tie up details with Kamini's intel from Jimenez's files. During his three-hour layover in San Francisco, Carrie Breun would meet him for last-minute arrangements. That meant passing through security again, but not a problem. Layovers would allow him to text the girls. Unfortunately, he wouldn't get into Chennai until 12:05 AM two days later. Not two days, he reminded himself, there was the dateline change, so only one day later. The problem was, while in first class, his body thought it was afternoon and was not ready to sleep. Once he got to San Francisco, the ticket would degrade to business class, and his body would scream for a bed. Didn't people fly first class to India? The best return flight available was twenty-five hours, leaving at two in the afternoon the next day. Getting home around four in the morning would give four hours of leeway for his eight o'clock Monday morning surgery. Business class, not first class, to Houston soured his mood even more. This was the best his ten-thousand-dollar upgrade bought? The numbers mocked him. In a seventy-six-hour period, he would fly twenty-seven hours west, remove a kidney, then continue another twenty-five hours around the world. For now, he reconciled himself to accepting whatever drink the pitiful minion gave him—at least it would be in a crystal glass.

****

As Charles and Marco headed with the donor to the end of the road to catch their ride to the hospital, a jeep with four Indian soldiers pulled up.

Charles let out a string of curse words and looked at Marco. "This doesn't look humorous like it does in the movies."

Marco turned to Charles, wanting to finish what they had started at the airport. Too terrified to move, he told Charles to shut up. The two Americans threw up their hands while the old self-appointed mayor walked up and pointed to them. The soldiers informed them India didn't condone organ sales—it was their luck this was the day the local government tried to make a point. Someone high up must have been under pressure—the soldiers said a tenant had protested about being solicited. Of course, the soldiers explained while pointing rifles at the Americans, the Chennai hospitals were the finest in the world and would help their Israeli and American friends get excellent kidney transplants if they bring their donor/friend with them—most bring their good cousins from Brazil. The neighborhood was saved for now, but the promise of money would go to another developing location for a time.

"Too bad for the poor in Chennai," snapped Charles.

"Yeah, well, you, me, and our lovely donor are screwed," said Marco.

****

Though uncomfortable, the flight was uneventful—the layover and terminal change in Hong Kong went smoothly. Ethan sighed with relief that he had finally touched Indian soil without even noticing the elegant brass icons of Hindu gods and goddesses that made the passageways to security and airport exits look more like a museum than a corridor. Engrossed in his mission, he checked his phone texts.

PATIENT DECEASED!

"You're fucking kidding me," he said, louder than he intended. This was the prearranged signal to abort and get the hell out of Dodge. He looked around. Everything looked right.

Then another text: *Do not leave terminal! Go back now!*

Ethan had to process this. He could not just turn around and get back on his plane, and his flight wouldn't leave for another twenty-four hours. He needed a story. The trip was already peculiar enough to explain to Indian immigration because his stay was so short. Fortunately, he had performed medical charity work in the country not too long ago, so there was a record of him, and he could say it was an emergency consult. He called his Chennai colleague and then hung up before it connected. What if his friend was arrested and the reason to abort? He and Ms. Breun arranged for the surgery through this person. Kidney trade was a small world—they both had collaborated with this man. Ethan had thought that comforting.

He called Nan. She suggested he tell authorities he checked on a patient in Texas and learned that his nurse had tried to reach him, but the plane was in the air. Their Indian patient had died, so no need for him to continue. It was unfortunate they didn't connect before he left Hong Kong. He would then tell them his nurse informed him his patient back in San Antonio was failing faster than expected, and, since they no longer needed him in India, he should return at once to the States. The condition of the Senator's dad qualified for such a conversation. They had to hope the authorities wouldn't check the Indian connection. With the story settled, he headed to immigration, looking all around for the feds to rush in to arrest him.

At first, he panicked when the line at security and immigration snaked on and on, but then he noticed signage said *Indian citizens and passport holders*. The line for foreigners was significantly shorter. He presented his story to the agents upon entering the country so they could back him up when he turned around to leave, and U.S. customs and immigration could verify the events if they came up. The whole process went better than he had imagined.

At the ticket counter, he told the reservationist about the poor man at the hospital in Chennai. He had been collaborating with the doctor there during his earlier visit, and all looked well; however, the man's condition declined for no apparent reason. The Chennai doctors tried phone consults but decided Dr. South needed to attend to him personally. It was regrettable that they had lost the man before he arrived. The woman behind the counter agreed it was a tragedy, but the only immediate flights were economy class. She understood the good doctor had just flown twenty-five hours, but there were no first-class or business seats for two days. It would cost him two hundred dollars to change his flight with no refund for the business class. He could wait and take the one he had reserved for the next day.

His phone buzzed with another text. *We need you at home at once. I hope you have no trouble returning.* More code talk from Carrie Breun. Ethan saw police cars arrive. He took the ticket and headed to departures where his plane was already boarding the business seats.

Hiding in the economy crowd boarding by groups, he had time to call Ms. Breun—he checked his seat assignment: the back next to the bathrooms.

Chapter 44

September 27, 2015, Dr. Ethan South's Apartment, San Antonio, Texas:
Ethan stood at the front of the living room where some instruments from Alex and Kamini's preparations covered the coffee table. "All right, with all of you present, Nan has an idea that will get us out of this." He placed his arm around Nan's shoulder and pulled her close. "That's more than you other whiners have."

He'd demanded an emergency meeting at his apartment/lab as soon as he landed in San Antonio. Nan brought Julissa along, which soured the others even more. Both Alex and Kamini stared with their mouths wide open. What they didn't know was how close he had come to spending the rest of his days in an Indian jail. And they didn't know he had spent the last of his wife's inheritance trying to pull this deal off. They didn't even know he had a wife. They attributed his mood to lack of sleep.

When Carrie Breun told Dr. South to abort, he demanded his money back. Carrie Breun berated him: "You dumb fuck. You're not even that, you're just a dumb shit. This isn't Kidneys.com— no refunds. Now get on that plane, you stupid shit. Soldiers have already picked up Charles and Marco. They've already raided the hospital in Chennai. And get rid of your phone!" Then the line dropped.

No one had ever spoken to him like that. That moment dominated his every thought right now.

In his apartment, the make-shift lab, all watched his face twitch erratically.

Nan took over. "The lab is ready to go. Correct?"

"Yes, about that," started Kamini, "we didn't borrow the equipment when you placed the abort call, but we have the photos from when we broke in the day before with the samples from India."

"Those samples won't do us any good now, will they?" Ethan hissed. "But you have everything else ready at the apartment—you just need to get those two things? Yes, or no—can you ready the lab?"

"Yes," murmured Alex. "With Jimenez still gone the rest of this week, we can borrow the equipment today after the custodians leave."

"Good," Nan said. "Julissa can retrieve some information that might just save this."

Alex's head swirled. She was trying to figure out why they made it sound like she and Kamini had caused the problem in India. Alex thought India was the legal part—she and Kamini were the ones committing crimes.

"But," interrupted Dr. South, his eyes glaring at Alex, "we will need Amir. I had time on the plane to study this lab work. You need an extra set of hands, and the rest of us will be busy at the hospital."

"Oh, I don't think he will join us." Alex shivered and wrapped her arms across her ribs. She had never planned to work on the antigens alone—she thought Ethan was going to do most of it.

"Oh, he will."

Alex could swear he growled. "Just give me time. I'll work on him," she said.

"Really?" Julissa spoke up from the back of the group. "And let's have tea and crumpets while we wait around for this grand conversion."

This brought a huge grin across South's face. "Now that's the spirit. Alex, learn from her."

Leaning over Alex like he had when he first caressed her shoulders that day in the lab, he did not caress her now. Instead, his breath was hot and muggy. "You are in this every bit as deep as the rest of us. In fact, you and Kamini are the only ones who have committed any crimes at this point."

Alex's eyes filled with tears as she nodded yes. Kamini just sat.

Nan took back the meeting. "There is a transplant on Wednesday's schedule, a couple from Julissa's clinic. She knows them well. She can get access to the reports and pre-surgery labs. I have been spending time in the hospital lab this month so as not to look out of place when needed. This way, I can put an added check on the lab work and retrieve the extra vials of blood when they draw for pre-op. Kamini will reschedule the Senator's father for the day after their surgery. You, Alex, will have a little less than twenty hours with the kidney we retrieve from that donor to tweak it and get it into the old man. That is more time than you would have had with the Indian kidney."

Alex ran to the trash can and threw up. India was so far away. The Indian donor had volunteered and would get compensation, all on the up-and-up, at least a crime ignored—people traveled to poor countries all the time. She didn't really approve, but desperation led to desperate acts. This was happening here, in her country, in her hospital. She wiped her mouth with her sleeve. "Who are these people?"

Julissa strutted forward, placing herself between Nan and Dr. South. "A pair of older friends who live together but claim no romance, just friends." She smiled as if she possessed secret gossip, the kind that makes or breaks dynasties. "They met on a dating site years ago and became best friends, so they say. When his kidneys failed, she volunteered to donate. She's a breast cancer survivor. There were months of conferences about whether to use her— doctors all around the nation said no, but Dr. Halabi said yes."

"Wait," said Alex. "You want to stop this transplant? It's a sweet story."

Three times Ethan closed his right fist and released it before he spoke. "Look, she had breast cancer and shouldn't be donating, anyway. She's perfect for the Senator's dad—he won't live long enough to get cancer."

"Actually," said Julissa, "it's only because the recipient is already seventy and she is in her sixties that the Institute considered this match."

South scowled at both Julissa and Alex.

Alex's eyes filled with tears again—Maura would be disgusted.

Kamini broke the spell. "What do you need from me? I'm in. Let's get this done."

Nurse Nan and Dr. South explained the details. Kamini would hack the hospital computers to switch the surgery teams to allow Ethan and Nan to perform the donor surgery. She would alter any records as they progressed through the nephrectomy. Alex would remain in the apartment with Amir, ready with the cellular conversions.

"Wait," Alex interrupted. "If we have more time than before, why do we need Amir?"

"Oh, shut up!" shouted Dr. South. "We needed him before, but you didn't see it."

Alex suddenly felt like a cast member on the television series *Leverage*—things always went wrong for them, but she told herself they always came through in the end. Sure, they did questionable stuff—in the name of the greater good—but they were there for the little guy, the one with no leverage. She wondered who the little guy was here. She hoped it was all the people who would later receive help from the research—it sure as hell wasn't the seventy-year-old guy receiving his friend's life-giving kidney.

Nan outlined the process. At the surgery, she and Ethan would place Ms. Clawson-Dawson's kidney into the transplant carrier case. "Kamini will report Ms. Clawson-Dawson's kidney had a suspicious spot missed during testing, so it will be sent to pathology and declined for transplant." Nan spoke as if this were a normal pre-surgery prep.

It was all precise. Of course, the kidney would never go to the lab. On record, the last place it would be seen was the lab where it was diagnosed as malignant and sent to the incinerator.

Nan continued. "Julissa will put the carrier in a backpack and take it to the apartment."

No cell samples or slides would be found, a tragic paperwork error discovered when the hospital investigates, so someone in the lab would get fired.

Dr. South said, "Think of the joy, Alex. We will save Ms. Clawson-Dawson from a tumor on her kidney. Mr. Deaux's surgeons will cancel, and the patient will end up on dialysis."

"His name is Jon Deaux. Could this get any better?" Julissa laughed.

The others stared—this was not a joke. The tone of the meeting implied it was unfortunate their *John Doe* would have to wake up at all.

Kamini quit doodling on her tablet and looked straight at Alex. "The hospital will apologize and pay off a legal suit."

Alex saw Ethan smile for the first time, but it was not meant for her.

"No one else in the OR will need to know anything," Nan said. "They'll be busy doing their own work. Kamini will see that the video sending from the donor OR to the recipient OR will conveniently go black as soon as Ethan removes the kidney."

"So, no one dies, Al-ex-an-dra." Ethan held out her name the way schoolmates did when they were tired of her questions. "The donor lives on with her one kidney, and the recipient goes to dialysis. All is well."

"Umm, Mr. Deaux has refused dialysis," noted Julissa.

Ethan scowled. "Too bad. With one injection of the prepared serum, the cells in the donor's kidney will lose all T-cell identity that would cause rejections. Alex, how can you doubt the goodness of that?"

"But that's Jimenez's work." Alex wanted to scream out the window for the world to hear, but she found her throat locked up.

Ethan grabbed Alex's shoulders again and shook her, hard. "Pull it together. You were the one who suggested we use Jimenez's stuff to begin with. You, Alex, will buy us the time we need to perfect the remodeled kidney so you can save thousands of lives."

Alex nodded consent. That was all she had the energy to do.

"Good," Ethan said. "You will have Amir to help make the serum. Thursday, you will deliver the prepared kidney to the OR that Kamini will have rescheduled." He paused and then addressed all of them. "You know what you need to do. If you will excuse me, I must sleep. I had a long flight."

****

The day before the surgery, Alex invited Amir to coffee away from the Institute. They met at Starbucks around the corner and sat at an outside table at the corner of the building. She sent him back in for extra napkins while she slipped a little ketamine in his drink. She thanked the coffee gods he liked lots of flavor, sugar, and cream. They talked about the sacrifices people make in their fields, how the public did not know what it took to save lives. As he became sleepy, Nan and Ethan showed up to help their friend get home.

At the apartment, Amir woke restrained with duct tape on his ankles and wrists. Nan had done her homework. She found out about Amir's disabled mother and had pictures to prove they knew where she lived and what medicines she needed.

Alex watched him look around the room, focusing on the instruments from his work.

And then he saw her.

Chapter 45

September 30, 2015, CiCi's Home, San Antonio, Texas:
The alarm went off unnecessarily at four thirty in the morning. CiCi had slept little and Jon not at all. Both had forced themselves to stay in bed so they wouldn't disturb CiCi's sister Amanda, who would be driving. CiCi's daughter, Kambri, and Jon's friend Cylene would meet them at registration in one hour. Three zombies gathered in the kitchen as the coffee grinder's Columbian Supremo wafted through the house. Only Amanda held a coffee cup. A morning without coffee was CiCi's ultimate sacrifice for this cause.

Staring at Jon holding his suitcase, CiCi laughed. "When did you pack that? Last week?"

"Of course, and where's yours?"

"I'm going to have surgery—what do I need other than my e-book and my toothbrush?"

"Uh, a bathrobe, change of underwear?" His face presented his well-practiced snarky mode.

CiCi had arranged all of that with Kambri earlier. There was no need to haul a suitcase around the hospital—all her post-op needs would be in her room when she got there.

At the hospital, the pair's story had preceded them. The nurses seemed more interested in their dating-but-not-dating story than their vitals.

"Your entourage awaits you," said the woman at the registration desk.

CiCi looked around as more pre-dawn zombies walked up with coffee. "Look. Our *subjects* have arrived."

Lark gave both CiCi and Jon hugs, but CiCi reminded him she was her nurse, not his. Lark explained, "I assured his crew I could see you both on your way. And now I have nothing pending until after lunch. I'm all yours." The truth was that Jon wouldn't back out—it was CiCi who could still change her mind as her gurney rolled to the OR.

All checked in, the king and queen of the moment strolled down the hall to the holding room, entourage in tow. Queen CiCi's hand lay lightly on Jon's in a ceremonial parade. Kambri and Cylene pretended to hold trains behind them. Jon whispered to CiCi he wanted to get her a plunger as a scepter but, for once, behaved himself and refrained from asking for it. Nurses asked questions and more questions—some actually focused on surgical needs. King and Queen then marched into separate cubicles, halving the entourage into two escort teams.

Follow-up care was another area where CiCi found difficulty in the system. Even though she and Jon lived together, they had to have separate caregivers. If something happened to one, the other couldn't be left unattended. They lucked out. Cylene was a physician's assistant between jobs, so who could be better? Amanda had retired and would care for CiCi on weekdays while Kambri would step in on the weekends. Other friends offered to drive for doctor runs or to bring food; however, these three were treasures. Internet stories told CiCi this was overkill since, in most cases, post-op was an easy recovery after two or three days. There were cases when healing soured, so the Institute had to protect itself. Besides, this wasn't the medical tourism as Eva had experienced. Here, caregivers were a real requirement for the surgery, and the Institute wouldn't consider them without a list covering at least three weeks. Ironically, the safety nets kept some patients out of the net entirely. What about the working class who didn't have *people* around? How did they manage recovery time?

Nobody verified CiCi's list, so she could have made it up for all they knew.

During the Q & A, one nurse tuned in on CiCi being a twenty-year breast cancer survivor. "We never get cancer survivors as donors." It was more a question than a statement.

"Our nephrologist said I'm the only one in America right now. It's a risk for both of us."

"Why for you?" another nurse asked.

"Because if I get cancer again, chemo is tough with only one kidney. Life-threatening risks increase. An oncologist gave me her blessing—she said there are safer chemo options now that don't have to involve kidneys. Besides, I figure any donor could come down with cancer sometime later."

The first nurse smiled. "I donated a kidney to my twin sister fifteen years ago and came down with pancreatic cancer five years later."

"Whoa!" exclaimed CiCi. "You survived pancreatic cancer? I've never met a pancreatic cancer survivor."

"Yep, ten years. And I did it with just one kidney."

"You're amazing. Usually, by the time they find it … whoa! And your sister?"

"Still going strong. They found my cancer in an early stage while looking at something else."

CiCi took her hand. "Thank you for sharing—I feel much more confident about blowing off the chemo thing."

Looking up from her phone, Lark suddenly announced she needed to get back to the clinic—she had forgotten about a staff meeting. She said her farewells and wished them speedy recoveries.

After she left, CiCi told the others she thought the clinic agreed to their donation because they were both old and didn't have to live forty more years. It certainly was against all existing protocols to let her donate.

The conversation was so friendly and supportive that CiCi hadn't even noticed they had taken yet more vials of blood. The vampires had to do what vampires did best. Someone mentioned it was unusual for the lab to have requested so many, but the conversation moved on.

Then they waited. The nurses and techs moved on to the next patients. CiCi's escorts were still there, but they had reached that moment when there was nothing left to say, so they stared at whatever as they shivered in the cold room.

Waiting for anything in normal circumstances triggered CiCi's restless imagination, usually toward the dark side. True to form, her mind wandered. Who would forget they had a staff meeting when she had just said her morning was clear?

"Well, hell!" she blurted out, catching her family off guard. "What can be taking so long? They had us get here at five thirty, and it's after nine."

****

As promised, Nan showed up at the apartment with the vials but had to race back to the hospital to prep with Dr. South for the surgery. It was already eight o'clock—they should have the kidney no later than eleven. Alex feared they would push the twenty-hour viability window with the time needed for mutarsanguicellation. Most specialists preferred no more than four or five hours for transport, but she recalled Harvard had done a study that showed no difference in success for kidneys transported fourteen hours. She scolded herself—these thoughts were irrelevant. And of course, she reminded herself, the kidney had to last only a brief time.

Holding the vials and walking toward Amir as if she were carrying a fragile eggshell, she saw him shaking. "Amir, I'm so sorry. You must focus on the ultimate good you'll be doing. We'll prove your team's research works and stall for our team to finish its especially important mission." She could hardly believe she said those words.

"But our research may not work." He looked so young and spoke in barely more than a murmur. "And if it doesn't?"

Ever so gently, Alex finished the extraction for him and then reminded him, "The man is going to die, anyway. He knows this. So much has failed in his body that nothing will save him. He volunteered to do this to better the lives of future end-stage patients." Her memory flashed that he didn't volunteer for the way things turned out. She had to put that out of her mind, paint over it.

"Then why do I keep hearing about the Senator's dad and the deadlines?"

"I assure you the Senator is conscious of her father's impending death. She's been a kidney research advocate ever since he became ill ten years ago. Now she has resigned herself to having her father be the first successful recipient of a remodeled kidney, knowing some other factor will kill him soon, even with the new kidney. We will name the procedure after her father, honoring his sacrifice."

"But it won't be a remodeled kidney, and even if my work today is successful, no one will know, not even Dr. Jimenez. This will all be a pointless fraud."

"You're right. And that is a terrible misfortune. But not pointless. He will still be the reason we will succeed, and you can return to your lab confident in your next trial."

Amir asked her, "Will I return?"

That thought never occurred to Alex. Of course, he would return. He would promise to remain silent about everything and go on with his life. Unable to speak, she looked at him like she wanted to hug a sad child.

Amir turned away, taking a vial with him to the make-shift lab at the kitchen table. Cluttered with the equipment Alex and Kamini had taken from the lab, Amir thought the doctor's apartment looked like an amateur mad scientist had decorated it, not brilliant researchers with a world renown institution. He wasn't afraid just for himself or his mother—he feared for the old man. He hoped the gentleman—someone's father, someone's grandfather, someone's loved one—would be one of the seventy-five percenters and not the twenty-five percenters in the experiments so far. All this just to buy more time for the desperate Dr. South.

As he drew out a drop of blood to place on the slide for initial observation—just checking cell formation, middle school biology stuff—Amir admitted to himself that in some odd way he was excited. He wouldn't legally see Dr. Jimenez's work in human trials for a couple of years, and by then he would no longer be on her team and not a part of the public release.

But that excitement terrified him. With revolution, there was always the fear of what would happen over time. With the real remodeled kidney, if something went wrong, there would not be rejection, just an engineering failure, in which case they would remove it and replace it with a West Coast artificial kidney or a pig transplant, or worst-case scenario put the guy on dialysis. Mutarsanguicellation, however? He thought about something his high school history teacher wrote on the whiteboard, something about there being known knowns and known unknowns, but the unknown unknowns defeat all. Not the right words, but close enough, had something to do with invading Iraq.

Amir asked Dr. Segel, "Do you know that with Dr. Jimenez's protocol, perhaps the donor kidney could become toxic, more devastating than rejection?" When he saw her eyes, he was certain Dr. Segel had learned that part of the research. How she learned it was not so clear. Yet, she was still doing this.

"The kidney only has to work a few days," she said once again. "If it fails, we can arrange for him not to suffer."

Amir had traveled to a different universe.

Chapter 46

September 30, 2015, CTMRI Hospital, San Antonio, Texas:
Escorts rolled CiCi and Jon to their respective operating rooms with grand fanfares from the entourage, minus trumpets.

The procedure required that the recipient crew watch the donor surgery in real-time video to know when, or if, to start. Jon, too, watched. As CiCi went under, he intended to stay awake to see them stitch her up. The surgeon inserted the ports for the camera and several instruments with long handles through half-inch cuts in CiCi's belly.

Curiosity trumped Jon's fear of blood when so little blood appeared. He could see the same images the surgeon saw and stared with awe as the surgeon made a two-inch incision just below CiCi's belly button. It was all very tidy. Then he saw Dr. Halabi and Lark wearing surgical scrubs enter CiCi's OR. Dr. Halabi asked Dr. South if he could speak with him for a moment. Jon grew drowsy.

The video was fine—he was what was out of focus. He resisted sleep to watch as much of the surgery video as possible.

The scene is full light inside the operating room, the heart of the hospital. A kidney transplant is taking place.

As Jon watched, South reminded Halabi that timing was critical in these operations—they didn't have time to chat. Halabi said they found something wrong with this transplant and they needed to cancel. In Jon's foggy state, he didn't register what that meant—he assumed they would cancel CiCi but continue with him. He returned to his joyful pre-op state of mind, trying to make sense of the *movie*.

> *Dr. South charges to the head of the table and puts a scalpel to CiCi's throat. Nurse Nan screams and throws both arms into the air. She tells South, "This is not what I agreed to." Lark takes over for Nan, watching vitals and the incision.*

Jon could see the anesthesiologist was a true professional, probably had been a M.A.S.H. doc and knew to keep the woman on the table alive during the chaos. Fighting to stay conscious, Jon reeled with the effects of his own anesthesia. This was an odd movie to show someone just before surgery. He wasn't aware his docs from the Institute were movie stars.

> *The camera pans to the door stage left, where two police officers enter.*

Jon thought it was comical to see police in uniforms with guns but covered in gowns.

> *Halabi holds one arm up as if to push back the police. Lark adjusts a knob on CiCi's vitals monitor. Halabi yells out to the police, "Stay back! Let me do this!"*

Puzzled, Jon wondered who would show the old melodrama *Perils of Pauline* to a surgery patient? No, this was more like *Rocky and Bullwinkle*. He loved *Bullwinkle*.

> *The camera zooms out to show the police stopped at the door.*

Not noticing that his team had left him alone with his anesthesiologist, Jon somehow knew if he blinked his eyes to better focus on the movie, he wouldn't be able to open them again, and he would miss the end. CiCi did a fantastic job of lying still, her big chance to be a star.

> *The camera closes in on the two doctors. Halabi tells South, "It's over, South. Stealing that organ will not help." Nurse Nan tells him, "Give up, you fool! You can't take on the fucking police!" The camera moves to close in on CiCi's open belly incision for dramatic emphasis, then zooms out. Halabi tells South there is no bargaining for an airplane and a million dollars. The camera fades to black.*

That's when Jon lost consciousness.

****

Nurse Nan began talking as soon as Dr. South handed over the scalpel, blaming the kidney theft on Alex and telling police where to find her, neglecting to mention Amir was a hostage. The police organized a team to head to Doctor South's apartment with sirens silent so Alex would not try to escape.

Earlier, Lark had called Maura's office as soon as she suspected something odd with Dr. South and Nan's taking over CiCi's surgery. The two women didn't really know each other but had once discussed Nurse Nan's addition to Alex's team. Adding that Alex quit showing up to coffee, and her text messages became minimal, Maura sensed something had gone seriously wrong at the hospital and that it somehow involved Alex. She ran out of her office and across the lawn to the surgical unit where she intercepted the police. As one car took off, she made the second car listen and convinced the police officers she could get Alex to tell all she knew if they let her enter Dr. South's apartment. They reluctantly agreed since counselor for Institute personnel was part of her job description, or so she said.

At South's apartment, Alex shouted through the closed door. "Coming! Julissa, you're late! I'm running out of time to do this."

The police pushed on through and saw Alex had no weapons, just some test tubes. They flanked Maura but let her do the talking.

Alex reached for Maura, but a police officer stopped her. "Why did you bring the police? We were so close to saving thousands of lives. You betrayed me!" Alex reached again for Maura, but another officer pulled her back, causing her to drop the test tubes. Alex sniveled and wiped her nose on her sleeve. "What about doing the greatest good for the greatest number of people?"

"Like the life of that lab tech over there?" Maura pointed to Amir.

Alex looked at the vials now shattered across the marble floor, then looked at Amir, who stood frozen. Two more officers had surrounded him and started putting him in handcuffs. Alex told them Amir did nothing wrong, that Dr. South kidnapped him to do the work. Amir fell to his knees, but the police caught him before he hit the floor. They read him his rights and said they knew nothing about a kidnapping.

Maura stood her ground and pushed. "When you didn't challenge those reports when we first talked, I thought you would figure it out and take care of business. You're a good person. You're not greedy and name hungry like Dr. South. I was wrong."

"Why couldn't you just leave it alone? I would have stopped them if it went too far."

"You aided in fraudulent reporting, a kidnapping, theft, and attempted murder."

Alex gasped. "Murder? What murder? No one was getting hurt."

Maura held up her hand and pointed to her fingers. "You say South kidnapped Amir—do you honestly think Ethan South would let him go with what he knew? South had a scalpel at Ms.

Clawson-Dawson's neck." She counted each item on her fingers for Alex to see. "Jon Deaux will die without his chance for a transplant. And what about the Senator's dad? You gave him false hope and would risk his life with a fake rebuilt kidney. You were going to kill him before he rejected." Four fingers. "What happened to *First, do no harm?*"

Alex's mind went numb—Maura had figured out everything. "But it was for a noble cause."

"You're a freaking medical research genius. You're smart enough to fix a kidney. You knew when those first reports were inaccurate that something was wrong. And what about Ms. Clawson-Dawson? What about stealing her kidney?"

Alex turned away. "Murder? Ethan wouldn't do that."

"How can you know? What do you really know? He's married. But you didn't know that. Or did you?"

"No, can't be." Alex was shaking all over. There it was, the flaw she had covered with paint took down the entire cause.

"There is an APB out for Kamini. Everyone else has been rounded up and hauled to the police station. It's time to go."

Defeated and exhausted, Alex stared at each of the room's walls for what seemed an eternity. What scars had Ethan added to those from previous renters? "I was saving lives. Can't you see it? People are dying every day, and I could end that. I was a guardian for humanity." Alex sobbed into her sleeve and collapsed against Maura.

"Ah," said Maura, "but *quis custodiet ipsos custades?*"

Alex shook as she sobbed. "Who guards the guardians?"

The two headed out the door with the police.

Chapter 47

September 30, 2015, CTMRI Hospital, San Antonio, Texas:
The hospital put CiCi in a large room because of all the people surrounding her. CiCi's daughter, Kambri, stood at the nurse's desk across from CiCi's room and collected the flowers—no uninvited visitors allowed. Everyone present knew the young woman was having a tough time—her mother, her superhero, was nearly killed. On top of that, a sick bastard pretending to be family called CiCi's hospital room to tell her she deserved what she got because she was donating to her friend instead of the next person in line with UNOS. Fortunately for CiCi, her daughter had answered the phone for her mom. So there she stood, gatekeeper, protecting her mom with the same vigilance her mom had while protecting Kambri as she grew up.

CiCi woke from a short nap, her anesthesia fog gone because the doctors had kept her in the recovery room for hours before letting her go to the room where she would have many questions. Brianna was sitting by her side, and Doctor Halabi and Lark came in to check on her. Then she saw Officer Jacob De Hoyos, a teaching colleague's husband, standing in uniform at her door. Beside him was Stan, her friend whom she had called to speak with Eva after the *non-kidnapping*.

Something was wrong—she felt it in her gut, but then Jon walked in dressed in regular clothes.

Brianna stroked CiCi's hair and bent down close to her face. "Everyone is fine, and both kidneys are intact."

CiCi switched from tears to a flood of questions. "What do you mean intact? Why is Jon standing here?" Questions were there, but they wouldn't come out of her mouth.

"Mom!" Kambri called out. "It's all over the news. Some bastard tried to steal your kidney!" The others stared at her. "Umm, but all is hunky dory, just grand now." Kambri returned to guard the door in case the police officer couldn't do it well enough.

CiCi started to sit up, but Brianna coaxed her back to her pillow.

Dr. Halabi whispered something to Lark who then adjusted CiCi's IV. Satisfied with her vitals, he clasped his hands in front of his belt in the warm teddy bear stance CiCi had liked when she met him. Dr. Halabi said, "Dr. South's research team here at CTMRI planned to introduce a remodeled kidney as an alternative to the upcoming artificial version. It would end the need for transplants."

"That sounds wonderful. When will this happen? Is that why you canceled the surgery?" This didn't seem right. She was sure they wouldn't have waited until she was sliced open to decide this.

For the first time since CiCi had met him, Dr. Halabi paced the floor as he spoke. "It turned out the team wasn't as ready as they had published and were under pressure to proceed or lose their Congressional grant."

CiCi's head spun. "Whoa. And that involves me how?"

Jon took her hand, which he normally would never do. "Lark was the one who became suspicious of dastardly deeds at Kidneys R Us."

Aware of Jon's affinity for the old cartoons, CiCi thought this was all silliness. "Dastardly?" Silence. CiCi looked around. No one was having fun.

Lark didn't pace the floor as her boss did—she shifted weight from one foot to the other. "While I was at a kidney donor awareness event, Maura from human resources mentioned she was delighted to place my good friend Nan with Dr. South's research team. But Nan wasn't my friend—I barely knew the woman—I could only say she was a nurse Dr. South had worked with in the past, before coming to CTMRI. I met her once at another conference."

Lark admitted she did not tell Maura about the nurse's soiled reputation. Nan had had an extra-marital affair with Dr. South years back. Dr. South was the married one. This was all juicy rumor stuff at that conference. Dr. Halabi, however, pointed out Lark was following professional protocol. Gossip didn't belong in the workplace and could have been slanderous.

Jon added, "And that's too bad because if she hadn't been such a professional and had provided a little juicy gossip, this Maura person would have investigated further."

"But I was concerned," said Lark, "so I did a little snooping around and sort of suggested things to see who would bite at rumors."

"It was Julissa. Julissa was the office leak!" Kambri was never known to hold back when she knew stuff.

Not understanding much of anything, CiCi glared at Jon. "And you fed her cookies?"

Jon performed his typical it-is-what-it-is shoulder shrug. "Yeah, and Julissa fed Nan details about Lark. Once, months ago, before the Institute hired her, Nan befriended Julissa in the cafeteria. Conning ran thick in Nan's blood, so she had Julissa chattering about Lark without Julissa even knowing it. During the HR interviews, Nan had enough information to appear as Lark's friend."

"Later," explained Lark, "when I had details and got back to Maura about Nan's shadiness, Maura felt guilty for not doing better due diligence on the background check. She had verified all the letters of recommendation, but she hadn't asked me anything because it all sounded true. By then, the hire had taken place, and Nurse Nan was working well with the team. We both screwed up."

"I still don't see what I had to do with all this." CiCi, exhausted, slid around a little, trying to get more comfortable. Kambri rushed to her side, rearranging and fluffing while Amanda tucked blankets.

Lark held up her pointer finger and tipped her head into the wait-for-it position. "I became full-blown suspicious when I found Nan's and South's sudden inclusion in the surgical team. South did transplants now and then to keep his skills sharp, but I had set you up with Dr. Kai and knew of no reason for a switch. I thought it might be a favoritism thing with South getting Nan some OR attention and almost blew it off. Except this morning, campus security showed Dr. H a video from the afternoon before with Julissa copying a patient's files. Your files."

CiCi studied Dr. Halabi's face. She saw fatigue in his teddy bear facade.

The doctor's pacing grew faster. "We were aware someone had been using the copy machine for several days because the counter was off. In fact, Julissa was the one to report it. I guess to make it seem like she wasn't the guilty one. When I texted Lark this morning about Julissa, she questioned the surgeon switch, which I knew nothing about."

CiCi nodded at Lark, recognizing a detail at last. "Your forgotten staff meeting?"

"Too many coincidences."

It was Brianna's turn to explain. "But it was Eva who saved the day with her own selfish form of altruism." The social worker always made sure credit went where it belonged. "Julissa had told Nurse Nan about Eva's kidney disease and that Eva had worked with two kidney runners, Charles and Marco."

"I remember their names from the day in the office when I hid from her in the hall." CiCi took pride in herself because she knew a detail in this ordeal. She also had heard about them in the cat urine shed. She thought it was part of Eva's past, intended to be forgotten.

Brianna explained Dr. South promised Eva a transplant if she fixed him up with a kidney through her old acquaintances Marco and Charles. He told her about his research and that they would end a need for living donors. Eva rationalized she would be helping an impoverished donor the way she had rationalized to herself years earlier, the remodeled kidney would stop illegal kidney trade, and South's deal would also help her. She gave South what little she knew about the broker Carrie Breun, and off to India the doctor flew.

"Wait, why did Dr. South need a kidney? Kambri was upset earlier because someone tried to steal mine."

Dr. Halabi skimmed the story of the Estes family, the remodeled kidney concept, the burned one, the near arrest in India, and ended with mutarsanguicellation.

Kambri threw in her two cents from the doorway. "And his people stole that research, too. Bastards."

"Fed Ex a kidney from India? You can do that?" CiCi discovered it hurt to laugh. "Next, you can get a kidney on Amazon with free overnight delivery." That brought about a lot of shoulder lifting and smirking from CiCi's fan club. "So, he wanted my kidney to fake his research? But he didn't get it, true?"

"He didn't get it," said Brianna. "This morning, Eva grew a conscience—or a streak of vengeance—and came to me about South's promise of a kidney. She realized this Dr. Ethan South was the same Dr. *Smith* in Thailand who had suggested to her during a brief coffee flirtation that she go to Johannesburg to work with an HIV group. He was the reason she left Thailand and indirectly got her involved in so many life-threatening events. She had been trying to figure out why she had recognized him at Denny's when they discussed Marco and Charles. All these years, she had his name wrong, not the first person to have done so."

When Lark rushed back to the clinic, upset about the surgeon switch, Eva and Brianna put it all together and called Dr. Halabi, who was still with campus security. He rushed to the OR while security called the SAPD.

"Ah, the police," said Jon. "That's where I faded out." He told CiCi he saw the beginning of her surgery on the video. "I started hallucinating a *Bullwinkle* TV episode. Dr. Halabi was Dudley Do-

316

Right. I imagined you, CiCi, were Nell crying out, 'Hay-elp, hay-elp.' But since it was a movie, I watched and didn't come to your rescue."

"After all I've done for you?" She attempted to slug him in the shoulder but couldn't reach him. The other baby boomers offered more casting ideas.

Jon told her he didn't notice while in his stupor that his team had left him alone on the surgery table with just the anesthesiologist. As he slept, his doctors took over CiCi's surgery and closed her incision. "Luckily, they had only made the first incisions—your kidneys remain virgins."

"Virgin kidneys?" CiCi wished they would quit making her laugh.

Jon once told her about a visit with the doc while planning the transplant. The doc lectured him about changes he needed to make to care for his new kidney. Jon asked the doc, "What new kidney? I'm getting an old used model." The doc laughed and proclaimed it was *certified pre-owned.*

CiCi teared up again. "So, no transplant?"

"No." Dr. Halabi took her hands in his. "You recover—then we'll revisit it."

She turned toward Jon. Much was at stake. Her soulmate. "And you?"

"I've agreed to dialysis until we can sort all this out."

"Why didn't you just go ahead? We were already on the tables and knocked out."

"Oh well, it was a bit of a mess with unsterile fields, shocked OR assistants, surgeons with shaky hands." Typical Jon, always seeing the practical side of events.

"And you guys figured all this out while I was asleep?"

Jon stretched and leaned back in his chair. "Well, not me." He drew his arms back to put his hands behind his head. Mister Cool. "I was sleeping a bit myself, dreaming about my role in the Academy Award-winning transplant movie."

CiCi called him an idiot.

Officer De Hoyos had been assigned guard duty without knowing all the pieces. Now he stepped forward to offer what he knew. "Nan started talking at once, right there in the OR. We don't know why she broke down so easily—she seemed like a tough cookie. You should have seen South's eyes flash fire when Nan announced he couldn't pull off the India thing. She had known she needed to find him a Plan B all along."

"And I was Plan B?" CiCi asked.

All in the room nodded in unison.

"Here's what I don't get." CiCi scrunched around a bit, bringing the entourage into pillow adjustment mode again. "Why didn't this Doctor South person just tell the volunteer man what happened? He had another kidney they could fix."

The IV Lark had adjusted earlier was giving CiCi more morphine. Dr. Halabi wanted her body to rest before the shock of all that happened could take hold. CiCi faded before they could explain why South felt he couldn't be honest with the Estes family. Dr. Halabi said he was glad they didn't get to the part about the scalpel held at her throat.

****

Kambri found a small conference room only five feet from CiCi's room. There were only a few chairs, so she commandeered seats from surrounding patients who had heard the news and were eager to help. Kambri also saw to coffee refills and a supply of plastic-wrapped muffins to make everyone comfortable while CiCi rested. This space became the entourage's command center, where they reviewed the details of Dr. South's dastardly deeds several more times.

Detectives were in and out of the room, asking more questions of anyone who could answer and giving information when they could, considering they couldn't compromise an investigation.

Police arrested Dr. South and Nan on the spot for conspiracy to traffic organs and so many other crimes. Kambri insisted charges should include attempted murder of Jon.

Jon pointed out the attempt on his life would be a tough one to prove. He didn't know the law on this, but he wondered if it would be attempted murder if nothing changed in his life. He was already dying, so taking CiCi's kidney would have been like finding out during the surgery that her kidney was not good for transplant. Nothing would have changed.

While in the apartment, Amir had filled in the parts about Jimenez's stolen research, his kidnapping, and the involvement of the other two on the team, Dr. Segel and Kamini Something-with-a-really-long-last-name. As part of her confession, Julissa revealed a plan to inject Amir with succinylcholine and then dispose of his body. Kamini disappeared. Police across the globe, especially in India, would search for her.

Things were happening quickly. Officer De Hoyos told them that because of the illegal kidney trade, the FBI stepped in. Dr. Sarah Wang had been working as an informant for many months because she became aware Dr. South had dealings with the illegal market for research purposes, but it had been all out of country. The FBI used Wang, hoping Dr. South would lead them to a U. S. connection. The entire research team was under investigation, but it looked like they were innocents trying to develop a great alternative to transplants and the shortage of donors. Ownership of the research belonged to the Institute, so maybe someone would pick it up again.

And Eva … what to do with Eva? She needed a psychological evaluation—that was a given. She had done terrible things through her ability to rationalize, but other than CiCi's unreported *non-kidnapping*, there was nothing illegal that would stick. And she saved the day. She didn't have long to live, anyway. The District Attorney was working on it.

319

Chapter 48

October 7, 2015, Carrie Breun's Home, Santa Barbara, California:
Losing Marco and Charles barely put a kink in Carrie's business. Her other recruiters eagerly stepped in. Anyone lasting over five years in her industry, other than herself, was extraordinary. The boys had made it ten. She wished them well during their stay in the Indian prison.

What was it about that Eva woman? She brought disaster to the medical tourism business across four countries. Moving forward, Carrie was on the phone with a tiresome new client. They had already exchanged blood samples and patient histories, but now the woman hesitated, wanting to hear it all again and asking more questions.

"I assure you, Ms. Wang, we thoroughly screen all organs for transplant, and the surgeries are safe with the best hospital care in the world." Carrie rolled her eyes even with no one present to see her. "Of course, DOCTOR Wang. ... Yes, Medicare will cover post-op in a Medicare approved facility. Look, do you have a donor to bring with you? ... Then you cannot use a Medicare approved facility. There are few of those overseas, anyway. ... Yes, immaculate, tops in the world."

Answered and answered.

"The doctors are all U.S. trained surgeons, and you'll receive excellent good American follow-up care with medications from American pharmacies. ... No, Medicare will not pick up the cost of the prescriptions and after-care, but most people ... no, really, most people who can afford to buy a kidney can afford those costs."

The sun going down outside her window called to her. Carrie could see herself at the beach watching the sunset, but not if this woman didn't let her go.

"You heard correctly—the prescription costs go down significantly as time passes. ... No, there are no U.S. grants or foundations to help when you go overseas, but some insurance companies might appreciate the lower costs. For insurance, you would need to bring your own donor. ... When you arrive in South Africa, there will be greeters to guide you to a lovely hotel."

It was called medical tourism—what part could this woman not understand? Thankful for speaker phones, Carrie walked around her office to stack files and clean up for the day.

"We want you to look upon this as a vacation, relax and know you will return home feeling well for the first time in years. ... Thailand is lovely, but we have a waiting period of over three-months there. ... Yes, you must meet your Brazilian donor. Your social worker will help you become best lifelong friends. ... No, that is the only way for transplants in South Africa because their laws require the donor to be family or an old friend. ... Yes, not family, so you must become lifelong friends."

She flipped through her photo album of Madras (or Chennai or whatever) and thought about her first interview with Charles. He came without Marco to get things rolling—smart move. Eva affected Marco's business savvy, even long distance.

"That's our job. You will do fine. ... Yes, the U.S. frowns on doing this, but sometimes one must look away to help people in need—it is my calling. ... No, you won't be arrested on your return. ... No, no, I prefer not calling it any color of a market. That sounds like sleazy hotel room care. You will be in a five-star hotel and the best hospital, so please call it *medical tourism*."

Working from home meant never leaving the office. Carrie Breun looked toward the beach but no longer saw the sun.

"Of course, I'm certain we can book you for next week."

Finally, she could set a date. As Carrie reached for her computer to view her calendar, there was a knock at the door. The woman on the phone told her she needed to answer her door.

"You could hear that? It's after hours, I don't need to interrupt us. Now, how about October twentieth?"

The computer screen flashed, replacing her calendar with *THIS SITE HAS BEEN SEIZED*. Words followed that showed a legal warrant was in place. Bold images of badges from the FBI, ICE, IRS, the Department of Justice, Homeland Security, and more circled the page.

She didn't have time to see all the badges. The door came flying toward her. At the door were three men and a woman in FBI jackets. The men had guns.

The woman had a cell phone at her ear. "Ms. Breun, I presume. I'm Dr. Sarah Wang."

Chapter 49

December 16, 2015, CTMRI, San Antonio, Texas:
It had been a year since Jon's first visit to a nephrologist while CiCi was off hula dancing. His disease progressed faster than most cases. CiCi was back at the Institute asking if they could still do the transplant. Her best friend was still dying. He had consented to dialysis just long enough to be sure CiCi fully recovered. Thinking the transplant option was over, he planned to follow through with his quality-of-life stance.

Dr. Halabi reminded her she had had cancer, osteopenia, all kinds of reasons not to donate that they were overriding, and then had this frightening event in the hospital. Transplant might not be in her stars. She told him she had had cancer, osteopenia, all kinds of reasons not to donate, and yet she still was an acceptable candidate. Now saved from this horrific event, obviously she was meant to give Jon her kidney. It was clearly in her stars.

****

They would both be home by Christmas Eve, in time for Jon's birthday on Christmas Day. The staff informed CiCi the surgery went so well it was boring, a relief for all. CiCi noticed an all-too-familiar pain in her abdomen as she awoke. This pain being far more excruciating than the one a couple of months earlier told her major stuff had moved around. Then it hit her—it was like the cesarean she had over three decades before. How vividly she remembered that.

"Well," she told the handsome nurse, "I lived through that. Women have a C-section and go back for more." She told him Jon's daughter had four C-sections, each two years apart on the dot. "Pain is okay when something great comes out of it."

"Umm, Princess, you talk a good talk," said Jason. "Let's see you walk that walk. Time to get out of bed. You must walk before we will remove the catheter."

"Ooooh, I call it the cesarean shuffle. 'Tis a dignified walk." She sucked in a deep breath. "So, let's do this."

CiCi held her stomach as Jason helped her to sit, giving her time to let her head stop spinning. Before she knew it, they had shuffled to the door. It reminded CiCi of the tiny steps she saw in movies of elegant Japanese women in their kimonos, only this shuffle required a tight hold on the stomach and an IV drip tree as the escort.

Mission accomplished, they returned to the bed and a couple of pain tablets. "Where is the morphine?" asked CiCi.

"Do you really need a drip? Every patient is different. You look good to me."

"I guess you're right—these Norco babies will do fine."

"You have those for now, and the doc will send you home with some to last a few days, but you'll be on Tylenol before you know it. You know abdominal surgeries well—I can tell you won't wimp around with this."

"Home?" she asked.

"Three or four days. Your friend, if all goes well, will get home a few days later."

"By the way, I am *not* a princess."

"No?"

"I am a queen." Somehow word got to Jon, who sent Kambri to buy a tiara for Queen CiCi to wear to rule her domain.

The next morning, donned in her crown with the IV pole as her scepter, CiCi had the nurse escort her as she shuffled down the hall. Time to check on her kidney.

CiCi stared at Jon's room. "Dang! You have a mansion here—my room barely holds my bed and one chair."

Jon was in the large ICU room because, as the recipient, he needed more monitoring and room to bring in a dialysis machine should it be needed, which it was not. The first thing CiCi noticed was color in his face that she hadn't seen in a year. And a spark in his eyes—the mischief was back. He pranced around like he had no pain, practically running laps. She held her tummy and shuffled to a chair.

"I've named her Bernice," Jon told her.

"Who?"

"Your kidney. And she is a real pisser."

The ICU nurse nodded her head. "Bernice has kept me busy emptying his bag all day."

Both patients doing well, Cylene had already assumed her post-op duties as Jon's caregiver and took pictures of the two friends in their look-alike hospital gowns. She had to admit Jon looked better for the wear than she did. That made sense. Jon's kidney function went from not even ten percent to sixty percent in minutes. CiCi's went from ninety percent— "excellent for her age," she had pointed out—to forty-five percent in that same moment. They all knew to expect this and that CiCi's single kidney would start compensating even before she left the hospital. And it did. The queen's fairy tale came true—she saved the king.

Cylene continued taking photos of the pair when CiCi's entourage arrived. CiCi and Jon entertained the post-op ICU nurses with their story about how they met.

Once again CiCi had to say, "Hey, *PairForLife.com*, this is *not* what I meant."

Chapter 50

December 26, 2016, Patong Beach, Thailand: It was Boxing Day, twelve years after the terrible tsunami. CiCi took Hilmi's hand in hers as she absorbed the sounds of Patong Beach. The fish tanks with tiny fish exfoliating tourists' feet tickled her fancy still. When she toured Thailand with her girlfriends four years earlier, she got herself a bad nail infection from one of those tanks. But she would do the fish tanks again this trip.

"Thanks for helping with this. I can't believe you remembered us."

"But of course. You were here not so long ago, and your travel friend spoke Thai—it is rare that an American speaks Thai. And Eva? Well, she would be hard to forget. It was a most memorable time in our lives."

CiCi noticed Hilmi didn't ask about Marco and Charles. "I'm grateful to you."

"So, you saved your friend's life?" Hilmi guided her toward the shoreline. "You know, in some cultures–"

CiCi cut him off. "I know. If I save a life, I become that person's keeper because I interfered with destiny. Do you believe that?"

"Of course not. Fire and ambulance crews could never function. Eva and I, along with hundreds of others, would have been overwhelmed with responsibilities after the tsunami." Hilmi smiled but sighed at the same time. "No, I think we are all responsible for our own lives, but a little help now and then is good. Tell me, are you well after this brave act of yours?"

"I'm great. No worries. After surgery, I hurt a bit for about three weeks, then my abdomen remained tender for another three weeks, but I needed only Tylenol by the second day I was home. No need for the hard drugs, so it couldn't have been all that bad. I was tired for a bit, but, shoot, I went scuba diving in Fiji three months later."

"That is a good ending, then."

The sun on the ocean invited CiCi to run into the surf, to immerse herself in some sort of purification ceremony, but she resisted. During her first trip to Thailand, she snorkeled at a teeny island an hour boat ride off the coast. She saw the broken coral bits from the tsunami years earlier, but she also saw all the new life growing there. She found herself in a school of tiny jellyfish and, diving under them, heard Nemo and Dori telling her, "Just keep swimming." Now with Hilmi beside her, knowing what he endured, and Jon at home fully functioning again, she reminded herself, "Just keep swimming."

She pulled herself out of her thoughts and back to Hilmi. "It's so odd, though. During all the testing and while in recovery, I was the center of everyone's attention. Now, I'm not even an afterthought—all the attention's on Jon. I've heard other donors say the same. It's a good thing—the deed is done, but it feels unfinished. It's like the party is over, and I don't even have to clean the house after spending so much energy getting there."

"It is as it should be. Why would you want to clean the house?"

"You're right. Eva spoke of the burden of the gift as a curse."

They both looked out to the sea, hoping it could bring answers with the waves. People so often find peace that way, forgetting those waves can bring destruction.

Eva kept her promise and stayed away from CiCi. Shortly after their transplant, Brianna told CiCi that Eva was in hospice care—she thought CiCi should know. Of course, she should know—they bonded that day in the disgusting shed. Even though Amethyst got Eva on dialysis through the Medicare kidney program, Eva's illness

327

had progressed further than anyone realized. She had been running on determination, not health. The dialysis helped, but she couldn't follow the diet and developed a severe infection that she couldn't overcome.

Brianna contacted Eva's parents, but neither showed up. CiCi visited Eva in the hospital several times and sat vigil as Eva died. They talked of Hilmi and hugged when CiCi told Eva the Buddha mask hung on a wall in Hilmi's new restaurant that he moved two blocks up the hill from the shoreline. That mask was all he had left from the tsunami, and no, he never found his partner. The only extended happiness Eva seemed to know was her time in Thailand, so CiCi contacted her own Thai friend who found Hilmi, who readily agreed to help CiCi with accommodations and friendship.

"Hilmi, what are the chances we all came together here in this story?" This had been tickling CiCi's thoughts ever since the *PairForLife.com* coincidence.

"My religion tells me it is *karma*," answered Hilmi.

"And do you believe that? Do you believe we're all bundled up with each other, hurting each other, loving each other because we have done bad things in the past?"

"Bad things? Not always bad things, just things to work out." The frown on CiCi's face asked for more. "But then, the whole kidney transplant thing is a small community for such an enormous world. There are not so many players—maybe you all got jumbled together just because."

They walked further onto the warm sand, such a wonderful place to spend winter. CiCi again stared out into the waves, letting the hypnotic sounds pull on her. "Are we really here learning lessons? Can't we just be? You know: *I think; therefore, I am?*"

"Not to belittle Descartes, but sounds boring to just sit around and think."

"I see your point," CiCi said, still transporting her spirit self into the waves. "Multiple lives?"

"I hope so. I hate to think we only have one shot at it."

"Forgiveness?"

"I hope so."

CiCi drew circles in the sand with her toes. "What are the rules? Eva lived strictly by trial and error."

Hilmi surveyed the shoreline with the new hotels and restaurants. "We learn best by errors—doing it right is just luck. And sometimes we still don't learn."

"You're an interesting man, Hilmi. I can't tell when you're serious or sarcastic." CiCi stared at him, soaking in his calm graces.

"What? You think, because I'm Buddhist, I'm the Dalai Lama? I'm just a misplaced Malaysian beach bum."

CiCi reached down to pick up some sand and teasingly tossed it at her companion. "Nice try, Mr. Bum. I remember your story about teaching at the University of Malaya before you and your partner dropped everything to live in Patong. You know, Eva pondered these questions in her own peculiar way. I hope she's pleased coming back to Thailand."

"Her work is done. She can rest." Then he added, "*Eva*, the name, means *life* or *living* and *mother of life*."

CiCi stared at Hilmi again.

The two walked into the bay with the *haft-seen* Eva had designed for herself before she died. It wasn't the Persian New Year, but Eva decided her death was her own *Nowruz*—she had cleaned house and was ready to start new. They leaned over into the wave to place the small board holding a small clay kidney, a bowl filled with flower petals, and a picture of her parents. CiCi added her ashes. Hilmi and CiCi watched in silence as the water washed Eva's ashes around in a swirl and out to sea.

329

A Call to Action (United States):
Write to your legislators for donor protection.

When people think of kidney transplants, they think of the miracle for the recipient. And it is a miracle. Many of us are aware of the difficulties transplant recipients have with anti-rejection drugs and their stripped immunities. And it is difficult.

What I don't often hear are concerns for living donors. Please don't misunderstand—our donation has gone perfectly even eight years later. A living donors Facebook group reveals wonderful stories from those who cherish their ability to help, and most say they wish they could do it again. Many donate parts of their liver after the kidney. The donors are called heroes and angels.

For a rare few, the stories do not end so well. I focused this novel on donors because even donors in affluent countries can face difficulty. A transplant is a miracle, but it can be—as CiCi and Eva decided—a brutal miracle for a rare few people. There is a Facebook group dedicated to donors with complications where people can discuss issues without feeling like whiners. Most complications are minimal considering a life was saved, but there are, occasionally, physical and emotional difficulties that interfere with the lives of the donors and their families. As it stands, there is little help for them.

The stories CiCi and Eva mention in the novel formed from real stories. Donors can die, though it is statistically well within the acceptable risk range. Donors can have pain from scar tissue that keeps them from holding their children. Donors can have had so much difficulty that they can no longer work. One story from Frye-Revere mentions a person going homeless because of medical bills. Medicare covers donor related side effects for two years, but, after that, the donors are on their own.

To keep this short, I assume you finished the novel and ran across examples of donation gone wrong. If the Affordable Care

Act is abolished, we must hope its improved replacement includes pre-existing conditions and elective surgeries. Back in the day, we could get insurance for pre-existing conditions, but it was phenomenally expensive. In 2024, our insurance cannot hold pre-existence against us. Life insurance is up to the issuer. Sometimes insurance policies have a post-condition waiting period. This surgery is, after all, elective for a donor.

Artificial kidneys and xenotransplantation (the use of pig kidneys) are on the way—please advocate for more research funding. In the meantime, we still deal with a shortage of kidney donors, with living donors still facing risks.

Some states have taken up legislation to protect living donors. There are groups who fund out-of-pocket travel and time off from work, but that is not consistent across the U. S.

Federal legislators have made several attempts over the last ten years to introduce living donor protection bills. In 2019, President Trump signed legislation aimed at prevention and early detection of kidney disease as well as more in-home services for patients. His bill called for improving support for living donors but did not specifically legislate the measures. President Biden signed a bill that modernized the organ procurement services, but nothing protected donors.

The latest living donor focused bill I found at my publication time is "H.R. 2923 — 118th Congress: Living Donor Protection Act of 2023" in the House of Representatives and the same bill S. 1384 in the Senate. It addresses insurance issues, paid leave, and updating educational materials.

You can search *NKF, take action ask: Congress for Living Donor Protection Act* for more information and form letters.

This bill has seen recent support with more cosponsors. It, however, has been floundering for years, so it may become the donor act of 2024 or '25, but please keep trying.

Acknowledgments

So many people helped me with this book—I apologize if I leave someone out. Some of my friends asked not to be included here due to privacy.

I need to start with our nephrologist, **Dr. Samy Riad**. Because of him, my *partner in crime* is still alive. I am a breast cancer survivor and was rejected as a living donor by two other San Antonio clinics. Dr. Riad listened to us. When I sent him the chapters involving Dr. Halabi, he simply wrote back, "You know that's not how it really happens." Okay, fine, but Bob really did get to watch the video during the first slice into my abdomen before he went under in his operating room.

Eve Porinchak, my editor, taught this old retired high school English teacher she still has lots to learn about crafting stories. **T.D. Storm** of Storm Writing and **Joan Dempsey** of Gutsy Great Novelist Writers Studio guided me through some particularly tough spots.

Caitlin B. Alexander designed my book cover and patiently answered my questions. I, also, thank **Hannah Willstrop** for designing the introductory art.

My dearest friend, housemate, and kidney recipient **Bob Golden** knew when to encourage me and when to stay quiet. My phenomenal daughter **Amberly Kurburski** was the first to read the opening chapters and changed my entire approach. **Karlene Pettit, Ph.D.**, a pioneer for women in aviation and a commercial airline pilot/instructor, inspired me with her six murder intrigue novels that spread public awareness about real dangers in commercial flight safety. She considers her nonfiction book, *Normalization of Deviance: A Threat to Aviation Safety*, the scariest of her works. **Rita Woodfill** cheered me on from reading my very first chapter outline to editing three times. **Kista Tucker** (of Kista Tucker Insights) and I discovered we were both authoring novels and guided each other through plot agony, character agony, point of view decisions, setting issues, the whole shebang.

English language teaching colleagues **Janis Tschirhart** and **Col. Janice Edgerson, Ph.D.**, applied their "red pens" gently but constructively. **Carol Siskovic** helped me with a critical title change and composed the title poem.

I asked numerous friends, colleagues, and wonderful strangers to help me with cultural sensitivity. I tried to follow their suggestions, but I am certain I missed things. I thank **Susan Dustin Hattan, Dr. Stan Schneider, Mary Muenster, Naghmeh Panahi, Rajee Thyagarajan, Dr. Nina Menezes,** and **Renganathan Vijayaraj.** The life and collegiate experiences these people selflessly contributed were invaluable. (It was a letter Stan sent to me forty years ago while he was in the Okavango River Delta studying bees—that were supposed to be in the Kalahari but were not, so he had to change locations—that inspired me to send Eva to Botswana.)

I thank the following for their help through the surgical and dialysis information: **Christine Stofle**, Director of Operations for Dialysis at the University Health Services in San Antonio; **Barbara Brock Burg**, my cousin and retired transplant nurse; **Johanna Manbeck,** a kidney transplant circulator who often scrubbed in for the surgeries at St. Luis University Hospital. My version is inaccurate, but Johanna said it is close enough for a novel. **Jesse Castro**, a professional computer geek, helped me with some details about hacking but pointed out that this is not how hacking really happens. He told me, however, television shows stretch computer reality all the time, so why not in a novel?

Finally, I need to thank **Maryann Patterson**, with whom I have traveled across the U. S. during the last five years with her clothing business. She has suffered through my many rewrites, listened to me read passages aloud, and heard me whine about marketing issues. She is not aware how many times a single word from her made me revisit my chapters and purpose.

I must express my gratitude to **Scott Carney** and **Sigrid Fry-Revere** for giving me permission to reference their information.

For more firsthand information please read:

Carney, Scott. *The Red Market.* New York: Harper Collins Publishers, 2011.

Fry-Revere, Sigrid. *The Kidney Sellers: A Journey of Discovery in Iran.* Durham: Carolina Academic Press, 2014.

Also, if planning to donate, join some Facebook groups for personal experiences. *Living Kidney Donors Support Group,* and *Living Donors with Complications* are two of the many sites I frequented when they became available (after I donated) and who gave permission for me to include them here. Search "kidney transplant" today, and you will find so much, not true when I first started writing this novel. That's a good thing.

Beth Willstrop and Robert Golden the day after the 2016 transplant at Christus Santa Rosa Hospital in San Antonio, Texas. (Photo courtesy of Celeste Thornton, friend)

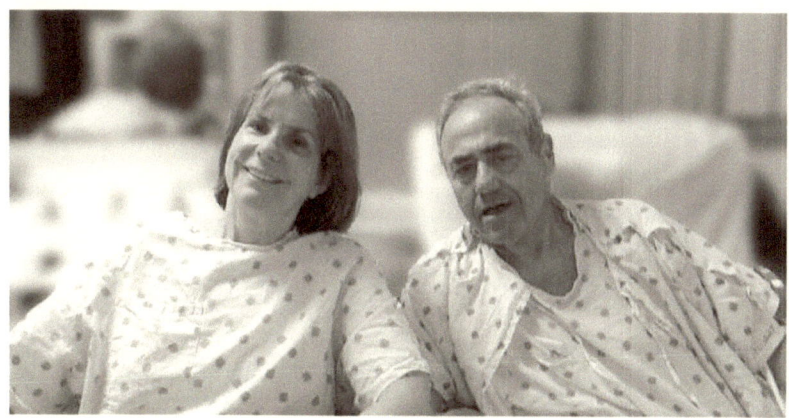

CiCi's fictitious quest grew from the author's experiences while saving her own best friend's life when he had chosen death with dignity rather than joining over 93,000 kidney dialysis patients living hooked up to life-giving machines and waiting years on a list.

(Search *Willstrop and Golden kidney transplant 2016* for 2016 press releases and video interviews with Texas Public Radio, KSAT TV, and Spectrum News.)